I0837867

Ridge & Root Publishing
West Rutland, Vermont 2025

ISBN 979-8-9898869-9-9

TROUBLED TIES

V. APRILLIANO

THIS BOOK IS DEDICATED TO ANGELO

YOUR MUSIC JOURNEY began before you could walk. You took risks, pushed yourself, and gained confidence in your skills. Your passion for the saxophone blossomed into such a talent that you were the top high school alto sax player in the state in 2023. Watching you play originals on stage with your own band is one of my greatest joys. Little did I know that your passion for music would someday inspire me to follow my passion for writing, and for that, I am eternally grateful.

Now on to the sappy stuff. I made it my life's duty to be the kind of mom for you that I never had, to listen, support your dreams, and create memories together that don't leave scars. I am grateful for our connection, and I am blessed to be one of your biggest fans. As you enter your junior year at UVM, I can only imagine all the places you'll go, and I can't wait to watch from the front row. Music is a universal language and you are fluent, you have touched the lives of many and this is just the beginning. There is nothing you cannot accomplish with a passion like yours.

Love, Mom

Troubled Ties

V. Aprilliano

PROLOGUE

THERE I WAS, sitting on my sun porch with a latte in one hand and a joint in the other, my calico cat rubbing her whiskers against my slippers. I was pondering life from the second story of an old brick building I owned in downtown Bunman, Vermont. Almost twenty-four, mature beyond my years, thanks to a shitty mother and some unthinkable childhood trauma. But somewhere amongst the untimely maturity was a bag of broken pieces masquerading as the Event Planner for the local mob boss. If you think that's a mouthful, you don't know the half of it. As I look back at all of this from the safety of the future, I have to give myself credit for not taking a toaster bath. I was, however, healing from an unprovoked gunshot wound to the face. Well, I might have provoked it just a little but, the point is, no one died. Well, that's not true either, but at least it wasn't me. It had been a month and a half, so I was healed up on the outside but my insides were another story.

As per usual, my personal life was a cluster fuck of epic proportion. I was deeply in love with a man who is almost as broken as I am. And despite my full set of emotional baggage, he drops everything and comes running whenever I need him. As luck would have it, last Valentine's Day, he told me he loves me. And before you tell me how sweet that is, let me clarify. We hadn't been sharing a romantic dinner when he said it, and we hadn't just celebrated our six month anniversary or some other such nonsense. He had said it about ten minutes after I almost got him killed. Classic.

The man in question is none other than Giuseppi Moretti, or Seppi to friends. And besides the fact that it was April Fool's Day, it was the day I set as my deadline for saying it back. So, there I sat, ringlets a frantic mess and last week's red nail polish looking whorish, at best. I hadn't slept, was hungover, and had a sizable chip on my shoulder. I took one last toke of my joint and startled the birds when I coughed the smoke out so hard that a drop of spittle hit my chin. I was a hot fucking mess, the epitome of grace and dysfunction, lost in my head, as usual. I had moved back to Bunman fourteen months earlier and still hadn't managed to find that fresh start I was looking for. No matter how hard I tried, most of the time, all I found was a case of the munchies and a hangover, thanks to my penchant for drowning my demons with whiskey and weed. After a little pep talk, I pushed off the porch couch, removed what was left of the chipped nail polish, and dragged my ass into the shower. That was the day I would say it, unless I chickened out again.

Don't get me wrong, I *wanted* to say it, but my demons had been wreaking havoc on my personal relationships. Back while I was busy realizing I loved Seppi, he was busy going through the motions with my sister while he prepared to reopen his ristorante. I had been caught between a quaint little cafe and the inner sanctum. My narcissistic mother moved back to town and the only saving grace was that my dad came with her. And if that wasn't enough, I had murdered a man, was unpacking my trauma with Isabella Rossi, and had dumped my first body. Those are the biggies, but there are a lot of little things that probably contributed to the list, I just suck at lists.

Fast forward twenty minutes and I was standing naked on the braided rug in the middle of my living room, raking curl cream through my ringlets. And while you're trying to picture what I look like without my clothes on, let me introduce myself. I'm Amelia Birch. I'm shorter than average, and right then, I was a comfortable size twelve. I have hazel eyes, curly brown hair, and one and a half dimples. I used to have two dimples but the one on the left is caught up in the aforementioned scar. Most days, my off-the-clock attire consisted of ratty vintage overalls and dingy white Chuck Taylors. That day, I was hiding behind the facade of a black tailored pantsuit, fitted white shirt, and black leather heels. The whole thing amounted to polishing a turd.

The fact is, I was pretty sure I wanted to spend my life with Giuseppi Moretti. That's a big statement about a man I had never even made out with. We had kissed a couple times but it hadn't amounted to much. In the handful of months I'd been Seppi's Event Planner, my attraction to him had shifted into overdrive. First it was his mob boss aesthetic, next it was his voice, and it got so bad that making eye contact with the man made me squeeze my thighs together. So, that day, April Fool's Day, my head full of crazy brown ringlets was wrangled and tended to, not just slammed into a frantic wad on the top of my head. I was wearing an expensive bra along with the suit and heels. I gripped the sink and stared at myself in the mirror. I loved him, there was no doubt about that. But the fact that he was in the mob caused me to take pause. As the icing on the cake, I did mascara, eyeliner, and a couple spritzes of Alien Elixir. To anyone looking in from the outside, it appeared I had my shit together. Boy, did I have everyone fooled.

CHAPTER 1
NOBODY'S FOOL

I SWUNG THROUGH the back door of Giuseppi's Italian Ristorante to the smells of yesterday's roasted garlic and marinara, but the back hallway always smelled faintly of Cuban cigars, leather, and dark mafia energy. In a couple hours, the place would come to life, but right then, it was still asleep. My office had cream colored walls and a cream colored leather sofa. It had edibles in the bathroom and a jar of fancy trail mix on the coffee table. My office had an incredibly comfortable desk chair, and most importantly, it was located right across the hall from Seppi's. It was somehow symbolic that my office was mostly light and his was mostly dark, from the walls, to the furniture, to the energy. I liked being a part of that world, being on that side of the glass, having access to the inner sanctum, the bat cave, the VIP lounge. Just some dumb girl with ringlets, one and a half dimples, and some PTSD. I needed to buy myself some time so I was headed to the kitchen to make a latte when Seppi's voice halted me in my tracks, an entire sentence in just one word,

"Dimples."

I changed course and entered the world of dark dealings and confidential conversations. Seppi swirled the remnants of some whiskey around the bottom of a rocks glass, gestured, and I sat in the leather armchair across the desk from him. He looked tired, or like he had a lot on his mind, which was nothing new. Giuseppi Moretti oozes sex appeal, the whole Tony Soprano vibe on steroids. Seppi was thirty-seven, six inches taller than me, sported a dark pompadour with a little gray at his temples. He's stocky but fit, has the typical Italian body type. Seppi usually smells like a couple puffs of a Cuban cigar, a couple shots of Johnny Walker Blue, and a couple spritzes of Tom Ford Tobacco Vanille. He usually had a faint tinge of sweat by the end of the night, but on him, it was sexy.

We made eye contact and I tried to read him but couldn't. I was undressing him with my eyes and wanted to push all his papers to the floor. There we sat, looking at each other, a little after nine in the morning. I'd been in that position with him a hundred times but it was April Fool's Day, and I had a job to do. I tried not to spiral and I was glad I was a little high, wondered if I would get the nerve to say it, get it out of the way right out of the gate so I could move on with my day. Instead of saying anything, I sat silent and listened to my guts gurgle. Seppi slid a shot of whiskey across the desk and I tossed it down the hatch to quell my nerves. I wasn't sure if chasing a latte with expensive liquor was our status quo, or if he was softening me up for something. Seppi held my gaze a little longer and then leaned forward like he was about to make a business proposition,

"I want to move forward with you, Amelia."

I had plenty to say, and I had thought long and hard about how I wanted to say it. But he had used my actual name, which made my butt hole pucker a little. I didn't say anything, so he clarified, all business and it made me squirm,

"I've put all my cards on the table and I've been very patient with you."

I nodded my head and swallowed the panic,

"I know you have."

Why couldn't I say it!? I was sure I loved him, more than sure, but I was chickening out, again. I stared at my lap, he was right, I needed to shit, or get off the pot, I was playing with fire and I knew it. I glanced up at him briefly, and then looked out the window at birds on the power line. This wasn't as simple as falling in love and galloping off into the sunset, he was in the mob, so there was an entire galaxy of moons pulling at the tides. There were different sides to him depending on who he was with and what he wanted. On one side he was ruthless and brutal, manipulative and dark, eyes on the prize. Right then, I loved the side of him that was in the mafia, but I was *in* love with the side that wore sweatpants and a hoodie at the breakfast table. Eventually, the dark side would mingle with the light side and he would idle somewhere in the gray. And while most girls who landed a man like him would be cooking up a way to lock him down, I was terrified I would disappoint him, as his Event Planner, in bed, and in general. It was going to take more than a half assed bathroom mirror pep talk to convince me I was worthy.

When you're part of the inner sanctum, there's an illusion of being untouchable, but it's a facade, and I'm all too familiar with those. I'm not about to pretend that I could ever live a bubblegum fairy tale life with Giuseppi Moretti. The truth is, I needed to be near him because it completed a circuit of some sort and my entire body vibrated in his presence. I made a deal with myself that I would count to ten and then blurt it out. I love you, easy peasy lemon squeezy. I had said it to people before, even if I realize now I had been wrong. Seppi's ice cubes clinked together and startled me back to reality. I glanced up at him and tried to read the look on his face, but couldn't. I chewed my bottom lip and tears came. It was time to say it back. Instead, I sniffled and said,

"It's complicated."

Idiot. I wanted him to pull the lever for the figurative trap door pit filled with alligators to put me out of my misery. At that point, I was about ready to call it a day and it wasn't even ten AM. It's complicated, what the fuck did that even mean? Seppi could have found it endearing that I was so naïve, or he could have backed me against the wall and told me not to fuck with him. He could have told me he was sick of waiting, and quite frankly, he could have just taken what he wanted, but he didn't. I felt vulnerable and didn't want his eyes on me from across the desk, he was too far away. I wanted to say whatever I had to say while our bodies were touching, while my face was buried in his collar, avoiding his eyes. I rose and removed my suit jacket seductively, but didn't do it on purpose, I was just trying to buy myself more time. Seppi was vulnerable and I understood the honor. I went to him, plucked the glass out of his hand and put it on the desk. I reached out to him and he pulled me into his lap.

I kicked off my shoes and climbed into the chair with him, one knee on either side. I straddled Seppi's lap and rested my head on his shoulder like I had dreamt a million times. My fear subsided a little as he wrapped me in his cage. My eyes fell shut as I took in the familiar scent of him, and I imagined falling asleep like that sometime. I can't count the nights I fell asleep imagining a moment like that, and there I was so close

I could feel the heat from his body. I could also feel that having me so close was doing something for him. I brushed my nose on the sensitive skin below his ear, kissed his neck, and nuzzled into his collar, the taste of Tobacco Vanille on my lips. I almost pinched myself. I sat back, Seppi's hands resting securely on my hips, and I wondered if he liked my body. My curves and imperfections, my ringlets, my broken pieces. I was on the edge, teetering there, losing my footing. I took one more deep breath and our eyes connected, my voice full of tears,

"I can't tell you the number of times I dreamt of being this close to you. I can't describe the way you make me feel, or how you hold all my broken pieces together. I can't fathom that someone like you, a man who could have any woman he wanted, would ever feel something for someone like me. And I'm terrified I will disappoint you."

Seppi rubbed my lower back as I spoke and my words tripped over my tears,

"What I'm saying is that, umm..."

I trailed off and noticed Seppi was holding his breath, trying to fight his own feelings. I squeaked out,

"I'm terrified this isn't real, or that you're not real, or that you're somehow taking pity on me, or that this is some cruel game you're playing, just because you can."

In through the nose, out through the mouth,

"I want to move forward with you too, I just need you to know how completely terrified I am that something will go wrong, or get in the way, or I'll let my guard down and it will all get ripped away. I can't have that happen."

Our eyes met,

"I have never felt these things for anyone else, but I feel them for you. Do you know what I'm saying?"

He nodded, waiting for more.

We sat there looking at each other, on the precipice of change, at the threshold of something more than what we used to be. As I looked at him, I realized I knew nothing about his past. He had an entire lifetime before me, he had been married at my age and I couldn't imagine what he was like back then. A wave of fear and panic crashed over me, what if he had loose ends or unfinished business that would come back to haunt him? Maybe that was the hardest part, knowing there could be debts he owed, or people who wanted him dead. In fact, there was a good chance both of those things were true, and maybe it was the fear of knowing eventually, I would lose him, or he would lose me because of our affiliation. But I guess when you think about it, that's no different than any other couple. I broke the silence,

"This is the point of no return for me, Seppi. Do you have any skeletons in your closet I need to know about before we do this?"

I blinked up at him and he shook his head, looking me right in the eye,

"No."

And I think when he answered, he thought he was telling the truth. I think, in his mind, all his loose ends had been tied, all the skeletons in his closet had turned to dust. Seppi was looking at the world through the rose-colored glasses you wear when you're in love. Seppi countered,

"Do you have any skeletons in *your* closet that *I* need to know about before we do this?"

The question caught me off guard, I had no idea what kind of skeletons he thought someone like me would have in my closet, besides the figurative ones. I shook my head and gazed at him with bedroom eyes, and I think I was wearing rose-colored glasses too,

"No."

I tasted my tears when we kissed and as our tongues touched, warmth rose to the surface. My body came to life as his body completed the circuit. I rested my forehead against his and remembered the night we danced in his office and it seemed like a lifetime ago. I placed one hand on each side of his face, rubbing his left cheek with my thumb as I got lost in his eyes, here goes nothing,

"I love you, Giuseppi Moretti, with my whole heart."

The power dynamic shifted between us and I didn't feel any fear about moving forward, he was the air I breathed and I was gulping him in like I had been drowning. Our mouths came together again and Seppi's hands began to explore new parts of my body, parts he would come to know like the back of his hand, parts he would be able to picture with his eyes closed. Seppi unbuttoned my shirt and traced the lace on my bra, brushing his thumb across my nipple. He nuzzled under my curls and took in the scent of me, exhaling his words,

"The smell of your skin makes me hungry, Dimples."

He sucked my neck and I felt it in unmentionable places. I squeezed his thighs with mine and squirmed around. Seppi kissed my throat and then my collarbone. I worked on the buttons of his shirt and laid my hands across his chest, my left palm squarely planted on his phoenix tattoo. I slid my hands to his shoulders and he buried his face in my cleavage. It was on. Seppi tossed my shirt to the floor and lifted me to the desk and our mouths came together again. I undid his belt and unbuttoned his pants. Seppi popped the button on my pants and the zipper followed suit, they were soon in a an awkward pile on the floor. Seppi carried me to the leather sofa, my legs wrapped around his waist. I pulled his belt out of the loops and tossed it, working at his zipper as we kissed. I squirmed as he hooked his fingers into the frilly waistband of my panties. Seconds later, my panties were on the coffee table next to a humidor filled with expensive Cuban cigars. Looking at me with bedroom eyes,

"Can I touch you, Amelia?"

On an exhale,

"Yes."

And then he touched me.

I squirmed around and frantically tried to free him from his boxer briefs. There were a couple rapid taps on the office door and we froze. I hoped it was locked. Shit. Not that he wasn't allowed to do whatever the fuck he wanted, he was Giuseppi Moretti. But still, it would be a little awkward depending on who it was and what they wanted. Seppi put his finger up and I didn't make a peep. Just then, Mary Moretti's voice came from the other side of the door as she tapped,

"Hello Darling, I brought you some delectable cheese danishes from Eliana Mazelli's place, they're to die for!"

How embarrassing to get busted by your mother, but Seppi kept his cool,

"I'm wrapping up a video call, I'll be right there, Mama."

He was an adult, but getting caught messing around by your mommy is a buzz kill. Seppi did up his pants and retrieved his belt from the corner. While I laid there, paralyzed with fear and embarrassment, Seppi buttoned himself back into his shirt. He was fully dressed and running his hand through his hair when I flew off the sofa, completely naked. I scurried around picking up pieces of my clothing, but mostly, I just spun around in circles and panicked. He waited while I darted into his bathroom with my clothes, he winked as I went by,

"We'll finish this later."

I nodded, but at that point I was so frazzled that I wasn't in the mood. I closed myself into the bathroom and eavesdropped as Seppi greeted his Mama. Standing there amongst the fancy soap and expensive towels, I stepped back into my panties, and scooped my boobs into the lacy bra. As quietly as I could, I shook out the expensive tailored pants and button up shirt, my suit jacket haphazardly thrown over the shower door. Where were my shoes? That's a good question. I'll tell you where my shoes were, my fucking shoes were out there on the floor next to Seppi's desk. Jesus Christ. I hoped he had kicked them out of sight on his way to the door.

Seppi was making small talk about pastries and I debated whether I should just swing the door open and walk out, or if I needed to maintain a level of discretion. I mean, he had his hand down my pants, we were practically dating. I stood there with my hand on the door handle. Ultimately, I decided to climb out of his bathroom window instead. I hoisted myself onto the window frame, my front half outside, my bottom half in the bathroom. I was in the process of rethinking my technique when Kane waltzed out the back door of the cafe, whistling as he swung a bag of trash, a bar rag over his shoulder. Perfect.

Kane's eyes went like saucers when he saw me and he swung the bag of trash in a high arc in the general direction of the dumpster before speed-walking in my direction. After all, no matter where we were in our on-again, off-again relationship, if I was climbing out of Giuseppi Moretti's window, there was probably a damn good reason. Kane put his hands under my pits and I slithered the rest of the way out. Kane slid the window shut and popped the screen into place. Between my emotions and the constant interruptions, it's no wonder I hadn't slept with Seppi yet. There was always a 'situation' or some other hyped-up crap that needed to be attended to on the double, or someone knocking on the door with gourmet pastries from Eliana Mazelli's place.

Kane slung me over his shoulder and carried me across the parking lot. I screeched,

"Don't drop me!"

He didn't say anything, but he gripped me a little tighter and I wasn't as scared anymore. He put me down on the porch steps and I turned to run inside but he didn't let me off the hook that easily. He rocked back on his heels and his eyes fell to my blouse,

"Whatcha doin'?"

I followed his eyes to my chest and noticed that my fucking shirt was buttoned crooked. Of course it was. I gestured in the direction I had come from,

"I was in a meeting."

I waved my hands around and I started over,

"I mean, I was..."

He reached for the door and held it for me,

"You don't say."

I pinched the bridge of my nose, went under his arm, and did the walk of shame up the stairs to my apartment. I retrieved the key under my welcome mat, unlocked my door, and tossed the key under the mat again. I frantically dug through the shit on my closet floor looking for another pair of black heels. I owned five pairs of black fucking dress shoes and couldn't find a matching pair. Whatever. I fixed my buttons and exchanged the black pants for Burberry trousers. I slid my feet into brown suede loafers that belonged to some lady the Morettis whacked. Retracing my usual morning procedure, I bounced down the stairs and went into the world. Ahh, what a beautiful day. I punched in the security code and swung through the back door of the ristorante, for the second time that day, and paused for a beat before proceeding. I went into my office like I was putting my shit down, and acted casual when I leaned into Seppi's doorway, waving,

"Morning! Anyone want a latte?"

Seppi made a face like he'd been caught with his hand in the cookie jar before dinner. He shook his head and gestured toward Mary,

"She knows."

I was mortified, and I'm sure my eyes bugged out of my head. For almost a year, I'd been sharing lattes and scones with that woman every Sunday. And, if you've lost track, or I didn't mention it, until a couple months earlier, Seppi was in a dysfunctional relationship with my sister. Hello everyone, roll out the red carpet, the whore has arrived. I shook my head at myself, and then at the entire situation. Whatever. I pulled up the cute little panties Seppi had been fingering, and walked my ass right into his office. But what if Mary was disappointed in me?

I glanced between the two of them, Seppi was sitting at his desk and Mary was perched on the arm of the leather sofa. Mary Moretti is a classy bitch. She has a dark blonde shag and white teeth. She smells like Chanel No. 5 , long skinny cigarettes, and brandy. Mary is like a mom to me, and I didn't want anything to come between us. She stood, so I went to her, and she kissed me on both cheeks. She gestured toward the chair across the desk from Seppi, I turned it to face her and sat down. Mary tilted her head a little like she was thinking. I moved my eyes, and saw the black leather pumps sitting askew on the floor next to Seppi's desk, like they had been kicked off, feverishly, by a woman on her way to pound-town with Mary Moretti's eldest son. I cringed. She broke the silence,

"When I was eighteen, just a senior in high school, I met Sally. He was the first person I was intimate with, and a year or two later, we were married."

She waved her hand,

"That's not the point."

She seemed to be finding her words,

"I'm almost sixty years old, and I only hope that someday I feel for someone, the way the two of you feel for each other."

Maybe I wasn't going to get in trouble after all. I sat very still, didn't say anything, and held my breath. She continued,

"There is something about the way you look at each other when the other isn't looking."

I let that sink in a little as I sat there without a suit jacket, in different pants, and the wrong shoes. My sister had said the same thing, and I wondered what people saw when they looked at us. And just like that, Mary kissed me on both cheeks again, and the whole thing was water under the bridge,

"Sunday for lattes, darling?"

With bewilderment in my eyes, I smiled and nodded. Mary kissed Seppi on the cheek, rustled his hair, and waved to us as she drifted out the door. He smirked and raised an eyebrow,

"Nice one."

Seppi dramatically shifted his eyes, from my eyes, to the heels, and back. I went palms up,

"I was panicking!"

He made a face and gestured toward the bathroom,

"Nice job climbing out the window and running home to change into something that doesn't require black shoes. That's amateur hour, Amelia, what are you, twelve?"

He gestured toward the hall,

"While you're at it, why don't you go smoke a cigarette in the bathroom, and cover it up with cheap perfume? Or perhaps you could drink half a bottle of Merlot, and top it off with some red Kool-Aid."

I smirked back at him and raised an eyebrow,

"You know, sometimes you really date yourself with your references. When I was a kid, Kool-Aid wasn't cool anymore."

Seppi smiled and then brought it back to the matter at hand, he gestured at the leather sofa,

"I can do whatever I want, you know."

Our eyes met again, and he flicked his eyebrow at me in a way that made my belly burn,

"If I want to touch you in my office, I can touch you in my office."

Right to my nipples. Jesus. I gestured toward the bathroom,

"Oh, Kane had to help me out of your window, all disheveled, and my buttons were crooked. So, I guess you inadvertently won that round of the dick swinging contest."

Seppi smiled and came to my side of the desk, the bag of pastries open, the smells of lemon curd and raspberries making my mouth water. I looked up at him and he closed the gap,

"Where were we?"

He bent down and put one hand on each armrest. Our mouths came together and I could tell he wanted to pick up where we left off. He sucked my neck, breathy and low,

"I want you."

He rubbed his nose against mine, and upped the ante, the smells of espresso and whiskey his breath, playfully,

"I *need* you, Dimples."

My nipples pressed against my bra, however, I wasn't in the mood anymore. I pulled back and swatted at his arm,

"Eww, no."

He was clearly confused and I waved my hands at him,

"No. I mean, I feel like your mom just gave us permission to make out in your bedroom while she's down the hall making Hamburger Helper."

Seppi looked at me like I either had a cactus growing out of the top of my head, or like I had lost my ever-loving mind. He clearly had no idea what I was talking about. His loss.

CHAPTER 2
BAD MEDICINE

IT WAS EARLY afternoon as I sat on the leather sofa in my office, with my feet crossed on the maple coffee table. I'd smoked half a joint with my latte. Since then, I'd had some whiskey, and tossed an edible down the hatch for the first time in weeks. I was picking through a glass jar full of fancy trail mix for the dark chocolate covered blueberries, pondering the fact that my left dimple was all kinds of jacked up. I felt a sense of loss, my dimples were my best feature. And then I had a very important question. When I got up from the sofa, I realized I had a little too much of something in my system, but whatever, I walked it off. I padded across the hall, and before I went over the threshold of Seppi's office I started asking,

"Does this mean I have a scrimple?"

I waltzed through the door in my stocking feet, the glass jar of expensive trail mix under my arm, eyes trained on Seppi's empty chair. A voice came from behind me,

"What the fuck are you talking about!?"

I snapped my head around and locked eyes with Vincenzo Moretti, perched on the arm of the sofa, the sofa where Giuseppi Moretti went down my pants. Anyway, Vincenzo, or Vinny as he is usually called, is a younger version of Seppi. Same classic Italian good looks and dark eyebrows, same presence when he enters a room. Vinny was twenty-seven and more baby-faced than his big brother, but I imagined Seppi looked like that when he was younger. I glanced at the bathroom and the door was closed. Anyway, Seppi's younger brother Vinny was a good shit, and I had a near death experience with him, so we had a bond, right? I continued sauntering, or whatever the fuck I was doing, and leaned against the back of the sofa, a couple half-chewed dark chocolate covered blueberries in my cheek,

"Does this mean I have a scrimple?"

Vinny went palms up and shook his head,

"I...I don't know what you're asking."

Like it was obvious, I gestured to emphasize the point,

"Half scar, half dimple. A scrimple."

Vinny's face did that thing you do, when you think someone's got a screw loose. A lot of good he was. I thumbed toward the bathroom,

"Is he taking a shit or something?"

"Who!?"

The door swung open, and my childhood best friend, Abigail 'Sunny' Solomon, came into view,

"What's up, fucker!?"

She ran over, lifted me off the ground, and spun me around. As a child, Sunny was the person I ran to when I needed to escape my dysfunctional life. She ran from her demons, and I ran from mine. We'd go into the woods and pretended we lived inside of hollowed out rotten trees. We made crowns with twisted twigs and flowers. Sunny was a strawberry blonde bad-ass, the girl with the nose ring and the hand-rolled cigarettes. She wore too much eyeliner, and had a bad attitude. Sunny was taller and thinner than me, she was a girl who turned heads. She was the one who could bring a boy to his knees, or hot-wire a car, if that's even a thing anymore. I needed to have my question answered, so I gestured toward Seppi's desk,

"Where is he?"

Vinny shrugged and Sunny sat on his knee, kissing him on the cheek. But, I really needed to know if I had a scrimple. We chatted for a few minutes and then I went back to my office to dig for dark chocolate covered blueberries. Jesus, I needed to sober up before opening time, what was my problem? My head was spinning and my hands were clammy. I closed my door, but something told me not to lock it. I sat there staring at the place where the wall meets the trim and just kind of went numb. The darkness closed in around me and I heard the jar with the fancy trail mix as it hit the floor. I opened my eyes to Seppi bent over me, slapping my cheek to rouse me,

"Amelia! Hey, wake up for me, Amelia!"

I blinked my eyes, but they were dry, and my tongue was glued to the roof of my mouth, he shouted through a long tunnel and it sounded like when you spin around in circles,

"What did you take!?"

I stared at him blankly, through slits for eyes. He saw the look on my face and rushed me into the bathroom before I threw up. I was sitting on the floor with my chin on the toilet seat, forehead sweating, acid churning in my empty stomach. Seppi stood there looking concerned, that had never happened to me before. I was aware he was on the phone, but didn't register who he was talking to as the darkness closed in again. I felt movement and when I opened my eyes, I was being rolled out the back door on a stretcher, an ambulance parked perpendicular to the Escalade. Seppi was talking to the paramedics, I could see that he was concerned, but I had more important things on my mind. When he came to my side, I reached up and touched the tip of his nose, before pointing to my mangled dimple,

"Scrimple?"

Seppi kissed me on the forehead and strode with purpose to the Escalade, I wondered where he was going. Where was *I* going? The darkness tried to close in around me but there were bright lights, people poking me with needles, people asking questions. I stayed awake but wasn't present. I had no idea where I was, or what day of the week it was. I failed two thirds of being alert and oriented times three, the only one I got right was my name, and I had to think about that one. I started to panic when I realized something wasn't right. I threw up in one of those kidney shaped basins in the ambulance, and by the time I got to the hospital, I felt like I was peripherally aware of what was going on around me. They had given me something that helped flush something different out of my system. Seppi was speed-walking toward me as I was wheeled through the VIP entrance you get to use when you ride in the white limo with the flashing lights.

Seppi looked concerned, and when the nurse retreated into the hall, he leaned close,

"Did you take something?"

I shrugged with my face,

"What!? Like, did I steal something!? No, I've been laying here the whole time..."

I panicked a little more, my eyes wide,

"Haven't I!?"

He shook his head,

"No, like, did you take something?"

Seppi made a gesture like he was tossing something into his mouth, and then shooting something into his arm, and then pushing one nostril closed. I'm not good at charades,

"Did I eat nuts, get a vaccine, and blow a snot rocket?"

I made a face like he was asking stupid questions,

"I can confidently answer no to all three."

Boy was I proud of myself, Seppi pinched the bridge of his nose,

"No, did you take any substances you don't usually take? Did you take any pills, or shoot anything up, or snort anything?"

Oh.

"No! I'm a creature of habit, I stick to my usual, you know that."

Very matter of factly, his voice was all business,

"Then someone drugged you."

I sat up in my uncomfortable stretcher bed and my eyes bugged out,

"What!? Who!?"

He shrugged and went palms up,

"You tell me."

My garbled mind rewound the day and tried to replay everything I did, or drank, or put in my mouth. Egg and toast, too many lattes, half a joint, whiskey, a handful of dark chocolate covered blueberries, edible, stale garlic knot. At that point, it seemed like a normal day, and if I had been more coherent, I would have been more freaked out. If I had gone about my normal business and had a normal day, why was I at the hospital? To make matters worse,

"You broke your jar of trail mix; I'll get you a new one."

Goddammit. And then I started to cry for the first time during all of this. I didn't really lose it all the way, but I was feeling my feelings, and I didn't like it. Why couldn't I remember that morning? Seppi stepped into the hall and made a phone call. When he came back,

"Your sister is coming to sit with you, I have to get back to the restaurant, we have a big party coming in tonight, and you're here, so..."

I was over the hump and in good hands, so he kissed me and went out the door. Fifteen minutes later, my sister came in with her baby bump, and a look of concern. Opal was a couple inches shorter than me, her eyes were bright blue, and her ringlets were almost black,

"What the hell did you take!?"

I shrugged,

"My usual, nothing out of the ordinary.

"Ya, well, you look like shit."

I didn't have an answer for her. She tried again,

"So, you didn't take anything different than usual?"

I shrugged and shook my head,

"No. I smoked half a joint before work, had maybe three shots of whiskey over the course of the day, less than usual really, and I don't usually feel like this. I tossed an edible about an hour before I started feeling funny, but they don't make me feel like this."

I paused and tried to focus on a sign hanging from the IV pole,

"I feel like things are wobbly, or like I'm spinning, and I threw up a couple times. My mind is garbled, and my reaction time is fucked."

The doctor came in, sat on the stool and rolled it over to me. Opal crossed her arms, she was over this shit a long time ago.

"We got your blood work back. In addition to THC and alcohol, we found Rohypnol."

My sister looked pissed,

"Like, a fuckin' Roofy!?"

The doctor nodded and my sister's eyes moved to mine, the color rising in her cheeks as panic set in. So, there I was trying to calm her down and she wasn't having it. This is a woman who's smoked her fair share of the Devil's lettuce, has experimented with nose candy, and shrooms. I could tell that she had ruled those things out before the doctor strolled in with my labs. All I know is that I felt like absolute dog shit and a bag of chips. I had a dull headache and felt like I wanted to sleep for a week. The doctor explained that the weed in my system interacted with the Rohypnol and caused more intense symptoms. I was being encouraged to drink fluids, and had three cups full of crushed hospital ice and cranberry juice lined up on my over-bed table. I was hooked to a bag of saline and had to pee every ten minutes, I needed help from my sister to make it safely, to and from the commode they put in my room.

I would be able to leave once the IV was finished, and my sister promised she would go through McDonald's for a large fry and a sundae on the way home, that sounded delicious. Opal stepped into the hall to take a call, and then came back in holding her phone out to me, I took it,

"Hello?"

It was Seppi,

"Amelia?"

"Yeah."

"I'm looking through the stuff in your office, to see if I can figure out what happened. Where did you get the edibles in the crystal jar on your vanity?"

"At the place across from the record store. I like the sour cherry ones, and that's the only place that sells them around here."

There was a pause,

"What color are they?"

"Red."

He paused again,

"What are the yellow ones?"

This is where I need to rewind a little bit. Remember the day I had some sort of heart to heart with Gretchen behind the restaurant, and we shared a joint? She gave me a handful of gummies, and I just tossed them in the jar with my other ones. I wasn't coherent enough to realize that it would have been very bad for me if I had taken one of those gummies when Lance and Gretchen were still alive.

"Umm."

Seppi didn't have time for my bullshit,

"Amelia, what are the yellow ones?"

I sighed,

"Gretchen gave them to me."

He let out an exasperated breath,

"Oh, for Christ's Sake."

The call ended.

I talked with the doctor about getting out. He told me I would sleep a lot, and I'd most likely have vivid dreams until the drugs were out of my system. I felt bad for ruining everyone's day, and hoped Seppi was having a good night at the restaurant, doing my job. I felt bad for worrying my sister, she was aware this could have been so much worse. Seppi had already tossed the jar of edibles, and made sure I understood that I needed to be more vigilant about exactly what I was putting inside my body. I wondered if that meant being vigilant about putting *him* inside my body. I was tired, and once I was in Opal's van, I took a little nap. I was fantasizing about my bed when she parked next to the mini mafia sedan. She pulled on the emergency break, and started crying, I put my hand on her arm,

"What's wrong? I'm going to be OK, you know."

Opal shook her head and didn't say anything, maybe she was overwhelmed with the situation like I was. She stared into the backyard, sobbing, something was wrong, something had happened. Why wasn't she saying anything? Seppi banged through the back door of the restaurant with purpose, and held me to his chest, his lips on the top of my head,

"I am so sorry, Amelia."

And I could tell he meant it. Oh, no, he had called me Amelia, I reassured,

"It's OK, I'm starting to feel better, the IV and juice helped. I ate a large fry and a sundae on the way home."

Opal shook her head,

"You slept all the way home."

I ate French fries and a sundae, what was she talking about? I waved them away,

"I'm going to take a shower so I can wash off the hospital cooties, and then I'm getting into some sweats. I'm tired and just want to sleep."

The two of them made eye contact, and I felt like there was something they weren't saying. I didn't understand. Seppi led me to the steps and sat down next to me. He swallowed hard, and I could see him stuffing his feelings deep down inside, shifting into a different gear. Opal was crying, and eventually came over to the steps. Seppi put his hand on my arm like he was bracing me,

"Amelia."

I glanced up at him expectantly, and he said,

"Kane is dead."

The world started spinning, and the darkness closed in, I threw up cranberry juice all over the suede loafers. I glanced up at Seppi and saw a look of deep sadness,

"He was on his motorcycle earlier today, and got in an accident, he was killed."

I couldn't understand what he was saying, my ears were ringing. I stood up, I'd show him. He rose from the steps, his voice filled with emotion, choking on his feelings,

"Amelia."

I went up the back stairs and stopped at Kane's door. I knocked and waited; he must not be home. Seppi grabbed my arm as I went to knock again,

"Amelia."

I pulled myself free, and knocked again, harder that time, more desperate, pleading,

"Kane!?"

I heard Kane's Staffordshire Terrier, Lola, on the other side of the door, her tail slamming against the wall. I fell to my knees and lost my mind. Seppi squatted down next to me and rubbed my back,

"I am so sorry, Amelia."

Opal unlocked my apartment and went inside; she didn't know what to say. Eventually, I peeled back Kane's welcome mat and picked up his spare key. Lola barreled past me looking for Kane, she didn't understand any more than I did. Seppi helped me gather up her food and leash and blankets. He took Lola out to pee, and then I fell asleep with my arms around her.

When I woke the next morning, I was groggy and starving, but I felt a lot better than I had the night before. I sat on my sun porch with a latte, and as I looked down at the back yard, I saw Kane's motorcycle. It took me a minute to make sense of things, and then it all flooded back, but it still didn't make any sense. If he got killed on his motorcycle, what was it doing in the driveway, there wasn't a scratch on it. I ran into the hall and pounded on Kane's door, yelling his name. I jiggled the doorknob, it was locked. I didn't even know what time it was, he had to be up. I was still pounding on his door when footsteps came up the stairs from the hallway of the cafe.

When Kane stepped into the hall, I squealed and wrapped my arms around his neck. He pulled away and looked at me with wrinkles in his forehead, gesturing toward the cafe stairs with a bar rag as he spoke,

"What the hell are you doing!? I could hear you all the way down there! You're making a scene!"

I was speechless, standing there in the hall staring at Kane Buchanan. Was he alive, or were we both dead?

"You're alive!?"

He looked at me the same way Vinny had when I asked about the scrimple,

"Excuse me, what!?"

I pinched him, he pulled away and yelped, my voice went up an octave,

"Oh my God, you're alive!"

I jumped up and hung from his neck, dangling there with my feet off the floor, his arms at his sides,

"Are you having one of your episodes!?"

Opal came through the door and shook her head before shooing me into my apartment. She explained that I had been roofied and it caused vivid dreams, and that I had dreamt that something bad happened to him. He came into my apartment and gave me a proper hug, tucked a curl behind my ear, and cupped the side of my face with his palm,

"I'd be sad if something happened to you, too.'

Kane kissed me on top of the head before retreating to the world of proper tamping methods and the perfect crema. I waited for him to walk away and then pulled the covers over my head.

CHAPTER 3
MURDER AND MONOTONY

WHEN MONDAY came back around, it was head-shrinking day. I blew the smoke out in little rings as birds circled the feeders, the wind chimes singing in the breeze. My birthday was right around the corner, and even though I was in my mid-twenties, I still felt like it was my special day. You know, something to look forward to. My sister would scour thrift stores for the perfect pair of vintage overalls, magnificently gaudy earrings or a wool sweater. Seppi would grill a steak and share some of his expensive whiskey, or maybe he would sweep me away in his mob boss aesthetic and make love to me on his yacht. And then there's my parents, I haven't recapped that part of the story, what was I thinking?

To go back to the very beginning, my mother was too busy watching soaps and smoking cigarettes to be bothered by the fact that the neighbor boy showed me his ding-a-ling, and what he could make come out of it. She also couldn't be bothered when she found out the kid's teen-aged relative chased me down the hall, pinned me to the bathroom floor, and ripped down the cute little panties with the day of the week embroidered on them. My mother found out and just told the neighbor kid's mother to make it stop.

So, as you can imagine, that, and the fact that overall, my mother was just an invalidating, self-centered bitch, our relationship wasn't great. Don't get me wrong, if we were drinking, we had a blast judging other people, and we'd laugh all night long. But for the most part, my mother is the reason I need therapy. When I made the decision to move back to Vermont, it was motivated by my need to get away from her. OK, nice job you're thinking, you got away. Nope. I moved back to Bunman and then my sister did too, and then she found out she was expecting. My dad is well-meaning, loves us, and wants to be close enough to babysit for his first grandchild. A couple months ago, they took us out to dinner and told us they were selling their house in Massachusetts and, as it turns out, they repurchased the same house we lived in when we were kids. In Bunman.

Sentimental, right? No. Whenever I went over there, I'd have to see the house that contains the hallway, that lead to the bathroom floor. I'd see the corn field I used to run home, I'd see the kitchen table I ate at that night, and the bathtub I was sitting in when I told my mom it hurt down there. Christmases would be in the same dining room and I was sure the tree would be in the same place it always was. I'd be surprised if some of our old ornaments weren't still in the attic. While I was dealing with healing my face, and everything else in my life, I had to do it with my parents fifteen minutes away. So far, I'd been able to hide some things, and make excuses for others, but a gunshot wound to the cheek is a little harder to explain than coming home, soaking wet, in my underwear and Vincenzo Moretti's wool trench.

At that point, the scar was still red, but I could cover it with concealer if I wanted to. Things had been weird and icky, and I didn't like it. And while I wanted to deal with all of that shit in therapy, I also needed to deal with my current situation. Like old times, I worked a shift at Muddy Waters and then went up to take a shower. I worked curl cream through my hair while Indie purred at my feet and rubbed her whiskers against my slippers. I didn't make much effort, but I didn't look like a complete slob, so I guess it landed somewhere in between. Overalls that didn't have holes, white V-neck tee, ocher colored cardigan, dingy white Chuck Taylors. I picked up a bottle of pills and gave myself a stern talking to about my mental health before returning them to the basket on my microwave. I removed the lid of a jelly jar and retrieved an edible. Hey, we all drown our demons somehow, and I keep mine pretty high most of the time.

I kissed Indie and bounced down the back steps to the parking lot. Oh, and I forgot to tell you about my car situation. I rolled into Bunman in an ancient Subaru Legacy that looks like Swiss cheese. Her name was Holly, and she ran like a charm, but she was held together with duct tape and tough love. My sister was worried I might need to make another hasty escape at some point, so about seven months ago, Seppi provided me with a sporty Cadillac sedan. It was black inside and out, had dual exhausts and a manual transmission. He even managed to get me a vanity plate that said DIMPLES. I affectionately called the thing, my 'mini mafia sedan.' I looked back and forth between the two cars, my past and my present, my sentimental side, and my bad-ass bitch side. Which was going to win that day? I plopped the key chain into my open palm; the key to the piece of Swiss cheese was pointed right at the car, and the fob for the mini mafia sedan was facing the ristorante. Fair enough.

The clicker shit the bed a long time ago, so I wiggled the key in the driver's side door. For your information, she started right up. I threw in a Slash and Myles Kennedy CD and made my way to the impressive office building of Dr. Isabella Rossi. I smoked half a joint in the parking lot before pushing through the tall glass doors into the lobby. I took the elevator to the sixth floor and checked in with the receptionist, a pleasant-looking middle-aged woman named Elaine. I flipped through a Martha Stewart magazine and scrolled on my phone while I waited. I had taken a break from my sessions, and it was my first time back since the stuff with Lance and the crowbar. I didn't really want to be doing therapy that day either, but whatever.

Someone performs an unspeakable act on me and I have to pay for it with years of climbing over the shit swept under the carpets, and wrestling with the skeletons crammed precariously in all the closets. Better yet, if I ever wanted to put myself back together, I'd have to sweep all that shit out from under the carpets and drag all the skeletons out of the closets. Oh, and I'd have to dissect all of it with a magnifying glass. Meanwhile, my mother was living her best life, clueless and ignorant, self-centered and entitled, that seemed fair. I hated her, but wished that she loved me.

The door swung open, and I passed Dr. Rossi on the threshold in a trail of Alien Elixir and weed. I sat in the overstuffed chair across from her and waited while she situated her notebook and pen. Isabella Rossi was trim, dressed well, and had soulful brown eyes. She went to high school with Seppi, so as far as I could guess, she was around thirty-seven. I was struggling with a couple different things. First, it was a big deal that I was moving forward with Seppi. Second, my parents were back in Vermont. And lastly, I had that horrible dream about Kane. I stared at my sneakers and realized I was clenching my jaw. Just rip the band aid off, Amelia, you're wasting her time and your own. Spit it out.

I looked at her and then glanced out the window at pigeons on roofs, it made it easier to find my words,

"Do you remember me telling you about the man who accepts me without the masks and the bullshit?"

Dr. Rossi sat forward,

"The man you're afraid will stop being your friend if you tell him how you feel?

"Yeah."

I watched a bird fly around, and glanced toward the almost naked ski slopes,

"Do you also remember the handsome stranger?"

She nodded. I squirmed around because I was trying to figure out how much information to give about Giuseppi. I was afraid she would run back and tell him everything I said,

"Everything I say stays between us, right?"

"Amelia, yes. Like I said before, you confessed murder and I didn't break your confidence."

It took me a second, but I laid it all out there in all its glory,

"For quite some time now, I've known I was falling in love with Seppi. But he's this powerful man and I was sure he wouldn't fall for someone like me."

She put her hand up to stop me,

"What do you mean, someone like you?"

I made eye contact with her, hopped up and spun around in my overalls and dirty sneakers. Once I was back in my chair,

"Anyway, I've had feelings for him a while now and never told him. I got shot in the cheek by the handsome stranger and Seppi saved my life."

Dr. Rossi glanced at me, and I gave her the information she wanted,

"Seppi went feral on the guy and bashed his head in with a crowbar."

She nodded like she was satisfied. I stopped talking so I could decide if I was going to let myself fall apart, or if I was going to hold it together. I took a deep breath and did a little of both, tears fell but I wasn't sobbing,

"I almost died and Seppi saw the whole thing play out right in front of his eyes. He killed Lance, and then told me he loves me."

She looked interested but wasn't prying.

"I didn't say it back, not until he cornered me."

She made some sort of acknowledgment with her face, and I continued,

"I was so overwhelmed with everything that happened that I didn't say it back. I set a deadline of April Fool's Day and made a deal with myself that I would say it by then. I almost chickened out but he put it all out there again and reminded me his cards are on the table. It was shit or get off the pot in my eyes, even if that's not what he was doing. I told him I love him, which I do,"

I stared out the window at the pigeons,

"All that aside, I haven't slept with him yet, don't you find that interesting?"

I waved it away,

"I keep telling myself the right situation hasn't presented itself."

I looked back at her,

"Does that make any sense to you, at all? Given the way I usually do things?"

She leaned forward,

"Do you think you're avoiding intimacy with Seppi because you love him? It sounds like making love with him would make you more vulnerable than you've ever been with someone."

I shrugged,

"I suppose. If I keep him at arm's length, I can be a part of his life without exposing all of myself or getting my heart broken."

"Really?"

Our eyes connected, I had to give her that one,

"Deep down, I just feel like there's no way it will ever work, look at us. I'm turning twenty-four in a couple days and he's a thirty-seven-year-old mob boss."

"Age is just a number, and that's not a big age gap. Once you're in your twenties, everyone is pretty much the same."

She offered a bit of insight,

"My husband is twenty years older and we have a fulfilling relationship."

I was uncomfortable and didn't wan to talk about her life, even though all she did was listen to me talk about mine,

"Okay, well, there's more. I do love him, like really love him. I want to see what it's like to be the one sitting across the table from him over pancakes, the one who falls asleep next to him, but..."

Dr. Rossi's voice was warm,

"But, what?"

I moved my eyes to the window again so I could find my words,

"But something happened recently that has thrown a monkey wrench in things."

I paused again and shook my head,

"It's a long story but someone who died a couple months ago, slipped me a roofy the other day."

She looked at me like I was crazy, which I kind of respected.

"Anyway, I had a bad reaction to it because I smoke a lot of weed. That night, I had a vivid dream that Kane was killed on his motorcycle. I'm talking, like it felt real, I felt the guttural pain and emptiness, the deep loss and how it would affect my life to not have him across the hall, or at the cafe."

I was hoping she had been listening to everything I'd said, but the only thing she said was,

"A dead person slipped you a Roofy?"

I waved her away and barked,

"Are you listening to me or not!?"

She put her hands up and told me to continue but I started over since I didn't think she had been listening,

"The night I was roofied, I had this vivid dream that Kane died on his motorcycle. It was so real, I mean, the feelings, the smells, his dog Lola and her things, it was all so real. And when I woke up the next day, I was disoriented and had somehow settled in that place between remembering the dream, and the fact that it felt like real life. Even after I found out Kane was living and breathing and going about his business with his on again, off again, I couldn't stop thinking about it."

"You're saying that imagining the loss of Kane made you realize how much you care for him?"

I stared out the window,

"Yup."

I glanced at my watch, we still had a half hour,

"I almost died, and the man I love saved my life, and then told me he loves me. But then, right after that, I had this dream that another person I care about, died, and I realized I don't want that part of my life to be over."

She nodded and waited. I continued,

"So, I finally have the chance to see what it would be like to be with Seppi, and I'm sitting around thinking about Kane. What is wrong with me!? I've already established that Kane is too comfortable and I can't deal with the on-again off-again bullshit with Alex, as sweet as she is, I don't need to be sloppy seconds."

Isabella looked at me and we both started laughing, I realized I didn't have that quite right,

"You know what I mean. I don't know what to do."

"Is Giuseppi putting pressure on you to decide one way or the other?"

I stared at my hands as they rested in my lap and picked at the skin on the side of my thumb, even though I would regret it later,

"He has been patient with me, but we recently had a conversation about his intentions, and mine."

I nibbled on my bottom lip,

"I am so scared something will go wrong, or that there is something horrible swimming in the periphery that will steal it all away."

She made eye contact with me,

"It sounds like you're afraid to let yourself feel loved, or truly connected to someone, even if you know they love you."

I ignored her and kept going,

"Like when you watch a cat stalk a mouse. They sit there patiently, watching, and then all of a sudden their tail straightens, and you see their butt wiggle, and you know what's coming."

I couldn't believe I needed to be concerned with Giuseppi Moretti's past, I never thought something like that would have any bearing on my life,

"We had a heart-to-heart last week, and I told him I love him. We've been in this limbo physically, but I started things last week and I probably would have slept with him, if his mother hadn't come knocking on his office door."

Dr. Rossi's eyes were like pancakes. That time I think she really did want me to spill the tea,

"His mother!?"

Lucky for her, I was ready to dump the whole tea pot right on the carpet, as I talked too fast,

"Yup, and then there was this whole thing where I climbed out of his bathroom window, and then pretended I just got there."

"What, are you twelve?"

I looked at her flatly,

"Yeah, I get it, amateur hour. Anyway, Mary knew what we were doing, and gave us her blessing, it was kind of a turn off."

I talked with my hands,

"Here I am, being encouraged by Giuseppi Moretti's mommy to jerk him off next to his baseball card collection and Nintendo."

"I guess I can see how that might put a damper on things."

"Anyway, and then I started obsessing about Kane. I'm talking real junior high shit, listening at his door, making sure we bump into each other at the cafe or in the driveway. I keep track of when Alex is there and when a couple days have gone by without her."

"So, you're confused because you wanted Seppi until you could have him and then you didn't want him anymore."

"No, it isn't that. I love Seppi, but deeply care about Kane, But like I've said before, I feel like life would be too monotonous if I was with Kane."

Isabella stepped out of her professional role for the first time, and I'm not sure she did it on purpose,

"You mean life would be boring without the car chases, gunshot wounds, and murder?"

Umm, no, that's not what I was saying. Was it?

"I see what you're getting at doc. There's a lot going on here. At first, I might have had a case of the 'want what you can't haves' with Seppi. And maybe the monotonous coffee bean and acoustic guitar life is safer and more comfortable, and maybe that's not a bad thing."

"I'm not going to ask you to compare your feelings for the two of them, but I want you to think about where you see yourself in ten years. Which one of them fits into that more naturally?"

I was pretty sure I knew the answer to her question, and quite frankly, it was a little disappointing. I had never loved anyone as deeply as I loved Seppi, but I wasn't stupid about what that would mean. It would be safer with Kane in some backward way, and I still had feelings for him. I was pretty sure if I laid all my cards on the table, he would tell me he felt the same. Deep down, I think Alex was just familiar and comfortable and kept him from getting lonely. All in all, the only thing I managed to do that time with Dr. Rossi was to scare myself back into my shell as far as Giuseppi Moretti was concerned.

My session ended and I made another appointment with Elaine. My car was like a fart in a hurricane in the sea of BMWs and Teslas. My other car is a broom, or whatever. And then my car wouldn't start. Goddammit. I slammed the back of my head against the headrest a couple times for good measure but it didn't do anything to solve my problem. I dug around for my phone and called Seppi, reluctantly.

"Dimples?"

Pinching the bridge of my nose, I sighed,

"Yeah, my car won't start."

"I wondered why it was still here."

"No, I was feeling nostalgic, so I drove Holly to therapy, and now she's dead or something. How ironic."

"I'll send Vin to give you a jump and follow you home. Hang tight."

He paused,

"You're the only woman I've ever known who would choose a bungeed-shut rattle-trap, over a hot looking Caddy."

Seppi chuckled to himself and then,

"You're cute."

The call ended.

I'm glad I serve as some sort of entertainment for that man. I sat in the passenger seat while I waited. I was really in a pickle as far as Seppi and Kane. The rational part of me knew that Seppi was the wise choice, but at the same time, I was already racking up the trauma and it had only been a year. What if my life revolved around lattes and running a community studio? No high-speed car chases or murder, or getting zip tied in the woods. No more high-anxiety or hyper-vigilance, no more concealed carry, no more panic button.

It would also mean no more across the desk whiskey in the inner sanctum. It would mean no more five o'clock shadow and Tobacco Vanille. And maybe it would mean I'd never get to know what it was like to be in his bed or sit across the table from him over pancakes. I let out a big sigh as Vinny nosed Seppi's Porsche into the spot in front of mine. What the fuck? Who shows up to jump start a piece of Swiss cheese in a Porsche, what a fucking douche bag. I rolled my eyes, crossed my arms like an asshole, and had to pee. It wasn't the battery. I ran inside to go to the bathroom while Vinny poked around under the hood. When I came back out, I could tell he didn't want to tell me what he had to tell me, and I didn't have time for his shit,

"Just tell me."

Nonchalantly, as he gestured like Italians do,

"This thing's toast."

Vinny's friend took Holly to his lot so I could clean her out and say goodbye before she went to the big scrap heap in the sky. On the way home, the two of us shared the ten-dollar pizza special at Bongiovanni's but we had it with a pitcher of beer and not the free two liter bottle of soda. On the ride home, Vinny offered me a cigarette and lit it with his fancy gold Zippo. I dug a silver flask from my bag and swallowed fire as I melted into the seat.

CHAPTER 4
CAREFUL WHAT YOU WISH FOR

THE NEXT DAY was weird, I was more anxious than usual and didn't know what to do with myself. I'd been thinking about what Dr. Rossi said, the part about where I saw myself in ten years. I was panicky and felt sick to my stomach when I thought about Seppi. No matter how much I loved him, I wasn't cut out to be a mob wife. I was honored to have gotten to know the parts nobody else saw, the parts that were vulnerable even when the rest of him was expensive whiskey and Cuban cigars. Being close enough to hug him was all it took to bring me back to life. My mind did one of those montage reels where you see all the big moments. I started with the first time I laid eyes on him and ended with how it felt when he finally touched me.

My stomach churned, and I had different flashbacks, scary ones, the ones I pushed into tiny little boxes on tiny little shelves in tiny little rooms, in the back of my mind. If you take a step back, you'll see that the deep love I had for him was constantly complicated by bullets and blood and bodies. There was an absolute pendulum swing, from the fiercest physical and emotional attraction, to the most intense fear I'd ever experienced, and I had a decision to make. But, knowing I had a decision to make was one thing, making an actual decision was something else entirely. I was being tormented by my demons and my own heart.

The day before my birthday, I worked at Muddy Waters. On my birthday, I had to meet with a couple about their reception, complete with tasting menu, phony smiles, and fake hellos. I pushed it out of my mind as I sipped a latte and smoked half a joint on the sun porch. Almost my last joint as a twenty-three-year-old child who wanted nothing more than to be loved by her own mother. Tears came and I rubbed my temples. I needed an answer, some direction, some reassurance I was good enough, strong enough, sexy enough to be with Giuseppi Moretti. When I glanced up, there was a crow on the edge of the fire pit and the two of us made eye contact. The crow tossed its beak toward the ristorante but I'm sure it was my imagination. I shook my head and rolled my eyes, whatever, I was trying to see things where there was nothing to see. I went to the screen and chittered at the crow. It launched from the fire pit and landed on the roof rack of the Escalade, making a big display of it with a full body flap. It cawed at me a few times to get the point across, you know, in case I'm stupid. And then it flew away. Whatever.

I showered and worked curl cream through my hair, slapped on some mascara, Carmex, and Alien Elixir. It was nice out, so I stepped into one of my vintage broomstick skirts and slid on a pair of Birkenstocks. I opened my jewelry box, and as I was moving things around, I uncovered a little drawstring bag, one of Maggie's birthday gifts from the year before. I had been such a mess that I hadn't even opened the pouch to see what was inside. I untied the ribbon and pulled out a scrolled piece of paper in my aunt's handwriting.

Amelia,

May these bells be a reminder that people notice your presence. You are light, and wit, and power. I love you, my dear, I hope you have a wonderful twenty-three.

Love, Maggie

I tipped the bag and dumped its contents into my palm. Maggie had gifted me two sterling silver anklets adorned with tiny sterling silver bells that made a gentle tinkling sound when they came together. Tears came and I felt bad for not opening her gift when she had intended, I felt sick I hadn't thanked her. My head was spinning and I was fighting a full on mental breakdown. I fastened the bells around my ankles and kissed Indie before bouncing down the stairs to Muddy Waters.

It was a busy morning for a Tuesday but there was a lull in the bustle, and I snuck away to Kane's office. I poked my head in and gave him a wave, he gestured me in and I pushed the door shut. Keep in mind that my head was full of gobbledygook, and that I was all confused because of the dream I had. Just keep that in mind, please. Either way, I caught him off guard and he glanced up from his papers with confusion on his face. I paused with my back against the office door and then went to him. Kane stood and I got on my tippy-toes so I could wrap my arms around his neck. He bent, his arms circling my waist, his body relaxing as he exhaled, like the weight of the world was on his shoulders. Kane was gentle, always gentle, he was never scary or intimidating, and I never feared for my life when I was with him. The parts of me that wanted to play it safe, found comfort in Kane.

"What are we doing here?"

I pulled away, pushed his chest, and he plopped in his chair. We looked at each other briefly and I wondered what was going through his mind. I bent and hooked my finger under his chin, tilting his face toward mine until our eyes met, but it was something more than that and we both knew it. I was trying to see if my future was in there, and in ten years, that is where I wanted to be, not swimming in fear and darkness. I had been looking for answers and it just confused me. I was at this precipice of darkness and light and I needed to decide which way to go. I was a deer during hunting season; was I going to run toward the vanilla safety of Kane Buchanan, or was I going to choose to stay in the line of fire?

Overwhelmed with the closeness and the feelings, I spun around and marched back to the counter, no one even noticed I was gone. I'm sure Kane was sitting there with his head spinning, but I hadn't crossed any lines or done anything I shouldn't. My mind was racing and I felt like I was going to shit my pants. I tried to push away the feelings I had for Seppi, but it was physically impossible. I didn't see him that day, and I didn't break the seal, and I'm sure he was busy because he didn't text me either. But every time my phone vibrated, I had a shot of adrenaline, wondering if it was him. I knew if I listened to my gut, it would tell me to run as far as I could, away from Giuseppi Moretti.

I hadn't mentioned it was my birthday the next day but Kane knew. That evening, we sat on his sun porch with weed and tequila and vintage vinyl records. He asked if he could take me out for a birthday dinner and I said yes. That simple decision would come back to bite me in the ass, and quite frankly, I have no idea what I was thinking. I'd had a deeply intimate conversation with Seppi, confessed my love and fears and apprehensions, and had every intention of moving forward with him. But there I was, panicking because Isabella Rossi asked me where I saw myself in ten years. There was some sort of irony in the fact that Seppi was paying her big bucks to cock block him.

It was my choice where we went for the aforementioned dinner, as long as it wasn't Giuseppi's Italian Ristorante. There was a nice steakhouse on the other side of town and a place we could stop for a couple drinks on the way home. I knew a couple drinks would lead me back into Kane's bed, but I'd made a hasty decision about my future and who I wanted to spend it with. We didn't cross any lines that night, but I fell asleep on Kane's couch because I didn't feel like being alone. I woke to Kane kissing me on the forehead as he placed a steaming latte on the coffee table. I looked at him with one eye open as he sang "Happy Birthday." Kane was showered and I smelled eggs and toast,

"I have to head down but I made you an omelet, just warm it up when you're hungry."

Kane kissed me and retreated to the world of crumpled napkins and empty coffee cups. I snagged the omelet and shuffled across the hall to get ready for work. My consult wasn't until ten and I wanted to avoid Seppi as much as possible, as far as he was concerned, it was just another day. I showered and worked curl cream through my ringlets, dressed in some tailored aesthetic, and did eyeliner, mascara, and Alien Elixir. I zipped my feet into some low-heeled boots and went to the world of piano wire neck ties and stiffs in trunks. I swung through the back door and dropped my bag on my desk. The pastry chef was making a flourless chocolate torte and I salivated as I walked past. A good flourless chocolate torte with fresh raspberries is my all-time favorite, and that particular flourless chocolate torte melted in my mouth as I sipped my latte,

"Wow, what's the occasion, I thought it was citrus olive oil cake this week."

The pastry chef nodded and smiled,

"Changing it up."

I was hoping I'd be able to snag a piece before I left for the day, and planned to eat it on my sun porch with a jelly glass of shitty whiskey and a joint. If I stayed in my office all day doing busy work, maybe Seppi wouldn't even notice I was right across the hall from him. I closed my door most of the way, sat at my desk, returned some phone calls and emails. Tried to stay busy and out of the hallway. When I went into my bathroom, I noticed a Diptyque hand soap and a small box on the vanity next to the jar of edibles. I lifted the lid to find two fancy looking joints with rolling papers that looked like hundred-dollar bills. When I passed the coffee table, I noticed a glass jar filled with nothing but dark chocolate covered blueberries.

I plopped on the sofa and spotted a small black gift bag tucked in next to the glass jar, it said Chanel in white letters across the front. I approached the bag as if it might bite me, unsure if there were strings attached to whatever was inside. I peeked inside to see black tissue paper surrounding a white and gold box. There was a small card inside with a note from Seppi, 'Dimples, I've never picked out perfume for anyone before, I hope I did good. Buon Compleanno. Ti amo, Seppi.' Nestled inside the fancy gift bag was a large bottle of Coco Mademoiselle. I removed the cap and sniffed, taking in the perfect amalgamation of my past and present. For a moment, I was swept up in the flattery of it all, the fact that Giuseppi Moretti had gone to Macy's on my account. I reminded myself to move toward the light and away from the darkness. A moment later, Seppi beckoned me from across the hall,

"Dimples."

If I tell you I froze in the middle of my office for a full minute, deciding what to do, that is probably an understatement. Finally, I went where I was beckoned and stood in his doorway as he motioned me in. I swallowed hard, crossed the threshold, and he gestured for me to close the door. I did as I was told as the dark mafia energy sucked me in. His eyes conveyed the same hunger and ferociousness with which he would devour me someday. But that day, I was trying to keep him at arm's length, my face to the sun instead of the darkness,

"Did you like your birthday gifts?"

I moved from one foot to the other, like a schoolboy getting in trouble for throwing rocks at little girls, my heart doing somersaults in my chest,

"Yes, thank you very much for thinking of me. Everything is very nice."

I was trying to stay behind a wall of some sort, an invisible barrier that wasn't really there. Where did I see myself in ten years? I gestured toward the door, my voice crumbling, tripping over tears,

"I, umm, I have a consult coming in a little while and...I, umm, I need to make sure everything is, umm..."

Seppi rose and closed the gap, walking me backward until my back hit the wall. He scooped the back of my head, and our mouths came together. My knees went weak, and he held me there with his body. I leaned into him, the bulge in his pants, pressing against my stomach, his voice like a snake charmer, and I was the snake,

"I'm trying to be patient with you, Dimples."

I glanced up at him, he was hungry and I knew it,

"I'm trying really hard not to scare you away, but I find you insanely attractive, and I'm having a difficult time thinking about anything but devouring you."

Jesus. I nodded and swallowed hard, my nipples pressing against my bra, my insides warm, my voice up an octave,

"Umm, thank you."

Giuseppi Moretti had me under his spell and I was spouting gibberish. I needed to get the hell out of there, pronto. Seppi backed away, and I dropped my eyes to the floor. He hooked my chin with his finger and our eyes met, I could tell he had sort of been playing, but something about it made me freeze. Seppi realized I wasn't just coming in to play wounded baby deer with him,

"What's wrong, my Amelia?"

I tried to maintain eye contact as I spoke, my voice tripping over my feelings,

"Isabella asked me where I see myself in ten years."

Seppi didn't look away but he took a deep breath and I knew he was putting up some sort of armor. He bent to me and our mouths came together again, only that time it was like he was teasing me; I made a sound low in my throat. I wanted nothing more than to go home with him and stay there forever. I almost pushed aside the fear and the apprehension, part of me almost gave into him that day, right then, in that office. Seppi pulled away so slowly that I chased after him with my lips. He separated himself from me and responded in his mob boss voice,

"I'm not interested in having something casual with you, Amelia, I'm way past that."

I wasn't interested in something casual either. Seppi looked me in the eye again,

"Let me know when you decide if your future includes me."

I stood there, doe-eyed, looking up at the man I loved,

"Seppi, I'm scared."

The dam broke and I sobbed in his arms with the heat from his breath on my scalp. After a long silence, his voice soft and gentle, as not to scare me back into my shell,

"You are safe with me, Dimples. You always have been, and always will be."

He held me at arm's length and examined me, trying to climb inside and read my mind,

"I am not going to lie and say there won't be complications along the way, but I intend to do everything in my power to ensure that you feel loved and protected."

I didn't say anything back, but I felt a little bit better, and knew deep down I would end up with him someday. Seppi held the back of my neck and kissed my forehead, keeping his lips there like I was of value to him,

"You are a treasure, and I cherish you."

He let me go and I retreated with the feelings in my throat. I closed my door most of the way, thirty minutes until my consult, the walls closing in, the room spinning. I kicked off my heels, hugged my knees to my chest, and fell apart. Almost too high to be conducting a consult, the last shot of whiskey soothing the parts of me that needed it. I was staring at the wall, popping dark chocolate covered blueberries in my mouth when there was a tap at the door,

"Hello, Darling!"

I swung my door open to Mary Moretti, she kissed me on both cheeks before handing over a bakery bag and a white paper cup,

"Dark chocolate raspberry latte and a lemon poppy seed muffin, darling, a special birthday treat from Eliana Mazelli's place."

I took the paper cup and pastry bag from Mary and we sat on the sofa. She pulled a gift bag and envelope from her cavernous designer handbag. There was a Burberry scarf in the bag and a five-hundred dollar gift card to Macy's in the little envelope. I threw the scarf around my neck and sipped the latte. And then Mary said she needed help situating a group that was coming in for a party that evening. I wasn't sure if Kane had made a reservation for dinner, or if we were going to play it by ear, but knowing him, we were playing it by ear,

"Sure, that's not a problem."

Mary smiled,

"Thank you, Amelia. I know it's your special day, but one of the girls quit last night and I want to make sure the guests have a good first impression of the place. If you can handle upstairs, I can handle down here. It won't be long, I'm sure you have plans this evening. Once everyone has been served, you can go. Does that sound OK?"

I put my hand on hers and nodded. She hopped up,

"Good then, I'll see you around four-thirty."

Mary blew me a kiss and strolled to the door, spinning around on the threshold,

"See you then, Darling!"

She winked and went on her way. A tailored suit and heels on my birthday, I made a face at the empty doorway, what a joke. I closed my door again. It was my birthday, I wanted sweatpants, a fat joint, and a big juicy steak, not a tailored fucking suit and heels. I pretended to gag myself. Whatever. I went to the kitchen and checked one more time that the tasting menu would be ready. Ten minutes later, I was unlocking the front door for the future Mr. & Mrs. Fairbanks. The man was good looking but not in an intimidating way, he had a strong jawline but nothing obnoxious. The woman was curvy and adorable and was wearing a cute gingham dress. When I asked where she found her dress she said she made it herself and I was jealous. They seemed like a sweet couple and I bet they didn't have a warm stiff getting cold in the back of their Subaru Forester. I ran to my office to get my folder and then gave them the grand tour. They loved the upstairs dining area and I told them it was my favorite too, it felt like Italy up there, for real, there was even a small stage for local bands. When we went downstairs, I gave them a tour of the outside seating area, complete with propane fire pit and tall gas lanterns. The outside seating would be opening on Memorial Day weekend and I was looking forward to seeing people out there again.

We settled in and the couple enjoyed the tasting menu. Seppi made an appearance, introduced himself, and told the couple they were in good hands. He winked before he walked away and electricity shot to my privates. The woman asked a lot of questions and by the time they left, I only had a couple hours before I needed to be back, polished, and dressed for the formal event. I asked about the menu for that night and the chef told me it was Antipasto salad, fresh pasta with Mama Moretti's marinara, and a choice of protein. Dessert was a Flourless Chocolate Torte with Raspberry compote. I was drooling. I made a mental note to bring a gallon zipper bag back with me so I could sneak a piece or two of that torte into my handbag on the way out.

In between, I spent time with Kane, trying to focus on the light, on the world that didn't consist of car chases and flying bullets, the one that didn't include perfectly square ice cubes. I knew deep down that the world with the light didn't hold my broken pieces together. It wasn't where I felt protected, and I would never love anyone like I loved Giuseppi Moretti, but I tried. We listened to records and I was looking forward to our steak date and drinks after, maybe the alcohol would loosen me up enough to commit to the wrong man.

When it was time, I showered and did the whole thing again, only that time I did a little more makeup before the lipstick. I dressed in a tailored dusty lavender pantsuit over a cream-colored silk camisole. I slipped my feet, begrudgingly, into a pair of nude leather heels. I spritzed Coco Mademoiselle on my pulse points before giving myself a once over in the mirror. I added a pair of dusty lavender, cream, and silver beaded earrings. I tapped on Kane's door to let him know I was leaving and he said I looked hot. I left a lipstick kiss on his cheek before retreating to the world of rubbing shoulders with rich assholes who have fancy parties. As I went for the stairs, Kane hollered after me,

"Hey!"

I spun around and he said,

"You smell nice."

He was right.

I strolled past the mini mafia, and it was the first time I wondered if gifts were Seppi's love language. Maybe he had never learned how to express love without flaunting his money and power and place on the food chain. Deep down, I knew the only part of me that wasn't sure about Seppi was the part that was scared of a life like that. But then I thought about how he made me feel, and that the gifts he'd given me were personal. I was so confused. Seppi and I came together in a way I had never come together with anyone else. He was the first person I knew who would kill for me, and I had seen it firsthand. With every step closer to the backdoor of that restaurant, my heart was knocked off its feet by a tidal wave of the feelings I had for Seppi. As I punched in the code for the back door of the ristorante, Kane hollered down from his sun porch,

"Don't be long!"

He blew me a kiss and I blew one back. And then I pulled the door open and went through a portal into the darkness. I put my purse on the desk and locked myself in the bathroom. My eyes fell to the new soap and fancy joints. I looked at myself in the mirror and I'm not talking about my appearance, I looked myself in the eye and I watched the darkness and the light as they swirled together like dragons fighting in the sky. I closed my eyes and imagined Seppi's hands on me, just the thought of it made my body react. I wondered if maybe he needed me more than I needed him.

I paused with my hand on the doorknob before taking a deep breath and going back to the real world. In the hall, I could smell marinara, roasted garlic, fresh bread, the house dressing, and espresso. Mary arrived in a swirl of Chanel No. 5 and skinny cigarettes. She kissed me on both cheeks and told me the party would be arriving soon. I made my way to the second-floor seating area, a string quartet warming up on the stage, playing something by Frank Sinatra. I did a lap around my favorite part of the restaurant and stood in the front windows, lost in thought. The place was decorated tastefully, and it seemed odd that I didn't know anything about it, since it was my job to plan the events. Was Seppi losing faith that I could handle the position? Was I so preoccupied with my own shit that he had his mother pick up my slack? Was I dropping the ball in the romance department *and* as his Event Planner!? There I was, still wasting his time, what an idiot.

I stood there, a fucking failure that needed to get my shit together. The hair on my arms stood up a split second before I felt his hands on my shoulders and his lips on my neck. I closed my eyes as the warmth from Seppi's breath spread over my skin. I turned and he was smiling from ear to ear, he winked and flicked an eyebrow,

"You smell good enough to eat, Dimples."

"I'm wearing the perfume you gave me."

I blushed and he upped the ante,

"I think you're on the dessert menu, Dimples."

Seppi flicked his eyebrows and that did something for me, so I flicked my eyebrows back,

"We'll have to see if you have room for dessert after you've finish your dinner."

Seppi leaned in, breathy in my ear,

"I always have room for dessert."

He took a step back and put his hand out to me, I took it. The quartet did a run through of Under My Skin as we danced. I felt like a princess in my tailored pantsuit and fancy perfume. I'd been transported to another world, another life, but I knew there was a reason I hadn't been part of planning that party and a searing need to apologize burned in my stomach,

"I'm sorry I've been so preoccupied lately. I guess I'm struggling with this thing between us, and with my parents moving back, just a lot of things. I'm sorry I haven't been holding up my end of the bargain around here."

I gestured around the room,

"I should have been the one to take care of all of this and I didn't even know there was an event tonight."

I teared up and Seppi hooked a finger under my chin. When I looked up at him, I felt it in my chest. The world stopped spinning, and my feelings for him flooded in so forcefully that I almost drowned. He put his mouth to my neck, and sucked a little, I knew it would leave a mark, and when he kissed me, I tasted my perfume on his lips. When he pulled away, he took my hands, and said,

"Happy Birthday, Amelia."

And everyone yelled,

"Surprise!"

I spun around to see my parents, Sunny and Vinny, Mary, and some of my friends from around Bunman. My Aunt Maggie had returned from her trip, and she introduced me to her boyfriend Clem. There must have been twenty-five people there that night, but Kane Buchanan wasn't one of them. I felt a pang of regret for how my heart was betraying me. Kane was waiting for me, and I was at the ristorante getting poured over with attention and toasts and my favorite meal in the whole world. I snuck away to text him that it would be longer than I'd planned. Kane felt far away, it felt like when I was in the dark world, the light one didn't exist in the same way. I was caught between a sinner and a saint.

My Dad jogged over and picked me right up off the floor,

"Happy Birthday Boo-Boo Bear! You look so grown up!"

Maggie was waiting her turn in a long flowy skirt and linen tunic, silk scarf, beaded fringe earrings, a waft of guaiac wood and weed,

"Happy Birthday, sweetheart, I am so glad I could be here."

Sunny bounced over to me and kissed my cheek,

"Happy Birthday, fucker!"

She spun me around and then Vinny kissed me on both cheeks and pulled me in for a hug, he smelled good as always,

"Happy Birthday, Amelia."

It was surreal that the upstairs was filled with people who wanted to celebrate me, that hadn't happened a single time in my whole life. Sunny snapped pictures as I enjoyed my meal, danced, and drank a couple glasses of very expensive champagne. Sunny, Maggie, and I shared a joint in my office bathroom, but Sunny didn't take pictures of that. Seppi made a speech about me and it felt like I belonged there, in that world. He'd swept me off my feet without even trying, no one had ever made that big a deal over me before, not even my own mother.

The flourless chocolate torte was the best I'd ever had, and I still had raspberry compote on my breath when I made out with Seppi in his office after everyone left. We didn't get interrupted that time, and even though we didn't go all the way, that was the first time we pleasured each other. I was in for a treat, if that experience was any indication of things to come, no pun intended. I made a mental note to report back to my mother that I had finally earned the fancy car.

CHAPTER 5
NATURAL CONSEQUENCES

I SNUCK UP the back stairs at two in the morning, carrying my heels, and I had Seppi on my breath. I tiptoed down the hall and held the doorknob so it wouldn't click when I pushed it shut, I turned the lock as quietly as possible. I waited but Kane didn't come tapping at my door to ask a million questions and smell my mouth. When I woke, I sat on the sun porch with a latte and my first joint of the day, watching birds circle the feeders. I looked at my phone and there were texts from Sunny, mostly pictures from the night before. You might think I was scrutinizing my appearance in all the pictures to see which ones I wanted to post on Facebook, but that's not what I was doing.

I'm someone who looks at every person in a picture, at the background and the things in it. And in one of the pictures of me dancing, was Giuseppi Moretti. He wasn't the one dancing with me, in fact, he was on the other side of the room. But when I looked at that picture, I realized what Mary said about the way we looked at each other when the other person isn't looking. I zoomed in and I would have known Seppi loved me even if he hadn't told me. The happiness in his eyes, the pure adoration and love radiating from his smile as he watched me dance from across the room. There was nothing scary about the man in that picture, there were no bullets flying, no stiffs in the trunk. There was just a man who loved a woman with his entire heart. As I sat there with my phone in one hand and my joint in the other, finally getting it, finally understanding how Seppi felt about me, there was a knock at the door. I padded through the kitchen and swung the door open to Kane. He crossed the threshold with a pensive look on his face,

"Can we talk?"

I gestured him in and he followed me to the sun porch. He sat, and then stood up and paced,

"What happened last night?"

I told him the truth but not all of it, and my head was still spinning from that picture Sunny sent me. I told Kane that it ended up being a surprise party for me and not just an event. He sat down like the wind had been knocked out of his sails,

"Who planned it?"

I waved him away and my voice cracked,

"Oh, I don't know."

He glanced at me,

"Who planned it, Amelia?"

I swallowed hard. Kane scoffed,

"I thought so."

He strode toward the door and I grabbed his arm,

"Kane, wait."

He looked at me again and I felt pain,

"I didn't know about the party, I promise. I guess Seppi planned it, but Maggie probably helped."

"Oh, yeah? If Maggie helped, she would have invited me and you know it."

Kane was right and I knew it. He threw his hands toward the ristorante, yelling,

"How am I supposed to compete with that!? With him!?"

My emotions hit me like a punch in the gut and I choked down the ball of tears in my throat,

"I'm not asking you to compete with him, I like you the way you are. You play it safe and don't take risks, you're gentle and predictable."

Kane's eyes did something I couldn't figure out, but I felt like I'd said the wrong thing,

"Amelia, I'm not dumb enough to get into a pissing contest with Giuseppi Moretti. For Christ's sake, I'll end up at the bottom of the lake."

"Kane."

He wagged his chin in my direction,

"What time did you finally get home? I stayed up until one-thirty."

I blurted out,

"Two."

He squinted,

"What took you so long?"

I met his eyes and swallowed the nerves in my throat.

"Amelia, what took so long?"

I dropped my eyes,

"Kane, please."

He turned around and disappeared down the stairs, to the world of basic bitches and burnt scones. I stood in my kitchen for a long time, just staring at the open door. I had to do some work at the ristorante, so I showered and brought my curls to life. I put on a tailored pantsuit, some black leather boots, and my fancy new perfume. I went through the back door of the restaurant like a bad bitch and put my purse on my desk. Seppi wasn't in his office and when my eyes drifted to his sofa, I blushed. Electricity shot through my body when I thought about the weight of his body on mine as we kissed the night before. I turned and ran right into Seppi, his chest like a brick wall, our eyes met and he flicked his eyebrows,

"Morning."

He kissed me on the lips like it was no big deal and strolled into his office with a cup of espresso. I made myself a latte and sat across the desk from him. He smelled like shower gel and Tobacco Vanille, fresh shave, top couple buttons unbuttoned, sleeves rolled up a couple times, I wanted to lick his face. That was the thing I had been wishing for and I finally got it, but all it did was complicate things. I wasn't just choosing between two men, I was choosing between two worlds. I also knew that without a doubt, I needed to stall before he put me on the spot.

I put my mug on the desk and went into his bathroom to stare at myself in the mirror, my phone vibrating in my pocket. I slid it out, another message from Sunny, I almost put it back in my pocket without opening it, but I didn't. That one had a caption, 'You love him, fucker. Telling you in case you haven't realized it yet.' I tapped on the picture and it came to life right in front of my eyes. That one was a picture of me looking at Seppi. First of all, I looked like a woman, a twenty-four-year-old woman, and not a broken little girl, it actually brought tears to my eyes. I looked at my hair and my makeup, the way I held myself, the way the tailored suit fit my curves. But then I looked at my eyes and my smile as Seppi told a story to my dad and Clem. I was staring at a woman who was looking at the man she loved and there was no doubt about it from that moment on.

A calm fell over me and for a moment, I knew everything would probably work out in the end. When I was in that world, things were dark leather, aged whiskey, and expensive perfume. There were handguns on hips, expensive cigars, whiskey on lips, lots of fast cars...blood on hands, skeletons in closets, stiffs in trunks. I was respected and protected and had access to the inner sanctum. I swung the bathroom door open and stood next to his chair. Our eyes met again and I needed to be close to him. I grabbed the front of Seppi's shirt and bent down to his lips, two could play at that game. I moved my hand to his throat and squeezed a little as I kissed him and I knew a pulse of blood was shooting to his nether region. On an exhale,

"What's gotten into you, Dimples?"

I chickened out so I kissed him on both cheeks and patted the bulge in his pants before I strolled out and closed the door behind me. I sat on my sofa and tried to slow my brain down enough to figure out what the hell I was doing, was I confident enough to be assertive like that with Giuseppi Moretti? And at this point, you're either thinking I'm completely confused, or that I'm a complete whore. And, either way, you're probably right, but in my defense, I didn't do any of it on purpose. Or, maybe you're just wondering if I gave him blue balls and then sat on my sofa eating dark chocolate covered blueberries until I had something better to do. The answer is no.

I came to my senses relatively quickly and went back across the hall. Seppi moved his eyes to the door as I locked it. He flicked his eyebrows and swirled his whiskey. I stood with my back against the door and made eye contact with him as I unbuttoned my suit jacket. I tossed the jacket onto the back of the sofa and started on my blouse, one button, and then another. Untucked it slowly, unbuttoned the cuffs, pulled it off one sleeve at a time, laid it on top of the suit jacket. Seppi was chewing on his bottom lip so I took a step closer and tossed my bra at him, it landed in his lap. I undid my belt and pulled it through the loops, tossing it at his feet. I undid my fancy tailored pants and laid them on top of the shirt. I took another step closer and hooked my thumbs in the waistband of my cute little panties. I slid them down, caught them on my right foot, and kicked them in Seppi's direction, he caught them and held them to his lips, I broke the silence,

"Penny for your thoughts."

Seppi was unbuttoning his shirt as he stood. He tossed it on his desk and undid his belt, the pants went on top of the shirt, his boxer briefs askew next to his shoes. We stood there completely naked together, neither of us carrying a single piece of armor. I went to him and we kissed there like that, naked in his office in the middle of the morning. Our hands grabbing, and squeezing, and getting acquainted, Seppi's lips against mine,

"I love you so much, Amelia."

I knew he meant it, and that time, I didn't hesitate, because I knew I meant it too,

"I love you too, Giuseppi."

We laid on the sofa, kissing, even though our bodies wanted more than that, breathy in my ear,

"Sleep over sometime, so I can make love to you all night."

Seppi kissed my neck and then my throat, collar bone and lower, worked his way down. He was a generous lover and he knew what he wanted in return. To this day, I don't know if anyone heard me, but I might have been a little too loud. And because I'm a lady, I returned the favor. I took my time and teased him, made him beg for it. Something about that exchange made me even more excited about that part of our relationship. And let me start by saying, I didn't set out to hurt anyone. And before you tell me I hurt Kane, let me remind you that I thought we were a couple when he strolled into the cafe with his arm around Alex one day. So, that road goes both ways.

I needed to talk to Kane though, I needed him to understand that I cared about him but that I couldn't go any further with him, I didn't even know if he'd talk to me. The truth is, when I was in the dark world, Kane didn't exist the way he did when I was in the one with the coffee beans and the acoustic guitar. That time though, I didn't get lost in my head, I wasn't confused about which man I wanted or which world I wanted to be in. I felt like I could take a deep breath and let it all out, relax for a change. It had been a roller coaster ride but I had finally made a decision. I spent time returning phone calls and felt good about my place in that world.

Not eight hours after we made out in his office, his voice came floating across the hall to me,

"Dimples."

I went over and perched on the arm of the sofa. Vinny was sitting across from Seppi in his beat up leather jacket and some black biker boots, the look suited him, and he smelled different than usual,

"Did you get a new cologne, you smell nice."

Seppi was all business,

"Amelia."

My eyes shifted to Seppi's side of the desk and I knew why I was there, so I closed the door. Twenty minutes later, I was riding shotgun with a stiff in the trunk. We wound our way past The Lakeside General Store and down the Lake Road. We parked at the Moretti's cottage and loaded the body onto a small houseboat. We made our way into the dark with a dead body on board. Vinny maneuvered the boat to the deepest part of Clover Lake and we floated there in pitch darkness. The two of us moved the body to the deck, it was wrapped in a tarp, weights inside the guy's shirt and strapped to his ankles. I kept stepping on the excess rope but at least I wasn't going to fall through the ice that time. We rolled the guy into the water and a loop of rope tightened around my ankle. I was pulled overboard along with the body, gulping in lake water, choking as I grabbed onto the ladder and screamed,

"VINNY!"

He screamed in response, I think we both felt a sense of déjà vu,

"AMELIA!"

He ran to the other end of the boat, came back with a search light and shined it in my face. I yelled at him as he blinded me,

"The rope is around my ankle, I can't hold on much longer, he's pulling me down!"

In a teary voice,

"Please hurry!"

Vinny dove in the water and swam over, wrapping his arm around me. I pushed him down, he needed to cut the rope, I was losing my grip and once I let go, I'd be pulled under with the dead body. Vinny dove into the darkness and felt his way from my thigh to my ankle, sawing at the rope with a pocketknife. My fingers slipped off the rung and I was sucked under. My face was six inches below the surface when the tension on the rope released and Vinny pulled me to the surface. I choked and coughed as he threw me on the deck like a sack of shit and knelt next to me,

"Are you okay!?"

I was gulping air so feverishly, I couldn't speak.

"Oh, Jesus, Amelia, are you okay!? Please tell me you're okay! You're okay, right!?"

I gagged, he rolled me over, and I threw up lake water. I cleared my throat and replied flatly,

"I'll be fine."

I lay on my back, staring at the sky. Vinny trolled back to the boathouse and twenty minutes later I would be in my apartment feeding Indie. But right then, the two of us were drenched, and there was a body sinking to the bottom of the lake. Just like that, another one bites the dust. What the fuck, right? Vinny dug through the tote of body dumping clothes in the back seat and we changed into something dry. For the second time, I almost died while dumping a stiff with Vincenzo Moretti. In his defense, he saved me both times, so that's something. Once we were back in the car, Vinny just sat there shaking his head. He pinched the bridge of his nose,

"I'm sorry this keeps happening, Amelia."

I put my hand on his arm and he glanced over at me,

"I know how much you mean to my brother."

I think he wanted to say more but he couldn't find the words. As we drove back into town, Vinny offered me one of his hand-rolled cigarettes. He lit it at a stop sign and I dug the silver flask from the bottom of my bag, melting into the seat as I swallowed fire. Vinny went through the McDonald's drive thru for a large fry and a McFlurry as an apology for almost getting me killed again. I finished eating before he pulled up the alley between Muddy Waters and Giuseppi's Italian Ristorante.

That time, I didn't run to Seppi. I clomped up my back stairs, carrying the wet pantsuit and heeled leather boots, my hair dripping with lake water, face wet with tears. You see the issue here, right? This wasn't as easy as, 'Do you want the chicken or the fish?' And I had already made my decision. But as I was unlocking my door, Kane opened his. I turned to him, completely deflated and exhausted. He saw something in my eyes that told him I needed to feel safe, so he came to me, and I fell in his arms and sobbed. I was not cut out for that shit, I just wasn't. How many more times would I almost die while I helped Vinny dump a body? I couldn't do it. I took a hot shower and came out to a bowl of popcorn and a scary movie. I fell asleep under Kane's arm and felt safe that night. We would have to talk about things, but I was sure that I never wanted to dump another body, or find myself in another kill or be killed situation.

The next morning, I sat on Kane's sun porch with my latte and joint, and pondered my life, I circled back to leaving Bunman. What other option did I have really? There was too much shit in that town, and there was no way I could exist in a place with both of those men, it was angel on one shoulder, devil on the other. To make matters worse, that was the night of my family birthday dinner and I wasn't in the mood. I needed to bring a distraction, I wasn't up for my mother's criticisms and general bullshit, and wondered if she would make some sort of meal I didn't like, since she had no idea what I'd want for my birthday dinner, and she hadn't bothered to ask. Maybe I'd dye my hair red, or wear something ridiculous to keep my mother's criticisms focused on one thing. I went through the motions at work and met with an older couple about an anniversary party. We talked about the head count and menu options, about Bunman, and how long they'd lived here. I admired that couple and wanted to be like them someday. If I chose the dark world, I'd probably end up dead long before that.

A while later, Seppi came into my office and kissed me on both cheeks on the way to his office. Maybe Vinny had told him and maybe he hadn't, but Seppi didn't act like he knew. As I sat there popping dark chocolate covered blueberries into my mouth, I got angry, livid even. I wasn't going to go along with something just because Giuseppi Moretti told me to, maybe this whole thing was a trap. I plunked the jar on the table, stormed across the hall, and plopped in the chair across from him. Seppi slid a rocks glass across the desk and it stopped right at the edge. I tossed it back and slammed the glass on the desk,

"I almost died last night."

I could tell he already knew, and wasn't sure if I was more upset that he hadn't said anything, or that he didn't seem bothered by the fact that I almost died.

He was all business, called me by my name,

"Look, Amelia, you're either in or you're out."

I narrowed my eyes at him like he was just some asshole I knew,

"What!?"

He sipped his whiskey nonchalantly and looked across the desk at me,

"I'm not going to play games with you anymore, you either want to be a part of this, or you don't."

He gestured at the wall,

"I'm sure your hippie friend can still use a barista in that hole in the wall over there."

Adrenaline burned in my stomach as he swirled whiskey around with the ice, almost antagonizing me, some sort of ultimatum,

"I can either trust you, or I can't."

I felt like he had been toying with me the entire time and the room started to spin. Just a cat batting at a feather, I was glad I hadn't slept with him. Do people leave normal lives to be a part of this? To be part of a world where you're ruthless and heartless and living on the edge? Do some people get off on that type of shit? Seppi came to my side of the desk, and hooked my chin with his finger as he kissed me, deeply, whiskey and espresso on his breath,

"Let me know."

I didn't understand what he meant and he knew it, so he clarified,

"You're either going to be a part of this, or you're not, and there's more at stake than you think."

I swallowed the lump in my throat,

"What do you mean?"

He looked down at me,

"Last I checked, you murdered a mob boss, so I don't suppose you'll last very long without me to protect you."

I was confused and hurt, my voice filling with tears,

"Seppi, I thought we were, something."

He was quiet for a minute, and when he moved his eyes to mine, they were filled with tears. He gestured for me to follow him out the back door to the Escalade. He drove to a place far away from there and I could tell something had shifted. Seppi cried quietly as he drove, and I could tell he was thinking. I wasn't worried he would hurt me, he left his armor back in that office, and I was with the man I'd fallen in love with. I wanted to make love to him, feel safe in his cage. I was with my strong protector, my second-best friend in the whole world, and not the patriarch of the Moretti mob family. We sat near the water, ate Chinese food, and sipped whiskey. Seppi lit a Cuban and blew the smoke out in rings. His voice had softened, and there was love in there somewhere,

"If you go back to your old life, I won't be able to protect you. This is bigger than me and you know that."

I started to say something, but he put his hand up,

"You killed my father, that's a big deal. It would be a big deal to kill anyone, but you killed a mob boss. Capiche?"

I nodded.

"Multiple people have already been sent here to find him."

Seppi came to me, cupped the side of my face and rubbed his thumb over my scrimple,

"Nothing can happen to you, do you understand?"

Our mouths came together and I came undone in his arms. It was simple, really. I wanted to stay alive and be protected, so I needed to stay, I needed to walk the walk and rub shoulders with the big boys. And I loved Seppi, but I had a deep fear I wouldn't be enough for him. And then he said,

"And I'm sorry about what happened the other night."

I hugged my knees to my chest and said,

"Listen, I came back to Bunman to get away from the bullshit in my life and it's been one thing after another since I got here."

He nodded. I lit a joint and blew out a stream of smoke, my voice had tears in it,

"I was worried about having to deal with my mother or running into my ex and his whore and their lovechild. But this!? Are you fucking kidding me!?"

"Amelia."

I waved him away and made a fatherly voice, playing both sides of the conversation,

"Hi Boo-Boo Bear, what did you do last night?"

"Oh, you know, I dumped a body and almost got sucked to the bottom of the lake."

I tapped my finger to my lips like I was thinking,

"Let's see, what else. Oh! And then I got high and ate some pizza bites."

"That sounds exciting, Boo-Boo Bear."

I glared at Seppi and threw my arms around as my voice rose,

"What the fuck, Seppi!? I didn't sign up for this bullshit! Suddenly, I'm Vinny's wingman when he has to ditch a stiff!? And both times, I almost died!? Is that how this is going to go!?"

Seppi put his arm around my shoulder and I shrugged away,

"Well!? I didn't sign up for any of this!"

I took another drag and coughed it out,

"I came back here to get away from shit, and all I've done is get sucked up in whatever the fuck you call all of this!"

He reached for me again and I pushed him away gently, my voice pleading,

"I just want to know what it would be like to be with you without all of this, because I'm not willing to do it this way, I'm just not."

And then I looked up at him with tears in my eyes,

"I love you with every shred of my being, but I don't like who you are when you're walking in your father's footsteps. I hated that man and I'm terrified I'll hate you someday."

Seppi wrapped his arms around me, kissed the top of my head and let me cry. I was trapped. If I wanted to live, I needed to stay. I was terrified about what that meant, and what it would look like. I was in over my head and I needed to figure out if it was worth it. It didn't make any sense; I was a broken little girl and he was a powerful man who could have any woman he wanted. Standing there in his arms, I felt like I was in the right place. I felt light years away from the car chases, the bullets, the dark water and the zip ties. I felt like Giuseppi Moretti was the most powerful man in the world and maybe he really was, but maybe it only felt that way because he held my heart in his hands.

CHAPTER 6
GROCERY STORE CAKE

I PULLED IT TOGETHER and when we got back into town, I called it quits for the day. I shut off my office light and waved to Seppi as I went for the back door. He waved me into his office, and I stood in front of him. He kissed me on both cheeks,

"Have a nice dinner with your folks, and say hi to your sister for me."

I kind of just said 'OK' and walked away. I felt like the wind had been knocked out of my sails, and here I was preparing for a family dinner at my parents' house. I needed a distraction. I sat on my sun porch smoking a joint and followed it up with a shot of whiskey. Kane strolled out onto his sun porch to light up a joint and glanced over, we made eye contact, fuck it,

"Wanna come to my parents' house for dinner tonight?"

He coughed out a cloud of smoke,

"I don't have anything else going on, I was just going to string my guitar and reheat some leftovers."

I finished my joint and went inside. I shook a bottle of pills and knew that sooner or later, I would have to give in. I was spiraling. I showered and worked curl cream through my hair. I didn't bother with makeup, but I slapped on some lipstick before spritzing on my new perfume. I stepped into my favorite pair of vintage overalls and slid my feet into the dingy white Chuck Taylors. I felt like a lost little girl as I looked at myself in the full-length mirror. I realized nothing had really changed in a year, but at the same time, nothing had stayed the same. The little girl staring back at me was not the same person who wore the dusty lavender pant suit. It was this bizarre yin and yang, this good versus evil, this ratty vintage overalls versus expensive tailored pant suits. This professional woman who functioned within the inner sanctum of the local mob, and this broken little girl holding all her broken pieces together with ripped overalls and dirty sneakers. At least I'd smell good while I sucked my thumb in the corner like a cry baby.

Off I went to collect Kane so we could venture to the world of veiled criticisms and cheap boxed wine with a spigot. He patted my leg as I sat in the passenger seat of Kane's Bronco, picking at the skin next to my thumb even though I would regret it later.

"How's it going, having her living this close?"

I rolled my eyes,

"I don't want to talk about it."

And that was all we said the entire trip over there. It was only fifteen minutes, but that's a long time when your head is swimming and you desperately want someone to throw you a rope. When we pulled in the driveway, neither my aunt and her boyfriend nor my sister and Auggie were there yet. Crap. It was just us. I leaned forward and rested my forehead against the dash,

"Fuck!"

Kane glanced over,

"What!?"

"Just, fuck!"

He nodded and we got out of the car. My dad swung through the door and picked me right up off the ground,

"Happy Birthday, Boo-Boo Bear!"

He kissed me on the cheek and rustled my hair. My mother came into view and I got sick to my stomach. She gave me an awkward hug and then gave Kane an awkward hug,

"Oh, after the other night, I assumed you'd show up with Giuseppi."

What the fuck was wrong with her!? We just got to the door, and she was already starting her shit. Jesus Christ. Kane put his hand on my back and pushed me across the threshold, my eyes filling with tears. Not two minutes in that house and I wanted to leave. I went to the bathroom and locked myself in, stood with one hand on either side of the vanity and cried into the sink. I was trying, I really was. My phone vibrated, it was my sister, 'On our way, see you soon.' And I thought, no you won't, because I'm getting the fuck out of here. There was no way I would make it to the part with the cake.

I splashed cold water on my face and patted it with a towel that wasn't nice like the ones at Seppi's. When I emerged, my mother was showing Kane her new iPad, and some other shit she got from the home shopping channel. She offered Kane a glass of shitty white wine and he politely declined, moments later, my dad brought him a beer. I clenched my jaw and it took everything I had not to walk out the door. I rooted around the liquor cabinet, made sure nobody was looking, and took a hearty swig of my dad's Southern Comfort before joining everyone in the living room. The warmth traced its way to my belly and it made me think of Seppi.

It felt like I had gone back in time. I was sitting there watching my mother chat with Kane and the world started spinning. A creeping dread churned deep in my soul, and the walls were closing in around me, dripping with black tar that would burn if you touched it. I wondered if I was going insane. I held my breath until I heard my sister's van. Action is a distraction, so I went out the back door to greet her and Auggie, I hadn't seen him in years. The first thing I noticed was that my sister looked happy, really happy. I could see that she was content deep inside and wasn't wearing any masks or playing any parts or worrying that she was going to be a mob wife. She was wearing a flowy gauze maternity dress and a pair of well-loved Birkenstocks.

August Ricard slid out of the driver's seat with his dreads and his beard and his flannel shirt. I was kicking myself for ever thinking she would have been happy with Seppi. My parents came out onto the back porch as Auggie jogged around the van and opened the door for her. Opal slid out of her seat and he put his arm around her shoulders, kissing her on the temple like a precious treasure. She looked up with light in her eyes,

"Do you guys remember Auggie?"

My dad came over and shook Auggie's hand and then gave my sister a hug, lifting her off the ground. He kissed the top of her head,

"You look so happy, Opie."

The little girl inside of her beamed up at her daddy. My mother stood there sizing him up,

"He looks like Sasquatch, where did you find him, living in the woods somewhere?"

Opal touched Auggie's arm,

"You could say that."

Opal looked up at him with love in her eyes. Auggie kissed her on the nose and put his hand on her baby bump. She put her arm around his waist and my dad offered him a beer. I watched the three of them chat while my dad lit the grill. Kane and I stood there in the driveway and my mother went back into the house, disgusted. I wondered what it was like to be such a miserable bitch. I went inside to get another beer and my mother was in the kitchen pouring crackers into a bowl, shaking her head,

"Can you believe she left Giuseppi Moretti for a mountain creature? I bet he doesn't even own a car."

I twisted the cap off my beer, dug an edible out of my purse, and washed it down with a swig of Corona. My dad smiled with his eyes and reminisced with Auggie as my mother stood in the window with her arms crossed. I drained my beer and retrieved another one. Whatever, this entire evening was going to be a shit show so I might as well be high and have a buzz. I knew Kane was going to want to talk about why my mother would think I'd show up with Seppi but that was a conversation for another time. I caught movement through the window and looked up to see my aunt Maggie and her boyfriend Clem pulling into the driveway in his Mazda Miata. My dad rushed over to greet them and picked his sister right up off the ground,

"Mags!"

They hugged like they meant it and not how my mother hugged people. My dad shook hands with Clem and then gave him a hug, apparently, they had known each other in college, way back when.

"Clem Babcock, how the hell have you been?"

"Maxwell Birch, nice to see you after all this time you've aged horribly."

The two of them laughed and joined Auggie at the grill with beers while they shot the shit. I elbowed Kane and he joined the other men awkwardly. That left me, my sister, my aunt, and my mother. If I haven't mentioned it lately, Maggie hated my mother, so I was looking forward to whatever kind of low blows I was going to witness over dinner. I threw crackers in my mouth to soak up some of the alcohol.

I went in to help set the table for my own birthday dinner and was impressed that my mother had pulled out the really fancy paper plates. I don't think she had enough of her real dishes to serve everyone and she'd rather die that have mismatched china. I had a pounding stress headache by the time we sat down to eat kabobs and roasted veggies and macaroni salad. My sister was hugging Auggie's arm at the table and my mother was rolling her eyes. What was her fucking problem? Maggie and Clem were swapping stories with my dad. I was sitting at the end of the table opposite my dad, with Opal on one side and Kane on the other.

Dinner was delicious, my dad used his special marinate, and the kabobs looked like a professional chef had made them. While I was sitting at that table, it healed my soul, and crushed it a little. Back in that house with those memories, trying to stay in the moment, enjoying the time with my favorite aunt and my dad and my sister and Kane. But nothing is ever as simple as that. I watched my mother as she watched my sister laugh and tuck a curl behind her ear. My mother shot daggers at Maggie across the table and Maggie scratched her nose with her middle finger. My mother had done this to herself. She was sitting at the table with her family, sitting there with her children and her husband and her sister-in-law and their significant others and she looked miserable. I suppose that's what happens when you're self-centered and the people around you are happy.

I felt bad for my mother for a second, until I remembered crying in my closet in the winter of first grade because I had been defiled on the neighbor's bathroom floor. And I thought about all the times she shoved my bad choices in my face, or made underhanded comments, all the while ignoring her own flaws. She had been this way the whole time, I just hadn't noticed it as a child. When you're little, you need your mommy, so you do whatever is necessary to keep her interested. If you're a baby bird and you fall out of the nest, you starve to death or get torn apart by the neighbor's cat. As long as you keep your tears behind closed doors, as long as you keep it together at the dinner table, as long as the curtains look good from the outside, everything is going to be alright. As long as you keep yourself quiet and don't talk about the pain, everything will be alright.

So, there I sat at my family birthday dinner, watching people I loved dearly, as they laughed and smiled at each other across the table. My eyes moved to Opal and Auggie and I saw how they looked at each other. Kane picked steak out of his teeth, he was vanilla safe and familiar. Things were in the process of changing dramatically. My parents had moved back to Vermont. My sister was going to have her baby in another month and my dad would be preoccupied with that. I was going to have to make a decision about whether I wanted the life with the espresso beans or the life with the dark chocolate covered blueberries.

When everyone was finished eating, my mother retrieved my birthday cake. Opal went into the kitchen to get smaller paper plates, it would be a waste to use the big ones for dessert. My mother came through the door with my cake, candles ablaze. She placed it in front of me and I looked at it. 'Happy Birthday Amy La.' What the fuck.

"I only had twenty candles but you can still blow them out for pictures."

I wanted to punch her in the throat.

"What's with the, umm, name?"

My mother laughed heartily like she was going to tell a real knee slapper,

"I told the girl over the phone and I guess she didn't hear me. I didn't notice it until I got home but it will make a funny picture."

You know what else would make a funny picture? My mother's ass at the bottom of a quarry. Idiot. Luckily that particular grocery store has good frosting and even though she got yellow cake instead of chocolate, it was still pretty good. When it was time for gifts, we moved into the living room. Kane leaned over and whispered,

"Was I supposed to get you something?"

I reassured him,

"No, just enjoy the show."

I took the place of honor on the center cushion of the couch. My dad sat down next to me with a newspaper-wrapped box. He kissed me on the cheek and I smiled up at him. I undid the twine and carefully removed the paper, folded it, and put it on the coffee table neatly in front of me. He cautioned,

"Be careful with it, it's fra-gee-lay."

I smiled up at him and we had a moment. I was a little girl and he was my daddy. I wondered where the time had gone, I wanted to sit on his lap and bury my face in his collar like I did when I was little. I wanted him to teach me how to ride a bike again, in the same driveway as when I was five. I wanted to pick strawberries and help him mow the lawn and watch him till his garden.

I lifted the lid and there was balled up newspaper inside the box, cushioning something. I worked the paper out of the box and my eyes filled with tears. When I looked up at my dad, his eyes looked the same. I reached in and pulled out a ceramic tea pot. This wasn't just any tea pot from T.J.Maxx, this was a tea pot my Gramma Birch made when she was in her twenties. I had admired it my entire life and it got lost in the shuffle when we packed up her house. I turned it over and looked at her name carved into the bottom, Melanie Birch.

My dad sat forward and prepared to tell me about the gift, that was his thing, his favorite part of gift-giving,

"OK, so, I know you used to love this tea pot and you used to have tea parties with your Gramma all the time when you were little. I know you wanted it when she died and we lost track of it."

He was pretty proud of himself,

"When we packed up the house in Massachusetts, I found it in the attic! Can you believe that? After all this time. And I know you used to love doing pottery so I thought if this was sitting on your counter, it would remind you to get back to it someday."

He teared up a little,

"It's important to do the things you love, Boo-Boo Bear. It's important to be true to yourself and it doesn't matter what anyone else thinks, you have to do what makes you happy."

"Oh, Dad."

We stood and hugged,

"I love you."

We were both crying and he said,

"It doesn't matter how old you get, you will always be my baby."

My aunt drained her glass of wine and sang,

"You guys, this is supposed to be a party and you're making all of us cry."

Maggie smiled up at us and I kissed my dad on the cheek before sitting back down on the couch. My mother wasn't crying. Opal jumped up,

"Me next!"

My sister handed me a fabric wrapped bundle tied with yarn. She kissed me on the cheek and sat next to me with her eyes sparkling,

"Open it!"

I unfolded the floral fabric to find an unsoiled and intact expensive sweater like the one that only cost me fifty cents. It was even the same color. I couldn't believe my eyes! I unfolded it and my jaw dropped. I hugged the sweater and squealed,

"OH MY GOD!"

Opal smiled from ear to ear and winked,

"I remember you got something on your other one."

That was putting it lightly. We stood and I wrapped my arms around her neck. I buried my face in her dark ringlets. It was so good to see her happy, she smiled as her blue eyes twinkle. Maggie moved over to the couch, patting the cushion next to her. She had a box wrapped in a beautifully painted silk. I took the box from her.

"I took a silk painting class when we were traveling, isn't it beautiful? I thought of you as soon as I made it, for some reason that color scheme and the swirls made me think of you and your crazy hair and your dimples."

I untied the silk to find a small box and an envelope. I lifted the lid and there was a set of keys inside, the key chain was a tiny little handmade ceramic mug. Maggie and my dad made eye contact and smiled at each other; great minds think alike.

"Those are the keys!"

I squealed,

"Really!?"

"YES! The building is finished."

She sorted through the keys,

"Front and back doors, garage, apartment, shed. Can you believe it?"

We hugged a real hug and my mother looked annoyed, like she missed an important part of the story, and it drove her nuts,

"What do the keys go to?"

I opened my mouth to tell her, but Maggie beat me to it. She told my mother that she had a studio space built on the lot of an old service center and that I was the owner. Where you would have thought a mother's eyes would have flickered with light, there was a flash of darkness and jealousy. My mother's lips drew into a tight smile and she moved her eyes to mine,

"Ya, well, try not to fuck it up. If you piss through money the way you usually do, the place will be out of business in a month."

She broke into a wine-fueled guffaw, proud of herself for putting me in my place, for knocking me back down where I belong. What the fuck was wrong with her? How about, 'congratulations' or 'good luck' or maybe 'now you can get back to the pottery I told you was rancid shit and a waste of your time.' I felt the heat rise in my cheeks. Maggie pointed at the envelope,

"That's just some paperwork, but I thought you should have a copy. I wrote down phone numbers in case you have problems with the plumbing or need some more two-twenty outlets installed for kilns."

She leaned closer and whispered,

"I put a couple joins in there, open that later."

My mother stood and retrieved a stack of three beautifully wrapped boxes and placed them neatly on the coffee table. The boxes were tied with an ornate ribbon that had curlicues at the ends and there was a dramatic gift tag with calligraphy writing. I undid the stupid fucking ornate wire-edged ribbon and clenched my jaw. I knew my mother would want me to roll the ribbon neatly so she could use it again, so I balled it into tight little wad and crushed it in my fist.

She ordered,

"Open the bottom one first, otherwise you'll know what it is!"

I unstacked the boxes and opened the biggest one first, just like she said. It was her old iPad, nestled in some tissue paper. I smiled at her but between the fucked up cake and not enough candles, I was trying not to cry. I set the iPad to the side and had a good idea what was in the other boxes. As I was opening the middle box,

"Oh, when you take the iPad out, my old case is under there too, it doesn't fit my new one."

I nodded and then looked inside the middle box, it was all the chargers she had accumulated and didn't need anymore.

"The way you keep track of your things, I'm sure you need more chargers. And, I put the one in there for the iPad, I got a new one."

I swallowed the anger and laughter and tears in my throat,

"That's very thoughtful, thank you."

Kane made big eyes at me like, 'what the fuck?' Opal and I made eye contact, and she said sorry with her face. I opened the last box and there was a drawstring pouch inside. Third time's a charm. I pulled it open and dumped the pouch into my hand, it was a tennis bracelet with fake diamonds all the way around.

"I ordered the wrong size, that one was way too big for my wrist. I thought about who I know that has a big wrist and I figured it would fit you perfectly."

What a fucking bitch. So now I have fat wrists!? Seriously!? I glanced down at my normal sized wrists and shook my head. What an absolute fucking asshole. I smiled and thanked my mother for the funny cake and gifts. I stood up and kissed her on the cheek but wanted to punch her in the throat and then hold her head under the water in the toilet until she stopped struggling. I excused myself and forty-five seconds later I was in the upstairs bathroom crying my eyes out. I meant nothing to my own mother, why would I think anyone else would love me? My eyes drifted to the bathtub I sat in after I had been defiled on the neighbor's bathroom floor. I went down the hall to my old room. I sat on the closet floor, hugged my knees to my chest, and completely fell apart.

CHAPTER 7
INTO THE DARKNESS

OPAL FOUND ME in my secret hiding place, just like she did when I was little. She sat down next to me and there was a lot less room in there now that we were grown. She put her arm around me and squeezed. We sat there in silence until one of us farted, and then we had to bail, it was bad, I'm assuming it was a pregnancy fart. I ran back and closed the door so the fart would be waiting for whoever opened it next, hopefully my mother. I helped clean up and gathered my things with a pit in my gut. As everyone was leaving, we gave our heartfelt hugs and kisses, we said our I love yous. Many of the people I held dear were together that night, and my dysfunctional little heart was happy on the outside while it cried on the inside. I didn't say anything when we got in the car.

At a stop light, Kane finally broke the silence,

"Why did your mother think you'd show up with Giuseppi Moretti?"

I was impressed how long he waited to ask but I didn't even know what to say. Was I supposed to confide that my mother was blabbing her theory to anyone that would listen? That she thought I 'performed fellatio' on Seppi to get the car? Maybe she was being sarcastic, I don't even know, but it doesn't matter. Either way, her words were meant to hurt me.

"When Seppi was with Opal, my mother accused me of doing sexual favors to earn the car."

Kane moved his hand from the steering wheel,

"I kind of wondered."

I rolled my eyes and was glad it was dark so he wouldn't see me,

"Look, my sister was going nuts about me getting hurt, so Seppi provided me with a car and a panic button."

I paused and Kane gave me some side-eye,

"A panic button?"

Here we go,

"After the shit went down with Sal."

Oops. Nope, that's fine...umm, I meant...what did I mean? I could see Kane making a face by the light of the dash,

"When what shit went down with Sal?"

I thought as quickly as I could, and knew he had already had some suspicion that I killed him, suspicions Seppi squelched on Christmas Eve,

"After that time he chased me around the lake and shot at me, my sister wanted to make sure I had a reliable car of my own."

I knew by his reply, he didn't buy it,

"Ahh."

It was mostly the truth, but Kane didn't believe any of it,

"What about the panic button?"

I gestured like it was no big deal,

"It's basically a button I can push if I get into trouble, you know, get attacked or something. Seppi is able to hear me, and the button shows my location on an app he has on his phone."

Kane was intrigued and a little jealous,,

"He tracks you on his phone?"

I gave him a bullshit answer,

"Well, I mean, if I push the button."

Have you ever pushed it?"

"Yeah."

"When?"

I could have told him about the time we met at Bongiovanni's and Seppi followed me into the woods, or the time I was freaking out that Kane asked if I killed Sal. I could have told him that, sometimes, I push it just because I can, or that I'd be paralyzed with fear if I didn't have it. All of those things were true, but I chose the path of least resistance,

"I pushed it that time I got attacked in the woods."

That shut him up. I pushed off my sneakers, hugged my knees to my chest and cried all the way home. Kane had no idea what my life was like anymore and I realized I'd been holding on to the idea of how things used to be, a daydream that I could rewind time, back to when things were simpler. If I knew then what I know now, maybe I would have asked Maggie to pick up her own lunch that day. If the circumstances had been different, would me and Giuseppi Moretti have become so close? Would I have murdered someone, would I have been shot multiple times, would I have all these new skeletons in my cramped little closet?

I stayed self-medicated and isolated all weekend. Seppi invited me to the hibachi place on the mountain and I declined, but he ordered something for me and had it delivered to my door. I think that was the weekend I realized I meant it when I told Seppi there was no turning back for me. I knew what I wanted and I needed to commit, move forward with him, tell him that's what I wanted, even if it would be complicated at times. On Monday morning, I worked a breakfast shift at Muddy Waters and dragged myself up the stairs to get ready for therapy. I showered, worked curl cream through my hair and spritzed my new perfume. I pulled on some linen overalls and a fitted white half-shirt, slid my feet into some Birkenstocks.

I drove to the impressive building of Isabella Rossi and smoked half a joint in the parking lot before taking the elevator to the sixth floor. I waved to Elaine and didn't bother with the magazines; I was busy being preoccupied with my horrendous mental health when Dr. Rossi opened the door and gestured me in. I crossed the threshold in a swirl of Coco Mademoiselle and weed. I plopped in the overstuffed chair and kicked my shoes off before I even got started, tucked my knees to my chest and hugged them as I cried. She was patient with me, but eventually,

"It looks like you are in a lot of pain."

I rolled my eyes. Yeah, you're a fucking genius, nice job. But I didn't say that,

"Really, what makes you say that?"

Sarcasm is the best medicine, isn't that what they say? No, wait, that's revenge. Well, whatever. Fuck this.

"Amelia, I think you'll feel better if you talk about it."

I looked right at her and felt the tears and anger boiling to the surface, I raised my voice for the first time since I met her,

"OH, YOU DO!? You think I'll feel better if I TALK ABOUT IT!?"

She stayed calm,

"Yes, I do."

I waved her away,

"Ya, well, what the fuck do you know!?"

The whole thing was completely fucked and I was over it. All she ever did was poke at my demons with her pen, so she would have something to write on her pad of paper. I stood,

"I'm fucking done here! Someone hurts me and I have to do all the work to fix it!? I'm being punished for someone else's crime!? This is bullshit!"

Dr. Rossi stayed seated, let me have the upper hand, her voice had a note of understanding,

"I'd like to help you, Amelia, but you are free to leave if that's what you want."

But it wasn't. The hour I spent with Isabella Rossi every week was something I had grown to rely on, it kept me sane most of the time, but just barely. I needed her way more than she needed me, and I knew it. Maybe I was just dollar signs to that woman, but she was so much more to me than that. I sat and she handed me a box of tissues.

"I can't even describe the week I've had."

She made her face look supportive,

"Try."

So, I did. I sat there for a couple minutes, trying to organize everything into a neat little package while I stared at pigeons on roofs,

"I love Seppi, but I can't be with him if he's going to end up like his father. And if I'm not with him, he can't protect me. And I care about Kane, he's vanilla safe and comfortable, but all we ever do is take turns hurting each other and I don't love him. And then my birthday was a mess, and I hate my mother."

She leaned forward and I continued,

"I left here last week and decided to see how things felt with Kane, you know, before deciding if that part of my life was over. Was he where I wanted to be in ten years, and everything. We made plans to go to a steak house and then out for a couple drinks on my birthday. No strings attached, but I wasn't going to feel guilty if we slept together. So, then I woke up on my birthday, went to work, and it was like I walked through a portal into the goddamn Twilight Zone. I was trying to avoid Seppi but there were gifts all over my office, including a bottle of expensive perfume."

Her eyes conveyed both personal and professional interest, I continued,

"Then Mary Moretti asked if I would help with a large group coming in for a party, but once they were settled, I could head out and enjoy my birthday. It was a formal event, so I dressed up and made sure I was there early."

I stared at my hands,

"It was a surprise party for me at the ristorante. And all of a sudden, I was in that world and there was no way out; you don't tell Giuseppi Moretti, thanks, but no thanks, for the birthday party. And I didn't want to tell him no thanks, it made me feel special. He twirled me and kissed me, and we made out in his office."

I stared out the window and sighed,

"And then I woke up the next morning to find that my best-friend sent me a bunch of pictures from the night before."

Dr. Rossi knew enough about the situation that she ventured a guess,

"You looked happy, didn't you? And so did he."

I fell apart and my voice squeaked,

"Yeah, I've never looked like that in my whole life, like a woman."

I shook my head,

"I know that sounds insane but it's true, it's like up until now, in my own eyes, I was just some broken little girl on the outside. But there was this one picture..."

I dug my phone out of my bag and found it, turned the screen to her, she took it. I watched Isabella Rossi's face as she looked at me looking at him. I took the phone back and found the picture of Seppi, handed it back. The only thing she said was,

"Wow!"

It gave me goosebumps,

"I thought I had everything figured out and then I had to help Vinny dump a body at the lake and almost got pulled under with the dead guy."

I shook my head like I was going to add the cherry on top,

"And then I had my family birthday party and it was a fucking disaster."

We sat in silence for the rest of my session.

"Amelia, this is a lot, no wonder you're overwhelmed. Think about which one of those things is bothering you the most and maybe we can focus on it next time."

I made another appointment with Elaine and got my reminder card. I sat in my car for a long time before I started it, and even though I hadn't used it in a long time, I dug my panic button out of the bottom of my bag, pushed it, and held it for three seconds.

The display on my dash lit up when he called me and I answered without saying anything.

"Dimples?"

And I lost it. How had I gotten there? I was sobbing and gasping for air and needed it to go away. I needed to feel something good, I needed to feel whole. I needed to feel like I mattered. I needed to feel loved.

"Go to my house and I'll meet you there."

The call ended and I'm not sure how I managed to make it to mafia mansion land. Big fat tears were swelling my eyes and burning my cheeks. I wanted to have a mother who loved me. I wanted someone to make me feel like I was valuable, because right then, I wanted to curl up and die. I got to Seppi's before he did. When he pulled in the driveway, I got out of my car and ran to him, he wrapped his arms around me, and I laid the side of my face on his chest. I was crying so hard I could barely stand. He kissed the top of my head,

"Come on."

He slung his arm over my shoulder and walked me to the house. I dropped my bag and kicked off my shoes at the door. I hopped up on one of the stools in the kitchen and we sat together sipping whiskey while the sun set through the sliding glass doors. He led me onto the patio and clicked a remote that brought the fire pit to life. I put my feet on the arm of his chair, he smoked part of a Cuban and I smoked part of a joint. Seppi rubbed the top of my foot with his thumb, caressing the bare shin under the hem of my linen overalls. I set my rocks glass on the table and put my hand out to him, he took it. We sat there like that, holding hands between our chairs as the sun went the rest of the way down. When we stood to go inside, Seppi stopped in front of me, his eyes speaking volumes, I reached up and touched his cheek, rubbed it with my thumb like he usually rubbed mine. He bent until I could rest my forehead against his. My voice filled with tears, I pleaded as I cried,

"Seppi, please love me."

He didn't hesitate, holding my face in his hands,

"I love you more than I have ever loved anyone."

I swallowed the tears in my throat,

"I need you to show me, I need to feel it."

Seppi led me up the back stairs to the master bedroom. That night was different than any other, that night we spoke without words, and I knew he loved me, really loved me. He accepted all of my flaws and broken pieces, my curves and insecurities, the scars on the inside and out. Seppi accepted the version of me without the masks and the bullshit. That night, I knew we would be together until the end. I knew because he showed me. Twice. When I opened my eyes the next morning, I was nestled in the crook of Seppi's arm, and he had been watching me sleep. I kissed him on the cheek. We needed to get up, but he showed me he loved me one more time before our feet hit the floor. That morning, I got to eat pancakes across the table from Giuseppi Moretti in his sweatpants, and it was everything I dreamt it would be. For the first time in my whole life, my heart was truly happy.

Seppi followed me into town, I went to my place and showered before working a late morning shift at Muddy Waters. When I went through the dining room, Alex was sitting in one of the booths along the front windows, enjoying a latte with her nose deep in a mystery novel. That was the first time I was happy to see her. I slid into the booth,

"Hi."

She looked up and smiled, I don't think she knew about my jealousy or how I felt about her history with Kane. But, from that day on, I never intended to interfere or slide into Kane's bed when they were taking a break. That morning, I smiled back,

"Take good care of him, he deserves it."

Alex put her hand on mine and released an invisible weight she had been carrying,

"Thank you."

I smiled again and waved as I swung behind the counter and pulled my apron off the hook. I had decided what I was going to do and it meant there were other decisions I needed to make. But, for that day, I just made lattes and paninis and wiped tables and got the basic bitches their fancy lattes. I wasn't obligated to pick up shifts there anymore, I was doing it to help out. And from then on, I planned to pull away from Kane Buchanan. He was right, if he had gotten into a dick swinging contest with Giuseppi Moretti, he would have ended up at the bottom of the lake.

CHAPTER 8
MOVING ON UP

THERE WAS a window of time before the ristorante opened, so I leaned into Seppi's office and asked if he'd come with me to the studio. He finished a phone call and appeared in my doorway, I grabbed my keys and when we got in the mini mafia sedan, my perfume swirled together with his Tobacco Vanille. It was this yin and yang of darkness and light, this mating of angels and demons. Seppi reached over and we held hands until I needed to shift at a stop sign. We had started something, he, and I, it felt exciting and terrifying but I guess that's true for everyone who falls in love. The electricity that had built in intensity for a year was finally given permission to zip back and forth, untethered, and there was a constant arousal just under the surface.

I had not driven to that side of town since the service station was demolished. The building was gone, and the asphalt parking lot had been pulled up. When I nosed the Caddy into the driveway of the new studio, there was a yard with new grass peeking through a later of hay, and a sizable space had been tilled for a garden. There was a garage and a shed. The backyard had bird feeders, and Maggie said teenagers from the local residential home were building round picnic tables to add some seating back there. I looped around to the back and parked facing the garden.

For the first time since I got back to Bunman, somewhere deep down inside, it felt like home. Seppi slung his arm around my shoulders and we went to the back porch. I unlocked the door of the studio; it smelled like cut wood and paint. It was a blank slate. As we went through each room, I imagined kids building birdhouses and hippie girls making macrame plant hangers or ceramic pot pipes, middle-aged women learning watercolor on canvas while drinking wine at a paint and sip. I entered the pottery studio and imagined shelves filled with wonky mugs with awkward handles. There were six brand new pottery wheels and a moderately-sized kiln. There were shelves for glazes and a closet for clay. There were buckets for tools and sponges for cleaning. Seppi went over and investigated the kiln,

"What's this thing? Like an oven for baking clay?"

I went over and explained the inner workings of a high fire electric kiln. The shelves and the stilts, the box of witness cones, the temperature chart. He squinted his eyes,

"Two thousand degrees!?"

"Yeah, actually a little higher than that for cone six, which is what I fire to."

Seppi made a face like he was impressed. I showed him the pottery wheels and told him about attaching handles. I was glad I had decided to use the place for things like that, pottery and painting and a place for people to gather. We finished our tour of the artisan studio and went up to the apartment. Holy crap. That place was perfect. The kitchen was outfitted with stainless steel appliances, including a commercial espresso machine. I opened a narrow door to expose a small pantry. The bathroom had a large window that looked out over the back yard and there was a skylight over the tub. The bedroom was spacious, and the closet was all drawers and shelves with a rod for fancy things that need hangers. The living room was in the front and there were windows facing the street. As I back tracked, I stepped onto the three-season porch that looked out over the back yard.

We made it back to the restaurant in plenty of time, not that he really needed to be there. Seppi liked to make an appearance and do a couple laps to make sure his customers were enjoying their meals. I pushed his office window open and the smell of spring filled the space that usually smelled like stale Cubans, leather furniture, and Tobacco Vanille. Seppi needed a hanging plant, I could start a philodendron for the patriarch of a mob family. I'd hang it in his window in a black macrame hanger. I didn't have any consults but stuck around anyway, so we sat there sipping whiskey together and it felt different, it felt like the beginning of forever. After Seppi locked up, I walked with him to his car and waved,

"I'll see you tomorrow, Boss."

As I turned for my place, Seppi latched onto my arm and pulled me into his arms. We swayed back and forth in the moonlight and our noses touched. I took in the scent of him at the end of the day, and when my lips touched his neck, he made a low noise in his throat. His voice was deep and hungry,

"I want to devour you, Dimples."

I pulled back and looked up at him with bedroom eyes, his hands hooked around my waist. Seppi rubbed his nose against mine,

"Why don't you pack a bag and come for a sleepover."

I liked that idea very much and knew there wouldn't be much sleeping going on,

"You can go ahead, I don't mind."

Seppi smiled and our eyes met again, he kissed me,

"And I don't mind waiting."

I kissed him on the cheek before I went inside but he pulled me close and we made out against the back of the Escalade. I jogged inside and pulled a backpack out of the closet, tossing in twenty-four hours' worth of clothing and toiletries. I threw in my laptop, Indie's food, blanket, and a couple of toys. Ten minutes later I was bouncing down the back stairs with my backpack and cat. I threw my backpack on the floor and laid Indie's blanket on the passenger seat of the mini mafia sedan. When I started my car and the headlights came on, it illuminated Kane and Alex, sitting on the Adirondack chairs looking at the stars. I backed out of my space and Seppi pulled out behind me. We made our way to the world of mafia mansions and pancakes for breakfast.

I brought my backpack upstairs and left my toiletries on the vanity in his bathroom. I looked at myself in the mirror and remembered the night I had been attacked in the woods by the woman with the cute hat and vintage bag who was really the red-headed woman in the pantsuit. I remembered the night I got shot. I went into the bedroom and found myself in Seppi's closet. I separated a row of expensive button up shirts and stuck my nose against the fabric. I scanned the hardwood jewelry box that held his watches and rings. After a glance over my shoulder, I pulled the cap off his cologne, and inhaled with the sprayer an inch from my nose. My God, that man made my juices flow. I stood there with my eyes closed in a haze of straight up Tobacco Vanille. When I opened my eyes, Seppi was leaning against the doorway of his closet, arms crossed casually, smiling slyly,

"Does my cologne do something for you?"

I couldn't even begin to describe to him how significant his cologne was in my sense memories of him. So many things really, swimming together to make the essence of him. The leather and whiskey, the Cuban cigars and Tobacco Vanille. Our eyes met, my voice breathy even though I didn't mean it to be.

"Yes."

Seppi flicked his eyebrows and pulled his shirt open,

"Come get it from the source, Dimples."

I pressed my body against his and then moved past him into the bedroom. I started the shower and stripped out of my clothes while he watched. I touched the tip of his nose and then closed the bathroom door and let the rain fall over me. I lathered my curls with his expensive shampoo and polished my skin with his fancy scrub. Seppi's conditioner was luxurious and did wonders for my ringlets. I dried my skin with one of his luxurious towels and shrugged into one of the plush robes.

I stood in the mirror with my pampered curls and my fancy robe, the smell of Giuseppi Moretti's shower gel on my skin. I knew at that moment, I would do whatever he wanted me to do. That man would let me play with the demons I normally kept deep inside, and I was willing to live that life if it meant I got to live like that. Maybe that's the moment I snapped, or maybe that's the moment all the pieces came together. When I swung the door open, Seppi was laying there in sweatpants, and I hoped nothing else. I went to him, and that was the beginning of the rest of my life, making love to Giuseppi Moretti at the end of a long day. We laid there after, fingers tangled together, bodies sweaty, the scent of sex in the air. There was a level of contentedness I had not anticipated, a realization that I could finally be myself with someone. I was right where I belonged.

The next morning, I woke up first and made Seppi a latte with a heart on top. I woke him up with kisses on his eyelids and he pulled me on top of him. We cuddled until our lattes were room temperature and then sat with our backs against the headboard, sipping them. While I drank morning lattes with Giuseppi Moretti, he put his arm around me and kissed the top of my head,

"Ti amo, Amelia."

I had to swallow the tears in my throat before I could reply, the whole thing seemed surreal,

"I love you too, Seppi."

That morning, we had smoothies instead of pancakes, and then he followed me back into town. I spent part of the day giving tours and facilitating tasting menus, and the other part trying to get last minute supplies ordered for the community studio. I would have members pay a monthly fee in exchange for open use of the studio and supplies. I pictured people buzzing around making art, within another month, I'd be able to plan an open house.

I wandered around, trying to get a feel for the studio, figure out if it was what my heart really wanted. I sat at one of the pottery wheels and mimicked the process of making a vessel. I centered the clay and opened it up, I pulled the walls and compressed the rim. Sitting on that stool reminded me how much I loved clay. I went over to the kiln and looked inside. It wasn't huge but it was big enough that I could fit inside, not that I tried. I inspected the brand-new exhaust system and the stainless-steel sinks. I imagined art on the walls and built-in shelves to display people's creations. Maybe that was why I came back to Bunman.

But somewhere deep down inside, before the place even opened, I realized my heart wasn't into it. I knew my aunt was doing what she felt she needed to do, to make up for the shit I experienced in Bunman, even though none of it was her fault. Maggie still thought of me as a little girl who loved pottery. But there I was, sort of excited and sort of ready to walk away from it all, because it felt like just one more thing to add to my to do list. At that point, I wasn't interested in teaching pottery to little kids and gaggles of wine-soaked women, I was interested in tailored suits and sexual tension and being untouchable.

CHAPTER 9
KIND GESTURE

I WENT BACK to the ristorante and finished that day just like I finished the one before, sitting across from a mob boss swallowing his well-aged fire. No, that's not a euphemism. I glanced at the window in his office and remembered I wanted to start a plant for him if I didn't forget again. My eyes moved back to Seppi, who was holding a rocks glass in his right hand, gazing at me. I raised my eyebrows, he raised his. I loved him. He loved me. Seppi was the only one in the world who had seen me without my masks and I was the only one who had seen him without his armor. I reached across the desk, and he squeezed my fingers. Maybe I would be the one who softened his edges, and maybe he would be the one who helped me glue my broken pieces back together.

That's when life started shifting. I don't know if it was the fresh start I had been looking for, but my demons and my heart and all my broken pieces were morphing and picking up steam. Within the inner sanctum, the dark parts of me were happy. I had experienced intense passion and fear, I had seen my life flash before my eyes, and I had beaten the life out of someone. All those moments and memories, all that energy mixed into my relationship with Seppi, fueling the fire within me. There was no way my mother would dare throw stones at me if I was accompanied by Giuseppi Moretti, she'd end up at the bottom of the lake. That hurt little girl who hugged her knees and cried in the closet was receding and growing and fading and being magnified, all at once.

Over the next month, Seppi and I fell into a rhythm and I packed up some of my things in preparation for my move to the apartment above the studio. I'm not sure who I was kidding, I spent most of my nights with Seppi. Most mornings, he would follow me into town, and most nights, he would follow me back to the world of mafia mansions and high thread count sheets. Alex moved into Kane's apartment. My sister and Auggie were taking one last road trip before the baby came. My parents existed in their old/new world, fifteen minutes away. My dad came to pick up a large pepperoni pizza and antipasto salad at the ristorante every Friday night and I made sure I was there. He would visit with me in my office and we'd snack on expensive dark chocolate covered blueberries while he waited. People in that world got to know Maxwell Birch, and something about that made me happy.

As far as Marco, he kind of fell off the face of the earth for a while after opening night. I think it was just too much to deal with. When he came back to help launch the new restaurant, he thought it was going to be 'out with the old and in with the new.' Without Sal at the helm, Marco thought things were going to be different. After what happened on opening night, it didn't take long for him to go right back to his sister's house in New Hampshire. He had been a part of the inner sanctum, and I think he sensed something between me and Seppi, long before anyone else did.

Sunny and Vinny seemed to be doing well, and I wondered how she dealt with his perpetual participation in ditching a stiff. She was the only one of us on the outside but I think she liked it that way, she had so much violence in her life as a child, and it was easier for her if she kept the bad stuff at a distance. She knew things were happening but didn't ask for details. I could talk to Opal, even though she didn't want to know about the danger I was in, or the things I had done. It's isolating when you do bad things and can't talk about it with anyone besides the people you do the bad things with. That left Vinny and Seppi, they were my sounding board, my voices of reason, the ones who kept me calm in the chaos, the one's who threw me a literal or figurative rope when I was in distress.

Seppi was so far into it that he didn't even need to talk about the things he did, or maybe he just compartmentalized like me. Sometimes, I wondered if he was going to lose it someday, but it seemed like even when I'd seen him snap, there was a level of control. That night in the warehouse, even while he had a clear disadvantage, something about who he was, exuded power. In the brief interaction I witnessed as I peered inside the warehouse, I could see that there was a battle of energies at work and I still wonder why Lance didn't just shoot Seppi between the eyes. But, Giuseppi Moretti has a vibe about him that's intimidating enough that it shook Lance's confidence, even though he had the upper hand in that situation. I wonder if it was the fear of retaliation, the sure demise, the world of hurt that would be coming his way if he killed Seppi. I hoped that someday my chaos would be under control like Seppi's, but maybe he had filing cabinets in the back of his mind too.

I shifted gears and focused on the studio, it was a nice distraction, but I was spreading myself a little too thin. I'm not saying I'm lazy, or that I mind working hard, but I don't like being pulled in a million different directions. I daydreamed about the new space because it was a blank slate, it wasn't wrought with chaos or death, it didn't have any dark mafia energy. Part of my distraction was the fact that I was still in the honeymoon phase with Seppi, we've all been there. That period of time when you don't want to do anything else but go to bed with the person you love, become familiar with every square inch of their body, get to know their innermost thoughts.

So, I guess even though that studio was a nice mental diversion, it was pulling me away from the inner sanctum. I like to pretend I'm all sunshine and moonbeams, but I have a lot of darkness in my soul, and I was thriving in the bat cave. It created another yin and yang situation, just like Muddy Waters and Giuseppi's, and I guess it was a nice break to go toward the light, even if it felt like I was forcing it. There was a part of me that was afraid I couldn't pull off the phony smiles and fake hellos of running a studio, but that was a worry for another day. As I received more supplies, Seppi mentioned that if I needed anything, he would help financially. I said,

"The kiln Maggie got is pretty big, but they never hold as much as you think they will."

He nodded.

"When I have people taking classes and coming in to work on their own, I'll probably need more space to fire things. And if I get another kiln, I'll probably need to upgrade the ventilation system."

Seppi offered to go back with me so we could assess the space. We piled in the mini mafia sedan and I made my way up the alley between Muddy Waters, and Giuseppi's Italian Ristorante. I glanced to my right before pulling out, and Seppi was waving at Kane with a few fingers, as Kane grabbed for the door of the cafe. I wondered if the exchange caused a burning in Kane's stomach, and wondered if it was sparked by jealousy or fear. Seppi rested his hand at the base of my neck and rubbed as I drove, I shivered with goosebumps, the good kind. I swung into the old Stanley's Service Center and pulled around back. Flowers were blooming near the trees, and there were birds circling the feeders. Seppi emerged from the car and gave the property a once over,

"It really doesn't even look like the same place."

I scanned the yard, nodded, and gestured toward the garden,

"No stiff in there."

I gestured at the shed,

"No stiffs in there."

And then I jogged up the steps and gestured through the windows of the studio,

"And, no stiffs in there."

He shook his head and smiled. We crossed the threshold and I went around flipping on lights,

"All that dark shit was bull dosed out of here with that old building. Out with the old, in with the new. Nothing but good juju from now on."

I turned to him and pointed at his chest,

"Capiche?"

Seppi smiled and pulled me to him, it felt intimate that we were there together, alone, but I'm not sure why. I grabbed his hand and brought him to the pottery studio. I explained the kiln in more detail than last time,

"You use shelves, and these little stilts and just make layers in there until it's full. Then you run a fire."

He circled the kiln and I propped the lid open, Seppi peeked inside,

"Are there bigger ones?"

I shrugged,

"Yeah, I mean, I think so. The problem with this one is that it isn't that wide but it's really deep. Any deeper and it would be hard to load for someone short like me. It gets to a point where even if you rest your stomach on the edge, you can't reach the bottom to load it, so there isn't any point."

I demonstrated, leaning in the kiln,

"I've seen big kilns at a rec centers so deep that you have to stand on a stool to load it."

I went through the motions of loading it, so he could see what I was talking about. He came close and I thought he was talking business, but he was talking pleasure. He leaned in and kissed me,

"These tables look pretty sturdy."

I smiled a little and broke free, moving to one of the tables, jiggling it to test how solid it was, raising my eyebrows in his direction. Seppi wrapped his arms around my waist, kissed my neck, made the sound he makes when he's hungry. So, while we were there, we christened the pottery studio. Fifteen minutes later, we were put back together, and he went back over to the kiln,

"Does a larger kiln need anything special, or does it use the same kind of outlet?"

"Most kilns, no matter what size, work on a two-twenty outlet. There's ventilation, and filtration installed, but if we have multiple kilns in here, I'll probably need something more substantial."

He gestured to the wall,

"Why is there such an elaborate ventilation system, does it cause a lot of smoke? Isn't it dry heat like an oven?"

"Well, yes, but have you ever gone outside while the Thanksgiving turkey is in the oven, and then come back inside? The whole house smells like there's a turkey in the oven."

He nodded,

"So, the fumes need to be ventilated out for safety purposes?"

"Yeah, there are people who have done pottery for decades and end up with asthma or COPD from all the fine clay particles, and off-gassing from the clay and glazes."

I could tell he was concerned about the fact that I'd be breathing in fumes and tiny particles of clay,

"Get me some information on the dimensions of the largest kiln, and the most advanced air filtration and exhaust system and the Moretti Family Foundation will make a generous donation to the new Community Studio to cover the cost."

For a while, whenever I was there setting things up, I was looking at it through the eyes of a hopeful dreamer. Someone who wanted to fill the place with laughing kids, groups of friends, and people expressing their creativity. Maybe it would be the thing I had dreamt of as a little girl, and maybe my aunt had made it happen for me. I wanted to make sure there were plenty of children's activities going on and I wanted to be involved in the ceramics classes, but knew I needed someone else. I had a demanding role at the restaurant and didn't want to lose touch with that life. I could involve the local community groups that promote self-sustaining practices and composting, I pictured a chicken coop near the tree line, veggies and roses growing in the garden, maybe there would be a farm stand next to the road.

It felt like things were coming together and I planned the Open House as part of my Event Planning position. There would be free finger foods like mini garlic knots and mini meatballs in Mama Moretti's marinara, provided by Giuseppi's Italian Ristorante, a local family business that supports artisans and the mission of providing activities for community members. Seppi and I were at the part where we finally had what we'd waited for, and it was hard to think about anything else. Our lives aligned in new ways, we were becoming familiar on a different level, a deeper level. He had made friends with my cat.

There were more of those nights where Seppi drank in the office with his associates and I was invited to join. I didn't flirt with Luciano 'Mozart' Cavallaro again, and he didn't flirt with me. Things were different, the dynamic shifted once everyone knew I belonged to Giuseppi Moretti, and I was untouchable.

CHAPTER 10
CHLOE WILFRED RICARD

NOW THAT I had packed most of my shit, and the studio apartment was awaiting my arrival, I started feeling wishy-washy about the whole thing. But, whenever I stayed at my apartment, I felt like I was in the way. I am a solitary creature, and having two other people in that place was driving me mad. The problem was, I knew eventually they would find a place. The other problem was that I didn't really want to move into the apartment above the studio. What was the point? But, I also wasn't about to ask Seppi if I could stay with him. I mean, most nights we had, what he called, a 'slumber party,' but that's a far cry from moving in. And, no way would I ever be the kind of person who would live in mafia mansion land.

The beginning of that night was normal. Making laps around the dining room with Seppi to make sure everyone was enjoying their meals. I was familiar with the regulars and had become friends with the bartenders. If you can count on someone to sneak outside to smoke weed with you, it's a bartender. Well, and a chef, but the chefs at Giuseppi's were a little too cliquey, and I think they did a little more than smoke weed. So, there I was, strutting my stuff in a tailored pantsuit, my curls were on point, I nailed the winged eyeliner, I was wearing the expensive perfume. I sauntered into Seppi's office but he wasn't in there, so I waited. I went over to his bar and fixed myself a whiskey over perfectly square ice cubes. He crossed the threshold and smiled with his whole damn face,

"I've been hoping we'd have a chance to chat."

He closed the door and sat across the desk from me, didn't hesitate, didn't stutter, didn't skip a beat,

"I think you should consider moving in with me, I'm not a fan of sleeping alone."

Our eyes met and I was momentarily speechless. He smiled, and I was uncomfortable, so I said,

"You'll get sick of me."

He locked eyes with me,

"Not gonna happen."

I swallowed hard and took a deep breath before taking the plunge,

"That sounds nice."

And that was the truth.

Seppi came to my side of the desk and I stood, he held the left side of my face and rubbed his thumb over my scrimple,

"Ti amo, Dimples, there is no turning back."

That night, it felt different when I drove up to the gate, it felt right, even though I had done it more times than I could count. We made love the way you do when you think you might spend your life with someone. Basking in the afterglow of yet another love making session, I was sprawled out, buck naked on Seppi's high thread count sheets when the house phone rang. He reached awkwardly toward the nightstand and answered, all business,

"Yes."

He sat up,

"Oh! OK, I'll tell her!"

The call ended. He looked at me,

"Opal is having the baby!"

I think Seppi was having feelings right then, because for a while there, he thought he was going to be a dad. He hadn't cared about her the way he cared about me, but he had still cared about her.

"You can come with me if you want to, unless you think that's weird."

He probably wanted to come with me but knew that it would make the actual father feel uncomfortable during the birth of his own child. I threw my covers back and Seppi put his hands behind his head so he could watch me run around like a chicken with its head cut off,

"Cute ass, Dimples."

I yelled back to him as I ran to the closet,

"Thank you!"

Five minutes later, I emerged in sweatpants and a Metallica t-shirt. I brushed my teeth, slammed my curls into a frantic wad on top of my head, swiped on some deodorant, and slid my feet into my dingy white Chuck Taylors. I kissed Seppi and left him there in his birthday suit with my cat, as I set off in the wee hours of the morning to watch my sister pop out her baby. Don't get me wrong, the whole process fascinates me, but my sister's blood, and maybe poop, and watching her vagina get torn to shreds, was something that would probably make me sparkly. Anyway, that's gross, there must be a better way.

Opal and Auggie had been staying, temporarily, at my apartment, so I essentially raced 'home.' I rushed up the stairs, and threw open the door. What on earth was I looking at? The futon was against the wall and a big blue tarp covered the living room floor, on top of the tarp was some sort of inflatable pool. Opal waddled out of the bathroom in just a sports bra, I wasn't ready for all of that, pregnant belly and armpit hair, full-bush swinging in the breeze. I started to panic,

"Why aren't you dressed, we need to go, I left the car running."

Auggie was heating water on the stove and a woman I didn't know was carrying steaming water from the bathroom. No one was freaking out; everything was under control. How could that be? My sister was about to push something the size of a watermelon out of something the size of a dime, why wasn't she freaking out? I was freaking out. In fact, I was getting bubble-gut and was afraid I was going to have the shits. I pointed at the swimming pool in my living room,

"Umm, what the hell is that thing?"

Opal waddled over and hugged me as I stood there like a deer in the headlights. Then she was bouncing on a big ball draped with a towel, to 'catch the fluids.' Nonchalantly, I might add, she replied,

"Oh, that's a birthing pool."

I looked at her with saucers for eyes,

"A what!?"

My sister laughed and then told me to stop it because she was going to pee if she kept laughing. Good thing for the towel. What the hell was happening? Why was there a swimming pool in my living room, and why was my sister bouncing on a ball without any bottoms on, instead of getting ready to go?

"YOU GUYS!"

Opal, and Auggie, and the woman I didn't know, stopped what they were doing and looked at me,

"We've got to go, what the hell is everyone doing!?"

My sister looked at me like I had three heads,

"Go where? I'm getting ready to have the baby."

I motioned from the towel-draped bouncy ball to the open door,

"Yeah, so let's GO!"

Opal waved me away nonchalantly,

"Amelia, I'm having the baby right here, we aren't going anywhere."

I sat down and put my head between my knees, the woman brought me a ginger ale. I was glad Seppi stayed home, it would have been a little awkward. I shifted gears, went out and turned my car off, and then ran back up the stairs. Kane pulled his door open to see what was going on, I waved at him and gestured like I was rocking a baby before I ran back inside and shut the door. OK, so there I was, not even a little bit high or drunk, staring at the tarp on my living room floor, eyes drifting to my sister in nothing but a sports bra, with her lady bits leaking fluids onto one of my towels. That was fine, I had a washer. Opal's contractions went from minor annoyance to full-on five-alarm fire. Auggie was cool as a cucumber, going back and forth with hot water when the woman said,

"If you want to help, there is another pot in that cupboard."

I wanted to say, yea, no shit, it's MY cupboard! But I didn't. She continued,

"She's at nine, so we need to get moving."

At nine what? I shrugged and grabbed my stock pot, filled it with water for the stove. I gave Opal a couple sips of water and a banana as she bounced there. And then she grabbed the hem of my shirt and twisted it as her face turned red. She breathed in through her nose and out through pursed lips like she was blowing out candles,

"That was a bad one!"

I felt helpless. And it went on like that for another half hour, it made me nauseous to watch her be in that much pain. But my sister was strong, she had a plan, and she followed it. Even though she lost control at one point, her body took over and gave her what she needed. Hard-wired intuition took over as the process grew more intense. I rubbed her back through contractions and pressed cool cloths to the back of her neck. I got to witness Auggie as he supported her and I knew he would take good care of them. In that moment, I was reminded how much happier she was with her mountain man than with a mob boss. She became restless but he didn't freak out, he calmed her, and reminded her she could do it. When Opal got into the tub, she quickly moved into the final stretch.

I think that experience was something I needed right then in my life, some reminder that good things happen. A reminder that new life and promise and love is constant, and sometimes a new life comes into the world. That little one was going to experience sand under its toes, and summers spent camping at a lake somewhere. That baby was never going to have to worry about their daddy getting wrapped up in some sort of mob war. Auggie would never be late for dinner because he was whacking someone. And that kid wasn't going to get dropped off at school in an Escalade. I wondered if I would ever have a baby, and watching Opal give birth, certainly made me want to wait a very long time. So gross.

That morning, I witnessed the most beautiful and most disgusting thing I've ever seen in my life. My sister's doula, apparently that's who the woman was, had worked as a labor and delivery nurse before ditching the rat race and focusing on a more holistic approach. She was soft spoken but served up tough love when she needed to, pushing Opal to keep going. I watched Opal and Auggie go from high school sweethearts to parents, and I had more than a tear in my eye when my niece came into the world. Well, after I threw up in the kitchen sink. At exactly five thirty-six in the morning, my sister Opal pushed one last time and little Chloe Wilfred Ricard came into the world. She weighed six pounds eight ounces and was nineteen inches long. She had a head of dark hair and was the most precious thing I had ever seen. As I sat there holding my niece, her new little fingers wrapped around my grown-up finger, I realized I had witnessed the whole process. I had seen someone come into this world, and I had seen someone go out.

CHAPTER 11
CUCUMBERS AND ROSES

THERE WE WERE, three days before the Open House, and I was sort of living in mafia mansion land. I can't really explain how it felt, but I was waiting for the ball to drop since that's how my life always goes. I hadn't changed my address to 2875 Hidden Hills Estates yet, it felt surreal that I would live anywhere that had a man in a gate. Opening my eyes every morning to see Giuseppi Moretti put a bounce in my step. Remember way back when I said I would sneak in and sleep with my body touching his if I ever spent another night in that house? Well, I was actually doing it, every single night. I was sleeping better than I had in my entire life, some nights I would sleep completely naked. If you've been the little girl on the bathroom floor, or if you've had any kind of childhood trauma,

I bet you'd never sleep naked, and you certainly wouldn't sleep on top of the covers. I can do that now, let that sink in. Not only was I sharing the bed with a mob boss, there were a fuck ton of guns in that room, one of them holstered to Seppi's side of the bed.

I was getting a little worried about the studio, and what I mean by that is that I wanted to drum up lots of business, but I didn't want to be there. I've said this before but I like it at the ristorante. I can sip whiskey, shoot the shit with the bartender, and smoke a j in the parking lot. I do not have to watch my mouth, lead by example, or teach anyone anything. I was having an epic case of stage fright. I was starting to feel more like a woman, after all, I was sharing a bed with Giuseppi Moretti. But, sometimes that lion looks in the mirror and sees a kitten. Less than seventy-two hours until the Open House and I was panicking a little.

I was sitting across from Seppi when Kane texted to tell me there was a woman at the cafe looking for Maggie's niece. I went out the back door of the restaurant and into the back door of Muddy Waters. Standing shyly with a vanilla cappuccino was a woman named Frieda Harper. Frieda was twenty-two, she had blonde dreads with big beads on some strands, and macrame on others. She had nose rings, an industrial piercing, and her arms were covered with beautiful tattoos. I shook the woman's hand and introduced myself. Kane handed me a maple oat latte and kissed me on the cheek. I gestured toward my favorite booth and we slid in on either side. Frieda was clearly nervous or something but after one more sip of her cappuccino, she found her words,

"Umm, I'm friends with Justine, the woman who runs the food co-op, and she mentioned that Maggie was having a studio built."

I nodded and smiled as she continued,

"Well, I used to belong to the rec center, but my ex-boyfriend works there so it's kind of become a conflict of interests."

She glanced out the window at a vintage Triumph Scrambler and I wondered if I would ever get the balls to ride a motorcycle. Her eyes shifted to her mug and then she said,

"It's a whole thing. Anyway, I've been selling my pottery for a couple years and now I don't really have anywhere to fire my things. Are you going to have pottery at the studio?"

Glad to meet a fellow mud slinger,

"Yes, my aunt knows I enjoy pottery, and I think she's hoping I'll go back to it. There are six wheels..."

She excitedly interrupted,

"I have a wheel. It isn't a professional one or anything, just an Artista Speedball, but it does the job."

She stopped talking and appeared to be attempting to put a leash on her excitement. I said,

"There's one kiln right now, but a friend of mine is going to make a donation that will cover the cost of a second kiln and an upgraded ventilation system."

Frieda spoke quickly as her feelings escaped the cage she had carried them in,

"Do you think you'll need any help? I heard that it would cost fifty dollars a month to be a member, and I don't really have that kind of money. But I've taught a couple classes before and I could help out like that or by volunteering my time, if that's OK."

She looked like she was mortified at herself, fiddling with her napkin,

"Or not, that's okay, I'm sorry for being so forward."

As it turns out, this blonde hippie chick with the dreads was exactly what I needed. I wanted to be involved with the pottery studio, but I had a job at Seppi's restaurant and even though it wasn't technically full-time, I spent well over forty hours a week in that building. And let's face it, that's where I wanted to be, not at a community studio. If that girl could hold down the fort, teach some classes, maybe run the kilns, it would be worth way more to me than a free membership. I didn't want to seem desperate so I played it cool,

"Are you available to follow me over there for a tour?"

Her face lit up,

"Really!?"

Well, gee, if that's all it took to make someone happy around here,

"Really."

Frieda slid out of the booth, I smiled and followed suit. We returned our mugs, and she followed me to the parking lot. I pointed at the back door of the ristorante,

"I need to grab my keys, you can come with me if you want, it's just over there."

Frieda glanced at the back of the ristorante and appeared to be contemplating,

"I'll wait here, I heard the guy who runs that place is in the mob. Eating there is one thing, going in the back door is another story."

She leaned in,

"My cousin's friend's ex-boyfriend said that guy left a horse head in someone's bed, like The Godfather."

I hadn't heard that one before, but managed not to laugh in her face as I gave her a thumbs up and jogged inside. On my way through, I poked my head into Seppi's office to tell him I was giving someone a tour of the studio. He saluted me and I blew him a kiss before retracing my steps to the parking lot. Frieda was standing there twisting one of her dreads, nervously. I asked,

"Do you want to ride with me so we can talk on the way?"

And then I wondered if that seemed creepy,

"I mean, or you can follow me in your car, I know you don't know me."

I pretended I wasn't a cold-blooded killer and made a face at myself, liar, liar, thrifted designer pants on fire. Frieda seemed to believe I was a nice person, and not someone who had killed someone with a shovel.

She replied,

"I rode my bike but sure, yeah, I can ride with you so we can talk."

Frieda got into the passenger seat of my car and hopefully she knew I wasn't going to kill her. I could tell by the way she was looking around that it was the nicest car she had ever been in. I felt uncomfortable or like she would think I was rich or trying to show off,

"Up until last month, I drove a twenty-seven-year-old Subaru wagon. It finally shit the bed."

Frieda was mesmerized by all the buttons and I felt like I needed to explain,

"This car belongs to my boss, I just drive it."

I told her there were heated seats and she seemed to like it when I chirped the tires. When we pulled into the driveway, I drove around back and her face lit up,

"There's a garden here!?"

She sprung from the mini mafia sedan,

"Can people plant things!?"

She ran over and touched the soil,

"Wow, this is great!"

I stood there smiling on the inside. Frieda was about the same height as me. She was beautiful, there's something about a woman like that, doesn't give a shit what people think. Dresses how she wants, gets the piercing she wants, the tattoos she wants. I stood in awe of her, hearing my mother's voice in the back of my head telling me how 'trashy' tattoos are, and 'what will they look like when you're older?' But this twenty-something did whatever the hell she wanted. Frieda seemed nervous socially, but I could tell she knew exactly who she was. She glanced back at me over her shoulder,

"Is the garden part of the community studio?

"Yes. I need to figure out how to divide it up for the people who are interested in planting things."

"Wow, that's so cool, I definitely want to grow a cucumber plant. Maybe some roses! I love roses."

I appreciated her enthusiasm. I unlocked the door and gestured her over the threshold. Her eyes lit up and it looked like she was in heaven. She was wearing sea foam colored linen pants and a crocheted top, no bra. I wished my tits were that perky. She squealed with delight when she found the pottery studio,

"Wow!"

Before we got back into the car, I told Frieda I would take her up on her offer to help around the studio in exchange for a free membership. I told her I hoped to eventually have classes two or three nights a week for things like watercolor, pottery, jewelry making, silk screening and other things like that. She had experience with some of those things and told me she enjoyed the classes she taught at the rec center. I told her the kiln was good to go, mentioned the second kiln again, and made a mental note to see what I needed to do to order the other one. I told her about my idea to have concerts in the garden to raise funds for supplies, and about maybe having a member farm stand or a booth at the farmers market where people could sell the things they've made.

When the two of us parted ways, we exchanged numbers and I told her Open House was in three days. Frieda said she would be there an hour early and would help with whatever I needed. She was such a doll. I waved to her before she walked up the alley with a bounce in her step. I couldn't wait to tell Seppi, this was going to be perfect. I bounced in the back door and swung into Seppi's office. He was on the phone and didn't see me so I retreated to my office. He hung up his phone and I appeared in his doorway,

"Hey!"

Seppi jumped out of his skin,

"Jesus, Dimples, you're going to give me a heart attack, what's the matter with you?"

You and I both know that if I ever give that man a heart attack, it certainly wasn't going to be from a jump scare. I went in and kissed him on the cheek but he turned his head, and we kissed. He slid his hand to my backside and squeezed. Had I not been preoccupied with my big news; I probably would have screwed him on his desk. Our eyes met briefly before I moved around the desk and plopped in the chair across from him.

"Guess what!?"

He pretended to be thinking really hard,

"You have a cute ass?"

I blushed and waved him away,

"No, really, guess what!?"

"What?"

"You know how I wanted to find someone to help with the ceramics and the kilns and things?"

I didn't bother to wait for him to answer,

"Well, a friend of the co-op lady showed up at Muddy Waters and heard that Maggie was building a studio where Stanley's used to be. This blonde girl with dreads named Frieda..."

"Breathe, Dimples."

I slowed down. Seppi went to the bar and put perfectly square ice cubes in two rocks glasses. He returned with whiskey and I took a sip, letting the heat trace its way to my belly,

"OK, the woman from the food co-op knew about the studio and told a woman who's looking for a place to fire her pottery."

He looked interested.

"I took her over and gave her a tour and we talked. She's going to help me with the classes, and kilns, and with other things, in exchange for a free membership, and use of part of the garden to grow cucumbers and roses."

We clinked glasses and Seppi winked at me, things were finally going my way. There I sat, across the desk from Giuseppi Moretti in the bat cave, the inner sanctum, the VIP lounge. I was an aunt, I was an Event Planner, I owned commercial property, I had a reliable car, I had a cat, I had a man. At that moment, I was sure that I was finally getting that fresh start I was looking for. The next day, I waltzed into the local ceramic supply place in a pantsuit and expensive shoes and they knew it. I looked like I had money to spend and they acted accordingly. When a middle-aged man came over to greet me, I told him the story about the studio and that I wanted to purchase a second kiln.

"Are you Ms. Birch?"

"Yeah, how did you know?"

"Well, ma'am, Mr. Moretti already took care of it, your kiln has been selected and paid for. And luckily, we had the model you were looking for, so we can deliver it tomorrow, if that works for you Ms. Birch."

Hell yes, that worked for me, but I played it cool,

"I'm sure I can leave work, if necessary, what time will you be delivering it?"

The man went behind the counter and flipped through a spiral bound notebook with coffee stains and tattered pages,

"It'll be afternoon, ma'am, but we can call you before we head over."

And just like that, I had a second kiln. I was hoping it wasn't deeper than the other one because I was going to need a stool just to load and unload it. I had faith Seppi that was watching when I showed him how I'd have to balance on the edge to reach the bottom. I shook the man's hand and got back in the mini mafia sedan. That was easy. The next day, I was sitting on my office sofa popping dark chocolate covered blueberries when my office phone rang. I scurried over and swallowed what I had in my mouth, clearing my throat,

"Moretti Events and Catering, Amelia speaking, how may I help you?"

"Yes, Ms. Birch, this is George from the ceramics shop. We are getting ready to head over to the service center to deliver the kiln."

I told George I'd meet him at the studio and two minutes later I backed out of the space next to Seppi's. I had moved up in the world. I pulled out of the alley and six minutes later I was pulling behind the studio. Five minutes later than that, a box truck backed into the driveway. I unlocked the back door and propped it open before jogging ahead to roll the other kiln over a little to give them space. One section at a time, the men carried in the layers of the kiln and as they constructed it. Seppi had managed to find a kiln that was the same height as the one I already had, but it was twice as wide. The SkuttKM1627 was shaped like an oval and would hold tons of pottery, it was reminiscent of an oblong coffin with it's lid propped open. I could fire tall vases and mugs and wonky little beginner wares in the same kiln, or Frieda could, or whoever ended up firing these things. George put his tools away and handed me the manual,

"Ms. Birch, I think you should upgrade your ventilation and exhaust system if you're going to be running both of these."

He seemed nervous to be the bearer of bad news,

"I know you just had this place built, but that exhaust vent isn't going to cut it."

I thanked him and didn't bother to tell the guy I'd already contacted someone about upgrading the ventilation and filtration systems. I waved him away and stood in the ceramics room with a big smile on my face. Shortly after, I was rolling into the alley between Muddy Waters and Giuseppi's Italian Ristorante. I swung through the back door and bounced in with a spring in my step. I felt light and happy, and tomorrow was Open House at my new community studio. I heard

Seppi's voice coming from the kitchen so I wandered in that direction. I could smell his cologne and watched him from afar.

Seppi was leaning against the stainless-steel counter in black pants and a dark gray dress shirt, the top buttons of his shirt open, his sleeves rolled up a couple times. He had a Rolex on the left and a rocks glass on the right. He had a fresh haircut and a clean shave. I nodded to him when he glanced up, and he gestured for me to join him. He pulled me in and kissed me, something about it made me blush even though he had done it before. He was discussing something with Guido and Carlo, so I excused myself and sat in the chair across the desk from his.

When Seppi came back in, his eyes were smiling. He came to my side of the desk and leaned on the edge, he brought a waft of espresso and Tobacco Vanille along with him. We made eye contact and Seppi flicked an eyebrow and I flicked one back. He put his hand out and I went to him, got close, kissed his neck. He said,

"I like wherever this is going."

I tousled his hair,

"Thank you, Seppi."

He played innocent,

"For?"

I smacked him and he grabbed me, pulling me close,

"You're welcome, I was able to find one that was bigger than the other one but wasn't any deeper. Did I do good?"

I put a hand on either side of his face, and we rubbed noses before we kissed,

"You did real good."

I put a finger up and closed the door. He smiled and I unbuttoned my shirt on the way back to his desk. And just for the record, I didn't have to push the papers to the floor because he did it for me. Once we were put back together, I retreated to the world of new voicemails from future brides, but I was preoccupied with the Open House. I confirmed with Carlo that the food would be ready and set up by five o'clock. And since I was the Event Planner, but also the owner of the community studio, Mary would manage the catering and the flow of foot traffic for the free mini garlic knots and mini meatballs in marinara. My mind was swirling with excitement and things were looking up.

CHAPTER 12
SPIDERS IN THE ROSES

I STAYED AT MY APARTMENT that night so Opal and Auggie could have date night and get some sleep. It felt good to be back there and it made me feel like a woman to take care of a baby. It helped me realize that just because my mother was a loveless bitch, it doesn't mean I'll be like that when I have kids. I spent most of the evening holding Chloe, I even figured out how to use that thing that straps the kid to your chest while you cook, and do laundry, and clean the toilet. My biggest accomplishment, though, was wearing Chloe while I took a shit, it was a stinker and she slept through the whole thing. Something about being with her felt natural to me, even though I was comforted by the fact that I could hand her over to Opal and bail if I needed to. But I didn't. Kids are good like that, they smell nice (most of the time), and they are a reminder of purity and innocence. I'm not going to lie and tell you that seeing her didn't make me a little sentimental for my own dysfunctional childhood. As I curled up on the couch and cradled her, I spent over an hour just watching her sleep, and wondered if I would ever be someone's mother, but I hoped I'd be their mom instead.

If I ever had the chance to be the one protecting a little girl, the world better watch out, because I had no intention of messing around when it came to keeping her safe. As Chloe cooed and made little sucking sounds with her perfect little lips as she slept, I let my mind wander off to my life with Seppi. I wondered if we would have kids someday, and I wondered what kind of shit show it would be. I pictured a mini mobster with a dark pompadour and Italian eyebrows, cruising around the back yard in a Power Wheels version of the Escalade with a diaper full of toddler shit. Or maybe I'd have a daughter and she would twirl around in a pink tutu with a flattened cloth baby doll in a matching dress. I let out a big sigh and hoped if I ever had kids that I would do a better job than my own mother.

As I fell asleep that night with Chloe in a bassinet by my side, a switch flipped somewhere, something hardwired into every woman. Every time she moved or squeaked, my eyes flew open so I could make sure she was safe. The next morning, I woke with a spring in my step, even though I had only gotten three hours of sleep. Opal stumbled out of my room at five-thirty with bed head and nestled in on the couch next to me. The three of us sat there in a forcefield of love and contentedness as Chloe made wet raspberries at Opal's breast. Things seemed different and I knew something good was about to happen. That morning, I smiled a little more than usual as I sipped my latte and smoked half of a sun porch joint. I showered and worked curl cream through my hair before some lip gloss, a little mascara, and my new perfume. I wore a dressy looking linen jumper that was really just fancy overalls, and wondered if the principal would scold me in the hall for not following the dress code. I slid my feet into some chunky leather ankle boots and bounced out the door.

By the time I swung into the back door of the ristorante, exhaustion was creeping in around the edges and Seppi's eyes smiled when he saw me. He closed the gap between us and wrapped me in his arms, kissing me on both cheeks and then the lips,

"I missed you last night, Dimples. Did you get any sleep?"

I shrugged,

"Maybe three hours, probably less."

He flashed a smile at me and winked,

"My poor baby."

Something about Seppi saying that, was sexy. I was his. He snuggled around me and I wanted to go to sleep, he was warm, and he smelled so good. He kissed the top of my head and I sat in the chair across the desk from him. He eyed me and then leaned out the door,

"Hey, Gweed, make Amelia a latte please, and thank you."

Seppi retrieved a small box from his drawer and slid it across the desk to me, I shook it,

"What is it?"

He smiled,

"You'll have to open it, Dimples."

I lifted the lid to find a little folded card that said, 'Dimples, there is nothing wrong with being sentimental. Ti amo, Seppi.' I put the card on the desk and my eyes moved to one of the most thoughtful gifts anyone had ever given me. Seppi had a piece of my twenty-seven-year-old piece of Swiss cheese made into a beautiful key chain. On the ring was an oval piece of rusty metal from my door, and the Subaru emblem from the front, both encased in resin to protect them. I didn't know what to say. I think that was the first time in my life that I was speechless. I was definitely not spending the night at my apartment that night, if you know what I mean.

A while later, I carried my empty mug back to the kitchen and made myself another latte. I double-checked that the food would be ready for the Open House and then Mary shouted from somewhere behind me,

"Amelia, darling, don't you worry your pretty little head about any of this. Today, you're not the Event Planner."

She flicked her hands at the dining room,

"Shoo! Shoo!"

I smiled and laughed,

"Well, I'm the Event Planner until after my consults, I'll hand over the reins after that."

Mary winked and retreated to the kitchen. I went back to Seppi's office and he pushed the door shut. Like the spider and the fly. He backed me up against the back of the sofa and kissed me, deeply. Put his nose up to my throat and inhaled,

"Is this the perfume I gave you?"

I answered as heat rose in my cheeks,

"Yes."

Seppi sucked my neck and made a noise low in his throat,

"Money well spent."

I let my body give in to his. He scooped the back of my head and we kissed like we were making love. I pushed him back,

"I'm coming home with you tonight; do you think you can wait?"

Seppi moved his gaze to the cushions and back, his eyes swimming with lust,

"Why can't I have dinner *and* dessert?"

The man made a valid point.

I reaped the rewards of smelling like a bad bitch, and planned on cashing in again later that night. I kissed Seppi on the cheek before retreating to my office, just in time to straighten myself up before I met with another set of newly engaged twenty-somethings. I made my way to Muddy Waters for lunch and then got ready to go to the studio. I didn't want to look like a mini mob boss, and I didn't want to look like a ragamuffin in ripped overalls and dirty sneakers. It was in the mid-sixties, so I wore my favorite pair of flare jeans, a flowy top, and my Birkenstocks. I spritzed Coco Mademoiselle in the air and spun around in the mist. I felt confident and like I had my shit together. I went over to see Seppi on my way to the other side of town, he kissed me on both cheeks and smacked me on the ass as I left his office.

"Dimples."

I spun around and went back,

"Yes?"

"Take my car. My Mama's MKX is in the shop and there's no way she'll drive the Escalade, she'd have to sit on a stack of phone books."

Was I delirious? Because I was pretty sure Giuseppi Moretti had just asked me to drive his Escalade V. And just to be clear, it wasn't just a regular Escalade, it was an Escalade on steroids,

"Umm, sure."

I was flooded with insecurity, could I even manage to get out of the parking lot without hitting something? We traded keys and I went on my merry way. Well, if you consider having the panic sweats and a case of the nervous shits, merry. OK, no problem, I got the seat adjusted, the backup camera was magnificent, so I didn't even back into any fences or cars or trashcans. I was driving, Giuseppi Moretti's mob boss aesthetic and something about it made me feel untouchable. When I looped around the back of the studio, Frieda was sitting crisscross applesauce next to the garden, smoking a joint, her vintage Triumph Scrambler parked next to the garage, her helmet hanging from the handle bar. Frieda Harper was my kind of girl. I joined her and she shared the last couple puffs of her Maryjane. I glanced at her bike,

"Is it scary driving that thing?"

She shrugged,

"Not as long as the roads are dry. My brother Seth is older and he's been working on bikes since I was knee-high to a grasshopper."

I said,

"I have a guy friend with a bike but it's bigger and seems more intimidating."

She gestured and we went over to her bike, she caressed the black leather seat lovingly, more relaxed talking about her bike than any other time,

"Sit on it, see how it feels."

She held the handlebar as I awkwardly swung my leg over the seat. The Triumph was lower to the ground than Kane's bike and the handle bars were more feminine. She smiled,

"We can go to the lot behind the high school on Saturday and I'll teach you. You'll have to get a motorcycle endorsement if you want to drive one on your own."

Impostor syndrome creeping in at the seams,

"Do you think I can figure it out?"

She nodded and I followed her back to the porch, we sat there swinging our feet. She said,

"Motorcycles have never scared me, Seth took me on my first ride when I was six-years-old and I've been obsessed ever since. He handed down his old Kawasaki dirt bike when I was nine and he gave me this bike when I turned eighteen."

She motioned to the bike,

"It was my Auntie Clay's."

Frieda blinked like she was trying not to cry,

"She had a lot of mental health struggles and isn't with us anymore."

I knew what she meant.

Freida shook it off,

"My auntie gave me a powerful piece of advice before she died, she told me,

"There is something about riding a bike that makes you feel free, you feel like you're flying. And there is something about a woman on a bike, there's something courageous about it."

She gestured at herself,

"I don't usually feel very confident, not really, you can probably tell I'm socially awkward. Most of the time I'm a ball of nerves and anxiety, but something about riding a bike, especially that one, makes me feel like I can do anything. I can be whoever I want to be. I wear her old jacket sometimes, it's black leather and has tassels on the sleeves that hang down and blow in the wind."

She shrugged,

"I feel close to her when I wear it and something about it makes me feel whole. It clears my mind and keeps the spiders out of the roses."

I was familiar with a desperate need to feel whole. I was also familiar with having spiders in my roses, I was pretty sure it was a lot like having demons in cages. She said,

"Seth is working on an Indian Scout right now, it's a smaller bike like mine. He was fixing it up for his girlfriend, Destiny, but they broke up,"

She glanced over at me and we had a moment, I could see the scars inside of her and she could see the scars inside of me. She tapped her temple and said,

"It will help you."

I nodded and wondered if I would have the courage to get the thing out of her brother's driveway,

"How much does he want for it?"

She shrugged,

"He just likes restoring bikes, it's the thing that keeps him out of the ground, he'll probably just give it to you."

So even more important than the open house for the community studio, I made plans to learn how to drive a motorcycle the following Saturday. Little did I know that owning a bike would evolve into just one more way to self-destruct, one more way to run away when I'm drowning. We sat there a little longer and then went inside to set out make-and-take activities for kids. Things went off without a hitch. Mary arrived in the mini mafia sedan and we carried in the cater gators filled with mini meatballs and Mama Moretti's marinara. Mary arranged mini garlic knots, lemon water, and a tray of Italian lemon cookies. There were moms with little kids, high school girls, college girls, and middle-aged women. But even though I was exhausted, I was happy that this was going to be a safe place for so many women. I soaked up the conversations and camaraderie. The laughter and the excitement about learning pottery or watercolor or how to make laser cut earrings with a Glowforge.

CHAPTER 13
FIRST FIRE

WHEN WE PACKED the folding banquet table and catering bins into the trunk of the mini mafia sedan, there wasn't so much as a garlic knot crumb left. Those women and their kids licked their plates clean. I glanced at the garden and thought about having a class on building raised beds so I could offer more space to grow things. I thought about having a farmstand at the end of the driveway so people could sell the things they made, or grew in the garden, maybe we'd even get chickens. So, already, I felt good about it, and I hadn't even asked anyone if they were interested. Sometimes the thought of something new is refreshing, it sparks creativity and motivation.

I loved my life in the inner sanctum, the darkness of it that spoke to the darkness in my soul, but I also liked having something that wasn't a part of all that. I liked the promise of cucumbers and roses, and back porch joints with Frieda. Sometimes I was dripping with dark mafia energy and sometimes I'd shed that skin in exchange for something brighter. A ray of sunshine that provided refuge from the perpetual game of 'ditch a stiff' I played with Vincenzo Moretti.

There were conversations about mugs and earrings and learning how to paint like Bob Ross. Groups of women asking about paint-and-sips, and a college girl who knew Frieda, asking about making stained glass sun catchers. So, right then, that place was a chance for something of my own, something creative, something that operated within the confines of the law. You've been here long enough to know that this kind of thinking never leads anywhere good, it leads to something dark and drastic and out of sorts. But right then, in that little sliver of time, I thought everything would be OK, I thought the studio would be an escape from the darkness when I needed it, and when I didn't, I'd have Frieda.

Mary kissed me on both cheeks and set off for the world of dirty pans and burnt-on marinara. I sat on the porch with Freida, our legs dangling as we shared another joint. It was dusk and it was a beautiful night. We sat there, just the two of us, in silence as we enjoyed each other's company and the sounds of kids playing in backyards. I smelled a grill and pictured a dad making burgers and dogs while the kids played on the swing set. It was going to be a nice summer and I was looking forward to it. The summer before, I had been adjusting to life in Bunman and there was a lot going on, so summer flew by in a swirl of chaos and confusion. But here I was with my own studio, a garden, people who wanted to learn stuff, a joint, a new friend, and Giuseppi Moretti's mob boss aesthetic. Frieda gestured at the Escalade,

"Is that your boss's car, that Moretti guy, the one in the mob?"

"Yeah."

I glanced over at her,

"We kind of see each other."

That was an understatement.

Frieda made the same face I used to make when I thought about the things he did, and I wasn't sure if she was approving or rejecting the idea,

"Is he really in the mob?"

I nodded,

"Yup."

She took a drag of the joint and passed it over,

"Is he scary?"

I shook my head,

"He can be. Seppi's a good person, but he's capable of bad things, just like the rest of us."

She nodded,

"Seppi?"

Maybe the fact that the scary Italian man had a nickname made him seem a little less scary. Frieda sat there silently, trying to find her words or get up her courage, she side-eyed me,

"Are *you* in the mob?"

It felt surreal,

"Yeah, I guess I am. *I'm* not scary, right?"

She shrugged and shook her head,

"No."

"OK, well, this is one of those don't judge a book by its cover situations."

And then we just sat there in silence, trying not to burn our fingers on the butt end of a joint. By the time the high had passed, we were sitting in complete darkness. I waited for Frieda to get to the end of the driveway before I backed out and went toward town. I was flying high in my mind, flooded with thoughts and feelings, daydreaming about that bike Frieda mentioned. I was imagining how it would feel to fly when headlights came up behind me, a little too close, and I thought about break checking the guy.

I was three minutes from the restaurant and once I pulled in the alleyway, no one in their right mind would tailgate. Suddenly, I felt uncomfortable driving Seppi's car. I made a right down a random street and the car followed. I was starting to spiral, latent PTSD from the night Sal chased me around Lake Road. I took another right and the car continued on, I was alone again. I let out a deep breath and wiped my sweaty palms on my leg.

I jumped out of my skin when my phone rang. When I reached for it, I bumped it and it slid into the pocket on the inside of the passenger side door. Crap. Maybe it wasn't important, I glanced at my left wrist and wasn't wearing my watch. I pulled over and went to the passenger side to retrieve my phone and it was ringing again. It was Seppi, I tried to be all come hither and flirty,

"Yes, darling?"

He sounded frantic,

"Are you OK, Amelia!?"

I reassured,

"Yeah, I mean I thought someone was following me, but they turned off."

Seppi cut me off in his mob boss voice, barking,

"Listen to me, Amelia."

Goosebumps crawled across my skin as he continued with his orders,

"Go to my house, I'll meet you there."

I squeaked,

"Did something bad happen?"

"Yes."

The call ended and my senses fired on all cylinders. I ran around and climbed in the driver seat, locked the doors and scanned my surroundings. I drove straight to the land of mafia mansions and cryptic phone calls. I sped past Gary at the gate and pulled in behind the mini mafia sedan, which had a couple bullet holes in the back of it. I slid from the driver's seat and speed-walked to the house while I rubbernecked the mini mafia sedan. Seppi swung the door open as I approached and he slammed it shut as soon as I was inside. Mary was perched on one of the stools in the kitchen, a glass of brandy in one hand, a long skinny cigarette in the other. I went to her and gave her a once over, she seemed OK on the outside but she was obviously rattled,

"What happened!? Are you OK!?"

I gestured toward the driveway,

"What happened to my car!?"

Mary moved her eyes to mine and then moved them back to her brandy. I was grasping for clues, for some explanation, putting the pieces together. Mary had been driving my car, the back had bullet holes. The emotions rose quickly, I put things together and knew she could have died. If it was supposed to be a kidnapping for ransom or some other such nonsense, whatever it was, it was meant for me. I didn't know how to handle the fear, the anger, the guilt. I put my hands on her shoulders,

"What happened!?"

I wanted to know because it could have been me, I wasn't wired for shit like that, and they were. I hopped up on the stool next to her and then immediately got up because I couldn't sit still. Mary took a long drag of her skinny cigarette,

"I swung by the cottage to pick something up. On the way back, someone came up behind me and tried to run me off Lake Road. And then the guy shot at me, but luckily, he had horrible aim. Just some punk."

She was being way too nonchalant, I was freaking out,

"Oh my God, are you okay!?"

"Amelia, yes. This isn't my first rodeo. I pulled over on that stretch with the trees, and the idiot pulled up behind me."

I stared at her like she had three heads,

"You pulled over!?"

Mary waved me away with the last of her cigarette as she blew smoke out through her nose,

"I couldn't see the guy very well but when he got out, he was swinging a gun like one of those gang banger assholes. I could see in the mirror that he was wearing droopy jeans and a big hoodie, just some fucking punk kid."

I was staring at her with saucers for eyes.

"He shouted at me, 'it's your turn, bitch, and then put a couple bullets in your trunk. He hollered and shoot into the air, calling me a cunt, so I grabbed my gun. I mean, I froze for a second, but when he came toward the driver's side window, I grabbed my gun and shot him."

Just like that, she shot the guy, without hesitation. Seppi slid a rocks glass across the counter and I slammed it back. I knew what was coming, I was going to have to help Vinny dump whoever that guy was. Goddammit. And let's not forget that whoever it was, could have pulled that shit with me, and my gun was mixed up with all the other shit at the bottom of my bag. Let's not forget I was running on like three fucking hours of sleep. Seppi said,

"I helped Vin load the guy into your trunk but need to stay here with my Mama. All you need to do is check his pockets for identification and personal effects, and make him disappear."

Fucking fabulous, there had been a dead body in my trunk. I slammed my glass on the counter and Mary jumped. I locked eyes with Seppi,

"Wonderful, now the mini mafia sedan has dead guy cooties and bad juju!"

Seppi refilled my glass and I tossed that one back too. I slid the empty glass across the counter, and without saying another word, went through the door to the garage. There was Vinny and a dead guy on one of those big blue tarps. Whatever. On my knees next to the tarp, I glanced at the guy and then pinched the bridge of my nose and shook my head, a statement more than a question,

"What the fuck."

Vinny looked over at me,

"I know."

But he didn't know. It was a long story, and I wasn't going to tell him. I was pretty sure that was the guy I shot in the cemetery. Same droopy jeans, same kind of body type. Only this time he had a bullet in his chest. Vinny put his finger up,

"I've got to grab my car, I'll be back."

Once he disappeared into the house, I pulled the guy's pant leg up and found the scar from the gunshot wound. I can't really explain how I felt in that moment, but it wasn't great. At the same time, I guess I was well enough acquainted with the system that nothing should have surprised me. The middle bay of the garage rolled open and Vinny backed in with the BMW. As he got out, the trunk swung open, and I said,

"Listen, I'm not cut out for this shit. Both times I've helped you do this, I've managed to fall into the water."

Vincenzo Moretti didn't really have time to worry about my feelings, he moved around me like I was in the way.

"Amelia, I'm sorry. Just be more careful."

I glared at him, and he waved it away,

"I'm not saying it was your fault, I'm just saying we need to be more careful."

I threw both of my middle fingers at him. Vinny didn't want to piss me off or he'd be doing it on his own. I crossed my arms and muttered,

"Fine."

I helped Vinny wrap the guy like a burrito and we loaded him into the trunk of the BMW. I went inside to kiss Seppi on the cheek before going for round three of ditching a stiff. Seppi grabbed my wrist and I spun around to face him as Mary lit another one of her long skinny cigarettes. He looked me in the eye and flicked his eyebrow,

"I like this side of you, Dimples, you're a good girl."

I made a face, shook my head, and walked away with my nipples pressing against my bra. Whatever. I didn't know whether to be flattered, insulted, or turned on. I mean, what the fuck was all this!? Was this why I moved back there? To help Vincenzo Moretti dump bodies? I'd completely switched gears in the span of an hour. I'd gone from 'local woman growing daisies in the community garden' to 'mini mobster, helping dump a guy who is literally pushing up daisies.' My bitch of a mother would be so proud. Not. I drifted off to some imaginary scenario where I'd been arrested for dumping human remains and being affiliated with the mob. I'm on trial and my mother is sitting there in her home shopping network pantsuit and fake diamond earrings, boxed wine on her breath. She clutches her fake pearls and responds to the newspaper reporter that she 'Never saw this coming' and, 'My daughter was such an angel until she got mixed up with that Moretti guy.' I rolled my eyes, 'that Moretti guy.' Yeah, the one I regularly perform fellatio on.

Me and Vinny went into town and I had a little epiphany. Well, I had been thinking about it ever since Seppi asked about the temperature chart for firing pottery. I investigated it, and crematoriums only get up to eighteen hundred degrees Fahrenheit, kilns get up to twenty-three hundred degrees. It made sense to me that I could cremate a body if I wanted to. I wasn't flying by the seat of my pants, but almost,

"Go to the place where the service center used to be."

He glanced over and I reassured,

"Trust me."

Vinny shrugged, and ten minutes later we were pulling around the back of the community studio. He got out of the car,

"Wow, this place looks completely different." And ever the smart ass,

"You mean completely different than the time when you were tied to a chair with a rag in your mouth?"

Vinny turned to me,

"You're the one who broke in that night!?"

"Yup."

He jabbed his finger at me repeatedly,

"I knew it, I fucking knew it!"

He shook his head,

"Yeah, that wasn't a good time for me."

He wasn't the only one. He nodded toward the back door,

"Let's get the guy inside."

So, we did. Vinny and I carried the dead guy wrapped like a burrito through the back door and into the pottery studio. I turned on the breaker and plugged in the coffin-shaped kiln. I sat in the almost darkness with experienced mobster Vincenzo Moretti, and was about to rock his world,

"OK, so listen, my kiln heats up even hotter than one of those furnaces they use to cremate bodies. So, I was thinking we could just cremate the guy."

Vinny stared back at me with saucers for eyes and didn't say anything for a long time. I scrunched up my eyebrows and leaned closer, waving my hand in front of his face,

"Hello?"

He shook his head,

"I just...that's really clever, I'm kind of impressed."

I waved him away,

"I mean, it just makes sense to me. The ventilation system is really good, and Seppi is footing the bill for an even better one. We can put him in this one,"

I gestured toward the oblong kiln,

"It's big enough that we can just curl the guy up in there and I can run a cone six glaze fire."

"A what?"

I waved at him apologetically,

"Oh, sorry. Cone is the temperature. You can fire kilns to different cones, or temperatures. I fire my things to cone six, and that's just about twenty-two hundred degrees."

"Fahrenheit!?"

"Yeah."

"Wow!"

The two of us proceeded to strip the guy naked, all of his personal effects. His wallet and watch went into a zippered bag and his clothing went into a trash bag. We used the tarp as sort of a sling to lower the guy into the kiln and then worked the tarp out from under him. It wasn't very graceful but whatever, we got him in. Vinny leaned in and curled the guy into the fetal position on the bottom shelf. I took one more look to make sure he wasn't touching the heating elements or thermocouple and I had full body chills as I closed the lid. I turned on the ventilation system and programmed the kiln. Three minutes later, the fire was underway and would be complete in eight hours and forty-nine minutes.

The two of us sat on the back porch with our heads spinning. Vinny offered my a cigarette and I took it, he lit it with his fancy gold Zippo. I fished a silver flask from my bag and we swallowed fire together. I told him that once the kiln got up to six-hundred-fifty degrees, most of the smell would be gone, if there was any. I reassured him I was fine, and he went back to the land of mafia mansions and mothers who can take care of themselves. Vinny snagged the tarp, the personal effects, and the clothing. He kissed me on the cheek and said he'd have an associate bring me some food. Then I just sat on a stool in the dark while some dead punk cooked in my kiln.

I heard fire trucks and immediately felt like I was going to shit my pants. My heart was beating in my ears and I was getting sparkly. What was I going to do? I didn't have a car. I stood and looked for a place to hide. The sirens were getting louder and I realized I could smell something burning. Oh my God, was I burning the floor or the wall or something? I ran to the kiln and there was nothing, I was so confused and paranoid. The sirens were getting closer. I went to the front windows and peeked around the blinds. Two fire trucks and a police car sped passed the studio. I opened the window and could smell a structure fire nearby. Well, not that I want someone's building to catch on fire, but it was going to make me less nervous that someone would smell the guy cooking.

CHAPTER 14
TOO HOT TO HANDLE

A CAR PULLED IN and I assumed it was Vinny with some spaghetti and marinara, or whatever Seppi had for leftovers at the ristorante. Or maybe he ran home and brought back some of Sunny's homemade mac and cheese. When the back door opened, I was surprised to see someone else, it felt like I was living in an alternate reality. Giuseppi Moretti, patriarch of the Moretti Mob Family, had just strolled into my community studio with take out and I wanted to stop time. He put the food down and shrugged out of his jacket. I knew someday one of us wouldn't make it home. Even if that day didn't come for decades, it would come someday, and I guess that was another one of those nights when I realized what love is.

I know I've said something similar before, but love, our capacity to give it and receive it, our ability to submit to its power, is something that changes over time. What was once our version of being head over heels at age ten, is soon nothing more than a crush. Some of that might not make any sense but that was the night I knew I loved Seppi in a way I never knew existed. We were in it for the long-haul. And even though I had no idea there was some major shit right around the corner, I knew we would make it through, until one of us didn't make it home.

We went to the kiln several times to stare at the digital temperature screen, its numbers aglow in the darkness. Things were going well, there wasn't even really an odor; the ventilation system was doing its job. The structure fire nearby had caused several gallons of paint and gasoline to explode so the odd odors and smoke in the air camouflaged the smell of the dead guy cooking in my kiln. Honestly, if that worked as well as I thought it might, I was pretty sure I'd never have to fall through the ice at the quarry again, if you know what I mean. We sat on the floor in the dark, eating Chinese food and sipping whiskey. An hour later, I had a revelation,

"Umm, what are we doing?"

Seppi was jumpier than I'd ever seen him,

"What!? You mean with the guy!?"

I waved him away,

"No, that's going to be fine. I mean, what are we doing sitting on the floor down here? There's an entire apartment upstairs."

"Oh!"

We gathered our dinner trash and I led Seppi up the back stairs to the apartment. I hadn't stayed there yet, but I had some furniture, there was toilet paper in the bathroom, and a twin bed in the bedroom. So, I spent that night curled up tight with Giuseppi Moretti, in a twin bed with secondhand Care Bear sheets and a thrifted quilt. By six in the morning, the kiln had run its course. Seppi was anxiously waiting for me to tell him the cycle had completed. When I confirmed that, yes, it was done, he went for the kiln like it was as simple as baking cookies. As he reached for the lid, I yelled,

"WAIT!"

Seppi jumped and spun to face me,

"I thought you said it was done."

I gestured toward the kiln,

"It is done, it's also at eighteen hundred degrees. You can't just open it, you need to wait for it to cool. It should be ready this afternoon. This isn't like the oven in your kitchen, Seppi."

His eyes got big,

"This afternoon!?"

I shrugged and went palms up,

"Yeah, or early this evening. Fucking relax."

Seppi started pacing, having an internal conversation, hands going, I had never seen him like that. What the hell was going on? He stood next to the kiln, I shook my head and said,

"Don't do it."

He opened his palm and laid it on the lid of the kiln to see if I was shitting him,

"Geez!"

I crossed my arms and shook my head,

"What did I tell you?"

"So, there's no way to get the bones out right now?"

"No! Do you have a pair of potholders that aren't going to burst into flames at that temperature!?"

He made a face and I waved him away,

"And anyway, you'll ruin the kiln. Calm down!"

Seppi made another face and chewed on his fingernails, he acted like a lightbulb went off over his head,

"I know, we can move the kiln into the garage!"

I scrunched up my face and went palms up,

"No, we can't."

He shook his head,

"Why?"

He gestured toward the driveway,

"There's a wheelchair ramp, we can just roll it into the garage."

"No, we can't! And anyway, the kiln weighs over eight-hundred pounds, the ramp isn't built for that kind of weight! Calm down, the body is cremated, all that's in there is a pile of bones. Seriously, calm the fuck down!"

I couldn't believe *I* was the one reassuring *him* that everything was fine. Seppi stood in front of me and gripped my shoulders,

"Amelia, I set up an interview for you with the Rutland Herald. It was going to be a surprise."

I looked at him like he had three heads. He started pacing again, reasoning, bargaining, disbelief,

"I thought it would be good promotion for your place and I had a guy that owed me a favor. He said he'd make sure the interview got on the front page."

I waited for the other shoe to drop and then he said,

"And I think WCAX is going to be here at the same time."

My eyes bugged out of my head, fingers gripping fistfuls of ringlets,

"WCAX is coming!? Here!? Today!? With cameras!?"

And then I spiraled, and I'm talking full-on spiral with crying, hysterical laughing, and the shits. Here I was with a body in the kiln of my new Community Studio and the six o'clock news was coming. Of course it was. I pinched the bridge of my nose and shook my head. That's fine, it was going to be fine, it isn't like they were going to open something like that without asking, people don't just open big kilns without getting permission. Do they? We stood there staring at each other, staring at the current temperature inside the kiln, seventeen sixty-eight.

"I have two meetings today, one with a bride and groom, and another with a woman who might want to have us cater her annual staff retreat. I can't sit around here with my thumb up my ass all day."

Seppi was in full panic mode and between the dead guy and the shitty night sleep, we looked like a couple frazzled assholes. Like, actual assholes, not like how people say, 'you're an asshole.' So anyway, Seppi had shit to do that day too. OK, that's fine. No one had a key to the studio and it wasn't even officially open yet, so it would be fine. And there was a Ring camera, so I'd know if someone tried to get inside. It was a six-minute drive from the restaurant, if everything went perfectly. I would just keep an eye on the cameras, no big deal. And I could install the Skutt app on my phone and link it to the thermostat on the kiln. That would make things a little easier and I wouldn't have to fight the urge to drive all the way there to see the kiln temperature.

We retreated to the world of mafia mansions so we could take showers, dress for work, and brush our teeth. I did not wear the expensive perfume that day, but while Seppi was in the shower, I snuck into his closet, sprayed Tobacco Vanille, and spun around under the mist as it fell. I drove by the studio on the way to the restaurant. Two consults, back at the studio by four-thirty, bones into a tote bag, vacuum out the crumbs, prep for the newspaper and the six o'clock news. I stayed on task, didn't smoke a j with my morning latte, didn't get sidetracked with the dark chocolate covered blueberries.

I did make time to visit with Opal and Chloe. Opal was feeling good and was back in her tiny little patchwork dresses with her breastfeeding boobs bursting from the seams. She looked tired, but that's to be expected,

"How are things going?"

Opal shrugged,

"Good, just tired. Oh, and mom is driving me crazy. Dad is being a little overhearing but I'm trying to give him a pass, at least he gives a shit."

She never let the spotlight stay on her for too long, she asked,

"How are things with you, how was the Open House? I was going to try to make it there but I was kind of a mess yesterday."

I swallowed the hot spit in the back of my throat and replied,

Open House was good, lots of college girls and little kids, I think it will be a big hit with the locals."

I looked down at Chloe, asleep in the crook of my arm. I traced her ear and then the profile of her nose. I stared at her perfect little eyelashes. She moved her mouth like she was sucking, and her hand gripped my index finger, she had paper-thin fingernails. I just stared at her while she slept. I don't know how long I sat there like that, but I had tears in my eyes when I blinked. My sister glanced over at me,

"I just watched it happen."

I glanced back at her,

"Watched what happen? Did she poop or something?"

Opal smiled,

"I saw the exact moment you realized you want to have a baby someday.

I blinked back at her through my tears. They weren't the kind of tears when you're sad, they were the kind when you love someone. I cleared the lump in my throat,

"I guess I never really looked at a baby like that before."

Opal sat on the arm of the futon and put her arm around my shoulder,

"I know, isn't she perfect?"

"Yes."

And then we both watched her sleep.

Eventually, I went back to reality, swinging through the back door and into my office. I almost ran into Seppi in the hallway as he lurched out of his office.

"And!?"

"Nine-hundred degrees."

"Is it taking longer than it should!?"

"No, Seppi, that's not how it works. It just takes time. And whatever, the news people aren't going to just walk in with their cameras and start touching expensive equipment."

Seppi didn't look convinced, but I had bigger things to worry about,

"How am I supposed to get around?"

He stared at me blankly and then made a call,

"Bring the Hummer for Amelia."

I recoiled in horror and Seppi put his hand over the mouthpiece,

"What?"

I made a face,

"A Hummer!? No! Those things are the same width as the fucking road! No!"

Seppi pinched the bridge of his nose,

"Bring my Porsche."

The call ended and I just stared at him like he had three heads,

"You can drive the Escalade until your car is fixed."

Say what now!? I wanted to shit my pants,

"I'll look like some mob asshole driving that thing!"

He met my eyes and uttered,

"Yeah, and?"

I reasoned,

"You can't possibly trust me with that thing. I mean, across town and back, fine, but all the time!?"

He put his hands on my shoulders,

"You're not going to forget how to drive just because you're driving my car."

I flailed my arms,

"Yeah, but."

He waited. I shrugged,

"Fine."

I don't know what I was complaining about, my mob boss boyfriend lent me his one-hundred-and-fifty-thousand-dollar Escalade. No big deal to him and thirty-seconds later he circled back to the bones,

"How are you going to keep people away from the kiln?"

We sat there looking at each other and then I had an epiphany and shouted, waving my hands,

"Frieda!"

"What!?"

I closed the door. He sat. I went to the bar, put perfectly square ice cubes in two rocks glasses and poured his expensive whiskey. I slid his glass across the desk and we let the fire work its way down into our souls,

"Remember that girl I told you about? The one who wants to work at the studio in exchange for a free membership?"

"Yeah."

"OK, I bet if I call her, she'll be all over it, especially if I tell her the news is coming for an interview. She's young and passionate about things

188

like that, I mean, you should have seen her blubbering about planting roses"

His interest was piqued.

"If I ask her to do a presentation about firing pottery, she will. She used to teach, so she has the info to explain it to people who aren't familiar with ceramics. I can hang a sign from the handle of the big kiln, something like, 'In Use, Do Not Open.' And I can put a display on top of it."

Seppi took another sip of his whiskey,

"That's a great idea, but are you sure you're not just afraid to do the interview yourself?"

He met my eyes,

"You're more capable than you think."

I put my hands on my hips, all dramatic,

"Listen, you...I...that."

Seppi smirked,

"You don't say."

I pointed in his general direction,

"I mean..."

He waved me away with my bullshit,

"I don't care what you do, as long as this interview doesn't involve the remains of the guy my Mama whacked last night."

I flailed my arms around a little, finished my whiskey, and left the room. I left a voicemail for Frieda, convinced I had succeeded in not sounding like a psycho.

She called back almost immediately,

"Amelia? It's Frieda, I'm so sorry I missed your call."

I tried to make my voice sound normal, friendly even,

"I know it's last minute, but I was wondering if you're free this afternoon."

"I can be!"

I smiled at her enthusiasm,

"My friend lined up a news interview to help promote the studio."

Frieda squealed loudly and I don't think that eardrum was the same since. I'm not kidding. She chirped,

"Oh my gosh, can I help!?"

"If you'd like to, that would be great."

"Oh my gosh, oh my gosh, oh my gosh!"

"Is that a, yes?"

"YES!"

"OK, I'm going to get ready, and I'll be over there a little after four forty-five."

Frieda was squealing in my ear when I ended the call. I changed into an outfit that was a little less, 'I fuck a mob boss,' and a little more, 'I make pottery and smoke a little weed.' I put my ringlets into two braids, and paired a denim skirt with a cream-colored top. I exchanged my heeled booties for my Birkenstocks. I kissed Seppi and went out the back door. I nosed the Escalade up the alley, and seven minutes later I unlocked the back door to the studio. I snagged the Trader Joe's bag I found folded in the pouch on the back of the driver's seat. I'd just grab the bones and lock them in the Escalade, I had plenty of time before Frieda got there. And then Frieda shouted out,

"HI!"

I might have actually jumped out of my skin, and if I didn't, I can tell you with complete certainty that I peed a little. I took in a lungful of air that sounded like a gasp. Frieda stood there snort-laughing but I could tell she was afraid she scared me. I took in a deep breath and reminded myself that this was a game show, and I was the host.

"Hi, Frieda!"

She followed at my heels and I went around flipping on the lights. It didn't smell weird in there but I opened a couple windows just in case. I glanced at the thermostat and could have totally opened it if I didn't have Nosey Nellie riding my coattails. I tried but drew a blank, there wasn't a single reason I could think of to get Frieda to leave, or check on something, or go outside for literally five fucking seconds. My cheeks were hot. To recap, all I did to 'help' the situation, was call Frieda, and now I couldn't get the bones out of the kiln.

Maybe someday, Frieda would know what I'm about, but right then, she was scared of Seppi because she heard he was 'in the mob.' I had her convinced I was just a normal girl, and even if she knew I was sort of in the mob, she had no idea what that really meant. I guess you really shouldn't judge a book by its cover, because I looked in the mirror, and from what I could see, I appeared to have my shit together. I gave off the vibe of a wholesome hippie chick who gave a shit about 'community' and 'studios.' While Frieda was pacing around, full of nervous energy because people were going to be coming for an interview, I was pacing around with bubble-gut because some guy Mary Moretti shot last night was a pile of bones in my kiln. As I spoke to the reporter, all I could do was think about how much better I'd feel once I put those bones through a meat grinder.

CHAPTER 15
GOOD GIRL

THE INTERVIEWS went off without a hitch. Both the Rutland Herald and WCAX got some great pictures, and the promotion would help bring members to the studio. Despite my nerves, and the acid churning in my guts, I was articulate during the interview, and my eyes didn't stray to the kiln while I was on camera. It was another hour before me and Frieda were ready to go. She had decided to walk there that night, so I offered Nosey Nellie a ride home. I wanted to make damn sure she wasn't going to catch me unloading those bones. Something like that would scare her off, and I needed her. It felt like forever to get to her house, but I dumped her off and went back to the studio.

It had been twenty-four hours since Mary put a bullet in that guy's head. The cycle was complete, he had gone from homicidal punk to pile of warm bones. I caught the smell of Tobacco Vanille on my clothes and my hair, and it made me feel invincible. I locked the doors and closed all the blinds before transferring the bones to a Trader Joe's bag. I shined the light around the interior of the kiln and decided to use my personal vacuum to clean out the crumbs, I'd do that later. I flipped the breaker for the kiln, locked up the studio, and made it back to the restaurant in six minutes flat. I sat in the Escalade with a canvas sack full of cremated remains. Now what? I had a year of experience working at a humane society, so I knew what happened to cremated dogs and cats and I assumed the same thing would work on humans. I called Mary, she answered on the second ring,

"Hello darling, how are you?"

To say this woman would help me bury a body would be an understatement. Not to mention it was technically *her* body.

"Well, I'm not sure if Seppi told you, but I, umm, I need to..."

"Hush. I'll turn on the porch light and the tea kettle. See you soon."

The call ended.

These people, however evil and ruthless, were the most loving and loyal people I had ever known. Very few people in my previous life would have even covered for a little white lie. I texted Seppi that I was meeting Mama, and I'd see him when I got back to his house later. I was heading to the home of a widow I'd created, and I had her back just as much as she had mine. That was one of the most profound moments of my life. I was a part of something, and it was something real, something important, something secret. I was on the other side of the secret keeping, I was in control. I *wanted* to keep this secret, nobody was shushing me or shaming me or telling me to keep my mouth shut. I nosed back up the alley again and ten minutes later I was pulling into Mary's gated community, the woman at the gate was expecting me.

I parked the Escalade next to Mary's Lincoln MKX. Fancy cars in that family. She swung the door open and hugged me. The air was scented with chai tea and long skinny cigarettes. I joined Mary on a cream-colored sofa and her long-haired, expensive-looking cat jumped onto her lap. We made anxious small talk while we drank our tea, and I think we both knew it. I don't know if we were stalling or just wrapping our heads around the whole thing. Mary led me to a screened porch and once she was settled, she lit a long skinny cigarette. A little dog came running out and jumped up next to her while the fancy cat rubbed its whiskers along the door frame. I dug around my purse, and she waved me away,

"Tut tut."

She handed over a silver case, a Zippo, and a

marble ashtray. I retrieved a joint and lit it with her fancy lighter. I got down to business,

"What the hell happened last night?"

Mary took a long drag of her cigarette,

"I handled the situation."

She blew the smoke out of her nose and I blew mine out in rings,

"Well, I don't know if Vinny told you, but we put the guy in my kiln and I cremated him."

I lifted the Trader Joe's bag of human remains. A couple bones clunked together and the fancy little dog sat and wagged.

"I used to work at a place that cremated cats and dogs, and I'd have to run the bones through a meat grinder when they came out of the crematorium. I glanced at the little dog,

"No offense."

Mary threw him a treat and looked over, I continued,

"I figure since you were married to The Meat Boss, you'd be the one to ask about getting my hands on a manual meat grinder."

A smile curled at the edges of Mary's lips, I assumed it was at the thought that I could handle a situation. I wondered how many times she cleaned up messes like that, or had to deal with a 'situation.' But I couldn't just toss a Trader Joe's bag of some guy's cremated remains in a trash can at the gas station. I took the last drag of the skinny cigarette and snuffed it out in a marble ashtray that reminded me of the counters at a bank. Mary pulled the bag into her lap and peeked inside,

"This is all that's left of the guy I killed?"

She glanced over at me and nodded, she was impressed,

"You did this in your kiln?"

I shrugged and went palms up,

"Yeah, it just made sense to me."

Mary gawked at me like I was a genius, she leaned forward,

"What did you do?"

I waved her away like it was no big deal,

"We just stripped the guy naked, curled him up on the bottom shelf of the kiln, and I ran a glaze fire. It gets to around twenty-two hundred degree and a crematorium only gets to eighteen hundred, so I thought it might work just the same. It's dry heat."

I sipped my tea, which was lukewarm,

"Vinny burnt the guy's clothes in his fire pit, and the guy's personal effects are in a lock box under Vinny's bed."

Mary brought the canvas bag into the kitchen. so she could inspect it in better light. She nonchalantly pawed through the bones, pulled one out and inspected it,

"This is probably going to make a bunch of dust, let's do it in the shed."

We didn't say much else about it, what was there to say? Mary carried the bag and I carried the meat grinder, which is exactly what it sounds like. It was a stainless-steel hand-crank meat grinder that gripped onto a counter or work bench with a vice-like clamp that tightened with a screw. It was bigger than the one at the animal shelter, but it was the same idea. I took my sweet-ass time with the clamp, I guess I was procrastinating a little. When I was sure the thing was on there good and tight, I reached into the bag and pulled out what looked like an arm bone. Bones are a lot lighter when they've been dehydrated, and a lot more brittle. One by one, I worked the guy's leg bones, and finger bones, and ribs through a meat grinder. The pieces fell into an old tobacco can and then I dumped the can into a gallon zipper bag.

We sprayed the meat grinder with the garden hose and went back to the porch for a while. It was surreal, really. Mary and I had crackers and cheese and berries. She scratched her elegant cat behind the ears and tossed a ball for her fancy little dog. What kind of nut job was I that I had just participated in that whole thing? I mean, seriously, I had figured out how to get rid of a body. I sat there on that porch and felt a sense of accomplishment, my mother would be so proud. Idiot.

On my way 'home,' I detoured back to the studio and pulled a five-gallon Home Depot bucket out of the shed. I filled the bucket halfway with topsoil and dumped the bone pieces on top of it, mixing everything together with a stick. Then I put that punk in a place where he could push up actual daisies. Frieda found it therapeutic to grow flowers and there I was putting a figurative spider in the roses. I turned the bucket upside down, tapped the bottom, and hosed it out in the middle of the driveway. Ten minutes after I rolled into that driveway, I was climbing back in the Escalade. I let out a cleansing breath as I set off for mafia mansion land. The gate swung open as I approached and I waved at Gary on my way by. I wound my way through Hidden Hills Estates and pulled the Escalade in next to the Porsche. I went through the front door, left my shoes on the mat, and hung my purse on a hook. I stood in the middle of the kitchen, stretched, and hollered out,

"Honey, I'm home!"

Seppi was there somewhere, but just for a second, I stood there alone with full access to the real inner sanctum, the bat cave, the VIP lounge. It didn't feel real, but at the same time, it felt like I'd waited a lifetime and I'd finally arrived.

From upstairs,

"Come to me, Dimples."

I jogged up the back stairs and found Seppi in the bedroom. By the sound of his voice, I knew I had pleased him. He curled his finger at me as he emerged from the closet in gray sweatpants and a well-worn Giuseppi's Italian Ristorante hoodie, hair damp from a shower. No one else saw him like that, in sweatpants and a hoodie, and I knew he was going commando. I locked eyes with him and closed the gap between us. Seppi reached out and grabbed my waist, pulling me closer, kissing me,

"I'm proud of you."

I wriggled free and stripped out of my clothes, Seppi followed behind me and smacked my ass as I got into the shower. He leaned against the vanity and watched as I worked his fancy shampoo through my hair, letting the ickiness of the day wash down the drain,

"You are proving to be a valuable asset to my brother, Dimples."

Seppi paused to watch me and then continued,

"I know you get scared but Vinny tells me you are willing to do what needs to be done. He also said you never complain."

I made a face at that one, I complained plenty. And if I wasn't complaining, I was giving Vinny attitude, or the finger, but maybe real families found that stuff endearing. He continued,

"You should know that Vinny cares for you like a sister, you are family."

A wave of heat flooded my body and I knew I had finally 'made it,' whatever that meant. I was naked in Seppi's shower and he was watching me like a lion watches its prey. We loved each other and he hadn't wasted his time on me. He came to the shower door and slid it open a couple inches, nodded his head in toward the bedroom,

"I have something for you when you're done in there."

Ten minutes later, I was in a plush robe, working curl cream through my ringlets. I lathered myself with luxurious lotion and spritzed on the perfume he got me. When I emerged, Seppi hooked his finger at me and I obeyed. I stood at the foot of his king-sized bed in nothing but a robe. I took a step closer, and he pulled at the ties, the thick terrycloth falling open. He touched my breasts, and then pulled me closer. I whimpered somewhere deep inside and he moved his mouth to my neck, leaving his mark, pissing on his territory and I liked it.

Seppi slid the robe from my shoulders, and it fell to the floor at my feet. I glanced at the sliding glass door to the balcony, wide open as I stood there bare naked with the lights on. He maneuvered me to the bed, and climbed over me, kissing my throat. I could taste my perfume on his lips when our mouths came together. He took his time getting where he was going, but it was worth the wait, and when I finished, in his breathy bedroom voice,

"Good girl."

I spent a good part of that night with my fingernails digging into Seppi's high thread count sheets. I had leveled up, I was holding my own and that meant something to him. Maybe it meant I was healing, or maybe it meant I was more fucked up than before. Either way, I was naked on Giuseppi Moretti's fancy California king, and he had just pleasured me multiple times, so I was pretty sure I was doing something right. I lay there with my body tingling, the Sandman sprinkling his magic dust over my mind, body, and soul, but Seppi had a better idea. He handed me the plush robe and I shrugged into it, the luxurious cotton caressing my skin. He disappeared down the stairs and came back with a charcuterie board and some whiskey.

I slid off the bed and retrieved my thrifted flip top tin before shuffling along behind him. We went to balcony you can only get to from the master bedroom. We sat there together and sipped whiskey under the stars as we picked at expensive cheeses and olives like it was no big deal. Seppi smoked part of a Cuban and I smoked part of a joint. We held hands between our chairs and he glanced over as he blew rings of smoke into the night,

"How did it go?"

"It went about like I thought it would, all of the skin, and fat, and hair just combusted, there was nothing but dried up bones left."

I took another drag and coughed it out,

"Your Mama still had one of your father's manual meat grinders, so I clamped it to the workbench in the shed and ground up the bones."

Seppi puffed on his cigar and I could see that his eyes were smiling, I continued,

"And then, on the way home, I stopped by the studio and mixed the ashes in with some topsoil, and then sprinkled that all over the garden"

I added,

"I looked into it and it's nearly impossible to retrieve DNA from cremated remains."

I shook my head,

"Even if someone noticed the guy was gone and thought, 'Gee, I bet Sal's widow killed that punk,' no one is going to be looking for minuscule pieces of bone ash mixed in with the very soil that's growing tomatoes and roses at a community studio."

Then I really went for it, sort of, but mostly I spun around in circles with my words,

"How fucking funny would it be if you made sauce for the restaurant out of some of those tomatoes."

I glanced over, eyes wide,

"Or is that messed up?"

I stared into the darkness,

"No, it's funny."

He thought I was done but I wasn't, I looked over at him again,

"No, it's fucked, what is wrong with me!?"

Seppi stared into the night with a smile on his face, nodding as he swirled the remnants of whiskey around the bottom of his glass. As we sat there under the stars, troubled ties worked themselves through the cracks in my broken soul. Seppi took a pull on his cigar and blew the smoke out in rings again. He squeezed my hand and I squeezed back.

CHAPTER 16
FRENEMIES

I WAITED FOR FREIDA in the lot behind the high school and she rolled up on my future motorcycle. She was a different person when she talked about bikes, the bad-ass side of her usually camouflaged with mania and social anxiety. On the coattails of dumping ashes in the community garden, I took another step into the darkness, my life forever changed by a woman I crossed paths with by chance. I did laps around the parking lot on an Indian Scout that was meant for a girl named Destiny, and I thought that was ironic. Before we parted ways, we made a date to do it again and she gave me the information to schedule a test for my endorsement. She pulled the helmet over her dreads and looked over her shoulder,

"Hey!"

I spun around and she smiled in a way that made my soul feel warm,

"You're going to be OK, you know. Seth has some cones, next time you can meet me at his house and you can practice avoiding obstacles and things, that's part of the test."

And with that, she threw up a peace sign and started the bike, the exhaust echoing off the cinder block building as she drove away. I stood there with tears in my eyes, swimming in a soup of overwhelm and growing pains, and then I went back to reality. Mary had killed a man two days earlier, the body was gone and there was no evidence. I had a creeping dread that someone would find out, but I pushed it away. I went back to mafia mansion land and got ready for work. Seppi followed me in his Porsche and we parked next to each other behind the restaurant. I detoured through the back door of Muddy Waters for two reasons. One reason was that I wanted a scone, but the other reason was that I wanted to strut into that place in my expensive pant suit, heels and makeup, and expensive perfume. I wanted Kane to see me, remember me, wonder if I could keep up with Giuseppi Moretti's insatiable sexual appetite.

I had my head held high, I felt confident, powerful, and untouchable. Wait until Kane saw my ass in those fancy pants. About five steps inside the back door, I heard Alex crying in Kane's office and my heart hurt for her, even though she was my nemesis. I slowed my pace and listened, pretending to look at a bulletin board full of business cards. What I heard felt like a dagger through my heart and almost brought me to my knees. I'm not sure why, really, I had someone better. I didn't have feelings for him anymore but that was a lie and I knew it. I remembered the day I met Kane Buchanan, the first time he tucked a loose curl behind my ear. I thought about how deep his eyes go, how deep his soul pulls me in. The world swirled and crashed, and I swallowed hard to push away the feelings in my throat.

I ordered a scone and a latte and chatted with the barista. I was peripherally aware that Kane was talking but I couldn't hear what he was saying. I could tell she was upset, even more than before. I had always liked her. That wasn't true. She was too pretty, too sweet, and she had loved him longer. Right then, Alex was just another woman who was in pain and something inside of me felt for her. It wasn't about me wanting him, I was on her side. I put myself in her shoes. I picked up my order and realized the two of them were in the middle of something that was going to take a while. I moved past the leather sofas and the fake fireplace. Three more steps and I would have been past Kane's office, but I didn't make it three more steps.

The door swung open, Alex stormed out and we collided. My feet flew out from under me, my latte did somersaults in the air and the bag with the scone slammed against the wall next to the fake fireplace. Alex tried to catch herself but landed on top of me. The latte rained down on us and Kane appeared at his door to see his two most recent love interests in a pile on the floor. Alex snapped her head around and barked,

"Don't!"

He didn't.

Kane spun around, went back in his office, and slammed the door. Well, that wasn't very professional. I moved my attention to Alex. Her cheeks were tear-stained and her eyes were swollen from a night full of crying. Her hoodie was covered with espresso and steamed milk. We made eye contact and I smiled at her. I was letting her know I was the calm in her storm. I was telling her that we were just two women and not adversaries. We laughed a little before I helped her up. We went up the stairs and I told her we could talk after we got cleaned up. Alex went into Kane's apartment and I went into mine.

I texted Seppi that I was taking a detour but that I was fine, I just needed to help someone. My sister and her little family were visiting Auggie's mom, so I had free run of my place. I showered and brought my curls to life, swiped on some eyeliner and mascara. I checked my reflection in Burberry slacks and a black satin camisole. I shrugged into a fitted cream-colored cardigan, and slid my feet into some leather booties. I dug the Coco Mademoiselle out of my bag and spun in the mist as it fell around me. When I opened my door, Alex was waiting on the bench in the hall. I knew that if it were me, I'd want someone to talk to. I didn't know her, not really, but right then, I felt like I knew her, I felt like we were the same person in some ways. We had both cared for the same man, so we had at least one thing in common. I hugged her in the hallway and she cried on my shoulder. I held her at arm's length,

"Do you want to get out of here?"

She nodded.

"Have you eaten breakfast?"

She shook her head and I gestured in a way that wouldn't reveal the amount of tears I shed over her hair tie and perfume in his nightstand,

"Let's go."

Kane had taken a walk to get some air and as me and Alex were pulling out of the alley in Giuseppi Moretti's car, Kane was reaching for the front door of Muddy Waters. The look on his face, what do they say? Scone: Four dollars. Fancy latte: Nine dollars. The look on Kane's face: Priceless. I drove to a pancake house and we sat there looking at each other for a while. I mean, up until then, that little breakfast date wouldn't have happened. I pulled up my big girl panties and called a spade, a spade,

"I didn't mean to, but I heard what you two were talking about."

She made eye contact with me and I reassured,

"Listen, I know there's this weird thing between us, but I'm not the enemy. I'm sorry you're going through this with him. I feel like it didn't go well in there and I'm sorry."

Alex seemed skeptical,

"Why are you being nice to me?"

Did she think I was some sort of an asshole? I was a little offended,

"What?

She looked me in the eye again,

"Why are you being nice to me?"

I scrunched my eyebrows together,

"Umm..."

She was crying again, silently, and put her hand over her eyes, but the rest of her face was crying too.

"Alex, listen, I don't know how you're feeling but I can see you're in pain. I'm not the enemy. Kane and I haven't seen each other in a while now. I'm in a relationship with Giuseppi Moretti, I'm not a threat."

Her eyes went wide as saucers when she heard that I was seeing Seppi, I tried to interpret what her face was doing. Maybe she was impressed. Maybe she was confused. Maybe she was jealous. Maybe she thought I was bat shit crazy. It didn't matter. What mattered was that she understood I didn't have some ulterior motive. The truth of the matter was that what

I heard hit me like a ton of bricks in the vajayjay but I was a compassionate person,

"When did you take the test?"

"Yesterday afternoon."

She was wringing her hands,

"At first I thought it was negative, so I threw it in the trash. I didn't even tell him about it. And then when I got ready for bed, I moved the tissue I put over it and looked at it again. I held it up to the light and I could see a line."

"Oh, boy."

"Yeah, so there we were, getting ready for bed and Kane hasn't been sleeping well. He's been stressed out in general and he was going to go to bed early."

She kind of just stared at the table,

"That's when I came out of the bathroom with the test."

I took a sip of my mediocre pancake house coffee and tried to make my face seem comforting, but I didn't know her well enough to say something profound. She continued,

"He couldn't see it until I used the flashlight on my phone."

At that point, considering what I'd heard when she was in his office, I was pretty sure I knew how the rest of the story went, but I was patient with her and wondered why this was such a big deal.

"So, we talked about it, and he said he's not ready."

I made a face like, 'yikes' and then reset and tried to appear neutral.

"We've had so many conversations about this over the last six years."

I felt for her, I felt for this woman who knew him first, a woman who had those conversations people have when they want to spend the rest of their lives together. I had those conversations with one of my exes, so I understood. And I knew the problem wasn't that she was pregnant, it was the way he had acted when she thought she was.

"When did you get it?"

Alex looked at her hands,

"This morning."

I sipped my coffee,

"Was he already downstairs?"

Alex nodded and stuck her hand in her bag to retrieve the pregnancy test. I took it from her and stared down at the one definite line and the very faint second line. I wanted to tell her I had done the same thing before. She said,

"I didn't know about evaporation lines."

I knew exactly what she was talking about.

"I didn't know that you have to look at a test after a specific amount of time or else it isn't accurate. I texted my sister about the test before I told Kane, and she told me that's what it was, but I saw the line."

I thought about holding Chloe and how mother nature started tapping on my inner chrysalis. I didn't know if that was what Alex was feeling, but I knew she was more ready than Kane was. I also knew that the conversation between them hadn't gone well. It's not that he raised his voice, but it seemed like a lot of, 'how could you let this happen,' and not much, 'I love you and I'm happy about this.'

Sitting across the booth from Alex was awkward, to say the least. My phone vibrated and it was Kane, 'WTF Amelia?' So now I was the bad guy? When did that happen? I wasn't the asshole here. I was trying to ignore Kane's text, but it was digging at me like the picky thing the dental hygienist uses when she cleans your teeth. His words were pulling my fingers to the keyboard like a high-powered magnet. 'Maybe if you hadn't acted like an insensitive prick.' Whatever. Men are fucking idiots. My phone vibrated again, and it was Seppi, 'You OK?' I replied, 'I'm OK.'

I moved my attention back to Alex. She swallowed the lump in her throat and used her napkin to wipe her tears. I stood and grabbed a new napkin from the adjacent table, hers was falling apart.

"I don't know how much he talked to you about us, but we've been on and off for six years now, and deep down I just kind of thought we'd end up together."

I didn't like hearing any of that. She continued,

"I didn't do this on purpose, but it made me realize that I want kids, and he doesn't. This is the first time in all this time that I've felt like we really won't end up together."

They had such a dysfunctional thing and I tried really hard not to judge, especially since I had been the other woman,

"I'm really sorry, Alex."

Her eyes fell to her lap and tears rolled down her cheeks when she blinked, her blonde eyelashes clumping together. She blew her nose and squeaked,

"Thank you for saying that."

"I get it."

She took a sip of her orange juice and a bite of her pancakes, but she was mostly pushing them around in a pool of melted butter and maple syrup,

"I guess I just thought he'd be happy about it, you know? I mean, we used to talk about it all the time, having kids someday. He said he changed his mind; he said the world is on fire and is too fucked up to bring a child into it. And he made me feel guilty for wanting to have a baby someday, like I'm not a good person if I want to have kids."

I made a face,

"I'm sorry he said those things."

And I meant it. I thought I wanted to spend my life with the man I dated after the narcissist, and since he wasn't a sociopath, I immediately wanted to talk about our future. And then he had a love child with his whore and I moved to Bunman. The End. I understood more than she knew. She wanted different things than Kane, but maybe he would let it sink in and would tell her he changed his mind. Things like that cause so many emotions, so many thoughts.

"Thank you, Amelia. And I'm sorry if I was ever standoffish or bitchy, I was always intimidated by you."

I looked at Alex like she had three heads, pointing at the center of my chest,

"By *me*?"

She spun her new napkin into a rope,

"I mean, you're doing it. You're independent, and pretty, and you're sure of yourself. You work for the mafia for crying out loud. You're this real woman who's waiting in the wings."

She paused and teared up again,

"I'm just this lost little girl or something."

You and I both know that I could have connected with that woman on a spiritual level, but I didn't. But, I leveled with her,

"There was a time when I'd notice you were gone for a while and my orbit would overlap with Kane's again."

"I appreciate your honesty, Amelia."

I defended,

"But that stopped a while ago, I need you to know that. My life has gone in a different direction."

She paused and I could tell she was finding her words or getting up the courage to ask me something,

"You mean, the mob?"

I almost spit my coffee out but reigned it in,

"Umm, no, I just mean that with my job at the restaurant and the community studio opening, my life is moving away from my apartment, and Muddy Waters. What I'm saying is that even if you weren't a part of this equation, I wouldn't be seeing him anymore."

She stared out the window and I knew she believed me, I continued

"I think you just need to give him some time. He's a good guy, deep down. You probably caught him off guard. You said he hasn't been sleeping, that can make a person irritable, Maybe just see how he is when he gets home from work. This kind of thing happens all the time, people thinking a test is positive when it's not."

She looked relieved for the first time since I'd laid eyes on her at the cafe. I think she was hoping I was right. She finished her fresh squeezed orange juice and pancakes with Vermont maple syrup. I was glad she had eaten. And then, about three steps from the passenger door of the Escalade, Alex blew chunks in the parking lot. Thirty seconds later and Seppi would have been dealing with the smell of pancake vomit in his car until the end of time.

"I am so sorry, sometimes I throw up when I get upset, it's my nerves."

Alex went into the bathroom to put a wet non-absorbent paper towel on her forehead and I walked to the gas station next door to get her a ginger ale. See, I'm not such a bitch after all. I was hyper-vigilant and threw her a side-eye with every little sound she made, for fear she was going to upchuck again. I very gingerly drove down the alley, and Alex exited the car without leaving any body fluids behind. I encouraged her to give Kane some time, and it reminded me of all the times I had told Opal to give it time. I felt like kind of an asshole but thought maybe I was right. Kane would let it sink in and tell her he wanted to have kids someday. Or at least maybe he wouldn't be mad at her for misreading the test.

I gave Alex my number and it felt like we were going to be friends but it never happened. I mean, deep down I knew I was too wrapped up in my own shit to cultivate a friendship with my ex's ex. But, we were two women who had been with the same man, and in some ways, that made us similar. Something about all of it made me really sad. When I swung in the back door of Giuseppi's Italian Ristorante, I didn't have a spring in my step. I wasn't strutting, I was overwhelmed, defeated, and sad. I plopped my bag on the desk, went across the hall, and completely fell apart in Seppi's arms. He didn't know why I was crying but he kissed me on the top of the head and held me. I was that hot sweaty kind of crying, when you just want to be in a ball under some blankets. I pulled away,

"I have to get out of here for a while."

Seppi kissed me gently and our lips parted. Our tongues touched but we weren't racing anywhere, he was telling me he loved me, and hoped I'd be OK. I left his office with tears in my eyes, retrieved my bag and the keys, and nosed the Escalade toward Clover Lake. I turned by The Lakeside General Store, onto the road where Salvatore Moretti shot me the first time. And it was the road where Mary shot that guy from the cemetery. I almost turned around but didn't. I went by the pull off where Sal had blocked me in with his Lincoln Continental and my mind flew into a storm of everything icky.

Goosebumps climbed my body like ivy, a chill creeping down my spine. I took the same dirt access road Kane brought me on the first week I was in Bunman, back when I had my whole life ahead of me. I was the only one out there so I climbed on a rock, lit a joint, and stared across the lake. So much had happened. So many feelings, so many wounds, so many demons. Oh, how naïve I was that day with Kane. Before I really knew him, when he was just some guy who worked at the coffee shop next to my aunt's gift shop. When he was just a guy with dark chocolate eyes and a dark chocolate voice. Just a guy who tucked loose curls behind my ear and made my knees weak. Just a guy who seemed to be the perfect fit for a while. Just a guy I outgrew.

I thought about Alex and hoped she would reach out, but she didn't, and I didn't reach out to her. I hoped Kane would be understanding. I hoped everything would work out. It made it easier that I was with Seppi but that ship had sailed, I had outgrown Kane. He was not the type I could come home to after killing a man or baking a stiff in my kiln. He wasn't the type who would find it amusing that I put someone's bones in a meat grinder and then dumped the ashes in the community garden. Kane was not someone who would get a kick out of the ways I had changed, the deep, dark ways I had changed. I hungered for things he couldn't give me, he was just a barista with a man bun and an acoustic guitar. Kane could never satisfy my appetites for expensive whiskey, being untouchable, or being dominated in the bedroom once in a while.

My mind drifted to the studio, and the bones in the garden. I wondered how many more bodies I would cremate in that kiln. Giuseppi Moretti wanted nothing but the best for me, but he was the patriarch of a mob family and had a job to do. If I hadn't been willing to experience that part of him, I should never have allowed myself to fall in love. But the reality was that I had enough anger deep inside that I was kind of OK with it. I was OK helping get rid of bodies, as long as they belonged to bad people. I knew that meant I had a screw loose and really, don't we all? But I also knew that if that particular screw wasn't loose, I would have had to walk away a long time ago. So, there I was, at the pull-off I had gone to with Kane, and so much had happened since then. Part of me wanted to rewind time and do it all over again. Maybe I'd make different decisions, maybe I wouldn't have gotten wrapped up in the stuff with Seppi. But that's not how things went, and I had made decisions along the way that brought me there. Deep down, Kane was safe, but I would have gotten bored with that life after experiencing this one.

My phone rang,

"Yeah."

"Dimples?"

I stared across the lake, hearing his voice made me cry again. I didn't say anything, I just sat there with a lump in my throat as tears fell. Seppi could hear that I was crying and knew I needed him,

"I'll be right there."

The call ended. I hugged my knees and cried. My current life circumstance was something I couldn't comprehend. I needed things to slow down but they didn't, and then the world started closing in. I grew paranoid and checked my surroundings, looked over my shoulder, here I was, a sitting duck and I didn't even have my handgun. I called Seppi and when he picked up, I was sobbing. I had locked myself in the car,

"Please hurry."

Five minutes later, I saw headlights as Seppi nosed the Porsche down the gravel road. As soon as he came to a stop next to me, I jumped out of the Escalade and climbed into the passenger side of the Porsche. I pushed the lock button on the inside of the door and scanned our surroundings. He reached over and put his hand on my knee as I squeaked,

"Why am I so stupid!?"

"Dimples."

"Why do I keep forgetting there might be people out there who want to kill me for what I did to your father!?"

I glanced over at him and threw my hands up,

"How do I keep doing that!? Why isn't it the only thing I can think about!?"

Seppi rubbed my knee,

"Because it's scary, and that's what people do with stuff like that, they push it into the back of their minds."

I swallowed the lump in my throat and replied,

"I have filing cabinets."

Seppi glanced over like he didn't know what that had to do with anything, and then I said,

"I think I need to be alone for a while."

I didn't know where I would go, but I felt like a animal, thrashing against the bars of its cage, a prisoner digging at a cinder block wall with a broken plastic fork. But at the same time, I didn't want that at all. I wanted to be with Seppi, right up next to him, like on his fucking lap with his arms around me. I wanted there to be guns, alarms, and safety nets. Crowbars, panic buttons, and bullet proof vests. I could tell he was nervous I'd run; he was assessing the situation. I broke the silence and he jumped when I barked,

"This is such fucking bullshit!"

Seppi nodded,

"Which part?"

That got a laugh out of me but I yelled,

"Just, why can't things be normal for once!? When am I going to get that fresh start I'm looking for!?"

I hugged my knees as I cried,

"How long am I going to have to worry that someone might come after me? Sometimes I can handle it and sometimes I can't. Right now, I can't handle it."

Seppi turned to me,

"From what I've heard, it sounds like they think my father took off to avoid a gambling debt he owed to another mob family. If that's true, then I think we're OK."

Then nonchalantly,

"Unless I have an old enemy out there with an axe to grind."

I glared over at him and threw my hands around some more, screaming as I cried,

"YOU MEAN LIKE A FUCKING SKELETON IN YOUR CLOSET!?"

There we were, back in the same place we were before. And there I was, sitting in the passenger seat of the Porsche, losing my mind.

He shrugged but stayed calm,

"I'm just saying, it's possible."

He thought about it for a second,

"I do not have any debts, or unfinished business with any of my exes. But given my position within the organization, there are certain risks, certain vulnerabilities that come with the job. And just as I can spot weaknesses in others, I am sure there are people who could easily fuck with my life if they wanted to."

The push and pull, the pendulum swing was unbearable. The depth of my feelings for Seppi, the range of emotions I had about the whole situation, the way I felt about killing someone, or grinding those bones. I was just this broken little bitch who was breaking a little more every day. How had I ended up there? Sitting at a pull off in Giuseppi Moretti's Porsche, wanting nothing more than to be wrapped in his arms and protected by the dark side of him. I crawled over the console and straddled Seppi's lap. Again, what is the point of a car that small? He was about one seventy and I was one forty, we were not big people, and I could barely fit my legs on either side of him. As an aside, I guess the reason the inside of a Porsche is so small is because most of the men who drive them, can't get it up anyway. At least they have an excuse, like 'oh, sorry honey, there isn't room in here to screw you.' I buried my face against Seppi's neck and cried while he held me. He kissed the top of my head and I wanted to stay there forever.

CHAPTER 17
THE PROPOSITION

I WOKE TO THE burr grinder and the smell of ground espresso. I laid there in a t-shirt and panties, Indie was curled up next to me on the high thread count sheets. On Sunday mornings, I'd been meeting Mary Moretti for lattes and scones for almost a year now, but this time, she was coming to me. When it all started, I would go over to The Meat Boss, where Mary ran the counter while Salvatore acted like a little man with a big key chain. Things had changed since then. Mary and I had grown close, but after I killed her husband, we became even closer, I'd given her a fresh start, and I hoped someday I'd get the fresh start I was looking for. I managed to free Mary from her demon, in the midst of battling my own.

I threw the covers back and padded to the bathroom, peed, and looked at myself in the mirror. I was in a pocket of time where I didn't have any bruises or wounds, and I leaned in to look at the scar running through my left dimple, my scrimple. I went down the back stairs with Indie following me. Seppi had food waiting for her. He was in a pair of gray sweatpants, steaming milk for my latte. I made an audible sound in my throat when my eyes settled on his ass. He kissed me on the top of the head and placed the latte in front of me. I sipped it and watched as he leaned against the counter sipping his. We made eye contact.

We were eating fresh berries out of a strainer that was situated in the middle of the dark marble counter. There was a quiche and a pan of thick cut bacon in the oven. I looked at Seppi again and didn't know if my mouth was watering because of his body or because of the food. That's a lie, I knew exactly why my mouth was watering. I went around the island and backed Seppi into the corner between the stove and the espresso machine, running my fingers through his messy pompadour. We made eye contact again and just stood there looking into each other's eyes. The longer we stayed like that, the more I fell in love with him. I saw a flash of things we had been through together, and it was only the beginning for us.

More than with my exes back home or with Kane or even with Marco Masiello, I felt love for Giuseppi Moretti with all of my body and soul. He was a tortured soul just like me, and we found each other in a world of separation between people like me and people like him. Our mouths came together, and I pushed my body against his. I ran my fingers through his hair and pulled him closer. We were kissing like we were making love, but also like we were fucking. He lifted me onto the counter and stood in between my knees, kissing me. He pulled the t-shirt over my head, I wanted him. I pushed him back and hopped off the counter, dropped to my knees, and hooked my fingers in the waistband of his sweatpants. Seppi was going commando and was already standing at attention. I ran my hands over his chest and stomach and lower. I took my time and teased him. He was bracing himself against the counter, his legs were shaking when the front door flew open,

"Good morning, darlings!"

So, there I was on my knees on the kitchen floor with Seppi seconds from popping, and Mary Moretti came through the front door with scones from Eliana Mazelli's place, what is it with this woman? I glanced up at him, scooped his manhood back into his sweatpants and he spun around so he was facing the espresso machine. As Mary kicked off her shoes, I grabbed my shirt, crawled to the stairs, and barely made it out of sight before she entered the kitchen. I peered around the banister for a second and watched her put something on the counter. She went around and kissed Seppi on the cheek.

"Hi, Mama, I wasn't expecting you until ten."

She spun around in a waft of Chanel No. 5, and skinny cigarettes. She smacked her oldest son on the arm,

"I want to speak with Amelia about something, so I figured I'd come a little early."

I could tell Seppi was trying to be welcoming as the blue balls set in,

"That's really nice, Mama."

Liar, liar, expensive gray sweatpants on fire. I wondered if she knew that was the second time she inadvertently cock blocked her eldest son. At least that time, my heels weren't sitting askew on the floor. I went to the closet and pulled on a white T-shirt and a pair of overalls. I twisted my curls into a semi-messy bun, spun around in a mist of Coco Mademoiselle, and bounced down the stairs, pretending I had just realized Mary was there. I kissed her on both cheeks and Indie rubbed her whiskers against Mary's leg.

"Good morning, Mama."

"Good morning, Amelia."

She came to me, kissed me on both cheeks,

"You smell delicious."

I was pretty sure she wasn't talking about my penis breath. I gestured toward Seppi,

"It was a birthday gift from Seppi."

Mary beamed her approval in his direction,

"Nice job."

Seppi smiled at his mom, and she smiled back. Mary was full of sunshine, and I knew I had never seen light in her eyes quite like that when she was with Sal. I remembered how Dr. Rossi said I did the world a favor and I knew she was right. The world is sometimes better without certain people. I let that sink in for a second before eating a couple more berries. Seppi was making fresh squeezed orange juice and checking the oven. We spent time drinking lattes and eating berries. Seppi served us quiche and bacon and we added scones and berries to our plates. Mary put her hand on mine,

"I'd like to speak with you about something, privately, come on."

She stood and gestured toward the patio. Seppi waved us off and sat on a stool eating quiche as he scrolled on his phone. Once we were settled by the pool, Mary made eye contact with me. She lit one of her long skinny cigarettes and blew the smoke out in a steady stream that spun and swirled over the heat from the propane fueled fire pit. I was in the process of taking a bite,

"Amelia, you know how much I appreciate what you did for me."

I moved my eyes to hers with a mouthful of cranberry orange scone. I knew she was living a life she never would have lived if she was still under the control of Salvatore Moretti. I knew it firsthand, not just because she told me. I saw a light in her eyes that wasn't there before, the bounce in her step, the peace, the happiness, the weight that had been lifted from her shoulders. I thought she might have been seeing someone. I chewed and swallowed,

"I know."

I felt a pang of something that Mary still felt she owed me something and she continued to thank me after all this time. All I really did was kill or be killed, but in the process, I freed her from her prison. I knew that,

"Mary, I know you appreciate what I did, but I was just trying not to die."

She took another drag on her long skinny cigarette,

"But you've freed me. You have completely changed my life. Sally would have been out of the picture sooner or later, but in the eyes of that horrible person, that hateful, spiteful, abusive man, you didn't back down like I always did."

Mary looked at her cigarette and flicked it,

"I wish I had the strength to do it myself, but I didn't, I was so broken and living on a tight-wire. I wanted nothing more than to cut ties, but I'd be using those ties like a noose around my own neck. You don't get away with leaving someone like that, you end up with your reputation destroyed or in the trunk of a car with a bullet hole in your forehead."

I mean, maybe leaving someone like that was impossible, but I'd done a pretty under the radar job of killing him. I finished my plate, and she handed me one of her joints. I lit it with her fancy Zippo, and let the feeling of self-medication fall over me,

"I know, I understand. I mean, I know I will never completely understand what you went through, but I do get it. I have an ex named Richard who's a narcissist, and he was horrible. I know it was nothing like what you went through, but now that I have separation from him, I realize I should have cut ties with him long before he cut ties with me."

I blinked away the tears I hadn't realized were brewing under the surface, staring at the side of the stone fire pit,

"Richard swept in like Prince Charming. He made promises and told stories. He made me believe he was going to save me, protect me, be everything I needed."

Mary uncrossed her legs and sat forward. I continued,

"I would catch him in lies, constantly, but he'd talk his way out of it, every time, gaslighting me. It took me so long to realize what he was doing; it was all a big game for him. Some sort of hyped-up car salesman bullshit, constant manipulation, and lies, and then fights and tears and apologies and gifts and blah blah blah, so fucking predictable after a while. I guess that's why men like that burn through women."

I stared at the fence at the back of Seppi's property because there weren't any pigeons,

"I was never crazier than I was when I was with him, he brought out the worst in me. Whenever I tried to break up with him, there was this onslaught of new promises and lies, and I'd fall for it every time. Or, if he sensed I was gaining strength and might actually leave him, he would start threatening me in subtle ways and sometimes not so subtle ways. And I knew he was cheating on me, but he lied about that too. I found out and had proof, he was kind of in a spot then. Even though he had been caught red-handed, he tried to make it my fault. He said the way I acted forced him into someone else's arms. Made up some story about all of his friends hating me."

I glanced over at her and she made a face, and I nodded,

"Like I should be worried if someone else's friends don't like me, who gives a shit?"

I stared across the backyard and Mary put her hand on mine,

"I didn't know."

I moved my eyes to hers,

"I'm not saying it was anything like what you went through, but I understand, in a way, what it was like. And I understand about the punishment part."

Mary settled in and I could tell she was about to say something important,

"You can see how my life has changed since Sally passed. And the other night, when I was in your car and that guy was tailing me and shot at the trunk, I had this sense of strength, I didn't hesitate."

She popped a berry in her mouth,

"I kind of wanted him to kill him."

I knew what she was saying, even though it was all kinds of fucked up. It felt good when I was beating the shit out of Wretched. Sometimes, taking your hate out on someone with your hands is very cathartic,

"I know what you're saying."

She rubbed her chin,

"Do you realize what a valuable gift you've given me?"

She had tears in her eyes, we were both falling apart. I think that's when I really got it, that's when I finally understood. I put myself in her place and I knew she had been living in hell, it's like if I had been with Richard for forty years, only worse. I imagined waking up under that roof, between those walls. Sitting across the table from that man or sleeping in the same bed. I wondered how many times she had to go along with things to stroke his ego, sexual and otherwise. I wondered how long she would have had had to live like that if I hadn't done the world a favor.

"I think I understand."

She seemed to change the subject,

"How did it go when you cremated that guy?"

I looked at her like she had three heads,

"What!?"

Why was she bringing that up? I thought we had already dealt with it. She lit a cigarette and started firing questions at me, no pun intended,

"Like, was it fast? Did it smell? What kind of process is it to run a kiln?

I bit my bottom lip and closed my eyes, I knew exactly where this was going before she even said it. I felt a shot of adrenaline but tried to calm myself. I mean, I didn't really know what she was going to say, I just thought I did, I kept going,

"The glaze fire program takes a little under nine hours. It didn't really smell; the ventilation system did its job. I mean it smelled like cooked meat and burnt hair for a while, but there was a structure fire close by so that might have helped cover it up."

She looked at me eagerly.

"As far as firing the kiln, I just program it, and press go. It's pretty simple."

"So, it's pretty easy to get rid of a body?"

Mary waved her hand a little,

"I mean, as long as the bones can be ground up after."

I shrugged,

"Yeah, I guess."

What the fuck was going on? Once the studio was open, and there were people in and out, there was no way we'd be able to use the kiln like that. I watched Mary's wheels turn and she needed to slow her role. The conversation moved to other things and eventually we brought our plates inside. Mary made her way to the cottage on Clover Lake, to the land of houseboats used to dump bodies, and curvy dirt roads used for high-speed car chases. I went back upstairs, stripped down, and stepped in the shower. About three minutes later, Seppi joined me, and I finished what I started. There wouldn't be any blue balls in the Moretti mansion, as long as I had something to say about it.

Later that day, I wandered into Seppi's office and sat in the chair across the desk from him. I curled my knees up and hugged them loosely against my chest. Our eyes met and he stood, pouring whiskey into two rocks glasses with perfectly square ice cubes. He slid one to my side of the desk and I took it. We swallowed fire together and our eyes connected,

"You saved my Mama's life."

"I know."

I teared up a little and so did he,

"She wanted to talk to you this morning."

"Yeah, she wanted to tell me how much her life has changed since your father died."

He took a deep breath and let it out slowly,

"She wanted to ask you something else, but I think she's afraid she'll freak you out or push you away."

I got nervous and immediately thought I had done something wrong. In my mind, Mary didn't want to be my sort of mom anymore. My demons made me spiral for no reason and then I panicked. Seppi sensed that I was getting nervous, triggered by the unknown,

"I'm just going to spit it out, I don't know why this is difficult."

I scrunched my eyebrows at him and got paranoid,

"Did I do something wrong?"

Seppi stood,

"To the contrary."

I shook my head and uncurled my legs from my little ball. I didn't know what to do with myself. I was freaking out a little. I got up and moved closer to Seppi,

"I don't understand."

He touched my arm,

"It's OK. You're OK, Dimples."

I let out the breath I had been holding but I still didn't feel much better.

"My Mama spoke with me about something, and I encouraged her to bring it up to you."

"...OK..."

"Sit down, Amelia."

He called me by my name, shit. I sat, he sat,

"Listen, you have given my Mama a fresh start. She couldn't cut ties with my father, and you were able to cut them for her."

I went to say something, but he put his hand up to stop me,

"Sometimes you need to look at things from different angles."

It's like people in that family couldn't decide if they needed to mollycoddle me, or give it to me straight. I wasn't one of them, I hadn't been born into that life, I'd just kind of stumbled into it. Mary knew I had baggage of my own, but at that moment, I knew what she wanted to ask me. I looked up at him,

"Just tell me."

A car pulled into the driveway and I looked out the window to see Mary's MKX. Seppi put his glass down and went to the door, Mary crossed the threshold, kissed her son on both cheeks, and he gestured toward the office. Seconds later, Mary emerged and sat on the couch. I got up from the chair and sat down next to her. She took a deep breath and then,

"I wanted to speak with you about something when I was here, and I didn't."

"I know."

She moved her eyes to Seppi, and then back to me. She started the way she always did,

"When you killed Sally, you freed me from a prison of sorts."

She didn't pause, or stumble, or beat around the bush this time,

"And I think it would be an incredible gift if we could do that for other women."

She paused,

"You know, if they find themselves in the same situation I was in."

I kind of thought that's where she was going, and where he was going, and where we were all going, but part of me wanted it to be, 'hey let's go to Disney.' I just sat there looking at her, she continued,

"If a woman is in a relationship like that, a horrible, abusive, soul sucking relationship with someone like that and can't get away, what if we could save her like you saved me?"

I wasn't sure if I should feel a sense of power or a sense of absolute fear and dread. Was this a good thing or a horrible thing? I hadn't signed up to be a killer...or maybe she would do that part.

"You mean kill horrible men and cremate them in my kiln?"

If I was sitting on the couch in Giuseppi Moretti's office, and Mary Moretti was proposing something like this, I probably didn't really have much of a choice. After all, I put everyone in danger by bashing 'Sally's' head in with a shovel, not telling Seppi about Lance, Gretchen, or the woman with the cute hat and vintage bag, who was really the red-haired woman with the pantsuit. I owed them something for covering up what I had done. I wasn't one of them but I had killed a mob boss, and instead of being whacked, I was part of the inner sanctum. Very matter of factly, Mary continued,

"Well, yes, but if we were to do this, we would have to designate a kiln for body disposal. I find it disturbing to think about little kids firing their maple leaf ornaments in the same kiln that held a dead body a couple days earlier."

I stared at her. What was happening!?

"If this is something we decide to do, we could install a kiln in my shed. I'm not saying we have to do this, I'm just saying, please think about it. I'm not talking about right now, I know you've got a lot going on with the studio, I just mean maybe sometime. We could burn up the bodies and grind the bones all in one place. You could use the bone meal in the community garden, or I could use it in my rose garden."

She was so matter of fact, but I knew she wouldn't push me any further. I also knew that somewhere down the line, this was going to come up again. Luckily, life got in the way for a long time. Think about how less than a week ago I was eternally grateful that the community studio would be a little break from the darkness, some glimmer of hope. Looking back, I'm kind of impressed with how fast things went off the rails. I mean, think about it. I hadn't even fired a single piece of pottery in that kiln yet. My head was spinning, but gradually, all of the ickiness was sucked into the filing cabinets I have in the back of my mind, where I keep all the things I don't want to think about. I sat there staring at Mary, wishing things had gone differently, but they hadn't, they had gone like that.

CHAPTER 18
HI, JENNIFER

MOST OF THE TIME, you don't really know what's going on in someone's life. You can make assumptions but usually, they're wrong. You can make judgments about where a person works, where a person lives, or the decisions they've made, but you really have no idea what you're talking about. I thought a lot about my ex and his whore, and their love child, and knew I was better off without him. The truth of the matter was that he was horrible, but part of me hoped he wasn't horrible to them. I thought about the narcissist before him and I guess what mattered most was that I had gotten away. I sat at my desk and replayed some of the things Richard had said to me. I got sucked back into the past, and the fear, and the bad memories. A surge of acid ickiness churned in my stomach as my nerves twisted and adrenaline poked its toe in the water.

It always bothered me that my mother was so incredibly judgmental of the men I dated. It seemed a tad hypocritical that she didn't care that teenagers molested me, but expected me to cultivate a strong sense of worth and self-respect. What if she had treated me like I was valuable, or maybe if she hadn't been focused on herself all the time. Maybe I would have been with better men. Maybe I wouldn't have started french kissing in junior high, and maybe I wouldn't have had a boyfriend until college. Maybe if I felt like I was worth being cherished, I would have stayed single, or I would have held out for someone who wasn't a complete piece of shit. I know enough not to beat myself up over it but sometimes, it makes me sick to think about the kinds of men I ended up with. I really hoped my decision to be with Giuseppi Moretti was motivated by something besides the demons I had in cages, the ones who guarded those filing cabinets I keep talking about.

I hadn't said yes to Mary's proposition, but I hadn't said no. Deep down, I knew it was the right thing to do, help women who were chained to horrible men. But for now, the whole thing was on the back burner, no pun intended. Deep down, I wish someone had stepped in like that as I squirmed and kicked on that bathroom floor. I wish someone would have kicked in the door and picked that kid up by his testicles. The heat of rage burned inside and warmed me to the core. Like coming in from a snow storm to stand in front of the fire, like when I turn my face to the sun, like when my body yearns for Giuseppi Moretti. But, I felt like my demons were under control, maybe I was finally working them instead of the other way around.

I kissed Seppi on the cheek and went out the back door of the restaurant. Kane was lugging out a bag of trash from the cafe and I slowed my pace to avoid him. I came to a full stop and just looked at him and he looked at me. I hadn't heard from Alex and I knew they had probably talked about things. I didn't see her car and he was clearly battling his emotions. He sort of looked like he needed me, so I started walking again and watched him toss the bag into the dumpster. Kane turned to me, and I closed the gap between us. I put my arms around his neck and hugged him. His hands worked their way around my waist, and he rested his chin on the top of my head. But he was the bad guy. If I was on her side, why was I comforting him? And why did he need comforting?

I only had a few minutes,

"Are you OK?"

Kane stepped back and looked down at me with his dark chocolate eyes and answered with the vulnerable version of his dark chocolate voice,

"Sure."

I put my hands on my hips,

"I don't believe you."

"It's over."

I didn't understand. Why would he throw it away over a misread pregnancy test? I drew in a big breath and let it out slowly,

"I'm sorry, Kane."

His eyes met mine.

"Like, really over."

I felt like he was working an angle but I didn't have the time to stick around and figure it out,

"I have to get to an appointment but if you want to talk later."

I thumbed toward the ristorante,

"I have to work tonight, but I can try to make time, OK?"

I was going to be cutting it close on the way back so I wore a tailored pantsuit and heels to the impressive office building of Isabella Rossi. My hair was all kinds of crazy curls that day and I was rocking it. That day, my curtains looked good from the outside. My mind was swirling with feelings and thoughts of the past and the present. The mini mafia sedan would be fixed that afternoon and I'd be back in the saddle again. I pictured all the teeny tiny little shards of glass all over the inside of the car and was glad it had leather upholstery.

I didn't have time to lean against the Escalade and smoke a joint, so I just locked up and pushed through the glass doors to the lobby. I took the elevator to the sixth floor and checked in with Elaine. I flipped through some of the magazines but my heart wasn't in it. It felt like I was growing into an actual mobster and I thought about Mary's proposition before cramming it into a filing cabinet in the back of my mind.

Dr. Rossi opened her door and gestured me over the threshold. I passed her in a swirl of Coco Mademoiselle, sat in the overstuffed chair, and watched as she settled herself into the chair across from me. She was taking it all in, reading the room, testing the waters.

"I burned someone up in my kiln and then ground their bones up in a hand-crank meat grinder. I mixed the little bone pieces in with some soil and put it on the garden at the community studio."

Isabella Rossi was speechless for a second, and looked at me like I had three heads, and I had never seen her look like that before,

"Is this real, or are you telling me about a dream you had?"

I looked her in the eye,

"Mary Moretti killed a guy, and I put his body in my kiln."

To clarify,

"I cremated someone in a coffin-shaped kiln at the community studio."

She looked at me but didn't say anything, she waited,

"And then after the news people left, I brought the bones to Mary's house and ground them up in a stainless-steel meat grinder until they were little pieces like this."

I measured with my thumb and index finger.

"I mixed them with some soil and dumped them on the community garden."

She inquired,

"After the news left?"

I moved my eyes to her, and waved her away,

"Yeah, the news was there."

She shrugged. I hadn't answered her question but didn't care. Very matter of factly,

"All a person boils down to is a gallon zipper bag, not even all the way full, of bone pieces."

I shivered. But then I thought about that guy we dumped into the quarry and the guy we dumped in the lake, and I thought about how those bodies weren't really gone, they were just out of sight, and hopefully being eaten by fish, or bacteria, or whatever happens to a body that has been sent to the bottom of a body of water. And then I thought about how much less traceable someone is once they're mixed in with soil and worked into a community garden. Once that garden was tilled again, forget about it. Part of me was a sick fuck and another part was proud I thought up a way to ditch a stiff with essentially zero material evidence. The guy's wallets and rings were in a lock box, and the clothing had been burned by Vinny and the ashes were scattered wherever. He could dump them down a toilet or into a dumpster or suck them up the vacuum at a car wash. The possibilities were endless.

"Amelia."

I met her eyes,

"And I don't really feel bad about it."

Dr. Rossi made a note on her paper and I didn't even care, I gestured at her pen,

"Write down that I'm certifiable."

"That's not what I'm doing."

"Well, then you're a fucking idiot."

Nothing. What a bitch.

"I come here and tell you all of this and all you've got is a scribble on your paper!?"

"Let's take a moment for a couple deep breaths. I'm not the enemy here. Would you like to see what I wrote on my paper?"

I wasn't sure if I wanted to see it or not, but I knew if she was offering, then it wasn't anything that would hurt me. I was being obstinate and defiant, pushing back against the reality of the situation,

"No."

"Alright, well, were you expecting me to respond in a certain way?"

"No."

"Well then what is it? You spiraled out of control because I wrote a word on a piece of paper. I write progress notes after our sessions, and sometimes I use shorthand notes to remind me of things."

Whatever. The darkness closed in,

"I don't understand why…"

I kicked off my heels, tucked my knees up to my chest and hugged them as I cried, hard. Like, I'm talking so hard that I was gagging and Dr. Rossi got me a glass of cold water and half an Ativan. I took the little yellow and drank the glass of water. Once I calmed down a little,

"I don't understand why, when I was a innocent little girl, that no one helped me."

She started to say something, and I put my hand up.

"I was just this innocent little girl and my mom threw me to the wolves so she could smoke cigarettes and watch soap operas."

Wet spots on the knees of my fancy tailored pantsuit,

"She never planned to have kids, she told me that. She had my big sister by mistake, and then I think she gave into it, the whole idea of the picket fence and family of four. Opal has always known she was an accident, and not a happy one, not as far as our mother is concerned."

I stared out the window, sniffling,

"My dad doesn't deserve someone like her, he deserves so much better. "

Dr. Rossi didn't say anything, she gave me the time I needed to find my words.

"He's this witty, intelligent man, the kind of gentleman they don't make anymore. He loves me and accepts me for who I am, he has never made me feel bad about a single thing I've ever done."

I had a rush of emotions, this avalanche of shit and death and demons, this cauldron of bubbling tar,

"Sometimes I wonder what his life would have been like if he never met her."

Then more than ever, I was just a broken little girl being held together with a thousand-dollar pantsuit that made me look like a million bucks. And even the fancy facade couldn't keep the little girl from crumbling to pieces right before my eyes,

"I couldn't pay that woman enough to love me, just an innocent little girl who trusted that her mom would protect her."

"Amelia, I am sorry all of that happened to you."

I shrugged dismissively,

"So, you've got that.'

"What does that make you feel?"

I stared back at her and shook my head,

"Yeah, we're not doing that now."

I kept going, fuck her questions,

"But then I came here. I can take a man's life and people still love me? What sense does that make? People protect me, they rescue me, even when I'm doing really bad things, it doesn't make any fucking sense!"

She put her pen down and rested her hands in her lap,

"I think I understand what you're saying, it feels backward that your own mother didn't love or protect the littlest version of you, the innocent version. But here you are, you've killed a man, and his own son is protecting you."

I moved my feet back down to the floor and put my head in my hands. I sobbed for the remainder of my session, made my next appointment with Elaine, and locked myself in the restroom. I threw cold water at my eyes and patted my face with a non-absorbent paper towel. Fuck this. Seriously. I rode the elevator with a pleasant looking Italian man who smelled expensive. Like, that guy was next level, right out of a magazine. And not one of the magazines in the waiting room upstairs, but like a magazine for people who had their shit together. I couldn't figure out if he looked like a detective or an executive level criminal. I made a mental note that I wanted to lick his face.

I got a text from Kane and my initial physical response to it was not a good one, I had a gut reaction that told me I shouldn't go there. His bed was easy to fall into and I was with Seppi, really with him, and I wouldn't do anything to mess that up. I opened Kane's text while I was walking down the alley to the parking lot, 'Dinner?' Fuck. I left it. The way I was feeling, it wouldn't go anywhere good. It wasn't my job to bail him out. I got in the Escalade and stared out the windshield for a while. I watched the pleasant looking man get into his car and wondered where he lived. He had busied himself with something when I joined the rats in the maze as they made their way home.

I got on the highway and turned up the radio, dug around in my purse, grabbed the panic button, and rubbed it like a rabbit's foot. I ran my thumb over the button and two minutes later I pushed and held it for three seconds. I had connected my phone to the Escalade, so the screen lit up when Seppi called. I answered and was trying not to fall apart, I just didn't get it. I didn't understand how people were covering for murder but my own mother didn't protect me from teenage boys. I wanted to kill her, and the boys who hurt me, I felt fire, but I also felt like a weak little girl. My voice squeaked,

"Seppi, I don't understand."

I fell apart in the safety of that car with Seppi on the other end. He was used to my after-therapy panic button pushing and it didn't faze him,

"Amelia, Vinny and I are in a meeting, can you make it back to the restaurant?"

I didn't feel rejected that time, there was something different in his voice, we had turned a corner, we were past the point of no return. I assessed the situation. I was safe in the Escalade and I would be at the restaurant in fifteen minutes. Big girl panties.

"I can make it to the restaurant."

"I'll see you soon, you're OK, Dimples. Ti amo."

The call ended. I was worked up enough that I wasn't paying attention to my surroundings. I didn't have my gun in a holster strapped to my stomach, it was rattling around at the bottom of my purse, and it wasn't even loaded. I had no clue I was being followed by the hot guy in the elevator. Either way, I made it to the alley between Muddy Waters and Giuseppi's Italian Ristorante, I was safe, I did it. I pulled into the space next to Seppi's and noticed the Porsche had been replaced with the mini mafia sedan. Headlights came up the alley and I assumed it was one of the girls. I reread Kane's text and I started to open the door, it was yanked open and I was pulled out by my armpit.

My phone bounced off the dash and landed on the passenger floor. My panic button, pepper spray, and unloaded gun were in the Escalade. I was drawn up close to a tall person's body, the man's belt buckle pressing against the middle of my back. I glanced up at Kane's sun porch and he was staring down at me, frozen in place, eyes like saucers. The man twisted my arm behind my back and pushed me toward his car. I dug my heels into the gravel and shouted, squirming,

"HELP! SOMEONE HELP ME!"

And then I screamed bloody murder. The man was calm and nonchalant, clamping his filthy hand over my mouth,

"Hello, Jennifer."

Genuinely baffled, I replied,

"My name isn't Jennifer, it's Amelia."

He chuckled and countered,

"Fenders sent me to collect your debt."

Fenders!? And who the fuck was Jennifer? I took a deep breath and the man's trunk popped open, he leaned into me and pushed me forward, I flailed,

"Wait! But, I'm not Jennifer!"

He loosened his grip, I could tell he was doubting himself. I thought he was going to spin me around but he didn't. The man hissed,

"I'm not stupid!"

And because I was under the impression I was kind of untouchable, I replied,

"Yeah, well, could have fooled me."

The stupid man snarled,

"Did you really think you were smart enough to pull this off? You're the stupid one!"

I was six feet from the man's trunk, heels dug in, engaged in a playground argument about which one of us was stupider. I heard Kane on the phone, frantically asking for Seppi from his post on the sun porch. I wondered what Jennifer had done to make Fenders so mad. The guy attempted to shove me down the final stretch to his trunk, adrenaline serging through my system. If he drove off with me in his trunk, I was screwed. I would be tortured or killed or worse. Kane flew through the back door and froze on the top step of the porch. I leaned into the man, my back pressed tightly against the front of his body.

I tucked my chin to my chest, jumped, and slammed the back of my head into the man's chin. Before he threw me away, I scraped my shoe heel down his shin and stomped the top of his foot with my heel. He grabbed his chin and I spun around to face him. I grabbed his shoulders and buried my knee into his groin. He grunted, grabbed his crotch and doubled over, blood dripping from his split chin. Seppi banged through the back door of the ristorante, clamped onto my arm, and threw me to safety. I stumbled backwards and slammed against the back of the Escalade. Kane ducked out of sight like a pussy. Seppi reached up and twisted the man's collar in his fist as the man squirmed. Seppi barked,

"Do you have *any* idea who I am?"

The man stuttered,

"Yes...yes...yes, sir. I know you...I mean, I know who you are. I've eaten at your place many times, you're Giuseppi Moretti."

Seppi emanated dark mafia energy, his voice conversational,

"What did you have for lunch today, pal?"

The guy swallowed hard,

"Leftover Chinese."

Seppi chuckled,

"I find it ironic that fried rice or a fortune cookie will be the last thing you ever eat."

A wet spot formed in the crotch of the guy's pants and he squirmed around like his life depended on it. Seppi inquired,

"What was the fortune?"

"Umm, umm, it said, you cannot shake hands with a clenched fist."

A calm had fallen over Seppi, he had figured out how he was going to solve the problem. I wondered if his pulse increased in situations like that, or if he was wired like a serial killer. Right then, Giuseppi Moretti wasn't the man who made love to me and then held me all night. He wasn't the man who danced with me in his office on Christmas Eve, or the man who rubs his thumb over my scrimple. A lifetime in the mob had trained that man to be confident and in control, not a shred of tremor in his voice, nodding his head in my direction,

"I made a promise to that beautiful girl over there and I intend to keep it."

The guy had just enough courage to ask,

"Wha...what was the promise?"

Seppi explained, very matter of factly,

"Well, see, someone hurt her one time and I didn't like it so much. So, I told her, if anyone lays a finger on her, I'll put them into the ground."

I swallowed the lump in my throat as it played out in front of my eyes. I was sick to my stomach. At the same time, I wanted to see what Seppi would do to the guy who thought I was Jennifer. Seppi glanced over and gave me a once over,

"You OK, Dimples?"

I nodded,

'In one piece."

I didn't tell him the back of my head was split and bleeding from smashing the guy in the chin. Seppi took the guy's keys and eyeballed the open trunk, the guy pleaded with him,

"This is just a big misunderstanding, man!"

But, I think at that point, he knew he was a goner. Seppi smirked, made a fist, and knocked the guy out with a single right hook under the jaw.

"You might not be able to shake hands with a clenched fist."

He shook his hand and wiggled his fingers,

"But it does a magnificent job of putting someone's lights out."

Seppi pinned the guy against the back of his car, I jogged over, and we folded him into his own trunk. Seppi slammed the lid and kissed me casually, like he was running out for a gallon of milk,

"Ti amo."

Seppi slid behind the wheel and moved up the seat. What had my life become? I was standing in the alley long after Seppi drove into the night with a man who thought my name was Jennifer. There hadn't been time to tell Seppi that the guy had the wrong person, and in his mind, it probably wouldn't have mattered. I gathered my things and scurried to my office without crossing paths with anyone. I locked myself in my bathroom and scrubbed my face with fancy soap. I looked like shit, or at least like someone who had been in a scuffle. I took a swig of whiskey, lit a joint, and made sour lemons into gourmet lemonade. I threw my hair forward, shook it out, and twisted it into a semi-professional messy bun that covered the cut and dried blood on the back of my head. I redid my makeup, swiped on winged eyeliner, mascara, and a layer of wine-colored lipstick. I did another round of pit-stick and spritzed myself with Coco Mademoiselle. Satisfied with the reflection in the full-length mirror, I took another shot of whiskey and went to the front of the house.

I greeted patrons and told them about the specials. I smiled and shook hands, did cheek kisses and thanked people for coming. I made my rounds with an inch long gash under my messy bun and no one ever knew it but Seppi. The man who thought I was Jennifer was getting a bullet in the back of his head or a piano wire neck tie. A couple hours later, there was Seppi, back at the helm like nothing happened. He found me upstairs and held me to his chest before leading me to his office. He closed the door and I sat in the chair across the desk from him. Seppi's hair was damp and he was wearing different clothes. Vinny helped him dispose of the body and the car had been run through the crusher at a junk yard. He poured two whiskies and slid one to my side of the desk. Seppi tossed his down the hatch and went back for seconds. I sipped mine and chewed on an ice cube. Seppi took a deep breath and exhaled it, slow and controlled as he melted into his chair. His voice tender and concerned,

"What was upsetting you earlier, Dimples?"

And just like that, I realized that's how it worked. There had been a problem and Seppi made it go away. He was one of those men who had been around it for so long that it didn't even trigger an adrenaline rush. I glanced over at him and hunger grew inside, I was attracted to the part of him that was ruthless and evil, a good man who did bad things sometimes. I went around the desk, rubbed noses with him, and answered in my bedroom voice,

"Whatever it was, I'm not upset about it anymore."

I put one hand on either side of his face and kissed him. Not like we were racing somewhere, but like I was saying thank you for keeping your promise. I knelt in front of him, untucked his shirt and ran my fingers over his stomach. I unbuckled his belt and held his gaze as I unbuttoned his pants. He leaned his head back and close his eyes as I worked on his zipper.

CHAPTER 19
THE WINE WITH THE SPIGOT

IT WAS ONLY A MATTER of time before my dad wanted to have a family dinner. That sounds like a nice gesture, a normal gesture that would lead to a night filled with joy and laughter. And unless you just stumbled into this fucking story five minutes ago, you know that's not how the family dinner would go. You know as well as I do that it would be a complete and total shit show, a cluster fuck of epic proportions, the big top circus of obligatory dysfunction. My mother was probably just trying to start trouble between me and my sister, who had sort of spent half a year with Seppi. Opal was infinitely happier, but as far as my mother was concerned, maybe there was animosity in the wings that she could encourage. You know, let's see what kind of drama she could serve up with the lasagna. And yes, you heard that right, my mother invited Giuseppi Moretti over for her homemade lasagna. What a fucking idiot. And if Seppi gifted my mother an expensive bottle of wine as a hostess gift, I would kick him in the nuts. I mean, come on.

I was all over the place but what do you expect. I had about twenty-four hours before the aforementioned dinner, so I had a little time before I absolutely had to tell him about it. The thing is, knowing Seppi, he would be more than happy to go to my parents' house for dinner. I sat at my desk and stared at the wall. I took an edible from the crystal jar on my vanity. I tossed it down the hatch and washed it down with a swig of whiskey. I plopped on the sofa and put my head back. Apparently, I fell asleep because I startled back to reality,

"Dimples."

I opened my eyes to Seppi leaning in my office door. I blinked up at him a few times to clear the cobwebs,

"Yeah?"

I sat up and fluffed my hair. Seppi asked,

"Why did a Sasquatch just come in to pick up a pizza and tell me he was looking forward to having dinner with me tomorrow?"

"Umm."

"Who's that guy? If that some friend of yours from next door?"

"I was planning on talking to you about it."

But then I didn't say anything.

"Spa-spa-spa-spit it out, Dimples."

I flipped him off with both hands,

"My dad invited us for a family dinner."

Seppi's face lit up just like I knew it would,

"I love your dad! That sounds great, but who's that guy?"

I looked at him flatly,

"With my sister and her baby daddy, and the baby."

His face went like, 'oh.'

"Things are fine between me and Opal, you know that, right?"

He nodded.

"I'm convinced my mother is encouraging this little dinner just so she has a front row seat to the cat fighting and territorial pissing, but my sister is happy where she is."

We both knew that was true, Seppi nodded. Our eyes met and it melted into a lingering kiss. I asked,

"Are you going to be okay seeing the baby?"

Seppi took a deep breath and held it for a beat before letting it out like a pressure cooker. He put his hand on the back of my neck and kissed the top of my head,

"I'll be okay. I want nothing but the best for Opal."

I knew that was the truth. I texted my dad to R.S.V.P. to his family dinner, the one where my mother would make some sort of horrible comment to someone and I would probably gain some new trauma. The one where I would cry in the bathroom or in the back of my closet. But my dad was happy, there was nothing Maxwell Birch loved more than having his girls under the same roof. It had been that way since we were born. Our dad may be flawed just like everyone else, but he loves his girls and his granddaughter had him wrapped around her little finger.

I told Seppi I'd never give him another blow job if he gave my mother a bottle of fancy wine. Instead, he decided to give my dad a nice bottle of whiskey, some gorgeous etched rocks glasses, and two Cuban cigars. Seppi was looking forward to it, I was not. I wasted mental energy thinking about what I was going to wear over there and whether I should wear makeup. Makeup for my parents' house. Why? I was just going to cry it all off. I wondered if Giuseppi Moretti was worried about what he was going to wear to the home of Max and Marta Birch, but I was pretty sure the answer was no. I scoffed at the thought of my mother serving him boxed wine after drinking a twenty-five-hundred-dollar bottle of aged Cabernet she found in his wine cellar. I was annoyed before we left the land of mafia mansions and only going to dinner out of obligation.

We took my car, but Seppi drove, don't even joke about the irony. Anyway, the mini mafia sedan was back to status quo, I hadn't found a single piece of glass anywhere and it smelled brand new. I popped a fuzz-covered edible I found at the bottom of my purse and eyeballed the bottle of whiskey in the back seat. Without taking his eyes off the road,

"Don't even think about it, Dimples, that's for your dad."

I crossed my arms like a kid having a tantrum, "Whatever."

We got to my childhood neighborhood and Seppi caught me staring at the neighbor's house as we drove by.

"Did one of your little girlfriends live there?"

Not exactly.

He waited patiently.

"Bad things happened to me in that house."

He put his hand on my knee,

"I'm sorry."

"Yeah, well, I have a lot of feelings about it, and I don't want to talk about it right before I have to deal with my mother. Someday, I'll pour you a big glass of your expensive whiskey over some of those perfectly square ice cubes of yours, and I'll tell you about my childhood."

A wave of nausea rolled through like a freight train, and I pawed around my bag for a wintergreen lifesaver. I squeezed the lifesaver into my mouth and stared out the window at nothing, a movie playing behind my eyes.

"Think of all the times your mom hugged you, or told you she loved you, or made you feel special."

I choked on the ball of anger and sadness in the back of my throat. When I blinked, big, fat tears fell to my lap and I plucked a used napkin from the cup holder,

"My mother never did any of that. You know how some people have a bonus kid, or they didn't think they wanted to have kids, and then they end up pregnant and it's the best thing that ever happened?"

He nodded and he said,

"That happened to my cousin, Ida, a decade ago. She was doing drugs and I think turning tricks under a train trestle for drug money. When she found out she was pregnant, she had a purpose for the first time in her life. The day Ida found out, she quit drugging and whoring around, she cleaned up her act that very day, and if it wasn't for that kid, she'd be dead in a gutter somewhere, I'm sure of it."

"Yeah, well, my mother didn't want either one of us. She drank and smoked the entire time she was pregnant, and never got to the magical point where she changed her mind."

"Amelia, I'm sorry."

It was genuine and loving, and he didn't push, but I wondered if he was thinking about tossing her into a mulcher.

"The short story is, I got hurt in that house when I was a little girl, and she didn't do anything about it."

I blinked and wiped away a couple more tears,

"And then she shamed me for something that wasn't my fault."

There I was, sitting in the driveway crying, off to a good start. My mother was going to assume that my sister and I had been fighting. Seppi and I sat there for a few more minutes and I inspected my face in the mirror on the visor. My eyes were puffy and I was splotchy but whatever. After one more deep breath, I got out of the car. Seppi grabbed the woven leather basket of shit for my dad,

"I hope he likes this stuff."

I rolled my eyes,

"Whatever."

I clamped an ugly bouquet under my arm and gripped the neck of the cheap chardonnay I got at the gas station down the street. It wasn't my idea, he insisted. As we approached the back porch, my dad appeared, smiling the way he always did when he saw me,

"Hi guys, come on in."

He picked me up off the ground and kissed me on the cheek.

"Hi Boo-Boo Bear!"

He eyed my ripped overalls and dirty sneakers,

"You look beautiful, as always."

My dad shook Seppi's hand and Seppi pulled my dad in for cheek kisses. The two of them wandered off to the den to enjoy expensive whiskey out of the fancy rocks glasses. My mother was getting ready to put her 'famous' lasagna in the oven. I bit my bottom lip and smiled to myself, I found it ballsy and clueless that she would serve an Italian chef her 'famous' lasagna. I mean, at least it wasn't Stauffer's, but I'd bet my life savings there was an empty jar of Prego in the recycle bin. I pinched the bridge of my nose and wondered if she was going to serve Little Debbies for dessert. Whatever. Thankfully, my sister pulled in the driveway a few minutes later. The baby was a good distraction. My dad and I were fighting over little Chloe, who was a carbon copy of my sister. Opal carried a bakery box into the kitchen and put it on the counter,

"I scored some gourmet pastries from Eliana Mazelli's place."

My mother peeked under the lid and turned her nose up,

"You spent money on gourmet pastries?"

She pointed out the window,

"You're driving your baby around in that beat up old hippie van, and you're spending who knows how much on gourmet pastries? Any excuse to waste money."

My mother scoffed to herself and rolled her eyes at what a failure my sister was for bringing gourmet pastries instead of getting a new car. Seppi gave Auggie a once over and I could tell he was wondering how someone like that was going to support Opal. When she was with Seppi, she had a Volvo and an expensive handbag. She had expensive clothes and anything her heart desired. It was obvious Opal was happier just by looking at her. In her thrifted dress and boots, with her flannel clad, mountain man, hippie boyfriend. Seppi kissed Opal on both cheeks and looked lovingly at the baby. He bent and kissed Chloe on the forehead,

"Bellissimo bambino."

Seppi shook hands with Auggie and then kissed him on both cheeks and pulled him in for a hug,

"I'm going to give you my number, if you ever need anything, please reach out. Any time, day or night."

I moved my eyes to my mother and noticed she looked annoyed that the men were not having a knock down drag out dick swinging contest in her living room. A mob boss, a mountain man, and my dad went out the back door to smoke a Cuban before dinner. What kind of alternate reality was this? Was I living in the Twilight Zone? That is when things started happening in a hurricane of just so many words and emotions and bad decisions. Or maybe it was the beginning of something that was a long time coming.

Opal breastfed the baby on the couch and I helped my mother finish setting the table. She kept her comments to a minimum, probably saving her energy.

"Go tell them it's dinner time."

I strolled out the back door and stopped at the top step, staring at the rag tag collection of men leaning against the garage. My dad was in the process of taking an epic rip on a big fat joint. Hands in my pockets, I rocked back on my heels, smiling. My dad realized I was standing there, pitched the lit joint in Seppi's direction, and waved the smoke away as he coughed out a cloud of smoke. Seppi juggled the joint several times before catching it, and he handed it back to Auggie. My dad stared at me with bloodshot eyes like I needed to keep my mouth shut. I laughed at him,

"Amateur!"

I gestured at the door,

"Time for dinner, assholes."

It was going to be a shit show now that my dad was high. Maxwell Birch was a man who bit his tongue a lot, and I was pretty sure the weed would disengage the filter. We settled in around the table to paper napkins. Now, don't get me wrong, I grew up with, and still personally use, paper napkins, store brand is fine. But this is a woman whose sole purpose in life is to make people think her shit doesn't stink, and she was fucking it up, oh so badly. My dad and Seppi sipped whiskey out of expensive rocks glasses while Auggie sipped from vintage Tupperware. The ice cubes were just regular like out of an ice cube tray, they were not perfectly square. My dad's cheeks were red and I gave Seppi the hairy eyeball to stop feeding my dad alcohol. My gaze moved to my sister, she and Auggie were staring at the baby, and both of them were smiling. My mother snapped,

"Why don't you put her down so you can eat?"

Opal moved her eyes to our mother and squinted at her,

"I put my baby's needs in front of my own, like it should be."

My mother looked at Opal like she had some nerve, but Opal kept going,

"You want me to be like you? No thanks."

My mother scoffed and looked at my sister disapprovingly, clutching her fake pearls,

"Opal, I am disappointed in your behavior, what ails you?"

Oh good, no one even had food on their plates yet. I made a face at Seppi, and then I really looked at him. The man was high as a kite. Oh my God. In all the time I had known Seppi, he had never smoked marijuana, or taken a gummy, or eaten a brownie. Giuseppi Moretti was so intimidated by Marta Birch, that he smoked weed with my father, and his ex's baby daddy, to prepare himself for dinner. And let's not forget that my dad is not accustomed to going shot for shot with someone like Seppi. Hell, I can probably handle more liquor than my father. The entire thing was a ticking time bomb. Lasagna was being served. You know, the kind with the jarred sauce, like a normal person makes on a Wednesday after work. Not the kind you serve to someone who owns a goddamn Italian restaurant and makes a generation's old marinara recipe. The kitchen timer went off and my mother looked over at me,

"Go get the garlic bread out of the oven."

My pleasure. I pushed my chair out, went into the kitchen, and wanted to keep going until I was in the fucking car. I would have left Seppi there, I'm not kidding. I grabbed the potholders and pulled the garlic bread out of the oven. Again, nothing wrong with frozen garlic bread that's sliced into two long strips but, come on. I moved the strips of garlic bread onto a plate, did a half assed job cutting it into slices with a steak knife, and found a place for it on the cluttered dining room table. I scanned the group of people sitting around that table, I never thought I'd see a Sasquatch man with a head full of dreads, and a mob, boss breaking bread together, and I never imagined the table they'd share would be in my childhood home. My gummy was wearing off, and I wished I had gone outside with the guys. I picked up what was left in Seppi's glass and tossed it back.

Whatever. And then my mother excused herself and came back with a chilled bottle of wine with a screw cap, at least it wasn't the wine with the spigot. I realized I was holding my breath as I pushed my wine glass forward, and my mother made her way around the table. Well, wouldn't you know it, by the time she got to my glass, there was just a dribble. Yup. I tipped my head back and slurped the sip of wine into my mouth like a vacuum cleaner. My mother made a disapproving facial expression, and some sort of a groan before getting up again. She returned to the table carrying the box of wine with the spigot, the one that lived on the counter next to the fridge, and Seppi didn't seem to give a single shit. I knew he wouldn't care anyway, and he already knew my mother, but his eyes were glazed over and he was examining a piece of something on the garlic bread in his hand. Oregano.

"It's a piece of fucking oregano, whoopty-doo."

I moved my eyes to my sister, and I could tell she was upset. I looked at my dad, who was making silly faces at the baby. He was sticking his tongue out and giggling at his granddaughter as he ate his wife's mediocre lasagna. And then Marta Birch threw her fork down, and it hit the edge of her plate dramatically,

"Maxwell, you have company, pull yourself together!"

I'm pretty sure everyone, including the baby, was staring at my mother then, and the color rose in Opal's cheeks,

"Daddy, you're fine, I like that you actually interact with my daughter."

Opal threw her eyes at our mother, and she was scowling. OK, everyone needed to calm the fuck down. I drank the glass of shitty wine from the box with a spigot, it tasted like room temperature vinegar, and a headache.

"Opal, your father is being ridiculous at the dinner table, we have company!"

Opal moved her eyes to Seppi, and gestured at our end of the table,

"Big fucking deal that Giuseppi Moretti is over for dinner, he's just a man, like daddy and Auggie."

Well, that did it. Our mother barked with laughter, which offended my dad, and Auggie. So, here's this mob boss who's used to killing people, and dealing with really bad shit. And sitting across the table from Marta Birch, I was pretty sure he was on the verge of a panic attack. That's when my big tough mob boss boyfriend began to spiral, for the first time since I'd met him. He was uncomfortable, so he looked down at his forkful of lasagna,

"This is really good; do you think I could have your recipe?"

And then my dad started laughing the way you do when you're high, I don't even think he was trying to be an asshole. Like, wheezing, with tears running down his cheeks. That's when I barked with laughter. My mother looked at me like we were at church, and I just farted. Fine. I pushed my chair back and went into the kitchen. I returned with the jar from the Prego and put it on the table in front of Seppi's plate. I gestured,

"Did you want the recipe for the sauce too, or...?"

I spun the jar, so the paragraph of ingredients was facing him. And then I put the crinkly plastic tube from the frozen garlic bread next to the jar, and made like it was a chore to flatten it out,

"In case you want her garlic bread recipe for Giuseppi's Italian Ristorante."

Seppi's eyes bugged out, and he felt like he needed to say something to deflect the situation,

"I like it."

He certainly was shoveling it in, you know, since he had the munchies. He crunched into a piece of garlic bread, dry pieces of crust raining down onto his shirt before falling into his crotch. Maybe I could hide under the table. My mother looked like she wanted to kill me and my sister. And let's not forget that this all started because she was a bitch to my dad about making cute faces at his granddaughter. It was only a matter of time before she pulled out the next weapon. To be more specific, it only took her three fucking seconds to reload. She tapped a fork on the side of her glass like people do at a wedding reception,

"Let's raise our glasses, this certainly is a special occasion."

For once, maybe Marta Birch was going to say something profound, something loving, and maternal, and kind. My dad was still making faces at Chloe, and she was still smiling at him, making milky spit bubbles. I could see the baby's dimples which made me smile. And then my mother geared up, or drew back, or pulled the pin,

"It isn't every day you get to serve dinner to a man who has had sex with both of your daughters."

OK. So, here is where things could have gone a million different ways depending on how people responded. My sister and I made eye contact like, 'yup, I could have seen that coming from a mile away.'

And since the gloves were already off, I tossed back some whiskey I found on the table and looked right at my mother,

"While you've got him here, why don't you ask Seppi if I performed fellatio."

I glared at her,

"You know, to earn the car."

All eyes were on me, and all eyes were like big round saucers, ask me if I cared. My mother didn't like being confronted, she barked,

"AMELIA!"

Whatever, bitch, I wasn't done yet,

"While we're at it, I wanted to thank you for moving back into this house."

My mother walled off the comment about the car, and looked at me like, 'thank goodness, someone is putting the focus back on me.' She smiled,

"I know how happy you girls were here, you had the perfect childhood."

Buckle up. My tongue was the bull and my words were the whip,

"Happy!? Are you out of your fucking mind!? Happy!?"

She gawked at me with her eyes like saucers,

"Amelia! You should be ashamed of yourself, acting like this! You had everything a little girl could want!"

And that was it, that was all I could take,

"Oh, I should be ashamed of myself!? You've done nothing but try to ruin the both of us since we squirted out of your womb!"

My sister's eyes were trained on me. I stood up and pointed across the table,

"You're the one who should be ashamed of yourself!"

And just like she always did, she pulled out the pity party mask. She dug through the costumes backstage and that's the best she could come up with. She threw her hands up, made herself cry, and in a whiny voice,

"I'm a horrible mother."

How predictable. She did the whole 'woe is me' bullshit, and not a single person at the table tried to make her feel better. There sat my sister with a smug smile on her face. Seppi looked like he was holding back a bunch of things. Auggie looked like this was about what he was used to at his own family dinners.

My dad who seemed amused by the whole thing.

My mother glared in my direction,

"I hope you're proud of yourself, Amelia, you've ruined dinner!"

She let out a dramatic sigh and brushed at her shirt like I had thrown rotten tomatoes. She ordered,

"I need you to shut up!"

I imagined a long black hook appearing from behind the perfect curtains, like the ones on the old comedy shows, when the person was kicked off the stage. I mumbled under my breath,

"I hope you fall into a trapdoor pit filled with alligators."

Seppi let out a bark of laughter that sent a mouthful of chewed garlic bread across the table, and it landed in right my dad's fancy rocks glass. My dad found that to be about the funniest thing he'd ever seen and started laughing harder than I'd ever seen him laugh in my whole life. My mother looked at my dad sternly,

"Maxwell, are you drunk!?"

He looked over at her,

"Probably a little, but I'm also really high."

She glared at him and he added,

"Just because you're miserable, doesn't mean the rest of us have to be."

Oopsies. That was the night I found out expensive whiskey and homegrown weed give my dad no filter, and a big ole pair of balls.

CHAPTER 20
WHEN ONE DOOR CLOSES

IN THE MIDST of all that, don't forget that the broken-hearted barista wanted to have dinner. I had been wishy-washy in the past, you know that as well as I do. But, both legs were securely planted on the other side of the fence this time, and I wasn't worried the grass was greener on the other side. Maybe people who have slept together can still be friends, but I hadn't had much luck with it myself. At one time or another, that person approved of me, or found me worthy. Listen, I'm not stupid, I know how things are, and I know that some men nail anything that walks, but I've convinced myself that I'm not in that category. I'm a nice girl, a funny girl, a good girl, according to Giuseppi Moretti.

I wasn't nervous that I'd make a dumb decision, but my stomach was doing somersaults just the same. I was pretty sure Seppi knew Kane wasn't a threat, but I told him about dinner beforehand, and not after. I caught Seppi as he was passing my office door,

"Hey, I'm having pizza or something with Kane later, there's some major drama going on with his girlfriend and he needs someone to talk to."

Not that I was expecting him to be jealous but you never know,

"Have fun, I'll be here until about ten, but if you're done after that, I'll see you at home."

Adrenaline burnt in my stomach when he said that, was I really living at Hidden Hills Estates? How had I gotten there? Seppi kissed me on the cheek and then retreated into his office. I sat on my sofa and popped dark chocolate covered blueberries into my mouth. Of course, Seppi wasn't worried or threatened or jealous, he was Giuseppi Motherfucking Moretti, Kane Buchanan didn't have a chance. Things were going well with Seppi and I felt like the ickiness was gone between me and Kane, maybe, just maybe, we could be friends without the benefits.

I did some actual work and made a social media post promoting the community studio. I finished up and went next door. I didn't unlock my apartment that night, the one across the hall from his. I tapped on his door and he swung it open with damp hair that smelled like his six-dollar coconut conditioner. His

Staffordshire terrier Lola barreled into the hall and danced around at my feet. Our eyes met and he kissed me on the cheek before we hugged, he got a little too close for a little too long and I could smell his leather and cedar beard oil,

"Thank you for coming."

When he hugged me, the warmth of his skin pulled me in, something inside of me reacting to something inside of him. But ultimately, we sat on the sun porch, and he told me his side of the story. I already knew she took a test and didn't know about evaporation lines. I also knew that, by chance, she got her period the next morning after Kane went down to the cafe. In his eyes, she had been playing games with him. Apparently, one of the reoccurring issues between them is that she acts out in ways like that when she feels threatened.

They had been arguing, and Kane had already made up his mind that he needed an actual break from her, that they wanted different things in general. That is precisely when Alex came into his bedroom with the pregnancy test. The 'positive' test led to a long conversation about the state of the world and Kane's opinion on having kids. She was feeling rejected and overwhelmed. They almost broke up but then because of the emotions and the tears and the connection, they sort of made up. They fought about it again before he went down to the cafe, and then an hour later, she came down in a flurry to tell him she got her period.

I understood it but he didn't. Mother nature is a cruel bitch that way. However the cookie crumbled, Alex thought he'd be happy when he found out she wasn't pregnant, but he thought the entire thing had been a game. I listened and knew that regardless of the situation and whether it was bullshit or not, he had already planned to end things with her. We ordered food and sat there drinking and eating and listening to the Eagles like old times. There was an awkward silence so I told him about the Indian Scout and about scheduling my endorsement exam. I immediately regretted it because it was clear it did something for him,

"That's great, Amelia, too bad you weren't riding when we were together, that would have been fun."

It felt like I had crossed some sort of boundary, for some reason, even though Seppi knew I met Frieda a couple times to hang out, I hadn't told him I was learning how to ride a bike. I'm not sure why, maybe because I thought he wouldn't like it, or maybe it would make me a bad girl instead of a good one. I was flooded with panic and hot acid crept into the back of my throat. I glanced at my phone, it was almost ten,

"Umm, I've gotta get back to the ristorante before Seppi leaves."

I hugged Kane and told him I'd be around if he needed me, but really, I hoped he wouldn't need me. Eventually, he'd catch me on a day I was feeling needy or nostalgic, he'd catch me on a night I was thinking of him too. He'd tuck a curl behind my ear and I'd melt into a puddle. That night, I realized I wasn't capable of seeing him as 'just a friend,' not really. There were times our eyes met that night that made me want to go to him, straddle him, kiss him like I used to. I missed the parts of him that maybe no one else had ever seen, not even Alex. And don't get me wrong, it wasn't just about sex, I reminisced about watching him play guitar, and about drinking his maple oat lattes. I saw something familiar in his eyes as I opened his door, something familiar that pulled my body toward his. I stepped into the hall in an attempt to break the spell and glanced at 'my' door, I sort of still lived there, even if I hadn't stayed there in a while. My sister and Auggie were in there, I could hear the TV and I imagined Chloe making wet raspberries at Opal's breast as they binged a series on Netflix. I decided not to bother them.

I needed to put distance between myself, those dark chocolate eyes, and that dark chocolate voice. It was more than just staying faithful to Seppi, it was that there needed to be an ending, and sometimes it's better to rip off the band-aid. I glanced at my watch, three minutes past ten. I hoped I could catch Seppi before he left so he could follow me 'home.' I bounced down the stairs and pushed through the door into the night, my head swimming. I heard an apartment door open and close and wondered if it was my sister, maybe she heard me leave and wanted to say hi. I spun around to see Kane descending the stairs with his wavy dark chocolate hair bouncing at his shoulders. Kane pushed through the back door and stood in front of me. He stood a little too close and when I looked up at him, he tucked a loose curl behind my ear. My eyes fluttered and my knees went weak. I knew those feelings never led anywhere besides his bed. He reached out and took my hands,

"Amelia, listen, I know things have been weird between us and I'm sorry. Alex was always swimming around the periphery but that's over now, it's over."

I squinted my eyes at him and held my breath. My eyes met his and I felt the things I felt before. I took my attraction out of it and focused on every time he had ever hurt me,

"It's over between us."

Tears welled in his eyes and I wondered if maybe it was the whiskey talking, the nostalgia. He let go of my hands and tucked another curl behind my ear, maybe out of habit, and maybe as a last-ditch effort to sway me. That annoyed me, the desperation, the neediness. And just like that, I didn't feel that way anymore. At one time, that would have made me nuzzle my face into his neck, or lead him to the bed. I said,

"I care about you..."

I dropped my eyes because I felt more than that and we both knew it. He took my hands again and swung them,

"I'd like to try again."

Our eyes locked and he closed the remaining gap between us. I took a step back, blinking away some emerging tears,

"I have to go."

I turned around and he grabbed my wrist, I spun around to face him,

"Amelia, I'm all yours now, we have a chance to see how this would go without anybody interrupting."

He was treading on dangerous ground, I knew someone who smelled like whiskey and Tobacco Vanille who wouldn't think twice about snapping him like a twig. I looked up at him again,

"I appreciate that but it's over between us."

Kane swallowed a lump in his throat and gestured toward the restaurant, his voice weaker than usual,

"Are you really with him?"

"Yes."

I watched as Kane's mind went to dark places, sad places, sentimental places, the places we used to go together,

"Do you love him?"

I looked Kane in the eyes,

"Yes."

And out of the darkness stepped Giuseppi Moretti. Just like that, he was on the porch next to me, it was like he flew silently from where he had been. Like when a vampire moves from one place to another in a movie. I thanked my lucky stars for making good choices. Seppi didn't usually piss on his territory, but he did it that night. He put his arm around me and kissed the top of my head, I bet he was looking Kane in the eye when he did it, as if to say, 'she's mine.'

"You ready to go home, baby?"

"Yeah."

And just like that, Kane was reduced to rubble right in front of my eyes. Part of me hurt for him, and the other part of me was glad he finally saw that my relationship with Seppi was real. I wasn't just some naïve girl who came back to my hometown to start over. I wasn't just some girl who made lattes. I wasn't just some girl he knew; I was one of the ones who had access to the inner sanctum. I was untouchable. I was Seppi's and he was mine. I didn't have room for a barista with a dark chocolate voice and an acoustic guitar. I didn't have time for Kane's maple oat lattes or for the way he tucked loose curls behind my ears.

As Seppi followed me to the land of mafia mansions and pissing on territory, I felt bad for Kane. He held onto that woman for six years, and in my opinion, had thrown it away for nothing. For the first time ever, I wanted them to make up. If Kane was ready for their relationship to be over, it was because he thought I was still waiting on the back burner. Only, that wasn't an option anymore. I wasn't waiting in the wings to climb back into his arms or into his bed. I wasn't living across the hall, bumping into him flirtatiously behind the counter at Muddy Waters, or making out with him in his office. He didn't have one of my bras in the top drawer of his desk from one of the times we almost got caught, and I didn't have tampons in his bathroom anymore. Even if I had still wanted him the way I used to, things had changed. In the time that passed since Kane and I parted ways, my relationship with Seppi, my life as a mini mobster, my plummet into the dark world of killing, and being untouchable, it had all made it impossible for me to ever be with Kane again.

I woke to the sun coming through the sheers on the balcony doors. Seppi was sitting out there, in pajama pants and no shirt, talking on the phone with an associate. I padded down the stairs to make a latte and then joined Seppi, with Indie trailing at my heels. The wood was cool and damp under my feet, a layer of dew on the wood. Birds danced around the feeders and Indie jumped onto the railing to spectate. We just sat there together and watched birds for a while. I sucked the steamed milk from the top of my mug and was grateful for the life I was living. Things were going in the right direction. I was making good decisions, I wasn't getting myself wrapped up in multiple relationships, or spinning around in my head, wondering what I should be when I grow up. I felt like I was home. I felt like I was capable, and intelligent, and part of something. I was an aunt. I was in therapy. I was in love. Part of me was getting harder, and part of Seppi was getting softer. I left my mug on the railing, stood behind him and wrapped my arms around his neck. I heard a low noise in his throat that he stifled into a cough because he was on the phone.

I settled in across from Seppi and lit a joint. He was talking about money and about someone who owed someone something. I went back to watching the birds at the feeders as the wind chimes tinkled in the breeze. It was different in the land of mafia mansions and balconies you can get to from the bedroom. There was a dog barking in the distance as a woman jogged by the house pushing a stroller. There was a weed whacker and a law mower nearby and I could peer across the fence and watch the neighbor's hot Hispanic pool boy as he skimmed the surface with a net. It seemed like a cut scene from a movie about people who lived in an exciting gated community. I snagged my empty mug and set off to retrieve another latte. I stood at the counter in my bare feet, popping berries into my mouth as the espresso brewed. I glanced out at the patio as I steamed the milk and reality set in, I was living in mafia mansion land and it was starting to feel like home.

CHAPTER 21
MIGHTIER THAN THE SWORD

I PADDED IN from the balcony and stripped out of my pajamas while the shower got hot. I was in the middle of working conditioner through my curls when the glass door slid open, and Seppi stepped in. He scrubbed his hair, the thick bubbles running down his chest, into his trimmed pubic hair. I liked that we could shower like that, shower together without needing to fuck. We were in that place where we were familiar with each other; he knew which tampons to get me at Walgreen's, and I knew which kind of pit stick and razor blades he used. After the shower, I watched him while he shaved, and put product in his hair. I followed him with my eyes as he put on his deodorant, and spritzed Tobacco Vanille. I really loved him. I don't mean the old lust I had for his looks, or his power, or his money, I'm talking about the part of him that eats pancakes in his pajamas. The part of him that snuggles with Indie, and feeds her cheese when he thinks I'm not looking. The part of him that makes love to me, and makes me feel safe. The part of him that grew up with a father that was just like my mother. We had things in common even though we were from completely different worlds.

That was the day the community studio was going to open. I was preoccupied, but excited about it. There was a part of me that wondered why my aunt Maggie had done this for me. I wondered if Freida was going to be my saving grace. I wondered if my mother would show up for the big night. I worked curl cream through my ringlets and swiped on some mascara. I had a couple phone calls with future brides, but otherwise, I had mostly desk work to do before going to the studio. I leaned on the vanity with both hands and looked myself in the eye. There was always a flood of both appreciation and internal criticism of my looks, and in my mind, 'love yourself, you piece of shit.'

I dressed in a pair of flowy linen pants and a crocheted top that tied at both shoulders, the ties had wooden beads at the ends. I slipped my feet into some espadrilles, twisted some of my hair and secured it with an ornate carved wooden hair pin. I spritzed on some expensive perfume and bounced down the stairs. As I watched Seppi rinse his coffee cup and put it in the dish drainer, I wondered why we always took two cars to work,

"Babe."
He looked up,
"Dimples."
I moved into the kitchen and knelt on one of the stools,
"Why do we always take two cars?"
He scrunched his eyebrows,
"What?"
"Why do you always follow me into town instead of both of us just riding in one car?"
He turned to me,
"Because my business can be unpredictable, and I don't want you to be stuck at work if I'm off putting a bullet in someone's head."
I know that sounds icky, but it was the reality of things. There had been times when he was otherwise indisposed when it was time to go home, and if I had to rely on Seppi for a ride, I would have been sleeping on the sofa in my office, or in my apartment amongst the baby's things. But it still made me feel a disconnect between us. I slid off the stool and stood in front of him,
"What if I helped you?"
He stepped back and looked down at me,
"Amelia."
No 'Dimples' that time,
"You know that's not possible. I understand you are familiar with what goes on, and there's really not much I don't tell you, but it's not as easy as all of that.

There are still some things I want to protect you from. I've provided you with a safe vehicle that's equipped with GPS, you have a panic button for emergencies, and you know how to get into my house. This is no different than if I had any other job with confidentiality constraints."

Seppi tucked me into his chest and kissed the top of my head. He breathed in my curl cream and the perfume he gave me. He filled his lungs and sighed it out in a long exhale. I knew he didn't want me as involved as I was, and I knew he wanted to keep me out of the line of fire, no pun intended. I was smarter than I was a year ago. I was darker, and deeper, and more broken, really. I was more angry, more resentful, and more willing to battle my demons on the daily. Seppi hooked my chin with his finger. I grabbed his wrist, moved my lips to his hand, and kissed his palm. He made a noise low in his throat, and our mouths came together. We kissed like we wanted to race somewhere but were already running late. When I looked up at him, I had tears in my eyes, he really was my everything. Maybe we could circle back around to that moment, later when we were in for the night.

Fifteen minutes later, Seppi was following me up the alley between Muddy Waters and Giuseppi's Italian Ristorante. Kane was walking Lola around the backyard and when I saw him, I had a pang of something deep in my guts. I waved to him, he waved back and held his hand there, like I had taken the wind out of his sails. Like he was waving to his true love as he drifted out to sea. Seppi swung out of the Escalade and escorted me to the building with his hand on my lower back, pissing on his territory. Once I was in the chair across the desk from his, he said,

"Cute top."

"Thanks."

"You'll be lucky if I don't cut those pretty little straps."

I gestured at the open door, my eyes like saucers. He pushed it shut and turned the lock. He closed the gap,

"Get up."

I just sat there and looked up at him like a deer in the headlights. He repeated himself using his mob boss voice,

"Get up!"

I stood. He was hungry; I could see it in his eyes. Our bodies came together and Seppi kept walking until my back hit the wall. He untucked my shirt and hooked his finger in the waist of my pants, and I reached for his belt. He scolded me with his eyes and moved his hand to my throat, not like he wanted to hurt me, more like he wanted me to know he was in charge. I dropped my hand and when our eyes met, a jolt of arousal shot to my privates. With the hand that wasn't on my throat, he hooked my chin so that my face was closer to his. I felt the heat of his breath and sensed something animalistic.

Seppi went after what he wanted and I hoped no one heard what was going on, hoped Mary Moretti didn't tap on the door with a bag of gourmet pastries. We were beyond the initial honeymoon period, we were beyond the awkward first time. There was an urgency about it and he had learned enough about me that we could steal away for moments like that. Ten minutes later, we were put back together and the office door was open. Whoever had been at the door had gone. I went into my bathroom and looked at myself in the mirror. Things were like that with Seppi, extreme and passionate, sometimes even rough, in a good way, sometimes we needed each other that badly. I knew something important was happening because Seppi was quiet after he got off the phone. I made my way back into his office, and sat in the chair across the desk from him. I tried to size him up, figure out what he was thinking. He looked serious, but not like something was wrong. He looked confused or something. I waited for him to find his words,

"A woman from the downtown business partnership wants me to attend a gathering this evening. She apologized for the short notice and said the ristorante is a big draw, bringing people to other local businesses in the downtown area."

"I think that's great, Seppi."

He seemed like a fish out of water,

"I'm not used to being asked to do things like this. Until my dad 'went away,' my family was feared, and avoided, and most of the downtown partnership leaders wanted nothing to do with a Moretti. I don't know how to act, or how to feel about it."

I went to him and sat on his knee,

"I think it's a sign of change, it means you have shown everyone that you're not like your father. It means you're helping the smaller businesses by drawing people in for fresh pasta with meatballs, and Mama Moretti's marinara. Your ristorante is improving the tourism, and the economy of Bunman."

The deeper and darker I seemed to get, the more Seppi's edges seemed to blur. He went to the mirror and brushed at his shirt, straightened his belt buckle, glanced over his shoulder at me briefly before going back to his reflection,

"What do you think of this outfit?"

Ladies and gentlemen, I've never known Giuseppi Moretti to worry about what he was wearing. I gave him a dramatic once over, he looked the same as he always did, hot as fuck. It was kind of nice to see him feel self-conscious and insecure. He picked up his rocks glass and took a sip, I boiled my critique down to four words,

"You have crotch wrinkles."

He spit out his whiskey and scanned his crotch. I wasn't sure if he was barking in laughter or surprise,

"What!?"

I gestured at his crotch,

"The crotch of your pants is all creased from sitting, you have crotch wrinkles."

But who cares? Don't we all get a good case of the crotch wrinkles if we sit in slacks? I reassured him that he looked nice, and did not need to change into something else before the downtown partnership gathering. He said,

"I'm sorry I won't be at the opening tonight, I planned to stop by, but I think by the time I'm able to get out of there, you'll be done for the night."

I put my hand on his,

"It's not a big deal, it's just the first day the place is open to kids after school, you're not missing anything. And you're going to do great, this is awesome, I'm proud of you."

Really, no matter what outfit he put on, they were all pretty much the same. He always wore dark slacks and a button up shirt to the restaurant. That day, he was wearing navy slacks and a gray button up shirt, the top couple buttons were open, the sleeves rolled up a couple times. Brown oxfords, Rolex, gold chain around his neck, phoenix tattoo peeking out when he moved just right. I kissed him on the cheek,

"I can't wait to hear about it."

I fired her up and made my way to the other side of town. I nosed the mini mafia sedan around the back of the studio and had a flash of the night I tried to break into Stanley's Service Center. So much had happened since the night I shined my purple pen light into Vincenzo Moretti's face to find him tied to a chair with a gag in his mouth. I got out of the car and beeped it locked, shouldering the vintage leather bag that used to belong to the red-headed woman with the pantsuit. Freida swung into the driveway and parked behind my car, I was in awe of her. She hung her helmet on the handle and swung her leg over the bike in gauzy overalls and a tiny little crocheted tank top. Her feet were in a pair of well-loved Birkenstocks and her toenails were painted with holographic polish. She wore pink lip gloss, and her blonde dreads had a couple new sterling silver and turquoise clips. She offered me a piece of cinnamon gum and I accepted. She saw me eyeballing her bike,

"How are you feeling about your exam?"

I nodded but didn't say anything. She said,

"I've been keeping track, you've had five hours of practice and Seth said you're a natural. I'll meet you at the DMV with the bike, you're going to do great. Maybe we can go riding after."

I nodded again, tears creeping up but I shoved them back, aware this whole thing was some trauma response, one more way for me to rebel. Seppi would have to be okay with it, he would have to understand that I could do whatever I wanted, even if I was his. I imagined myself in a thrifted biker jacket and leather boots, frantic ringlets mashed down by a sparkly black helmet. Freida moved on to other things and started talking fast like she always did when she was nervous,

"I tried on like ten outfits before I decided on this one, and it was the first one I put on, can you believe that? Do you ever do that?"

She made an 'I'm crazy' hand gesture, and I nodded at the question,

"Yeah, I've done that."

"And then I decided to take everything out of my closet, and then I didn't want to do it anymore, so everything is in worse shape than it was to begin with. Everything is in a pile on the floor."

I glanced over at her as we made our way to the back door and she kept going,

"My mom was saying that I should find something to teach at the studio and I told her I was going to teach pottery and help with the classes. She always tells me I should be a teacher; do you think I should be a teacher? I mean, not like at a community studio, I mean like, should I be a teacher?"

I moved my eyes to her backpack and wondered if she brought some duct tape for her mouth. I said,

"I think you should try to calm down a little bit, you seem a little manic, are you okay?"

We had about a half hour before the kids would arrive for crafts and poetry, and Freida needed to calm the fuck down. The next time I glanced over at her, she burst into tears. Come on. I pinched the bridge of my nose and let out an exasperated sigh. She glanced over at me,

"Are you mad at me?"

Oh, for Christ's sake, were we in junior high? I imagined putting *her* in the garden,

"No, I'm not *mad* at you, I just don't understand why you're so worked up. Twenty kids are coming to make pipe cleaner bracelets, this isn't rocket science."

She waved me away,

"No, I know, I just want to do a good job."

"Freida, you're enthusiastic and want to be here, that's all I could ask for. You've offered to help me teach classes and wrangle grubby-handed elementary school kids. I'm not looking for you to do anything more than pour apple juice into paper cups and help me keep the little crotch gremlins from destroying the place. Why are you crying?"

"I just, this is something I've always wanted, so it's making me emotional, I'm sorry."

I knew right then that Freida wanted the community studio *way* more than I did. At that point, it seemed like a huge pain in my ass. I tried to be reassuring, maybe she'd shut the fuck up if she felt better,

"If there's one thing I've learned, it's never apologize for the way you feel, ever."

She looked over at me and I knew she understood that I was talking about life in general and not just that situation. It seemed to soothe her a little. I glanced at the garden before going up the steps. We set the tables with snacks and cups of juice and things to make a craft or write a poem. From about three until six, we'd be molding little minds. I didn't really have my heart in it, but when the first kids came through the door, I got excited for what the place would become.

Most weekday afternoons, kids could come for an activity, and some evenings we would offer classes for adults, I'd figure that out over time. I wanted to have watercolor classes, and pottery classes, and nights where people could learn how to make jewelry. I had a grandiose daydream of having steadfast members who were in the studio multiple evenings a week, or maybe all day on a Saturday. I imagined people selling their wares at the farmers market, or in a stand at the end of the driveway. Bouquets of flowers in painted mason jars and corn husk dolls with pretty dresses. The maternal part of me smiled as I helped a kindergartner named Walter open the glue. There were googly eyes and glitter on the table and the floor. There were broken goldfish crackers in the seats of plastic chairs and apple juice rings on the tables.

A little girl sat quietly at the table with the paper and pencils. She was alone and I had no idea what an important decision it was making when I sat in the chair across from her,

"Hi, my name is Amelia, what's your name?"

She had curly dark hair and deep brown eyes. Her dimples were more subtle than mine but they came to life when she smiled. She had a round face and a sprinkling of freckles across the bridge of her nose. She had dirt under her fingernails, her jeans were too short, and her shoes had seen better days. She didn't seem the least bit bashful and it intrigued me. She answered confidently,

"My name is Gabriella, but everyone just calls me Gilly."

I guessed she was about six years old,

"How old are you?"

She beamed up at me, excitedly,

"I'm five and my mommy said that when I'm six, I'm going to be a big girl!"

I wondered if I would ever feel like a big girl,

"Being a big girl is a big responsibility."

Gilly smiled up at me again and very matter of factly, she said,

"I know."

She paused to scrutinize my appearance,

"How old are *you*?"

"I just turned twenty-four."

Her eyes went wide,

"You're even older than my mom!"

I tried to see myself from her perspective, I had never cared what a little kid thought of me before. For some reason, I wanted her to think I was cool, or something. When I was that age, I thought people in their twenties seemed old. It reminded me of when I was almost six and hadn't been hurt yet, I was innocent and my head didn't have any demons in it. Back when I thought the world was filled with good and I thought my mother loved me. My mind flashed to my routine escapes into the forest with Sunny to pretend we were fairies. Running away from the pain and the yelling, running away from the lies. Hiding in The Fortress, pretending we were surrounded by vines that would throw out sharp barbs if anyone tried to hurt us. I grew up in a house that looked pretty from the outside but the forest was ugly and broken and damp, and I preferred how it made me feel. I put my hand out to Gilly and she shook it confidently. When we made contact she gave me a more detailed once over,

"You don't look like an Amelia to me."

She had my attention and I could tell she was wise beyond her years,

"Who do I look like to you?"

Gilly knelt in her chair and leaned on the table with both elbows. She didn't scrutinize me in a way that made me self conscious, it was as if we had known each other in another life, as if recognition was registering somewhere deep inside,

"You're Adeline, but your nickname is Adele."

And after that day, that little girl called me Adele, even though my name is Amelia. I wondered if she had the same life as me, I wondered if she was at the writing table because she was broken, or if she just preferred writing over googly eyeballs and glitter,

"Can I sit with you and write a poem?"

Gilly smiled so wide that she activated her . I was smiling with my whole face as I picked out the pencil I wanted. Mine was purple and Gilly's was bright pink, she looked up at me,

"I'm going to write about my sweet dreams room."

I thought about my old bedroom, the one I ran to when the world closed in. The back of the closet where I would sit on the floor and hug my knees, I heard the echoes of being told to shut up, I would run to my room in tears, wondering why she didn't love me or want to hear what I had to say. I was flooded with feelings, and whenever I felt a lot of things, I wrote good poems. I stared down at my paper and envied her, the way the words flowed through her pencil. I wondered if good memories flowed into poetry more easily than bad ones. Maybe a new crayon draws prettier pictures than a broken one. I closed my eyes and thought about the things I felt, and smelled, and heard. The things I saw, and touched, while I was being hurt on that bathroom floor.

It was winter, maybe Christmas Vacation from school. I remembered the way my socks slipped as I tried to get away, as I ran down the hall in the wrong direction, on the hardwood floor that had been polished with lemon Pledge. A wave of nausea flooded over me, and I swallowed the warm spit in the back of my throat. I tossed back a little paper cup of apple juice to stave off a full-on vomit. The smells of the room and the cold from the bathroom tiles. My pants had an elastic waist and my underwear had the day of the week embroidered on them. Words started to come when my pencil hit the paper, and those words flowed into poetry. I used to love writing poems, the pen was always mightier than the sword, it helped me when people didn't.

CHAPTER 22
BOXED CHARDONNAY

IF YOU DON'T HOLD BACK, writing a poem is a therapeutic experience. Other people don't have to like it, they don't even have to read it, a poem is really for the person who wrote it. I think poetry is like a valve, a river of thoughts and emotions. It's sort of like bleeding feelings onto a piece of paper. It's giving yourself permission to let your wounds seep out into words, to tell your story without watering it down. And if it isn't poetry, then let it be something else entirely, but for the love of God, let yourself be free like that once in a while. There is nothing more cathartic than telling your story. Use your heart, use your soul, use your voice. That is exactly what I did that night and this is what I wrote.

Boxed Chardonnay
By, Amelia Birch

Wood stove, pine needles, a mug shaped like a bunny,
snowmobiles and ice skates in the winter of first grade.
When the first frost came that year, I was still unbroken,
I was still unscathed, the wounds hadn't yet been made.

I'd run through the row of corn they pushed down for me,
what a good place for the boogeyman to hide.
I'd break into a run until I was safe and sound,
inside the house that looked happy from the outside.

He showed me something I shouldn't have seen,
he tried to get me to do things no little girl should.
I think back and remember it all in slow motion,
the fear and the confusion, little girl misunderstood.

Secrets were kept and shame was laid,
I would cry in my closet until I felt safe.
When you're a little girl just in the first grade,
You shouldn't be hurt so bad, or need to escape.

As long as the curtains look good from the porch,
and there can't be any dust bunnies, or things out of place.
The way you shushed and shamed me when I needed you,
is the reason I hate you, you're such a disgrace.

I'm not the one who deserves to be hurt,
I hope you drown in your boxed chardonnay.
You don't deserve to have a daughter like me,
maybe I'll kill you with a shovel someday.

Eventually, I would write a book filled to the brim with poems, but right then, I wasn't ready. Poetry is like music, the same poem is different to everyone who reads it, and I kind of like that. I realized Gilly had finished her poem and was drawing on her paper. She wanted me to read it, so I did.

The Sweet Dreams Room
By, Gilly

My room is nice because it's pretty,
there are fairies and sparkles and leaves.
I pretend I'm a famous author,
twinkle lights when I have sweet dreams.
I like when I'm in warm pajamas,
reading with a quilt in my big comfy chair.
Fluffy pink rug, stars I can see in the night.
I listen to music and dance sometimes,
but mostly I just like to write.

Gilly had very nice handwriting for a little girl who wasn't going to be a big girl until her next birthday. Her poem brought tears to my eyes because it seemed like she had a normal life, not a care in the world. She had sunshine in her big brown eyes and it didn't seem like she was crying on the inside.

She perked up,

"Wanna see my loose tooth!?"

I smiled with my whole damn face,

"I would love to!"

Gilly adjusted herself on the chair, swallowed, and opened her mouth,

"This one!"

She wiggled one of her front teeth, and asked,

"Do you think the Tooth Fairy will come this time?"

I didn't really know her financial situation and didn't want to write figurative checks her parents couldn't cash,

"Did she come when you lost that one?"

I pointed at the space on the bottom with a big girl tooth growing in.

"No, but my mommy said it was because the Tooth Fairy had to pay rent and didn't have any extra."

She paused,

"But today is the fifteenth, so maybe she has it this time."

Oh God. I was driving an expensive car I didn't pay for and this little girl's mom didn't have money for the Tooth Fairy. I felt sick to my stomach so I tossed back a random paper cup full of goldfish crackers I found on the table. Thankfully, that's when Freida made her way over,

"Hi Gilly-girl! I didn't know I was going to see you here!"

Gilly pushed her chair back and threw her arms around Freida's midsection. I took the opportunity to dig around the bottom of my purse for some change. I folded a piece of paper into a tiny envelope and wrote 'Gilly' on it. I tucked seventy-five cents inside and folded the flap over before dropping the bundle in my purse. Gilly waved, and I waved back. A little boy was tugging at Freida's shirttails, so Gilly hugged her and ran back to the table. I swallowed my feelings down hard and pretended I remembered something,

"OH!"

Gilly looked over, I pulled out the folded wad of paper,

"This was under my pillow a while ago, and I knew it belonged to someone, so I saved it. I just realized it says Gilly on it, do you think that's you? Maybe it's for you! I bet the Tooth Fairy found money for your tooth and delivered it to the wrong house by mistake! I bet this was supposed to go under *your* pillow!"

Gilly glanced at me inquisitively, and took a step closer, I handed it over,

"Do you think that's you? Do you know any other little girls named Gilly?

She thought long and hard, and then very matter of factly replied,

"I'm the only one around here."

Her eyes lit up as she peeked in the little envelope,

"Oh, wow, there's a lot in here!"

I jumped up and down, and clapped my hands,

"How much did she bring you!?"

Gilly held her palm out, three quarters,

"That's like enough for three teeth! Holy cow!"

I giggled,

"I'm really glad I ran into you!"

She beamed up at me,

"I'm glad I ran into you too!"

I thought about having a little girl and about Opal and Chloe, and wondered if I would ever be a mom. I got sentimental for a childhood I never knew; I lived vicariously through a little girl that day. Before Gilly left, she asked if I wanted to keep her poem, and it just about brought me to my knees. She picked up a crayon, drew a smiley face, and then added googly eyes,

"I autographed it for you."

And then she leaned in,

"That's what authors do."

"Thank you, Gilly, I will cherish it."

And I meant it. As an aside, I put Gilly's poem in an antique wooden frame that night, and it's on my dresser to this day. I didn't know it then, but I Gabriella 'Gilly' Graves would be the reason I started writing again someday. In fact, that little girl inspired me to do a lot of things a little further down the line. Sometimes the stars align and you cross paths with someone who changes your life. For the first time since I moved back to Bunman, a ray of sunshine had come into my life and there weren't any strings attached.

The kids were picked up by the same parents I met at the open house, before I burned up a body and ran it through a meat grinder. I cringed. I shook hands with mothers and fathers, and waved as the kids retreated to the land of supper times and bedtime stories. We picked up the mess, wiped the tables, and ran the vacuum. Freida sat on the porch to smoked a joint and I joined her. As she blew out a stream of smoke, Freida explained,

"She's my neighbor."

"Gilly?"

Freida nodded,

"Yeah, she and her mom live in the apartment building two up from my house, what a sweetheart. Her mom, Tina, does her best to make ends meet, but its hard. Sometimes I make them a big pot of spaghetti and meatballs and bring it over, Gilly-girl loves spaghetti and meatballs, she'll eat it, breakfast, lunch, and dinner for days. Tina is about the same age as me, I think she had Gilly in high school, I can't imagine. They don't have any family around here, so I'm glad she's doing this."

We finished the joint and sat there until the high receded. She hugged me and gave me a little wave as she went for her bike. I went back inside and did one more lap around the place, making sure things were in order. The following week, I would have a couple afternoons of clay crafts. The place was already a big hit with the kids and I thought maybe the whole thing would work out. I was heading for my purse and keys when I heard a familiar voice,

"Am I too late? Did I miss it?"

I turned around to see Kane standing in the doorway. Considering our last encounter, I wasn't sure what he was doing there. He shifted from one foot to the other, his dark chocolate eyes were lonely,

"I was hoping to get here in time for you to show me around."

I forced a smile,

"Sure."

I flipped on some of the lights and gave him the grand tour. He stopped in front of me,

"You look really happy, Amelia, I'm glad."

Part of me wondered if he was telling the truth, or if he was lying. Did I look happy? Was he glad? I knew something was on his mind, but it looked like more than that, he looked drunk, or high, or something,

"Are you OK?"

Our eyes met, and I could see he was begging me to love him, I could see it in his eyes. I had love for him, in my own way, but he was skating on thin ice.

And I was feeling vulnerable, sad, and triggered by the past. He hugged me and kissed the top of my head. I brought my eyes to his and he tucked a loose curl behind my ear, my kryptonite, especially when he did it. I moved away and changed the subject,

"Look at this little girl's poem."

I handed over Gilly's poem about her room, and her innocent little childhood. Kane read it, and I could see he understood the pain it stirred up inside of me. He looked at it long after he finished reading, and then he put it on the table and tried to hug me. I smelled coffee beans, and beard oil, and his six-dollar coconut conditioner. I pulled away. He bridged the gap between us again, and our lips came close to touching before I moved my face to the side and backed away from him,

"Kane, things are complicated, I can't do this."

He stepped forward, and I took another step back. He stopped, but it looked like he was getting agitated. The next time Kane spoke, his voice was a little deeper, a little louder, and a little more emotional,

"Things are over with her, isn't that what you wanted!?"

Was he putting that on me? Their breakup? What the fuck was going on? I scrunched my eyebrows at him, and realized I was clenching my jaw,

"There was a time when that was what I wanted, but I'm with someone else now."

Kane took another step forward, I stepped back, he threw his hands around as he talked,

"Are you fucking kidding me!? Are you going to tell me that you're happy with someone like Giuseppi Moretti!?"

It seemed like he was assessing my reaction, and then he continued,

"I'm sorry it took me so long to realize how I feel about you. You were right in front of me the whole time, across the hall, making lattes next to me, why didn't I see it?"

Maybe he loved me, and maybe he was just lonely, either way, I needed to draw a line in the sand. He took another step closer and I couldn't tell if he was turned on or ready to choke me. I had never seen him like that. Maybe he was regretting the breakup, or freaking out about being alone for the first time in six years. Kane had both of us, and then he didn't have either one of us. He raised his voice a little and seemed to be panicking, tears were coming. I wasn't going to fall for it, I wasn't going to fall for his dark chocolate eyes, and his dark chocolate voice, and his six-dollar coconut conditioner. At that point, I wasn't really freaking out because it was just Kane, but I wasn't exactly comfortable having that conversation. I felt like there was a time and place for everything, and I was already raw, and poking at my wounds with a chop stick.

I caught movement in the door, made eye contact with Seppi, and gave him a low wave. That was about the time Kane took one more step toward me, closing the gap completely,

"I love you, Amelia,"

He bent to kiss me, and I don't have to tell you that he probably shit his pants when Seppi clamped down on his shoulder, offering a couple words of wisdom,

"Watch yourself, pal."

Kane's adam's apple bobbed up and down as he swallowed. He took a step back and turned to Seppi,

"I didn't mean anything...I...I was just..."

Seppi doesn't play like that, and Kane Buchanan is not equipped to get into a dick swinging contest with him, literally or figuratively. Seppi put one hand on each of Kane's shoulders and looked up at him.

"I know what you were trying to do, buddy, and unless you want to end up in the ground, I suggest you find a new hobby. Amelia is mine now."

Seppi backed Kane the to the wall just like he had done with me a hundred times, but he was rougher with Kane. I wondered if anyone had ever done that to Kane before, he didn't seem like a person who got his ass kicked. Seppi held him against the wall with his body, a hand at the base of Kane's throat.

Seppi barked and it echoed off the bare walls,

"Capiche!?"

Kane just looked down at him with eyes like saucers, clearly realizing his mistake, his overstep, the feelings he should have kept inside. But he didn't say anything, and that made Seppi even angrier,

"I don't want to see you around here again, you understand me?"

Seppi pointed at the door and Kane retreated with his tail between his legs.

"Are you sure about this, Dimples?"

I went to Seppi and held the left side of his face in my hand, rubbed his cheek with my thumb. I could see the insecure parts of him, even though he pretended he was strong where I was concerned.

"I'm sure."

And I meant it.

Seppi wrapped me in his arms and kissed me deeply,

"You need to let your little friend know that it won't end well for him if he keeps it up."

He added, very matter of factly,

"You're *mine* now."

I felt like property, the belonging of a powerful man. He followed me back to the restaurant and we sat at the bar eating antipasto with pasta and Mama Moretti's marinara. We sipped expensive whiskey and I was glad my mother wasn't there because Giuseppi's Italian Ristorante doesn't serve boxed Chardonnay.

CHAPTER 23
FOR BETTER OR WORSE

LATER THAT WEEK, I woke to Seppi talking to Indie. I looked out the sliding door to see her standing on the table. Seppi was hand-feeding her tiny pieces of fried egg and cheddar cheese. I made myself a latte and joined the party on the balcony. Birds circled the feeders and the wind chimes sang their songs. I squeezed Seppi's fingers across the table and with my free hand, I snagged what was left on his plate. I liked my life, I liked waking up to that, and I liked waking up to him. I showered and then scrutinized my reflection in the mirror, I leaned in and looked myself in the eye. I could no longer see the person I had been the day I rolled into Bunman, and I didn't even know if she was still in there. A year and a half had changed everything.

Seppi got ready for the day and I helped him pick out a nice outfit for the Downtown Partnership dinner he would be attending that evening. Most of his clothes had the same mob boss aesthetic, but he dug out a pair of tan slacks that transformed his look, a little less mob boss, and a little more local businessman. We stood in his huge closet and kissed, running late again, so it was nothing more than kissing that time, but it set my soul on fire and I wanted more. I put a mental pin in it and would have to wait until we were back home that night.

The day was nothing out of the ordinary, besides the pep-talk I gave Seppi about the dinner that night. It was unsettling to see him that anxious but I understood. His family was a big deal in that town, and most of the time people went the other way. Even as a kid, Seppi got the cold shoulder from people, just because he was a Moretti. And here he was, preparing to become one of the fold, just a broken little boy in a pair of tan slacks and his buttons buttoned for a change. He had a clean shave and a hair cut, and something about that costume made him look like a nerd. I guess it's like if you see a nurse in her scrubs all the time, and then you see her in sweatpants. And as he stood there, inspecting his reflection in the full-length mirror for the seventh time, I caught a glimpse of the broken little boy.

It was a reminder that we all have a past, a reminder that we all have things that broke us a little, or maybe a lot. But as I sat in the chair across the desk from his, watching him being confidently insecure, it reminded me that he is just a man, and not a superhuman. Sometimes, I still forget that. After all this time, after more than a decade of knowing him, once in a while, I forget he isn't untouchable, I forget he isn't immortal. And you'd think that after all this time, maybe I'd know him enough that I'd know better, but there is always a broken little boy just under the surface. Being someone with childhood trauma makes me so much more understanding of what he went through, it's that thing about finding the puzzle piece that fits next to yours. And sometimes, like when he was having stage fright, I'd remember how much we needed each other. You know how it is, sometimes life gets in the way, I went to him and touched his arm,

"You look really nice, babe."

Seppi didn't take his eyes from the mirror, as he held first, one tie, and then another in front of his shirt,

"Which one do you think?"

I turned to face him, pulled the ties out of his hand, and tossed them over my shoulder. I stepped back to give him a once over, unbuttoned the top button of his shirt and then moved to the cuffs,

"I think you should be yourself and not some watered-down facade."

I put my hands on his shoulders,

"Listen, they invited Giuseppi Moretti so give them Giuseppi Moretti, not Crispin Maffettone, a professional pocket protector collector who gets black out drunk on Appletinis. Capiche?"

Seppi smiled with his whole damn face and put his forehead to mine. In the voice he saved for me,

"I like sharing my life with you, Dimples, you're good for me. You don't put up with my shit."

I closed my eyes and smiled with my whole damn heart as a tear rolled into my cleavage. Just maybe I had found my person, the yin to my yang, the moon to my sun. When Seppi left for the dinner, I kissed him goodbye at the back door and he waved back at me as he got into the Escalade. It reminded me of my Gramma waving from the porch with a hanky when we backed out of her driveway.

I managed the chaos while Vinny banged around somewhere, he was probably getting high with one of the chefs. Anyway, before we opened the house for the night, I gave myself a once over. My hair looked great, my mascara made it through the day without any major meltdowns to contend with. My charcoal gray suit flattered my curves and the blush camisole reminded me of the day I met Isabella Rossi. I had been hoodwinked, or seduced, or whatever you want to call it. I was all in. I put on another coat of lipstick and spun around in a mist of Coco Mademoiselle before going to the front of the house like a bad ass. It was time for the show, and I was the host.

Eventually, the smiles and cheek kisses wear on me and I go on overload. I just don't like people that much, it's nothing personal. I hopped on a bar stool and fingered a carved wooden bowl for the last three pieces of popcorn. The bartender, a guy named Joey, poured me a whiskey and slid it across the shellacked hardwood bar on a square napkin. He winked at me, I winked back. Joey was gayer than a two-dollar bill, as my dad would say. But he wasn't flamboyant, or one of those gay guys who make it their whole personality. He was one of those men who was manly without being chauvinistic about it. He has a soft-side but can throw a belligerent drunk out on the sidewalk if needed. I blew him a kiss and he pretended to catch it. He bit my kiss like an apple and pretended to gag, grabbed his throat like he was choking, and threw himself on the floor behind the bar. I leaned over the bar, peered down at him, and flipped him off. Joey sprung to his feet and blew me a kiss. I caught his kiss as it flew over my head, hopped off the stool, and proceeded to wipe my ass with it. He flipped me off.

We pulled it together as a breathtakingly beautiful woman approached the barstool next to mine. Joey moved his eyes from mine, to the beautiful woman, and back. I shrugged and went palms up, I hadn't seen her before either. She seemed hectic and manic and out of sorts. Joey moved his eyes to mine and wiped his nose with his finger. He complimented her blouse and designer handbag, it was obvious she had money. She had shiny dark hair that looked like she frequented high-end salons. Her teeth were perfect, she had pretty fake eyelashes, beautiful brown eyes, and looked Italian. She ordered a double of vodka and a glass of well-aged Cabernet Sauvignon. Joey slid the wine glass and vodka across the bar on a little square napkin. She picked around in the bowl and chewed a burnt popcorn kernel. She was inside her own head and I could relate. She was one of those women who woke up looking prettier than I do after an hour of goat-hair plucking and concealer. She also seemed to be the tiniest bit unhinged. OK, she seemed a lot unhinged, and I had never known anyone who did cocaine.

I had a really nice conversation with the woman and we could relate on a lot of levels. Her name was Giulianna and I thought that suited her. Apparently, there was a death in her family and whoever died, left something with their estate lawyer for her ex-husband. I asked if she was on good terms with her ex and she shrugged. I told her my ex and his whore had a lovechild. She told me she understood why I needed to move and she talked with her hands. Giulianna finished her wine and slid the glass to Joey's side of the bar, he filled it and slid it back. She seemed sad or tormented or something else entirely. I felt like I knew her, I felt like I *was* her, minus the cocaine and whatever else she was taking. I could tell the drugs and alcohol were helping, but she wasn't drunk or high, the stuff just seemed to level her out,

"I know he meant well."

She waved her hand at the empty bowl and Joey refilled it,

"But it felt like he didn't have time for me."

I made a face like I understood.

"My in-laws were bat-shit crazy, especially my father-in-law, he was a real piece of shit. Why can't people just be decent?"

I told her about my life, and she told me about hers. She said she always wondered if her ex found someone new and I told her I wonder about that too sometimes. She picked at the popcorn and took a sip of her fresh glass of wine,

"Anyway, this is kind of a surprise visit. I came to Vermont for the reading of my uncle's will and I figure I might as well get this over with while I'm at it. Besides, maybe he's changed."

I wondered what it would be like to have an ex-husband and ex-in-laws. I wondered if her ex was horrible, maybe he didn't have time for her because he was off committing crimes, or screwing his secretary. It would be awkward to see someone after all that time, just to tell him that her uncle left something for him. Numbers and shapes swirled around in my head and I think I smelled smoke. Giulianna patted her mouth with the napkin, and I noticed she had pretty lips too.

She tucked a lock of hair behind her ear and licked her lips, she couldn't sit still. Giulianna was wearing one carat diamond studs in her ears and had a fancy looking nose ring with a diamond in it. I moved my eyes to her left hand and there was a solitaire on her ring finger, three carats if I had to guess, maybe more. She had freckles that lent a Mandy Moore vibe and I was there for it. I had my chin on my fist, listening to her talk about Manhattan. She was the epitome of being put together, besides the nose candy. Her nails were fingertip length and painted with taupe polish. Her breasts were the perfect size, a little smaller and a little perkier than mine. I subconsciously adjusted my bra and felt like my boobs were saggy. Call me, good ole 'droopy boobs.' I broke into a mental rendition of 'do your boobs hang low, do they wobble to and fro.' Giulianna stared at the stem of her wineglass,

"Sometimes I wonder if maybe it would be different if we tried again."

She held out the large solitaire,

"I'm engaged, but I just mean I think about it sometimes."

Giulianna slid the glass back to Joey and continued as she waited for her refill. She pulled a bottle out of her purse and washed a yellow pill down with her red wine. I don't think it was physically possible for that woman to sit still. If her hand wasn't moving, she was jiggling her foot, or bouncing her knee,

"We really loved each other I think, life just got in the way. We were married in front of my in-law's beach house, I had this beautiful gown, everything was perfect. I'm hoping to dig out our old photo albums while I'm here, maybe he'll look at the pictures and he'll remember how he felt about me."

"That sounds nice."

She played with her little square napkin,

"Our families don't get along very well, which caused constant tension. My father-in-law was just so awful and he had my husband on a short leash."

She waved her hand again,

"He works in the family business and my family is in the same business but is a little higher up on the food chain. My husband never felt like he was good enough."

I hoped she and her ex would get a chance to talk, maybe they would get a second chance. Maybe they would look at their wedding album and rekindle dormant feelings, maybe they had both grown. I slid my glass to Joey, he refilled it and slid it back, all while immersed in a debate with Giulianna about thin crust or thick crust. There was no doubt Giulianna was on something, her personality changed as the alcohol ebbed and flowed with whatever else was in her system, and the yellow pill began to calm her. I caught movement in the hall and gave Vinny a low wave as he approached. He stood on my left and Joey slid a whiskey across the bar to him, no little square napkin.

Vinny tossed it back and slid the glass to Joey for a refill. Vinny's eyes moved to the woman on the stool next to me and it looked like he had seen a ghost. I shook my head, went palms up, and mouthed, 'what?' Vinny grabbed my wrist and speed-walked to Seppi's office with me trailing behind him. He stood with his back against the door, muttering to himself. And then he started biting his fingernails and spitting the shards to the floor like a savage. He gestured,

"You might want to sit down."

I sat and spun the chair so I could watch Vinny pace back and forth, chewing his fingers to bloody stumps. I waved my arms over my head to get his attention,

"YO!"

He stopped and looked at me, I said,

"What is it? I'm sitting down!"

Vinny lit a cigarette and blew smoke through his nose as he stared into his empty glass. I had been in some pretty sketchy situations with Vinny and I had never seen him act like that, it wasn't instilling much confidence. He plopped in Seppi's chair and opened his mouth to say something, but all he could managed was,

"Umm."

CHAPTER 24
WASBAND

VINNY SAT SILENT, incapable of finding his words, his eyes rolling around in their sockets. It was as if he had just seen a ghost and I snapped my fingers at him,

"Hey! Over here!"

Vinny met my eyes and proceeded to go into a full-on panic. Vincenzo Nunzio Moretti is someone who nonchalantly dumps bodies on the regular, so the fact that he was panicking was making me panic. He was having a fit of some sort, something akin to some of the fits I've had. He tossed some whiskey down the hatch, slammed the glass upside down on the desk, and dialed someone. I waited impatiently as Vinny left a voicemail,

"Dude, your crazy ex is at the ristorante!"

Vinny tossed his phone as if it was the hot potato. He retrieved it from the Oriental rug and left another voicemail,

"Dude, don't come by!"

I started fantasized about the whiskey waiting for me at the bar,

"What the fuck is going on here, Vin!?"

He fished another cigarette from the pocket of his leather jacket and lit it with his fancy gold Zippo. He pinched the bridge of his nose and blew smoke through his nostrils. I thumbed toward the door,

"Is that your friend's ex or something? She's here to talk to her wasband about something her uncle left for him when he died."

He moved his eyes to mine, question marks over his head,

"Her wasband?"

Very matter of factly, I gestured at the air,

"Yeah, the person *was* her *husband* and now he's not, he's her wasband."

I was getting impatient. I had forfeited a perfectly good glass of whiskey in exchange for watching Vincenzo Moretti spin his wheels. I got up and went for the door,

"Let me know when you remember how to string words together into a coherent sentence, I'll be at the bar talking to your friend's breathtakingly beautiful and moderately unstable ex."

Vinny clamped onto my arm,

"Stop!"

I spun around and as soon as our eyes met, I knew. I knew before he told me, but I hoped I was wrong. He dropped the bomb,

"That's Seppi's ex-wife, Giulianna Genovese."

Goddammit. My heart raced and things got sparkly. I did a u-turn and plopped in the chair like I had been punched in the gut. I put my head between my knees and hyperventilated, I had just changed my mailing address that morning. Vinny brought me a bubbly water and sat on the desk in front of me,

"Amelia, I'm sorry, but it's worse than that. The Genovese family is big-time mob. You think my father was a tyrant, you should meet Valentino Genovese, this isn't good!"

I waved him away,

"No, her dead uncle just left something for Seppi."

I paused and then gestured nonchalantly,

"Well, and she mentioned wanting to look through old photo albums or something."

He acted like his ass was on fire, flailing,

"Amelia, she's bat shit crazy! She's mentally unstable and does coke, she mixes benzos and alcohol! She's self-destructive and suicidal half the time! And she has a way of twisting things, and playing the victim, she's bad news!"

I went palms up and grasped at a straw,

"People change."

He shook his head,

"I was thirteen when they got married. I was an usher, and I remember this absolute freak out over the sea green bow ties being too green! It was fucked, *she's* insane! You wouldn't believe the bridezilla-level tantrums she threw. Seppi would tell me, 'whatever you do, don't mention the wedding around Jules. she'll never shut up!'"

He amped up a little more,

"Amelia, I love you like a sister here and, ahh, that bitch is fucking nuts, you should lay low or some shit until she's gone!"

I tried to be the rational one even though I was about to shit my thousand-dollar pantsuit,

"Relax, it's fine."

His hands flew around in the air,

"Sometimes Memory Lane needs to have a dead end, capiche!? She has profound insecurities and the nose candy gives her a false sense of reality, especially mixed with everything else. She could have called my brother, or sent him a text, she didn't need to come here. She's full of shit. She'll pull her mafia princess bullshit."

He looked like a light bulb went off over his head and he started shoving me toward the door,

"I know, lock yourself in your office until closing!"

I countered with,

"What are you doing, dude? Calm the fuck down! You should see the rock on her finger, she's clearly engaged to some rich guy!"

Vinny put his hands on my shoulders again,

"You need to be prepared for shit to hit the fan."

I opened Seppi's office and peered into the hall, I could hear her laughing from her place at the bar. I swiped around the bottom of my bag, retrieved the panic button, and pushed it for three seconds. Twenty seconds later my phone rang,

"Seppi!?"

In a hushed tone,

"Are you OK, Amelia!?"

There were glasses clinking, silverware hitting plates, and the low hum of ambient conversations. I had abused my panic button privilege, so I lied,

"I'm sorry, Seppi, I pushed it by mistake. I'm OK."

The call ended. Little did I know that at that very moment, Giuseppi Moretti and his rolled up cuffs were being praised for the generous contributions to downtown Bunman. Seppi was thanked for his sizable donation to the community studio. And most of all, he was being showered with gratitude for being one of the good guys. Little did they know that his sizable donation had already cremated a body. Boy did he have everyone inadvertently fooled. And for a second, I convinced myself that all of this was normal, that all of this nonsense was above-board.

I went back to Seppi's office and deflated into the chair across the desk. By then, Vinny was sitting in Seppi's chair, staring at his empty glass of whiskey like it was going to give him guidance. He lit another cigarette and I accepted when he offered me one. Vinny leaned across the desk and lit it with his fancy gold Zippo. I let the poison hit my system,

"Whatever, people have exes. I'm not going to worry about this, she seems nice and she just stopped by to tell him something."

When I was finished with the cigarette, I went to the door and he didn't stop me, I turned to him before I went out,

"You know, sometimes there's not some major catastrophe looming in the shadows, sometimes you can take things at face value. I think you're blowing things out of proportion."

Famous last words.

I went to the front of the house, did a lap to make sure everyone was enjoying their meals. I shook some hands, gave some cheek kisses, and made my way back to the bar. I hopped onto my stool and a half hour later, the back door swung open. Seppi's keys hit the desk and I followed him with my eyes as he approached. His face seemed happy, the weight of the world had been lifted a little. He hadn't listened to his voicemails and hadn't crossed paths with Vinny between there and here. Maybe Vinny was wrong. It had been a long time, maybe she was just someone who looked like Seppi's ex, maybe it was a coincidence they had the same name. Seppi put his arm around my shoulder and kissed my temple, I nestled into his chest and breathed in the scent of him. Joey and Giulianna were debating tie up versus slip-on sneakers. She tossed her head back and let out a bark of laughter,

"Oh my God, you're a gas!"

Seppi stopped breathing. Shit. That was the moment he realized his ex-wife was at Giuseppi's Italian Ristorante, and I felt the trapdoor close. He pulled free from my body and went to hers,

"What are you doing here, Jules?"

Giulianna spun around,

"That's not very nice."

She looked like one of those cartoon bad guys, deep in thought about how she was going to blow something up. Her eyes were dark and mean, and it looked like she was holding the cards,

"I'm here to take a walk down memory lane."

He didn't kiss her on both cheeks or hug her, it was clear that he wasn't happy to see her,

"Why are you in my restaurant?"

She glared at him and he turned to me,

"Excuse us for a moment."

Seppi grabbed Giulianna by the armpit and maneuvered her toward his office. She trotted along behind him in her expensive leather pumps and mafia princess aesthetic. Joey and I made eye contact when the door slammed. The ristorante and bar closed, the staff went home and I sat in my office waiting for Seppi. He would follow me back to the land of mafia mansions and feeling like you're in the Twilight Zone because your mob boss boyfriend's crazy ex showed up. I swung my head to the hallway when the office door finally opened and Giulianna strode down the hall like she owned the place. The back door opened and closed. Finally. I stood and hollered,

"Geez, what the fuck was that all about!?"

Seppi appeared in my doorway and I did the crazy sign next to my ear. It took him a while to say anything, so I winked and added,

"I'm looking forward to finishing what we started this morning."

Seppi's jaw tightened,

"You'll need to stay at your place tonight."

And just like that, things changed. I woke up that morning, had a latte on the balcony, and then went to the post office to change my address. It was late and Opal was probably sleeping, hopefully she was sleeping. My mind raced. I was letting my thoughts go into catastrophic places and texted her, even though I was sure Seppi and I would work it out, and he'd follow me back to mafia mansion land.

"That woman is my ex-wife. We need to discuss some things, and if memory serves, it's going to take a while."

I didn't say anything. I wrapped my arms around him but he stood with his hands balled into fists at his sides. I kissed him on the cheek and it felt like I didn't even know him, like it had all been a dream,

"I love you, Giuseppi."

I waited but he didn't say it back. I dropped my eyes and went out the back door with my tail between my legs. As I crossed the parking lot to my porch, I heard dog tags jingling and looked over to see Kane and Lola in the back yard. He waved and I waved back. I went over and sat in one of the Adirondack chairs that circled the fire pit, staring at the burnt corner of a brick. Kane sat in the chair across from mine and Lola curled up at his feet. And then we just looked at each other for a while.

The back door of the restaurant slammed open and shut, and the alarm system engaged. I sat under the cloak of darkness and followed Seppi with my eyes as he climbed into the Escalade. He sat there for a while and the screen of my phone lit up. He backed out of his space and spit up some gravel, on his way up the alley. I glanced at my phone, 'Ti amo.' But that time, it felt hollow, or like it lead to a dead end. But maybe he would change his mind, maybe he would throw it in reverse and come back for me, but he didn't. As his taillights turned and disappeared, the wind was knocked out of my sails. What I thought was, was not. What I had envisioned, had been a naïve fairy tale of a sexy powerful mob boss and a stupid twenty something with no filter, gorgeous ringlets, and one and a half dimples. Kane knew me well enough to know something big happened, and that I was trying to figure out how I felt about it.

"Doesn't he usually follow you back to the secret lair?"

My phone vibrated again, it was Opal. She said the baby was sleeping, to be quiet when I came in, and that she would see me in the morning. There was a pillow and quilt on the couch, and a new toothbrush on the bathroom sink. If I was sleeping at my apartment, I wasn't sleeping with Seppi. It meant that when I got up that morning and sipped a latte on the balcony, maybe it was the last time. What if they got back together? I mean, they had been married for crying out loud. I sighed,

"A beautiful woman came into the restaurant tonight, and it turns out, she's Seppi's ex-wife."

Kane raised his eyebrows and said,

"Look, I know you're probably spiraling and feeling like she's got her shit together more than you do and that he's going to get back together with her."

I looked him dead in the face and waited,

"But exes are exes for a reason, maybe they just have some loose ends to tie up."

Giulianna Genovese seemed nice, but I've been fooled before. You know what they say, fool me once, shame on you. Fool me twice, three times if you want, I'm on the slow side. Maybe she was acting, like when someone sleazy runs for office or tries to sell you a piece of shit used car that won't last a week. Maybe I wasn't such a good judge of character after all. Kane gestured toward the porch,

"Wanna come up for a nightcap?"

Why not, what did I have to lose by having a drink, and probably some really good weed, with Kane. He was safe.

"Sure, that sounds nice."

And I meant it. It was familiar and comfortable. It felt like the world wasn't spinning as fast when I was with Kane. It felt like maple oat lattes, acoustic guitars, and six-dollar coconut conditioner. We ascended the stairs to the apartments. I texted Opal that I might be a while and that I had a key. It hadn't been long, but there was a different vibe in his apartment and I couldn't put my finger on it. Maybe it was the smell of untapped testosterone or maybe Alex's perfume has finally faded for the last time. Kane poured two glasses of wine and made a small charcuterie tray as I spun around in my head. I carried things to the sun porch and we sat, staring out over the back yard. The mini mafia sedan sat all alone in its spot next to Seppi's. I sipped my wine to dull the pain.

Kane put on some records and we sat in the cool evening air on the sun porch, finishing a bottle of wine and every last bit of sharp cheddar cheese and berries. We shared a joint and that's what took away the barrier. We talked about life, and feelings, and exes.

We had both been in situations where we thought something was one thing, but it was really something else. By the end of the night, we were sitting side by side, his arm around me, my head resting in the crook of his armpit. I let out a big sigh, and released more tension than I realized I'd been holding.

Kane kissed me on the cheek and when I smiled up at him a little, he tucked a loose curl behind my ear. He knew that drove me crazy, and I knew we needed each other, I had him and he had me. It was really late, we were both a little drunk and a little high. I stood in his bathroom mirror, staring at myself, trying to make the right decision. When I came back from the bathroom,

"I should probably get going before we do something we'll regret."

But the more I thought about it, that might have been the first time we were both free. I was sure things would never be the same with Seppi. We stood there looking into each other's eyes, the safe comfortable place beckoning me between his sheets for some vanilla sex. The world without bullets, and bodies, and ex-wives. Kane wrapped me up in his arms, and kissed the top of the head before opening the door. I turned to him and waved before I tiptoed into my apartment.

CHAPTER 25
BACK TO LIFE, BACK TO REALITY

AT FIVE THIRTY-SIX in the morning, Opal and the baby came out of the bedroom. I sat up and Opal nestled into the warm spot where I'd been laying. There was a long silence with nothing more than the sound of Chloe suckling at Opal's teet. There I was, wondering if it would be acceptable for me to crawl into the dark recesses of my mind instead of facing the day. I went into 'my' room and assessed the closet situation. It was still a mess, I'm not sure what I was expecting. Opal's dresses and skirts were on the right, my vintage overalls and other miscellaneous thrifted jeans, dresses, and sweaters were on the left. Of course there was a pile of clothes on the floor in there too, I'm not a big fan of dressers, they annoy me. My eyes landed on the green velvet dress I wore on

Christmas Eve, the night Seppi danced with me in his office, before he was mine. I tried to stay calm but the world was spinning. I sat on that pile of miscellaneous garments and had a good cry.

Surrounded by secondhand clothes, I made a decision. It might have been rash, or it might have been the best decision I ever made. I pulled my favorite overalls off the hanger and held them to my chest like an old friend. I had inadvertently abandoned the sentimental thrift store hippie. And all at once, I realized I preferred this world over that one. Life was not greener on the other side, it was dark and scary and disgusting. A naive and traumatized twenty-something with no filter, had no business sharing space with the patriarch of a mob family. I could never compete with Giulianna Genovese and I knew it.

I showered and ran some of my sister's curl cream through my hair, let it air dry a little, and smashed it into a disaster on the top of my head. I dug through the bin of makeup I'd left behind when I went to live in the land of mafia mansions and alternate realities. I swiped on some waterproof mascara and pulled my ratty vintage overalls over a fitted white half shirt. I slid into an old pair of dingy white Chuck Taylors and they felt like a long-lost friend. Opal glanced up at me and noticed the tattered overalls,

"I see you pulled out your security blanket, are you trying to make a difficult decision or something?"

I made lattes and sat next to her on the couch. Opal handed Chloe over, she snuggled into me and I sniffed her head. The scent calmed me and stirred the part of me I never felt until I became an aunt. I took a sip of my latte, and licked steamed milk from my top lip,

"You could say that."

Opal put her hand on my knee,

"Why did you sleep here last night?"

I answered her question in a roundabout way,

"I woke up yesterday and it was a normal day. I sat on the balcony with him and watched the birds circle the feeders. Seppi followed me into town like usual. He was invited to a dinner last night and he wore these tan slacks."

Opal cut me off, her eyes wide,

"Giuseppi Moretti owns a pair of tan slacks?"

I nodded,

"Yeah, and he looked like a fish out of water. I even caught him trying to pick out which tie to wear."

She recoiled in horror and clutched her beaded hemp necklace,

"A tie!? Gross!"

"I know! He had all of his buttons buttoned too. I told him, they invited Giuseppi Moretti, give them Giuseppi Moretti. He unbuttoned and rolled up, but he wouldn't change out of the pants."

Opal shrugged and went palms up, I went on,

"I managed front of house last night and when there was a lull, I grabbed a drink with Joey. We were up to our usual shit when this drop-dead gorgeous sex-pot hopped onto the stool next to mine. I've never seen a woman like that in person. Anyway, we had a couple drinks, talked about life the way you do with the stranger on the barstool next to you, no filter."

Opal leaned forward,

"Who was the woman, was it someone famous disguised as a regular Joe?"

I shook my head,

"She told me she was here for the reading of her uncle's will and he left something for her ex-husband."

Something went dark in Opal's eyes and I think she knew it wasn't good. I continued,

"Vinny saw the woman, dragged me into Seppi's office, and told me it's Seppi's ex-wife."

Opal gasped and made a face, even though I think she tried not to, her eyes went wide,

"She's here!? Like, here!?"

I raised my eyebrows at her,

"Buckle up, it gets worse. I had to sleep here last night because she went to his house for a 'long talk' and I never heard from him after that.'"

I was afraid I knew what 'long talk,' was code for, and wondered if Giulianna cashed in my rain check. It's strange because I cared but I didn't, it was almost like I'd dodged a bullet, figuratively. Well, you know that's bullshit, I really cared, but the part of me that cared was locked up tight in one of the filing cabinets in the back of my head where I put things I don't want to think about. Opal leaned forward and talked with her hands, made horns on the top of her head,

"She's the devil! She needs to be as far away from here as possible. She's rich and powerful, and she's incredibly unstable. Her last name is Genovese."

I shrugged and went palms up, that didn't mean anything to me,

"The Genovese family is big-time mob. I'm not saying the Morettis aren't a legitimate mob family, but in the grand scheme, the Morettis are mafia-lite. The Genovese family is hard core mafia like the Gottis and the Gambinos, bullet in the back of your head without batting an eyelash mafia."

I swallowed hard, Opal continued,

"There was a beef between the Genovese family and the Morettis, I think Sal owed money or favors to cover some gambling debt he owed. Seppi mentioned he was afraid the Genovese family would assume Sal went MIA to escape his debt. If that was the case, they could send a goon to capture and torture someone close to Seppi as a way to force him to give up Sal's location. Seppi isn't about to tell them that his father is toe-up with the plankton."

I was spiraling, too much information was flying around in my overflowing mind. I was so naïve. But when it comes to the mob, there's always someone waiting in the wings to take your place if you fuck up.

I haven't seen it personally, but I bet it's like a dark and deadly game of musical chairs, except everyone is packing heat. I was a normal girl with stretch marks and a pooch, Giulianna Genovese was one of those women who probably got her crotch waxed and her asshole bleached. I'd been deep in disguise, strutting around in leather heels, drinking well-aged whiskey, wearing expensive tailored pantsuits, driving the mini mafia sedan. As if an invisible foot had kicked me in the ass.

"I'm going to quit."

Opal scrunched her brows and sneered,

"Say what now!?"

I handed her the baby, jumped up like my ass was on fire, and paced, talking with my hands,

"I made a mistake, that's all. Nothing I can't fix."

I sat down hard and then sprung up again,

"I want my old life back. Not my old-old life, but the life I had before I got involved in all this."

Maybe Seppi didn't even exist, maybe this whole thing had been a fever dream. Chloe made little sounds as she slept, and it snapped me out of my PTSD-fueled delusion. I let it sink in that I had slept with a fucking mob boss, like a lot. Oh my God, what if I was pregnant with his kid!? What the fuck!? I grabbed my head like a lunatic and started spinning, like the lady in The Sound of Music. Don't ask, I have no idea. Anyway, that's fine. It's fine that I was in a sexual relationship with a fucking mob boss. What the hell was I thinking? I thought about Giulianna Genovese, you should see her, we don't even rate in the same hemisphere! I would do her and I'm not even into women! I put my head between my knees and Opal put her hand on my back, rhetorically,

"You gonna bail?"

"You bet your ass, I'm getting the fuck out of here, pronto! I'm over it."

She handed me a can of lemon seltzer. I drank half of it and woke the baby with an epic burp, I continued,

"This isn't my life any more than it was yours. I've traded my ratty vintage overalls and dingy white Chuck Taylors for tailored suits and heeled leather boots. I wear expensive perfume and drive a Cadillac with leather interior and vanity plates. I have a panic button I can push, and most of the time, the patriarch of a mob family comes running!"

I was in full panic mode and Opal pointed toward the sun porch,

"Go rip a doobie, you're making me anxious and Chloe will feel it when she eats."

I grabbed my thrifted flip-top tin and moved my pity party panic attack to my sun porch. While I was out there self-medicating, I followed Kane with my eyes as he went to the dumpster. He spun around and reversed course, I shouted to him,

"Hey!'

He stopped in his tracks and look up at the sun porch,

"Guess what?"

He smiled and gestured toward the Indian Scout parked next to his bike,

"You passed your endorsement?"

"Yup!"

"We'll have to go riding sometime, there are some beautiful spots around here."

There was an amalgamation of emotions in that moment. If I had started riding sooner, I would have had something with Kane that Alex did not. I imagined riding our bikes to a secluded place, messing around before we made the trip back home. I wondered if we'd get the chance now that Seppi had dropped me like a hot potato. I went into the living room, high on weed, motivated to make hasty decisions, I plopped on the futon and pulled on my sneakers,

"I have to do a couple things, I'll be back."

Opal hollered after me as I went out the door,

"Don't do anything stupid."

I bounced down the stairs to Muddy Waters and leaned into Kane's office, he finished a call and gestured me in. I sat in the chair across the desk from him, it wasn't expensive or made of leather, it was wooden and wobbly and had chipped paint. He found it at a yard sale and thought it had character. I glanced over at him and let out a sigh. His dark chocolate eyes still looked at me the same way,

"You OK?"

I nodded,

"A girl I know is looking for some barista work, do you have anything available?"

He doodled on his desk calendar,

"I'm making do but it would be great to have another barista. What's her number, I'll reach out and see if she wants to come for an interview."

I acted like I was trying to remember the person's name,

"She's really cool, I've known her my whole life."

Kane had shit to do,

"OK, great, what's your friend's name and number? I'll get in touch with her about an interview."

"Her name is Amelia."

He wrote 'Amelia' on some free space next to the month, and chuckled,

"I've never met a single Amelia in my whole life up until I met you and now I'm going to know two. I hope she isn't as nut-so as you are."

Kane winked at me and waited with his pen. I could have dicked him around for a lot longer but I had something else I needed to do,

"Her last name is Birch."

He started writing and then put his pen down and looked at me, gesturing toward the ristorante,

"Don't you work for Tony Soprano?"

I made a face,

"Yes, but I'm quitting."

"What!?"

I repeated myself,

"I am currently Seppi's Event Planner but I'm quitting."

A worried looked crept over his face,

"Do you think that's a good idea, Amelia?"

"Seppi's ex-wife is here and he told me I should sleep at my apartment last night so they could talk. I sent him a text last night and he still hasn't replied."

Kane's eyes went like saucers,

"Are you sure he isn't dead in a ditch!?"

I nodded,

"Yeah, someone would have told me."

"OK, but that's not a reason to quit your job! As much as I don't want you with, or working for, Giuseppi Moretti, it's solid work. He's paying you big bucks, gave you a car and he comes to your rescue whenever you push that button. I can't protect you they way he can."

Kane shifted in his chair,

"Look, the thought of you sleeping with that man just about kills me, but he's powerful, he's rich, and he can pull a lot of strings. He'll make her go away, be patient."

I closed his office door and sat in the wobbly chair hugging my knees to my chest while big fat tears fell onto my ratty vintage overalls. Kane knelt in front of me, tucked a loose curl behind my ear and tried to change the subject,

"I haven't seen you wear your hair all crazy like this in a long time, it looks cute."

"Thanks, I used Opal's curl cream."

He put his hand on my knee and rubbed the sliver of skin peeking through the shredded denim,

"What else is going on, Amelia?"

I moved my eyes to his and knew that what I was going to say next would change our relationship, it would change the way he looked at me but I said it anyway,

"Remember when you asked me if I killed Salvatore Moretti?"

Kane stood and waved his hands around as he talked,

"Yeah, I'm sorry about that. I just…things were weird and I wasn't thinking straight."

We made eye contact,

"Kane, I killed him. I beat him to death with a shovel after he shot me in the shoulder."

Kane had a thousand-yard stare as everything registered. He pulled me out of the chair and held my body close to his, there were tears in his voice,

"I am so sorry."

It didn't make sense, I killed a man and people were telling me I did the world a favor. They were sorry I had to experience it. I had people in my life who would die for me and people who would give me a place to stay, no questions asked. I had people who would drop everything if my heart was broken, people who loved me, and none of them were my mother. I was floating around in a soup of overwhelm, this Twilight Zone of realization, of putting two and two together. I was just a little girl who wanted to be loved and protected.

Once Kane was back in his chair, I pulled my phone out and texted my aunt Maggie. I had the Scout but I wasn't ready to use it as my only mode of transportation. Maggie and Clem were on their way back home in the RV but I was hoping I could use her vintage powder blue VW Beetle in the meantime. Maggie quickly replied, 'Of course.' Just like that, no questions asked, one more person who loved me unconditionally. Maybe I wasn't worthless after all, even if my mother didn't see it. I felt the shift, I felt all the feelings. I wiped my eyes and went to the mirror, glanced at my reflection and fluffed up my hair,

"I'll be back, I need to take care of something."

I went out the back door and made my way across the parking lot to Giuseppi's Italian Ristorante. The Escalade wasn't in its spot so I punched in the code and went inside. I crossed the threshold of Seppi's office and took it all in, remembered the times we talked over whiskey, the times we made love on that sofa. I put the panic button and the key fob in his top drawer. What choice did I have? I slid the drawer shut, kissed the palm of my hand, and touched the top of his desk before I left his office.

Action is a distraction, so I put the jar of dark chocolate covered blueberries in my tote and pulled my chair out so I could unplug my laptop. My eyes fell into the seat of the chair, and my heart fell into my stomach. Nestled on the seat was a reusable shopping tote with all the things I had left at Seppi's. Even though we had come to the same conclusion, it hurt me knowing he realized it too. Or maybe this was all a dream, I'd wake up and have a latte with Seppi on his balcony. When I opened my bathroom door to get my expensive soap and jar of edibles, Indie ran out. I scooped her up and cried into the top of her head. I slung a tote over my left shoulder and a tote over my right. I hugged Indie to my chest and took one more look around the room before hitting the light switch with my elbow and going out the back door. I reset the alarm and retreated to the world of maple oat lattes.

I went back to my apartment and Indie ran straight for her spot. I dumped my bags on the floor and realized the place was too small for four people. As I unpacked my things, I realized I was right where I belonged. Maybe the last year had been a lesson, maybe I searched my soul and it led me back to where I started. I took in the hardwood floors and tall windows. I remembered how I had things arranged when I originally settled in. I laid on the floor and looked up at the ceiling. What was important was peace, not killing, cremating someone and then putting them in the community garden. What mattered was maple oat lattes and acoustic guitars, not expensive cars, and constant chaos. Right? I got a little too high, ate leftover pizza from Giuseppi's, and stared at the mini mafia sedan in its space behind the ristorante. I threw up in my mouth. My phone vibrated and I had an adrenaline rush, it was from Kane, 'You, OK?' I wasn't, not really. I folded the bags and slid them in the basket next to the door. I went back down the stairs to the cafe.

Kane chatted with some customers, answered the phone, and made an Americano. I don't know what I was waiting for. Finally, I went up to him and waved,

"Hey, what time can you take me to get the VW?"

He was steaming milk for a latte,

"I'm all yours after closing."

And I knew he meant it. A late morning rush fell over the cafe and I noticed Kane was the only one working the front. While he was ringing someone out, I snagged my old apron, it was black canvas with a white Muddy Waters logo. The black name tag said, 'Your barista is: Amelia.' I pulled it over my disaster of a messy bun, the one with the loose curls, the one that made me look crazy. As Kane took a large coffee order, I slid into my old place at the espresso machine and did my thing. We hadn't spoken besides 'thank yous' and 'you're welcomes,' but I knew he was happy to have me back in the saddle.

When the late morning rush ended, there was a small window of time to prep for the lunch rush. I'm not sure what Kane would have done without me, because it's impossible to make wraps and paninis in the kitchen, and make coffees, warm scones, and squeeze fresh OJ up front. In that window of time before the rush hit, in that sliver of time when it was just the two of us, he leaned over,

"Thank you."

I shrugged,

"You were in the weeds."

He shook his head,

"No, I mean, thank you for being honest about what happened. I knew deep down when you came back after, you were different, your eyes were different for a while."

I swallowed hard but didn't cry,

"It's been a lot, maybe I'll tell you about it sometime."

That was either the truth or a lie. Kane kissed the top of my head,

"I'd like that."

And that was either the truth or a lie. Just like that, the lunch rush started and we barely spoke until the wave passed. By three o'clock, we were heading to my aunt Maggie's house, I gestured on our way to the Bronco,

"Wanna take my bike?"

Kane smiled with his whole face and we trotted back inside to get our helmets. He met me in the hall with a beat up biker jacket,

"Hey, this was my first jacket. It's too small for me now. Here, give it a try."

I shrugged into Kane's old jacket and surrounded myself with the smells of warn leather. It was a real Harley jacket, black with silver hardware. I spun around in the hallway and he nodded his approval, fuck it. We trotted back down the stairs and I slammed the helmet over my crazy ringlets before swinging my leg over the Scout. Kane situated himself on the seat behind me as nerves simmered in my belly. I started her up and as I was waiting to pull out, a black Escalade was waiting to pull in. Even though there was no way Seppi would recognize me with that helmet on, my stomach dropped into my asshole and my heart pounded in my ears. My mind spiraled as a highlight reel of the last eighteen months flashed before my eyes.

Mistakes had been made, triggers had been pulled and shovels had been swung. Ropes had been tied and crowbars had been buried in skulls. I knew what it felt like to be punched in the face and left in my stocking feet in the woods with quick ties around my wrists. I knew what it was like to do a lot of things. I thought back to the night I danced with Luciano Cavallaro, I had no business dancing with someone like that. I would never be the same after all I had been through, but the people who loved me would love me anyway, and one of those people was Giuseppi Moretti. It was this disgusting yin and yang of darkness and light, this sloshing around of feelings and decisions to be made. The demons in those cages were backed against their bars as I dodged bullets and bodies, and got lost in the undertow. Tears rolled down my cheeks, swept away with the wind as we made our way to Maggie's. Love is a cruel mistress and I wanted nothing more than to be sitting on her lap. I got off the bike and Kane slid forward so he could drive it home. I went in through Maggie's front door and came out through the garage.

Kane followed me back home and I hung out at his place until Opal came knocking,

"Dinner's ready if you want to eat."

I waved to Kane and went across the hall. I took my place at the table and observed the three of them. As we devoured roasted chicken and a slew of roasted veggies, I made a decision,

"You guys should take the apartment over the studio. It's bigger, has a garage, and you guys can have a garden."

They glanced at each other and Opal said,

"Are you sure?"

I put my hand on hers,

"Opal, yes, you need it more than I do."

She got up and hugged me with the baby strapped to her chest, and since I wanted my space back sooner than later,

"Feel free to start moving things tomorrow, I can help if you want."

Auggie wiped his mouth and put his hand across the table, I took it and he said,

"Thank you, Amelia."

I nodded but just wanted things to stop changing so fast, and that brought me back to my situation with Seppi. Our hearts play games on us sometimes, we feel one thing and then we feel something else entirely. Vulnerability creeps in and we run for the hills, terrified the other person doesn't feel the same. But then one day, you realize the person you'd die for, would die for you too. You feel something you've never felt before and the energy passing between you is palpable, your entire body reacts to the sound of their voice. I had allowed myself to fall in love with someone who was larger than life, but maybe it only felt that way because he held my heart in his hands.

CHAPTER 26
DOING A DANCE

SUNNY INVITED ME over after dinner. It was a beautiful night, so I decided to walk. I took in the smells and the sounds, it was the perfect temperature as the sun made its journey to bed. It felt good to be outside, to be free of the confines of the inner sanctum. Sunny had something for me, and I wondered what it was. Maybe some thrifted earrings, or a mug she found at the new consignment shop in town. Maybe she made me some cookies. No matter what it was, I was happy to have any token of her mutual affection. Life had gotten in the way, and we needed to make more time for each other. I went down the alley between Sunny's building and the store next to it. Sunny swung the door open and gestured me in,

"What's up, fucker?"

We hugged on the threshold and chatted for a few minutes. Sunny glanced at her phone and then grabbed her keys,

"Do you need to pee before we go?"

I shook my head,

"No, I'm good."

She knew me better than that,

"Why don't you try."

So I did.

We slid into Sunny's nineteen-seventy-five Mercedes Benz. She handed me a freshly rolled joint that smelled skunky and cheesy and amazing,

"It's my latest strain, it should knock you right on your ass."

I nodded and ran the joint under my nose. I'm a lady, so I waited until we were moving before I lit it. I had no idea where we were going, but wherever it was, it appeared Sunny thought I should be high. Maybe Vincenzo told her what was going on with Giulianna and that I was back at my apartment. Or, maybe Sunny knew I quit my job and walked away from my entire life as a mini mobster. I stewed about Seppi and wondered what he was doing with that beautiful rich woman who did cocaine. I wondered if she had seduced him into making love to her. I tried to have more faith than that, I tried to have faith that he loved me. He had told me I was good for him. He had said it in passing but once the weed set in, my mind went to bad places, dark places, scary places. I panicked and turned to Sunny, shreeking,

"Is this sativa!?"

Sunny shrugged nonchalantly,

"Yeah, so?"

I took in a sharp breath and clutched my chest,

"I think I'm dying!"

She chuckled and I started hyperventilating, Eventually, she pulled over,

"Amelia, you're not dying, you're just high."

"You can't give me sativa, are you fucking nuts!? Not unless you give me a project to do!"

I paused long enough to take a big breath,

"He's fucking her, I know it, he's probably fucking her right now!"

I gagged and Sunny handed over her Coke. I took a swig, and handed it back, frantic, panicking. Sunny dug around the bottom of her purse,

"Put your hand out."

She dropped three peppercorns into my palm.

"What the fuck am I supposed to do with these?"

She shook her head like I was stupid,

"You chew them, asshole, they'll kick you out of the panic and paranoia. "

I chewed the stupid peppercorns and made sure to be dramatic about it but it helped almost immediately. Sunny glanced over,

"You good?"

I nodded,

"Yeah."

Sunny lit a cigarette and eased the car into traffic. She didn't tell me where we were going, and I didn't ask, I just enjoyed the feeling of being free from it all. We got on the highway and crossed the border into New York. A half hour later, we pulled into a snack bar that had custard ice cream. I ordered a maple creemee and Sunny got a hot fudge sundae. She led me around the building to a patio that sheltered several picnic tables. I couldn't stop thinking about Seppi and Giulianna, and how he dropped me like a hot potato. I was a regular girl. No Botox or expensive manicures, I don't wear fake lashes. I was the girl with the stretch marks who could burp louder, wheeze-laugh harder, love more passionately. I was the girl with the scars, and the questions, and the genuine heart,

"What are we doing here?"

"We're eating ice cream, fucker."

There was more to it than that, but I didn't have the mental capacity to ask any more questions. I ate my ice cream and didn't even spill any on my overalls.

Sunny drove to the lake and we sat on a shelf of slate to watch the moonlight reflect off the ripples. A couple other cars came and went, mostly people walking their dogs, but then a familiar car pulled in. Sunny waved as Vinny exited his BMW. Maybe he dumped a body in that lake for a change of pace. I turned to face the water, and the two of them sucked face behind me. Goosebumps rose to the surface a split second before I felt a familiar hand on the small of my back. I whipped my head around to see Seppi standing there. Afraid he was there to end things, I beat him to the punch. I slid off the rock and shoved Seppi square in the chest, he grabbed my wrists,

"What's the matter with you!?"

I got all teary and full of fire. I twisted my wrists and pulled them away, pointing at the middle of his chest repeatedly, voice full of feelings,

"Fuck you!"

I stormed toward the car so I could curl in a ball and have a temper tantrum. Seppi's voice pleaded,

"Amelia, wait."

I flipped him off with both hands as I walked away. I repeated myself as I approached the Mercedes, windows down, doors unlocked,

"Fuck you, dude."

Vinny reassured him,

"She'll come around, man."

Whatever, what did Vincenzo Moretti know about anything!? Idiot. Seppi grabbed my arm, and I lost my fucking mind. I yanked free and spun around. Seppi blocked my way to the car so I scoffed at him and turned around. I took a path near the water that curved into the woods. Maybe I just needed to sit on a rock and cry it out. I heard the soles of Seppi's fancy fucking oxfords on the paved path and geared up for his bullshit. I stopped walking because what was the point. About fifty feet in, Seppi caught up with me. I spun around and looked up at him, my heart broken in a million tiny little shards and I didn't have anything to put them in. Seppi reached out for me and I pulled away. He reached out for me again and wrapped his fingers around my arm, firmly, pulled me close,

"You need to listen to me, Amelia."

Whatever. I pinched the bridge of my nose and listened. He released his grip on my arm, and took my hands,

"There are two things going on here. One, Giulianna is pulling her mafia princess bullshit, trying to weasel her way back in. I promise you, that bridge burned a long time ago."

I met his eyes and took my hands out of his, moving them around frantically as I talked,

"Why are you telling me all of this? I'm out! I loved you, and you tossed me out like an apple core. I'm not going to beg you to love me, it wouldn't have worked out anyway. Go have fun with your rich ex, her bi-polar disorder, perfect tits, and cocaine addiction. I returned your stupid car and panic button"

His voice had hurt in it,

"Amelia."

"Oh, and consider this my resignation from the Event Planner position."

I wiped my hands together like I had flour on my palms,

"You're clearly on the same page since you gave me back my cat."

I looked him in the eye,

"I thought you loved that cat, or at least that's what you told her. And just like that, she's out of your life just like me."

His voice broke,

"This is bigger than me this time, Amelia. I'm on the hook for my father's debt. The Genovese family thinks I know where he is, I can't very well tell them he's somewhere off the shore of Kimbrook Beach."

He had my attention. Seppi put his hands on my shoulders and looked me in the eye,

"I need, and I mean *need,* to play the game for a while, but it's just a game, I swear."

I crossed my arms,

"What about the thing you got from Cuntypant's dead uncle?"

That surprised him so I enlightened him,

"I spent an hour drinking with her before I knew who she was. We chatted about life and she told me she was here about her uncle's will. She also said he left something for her ex-husband."

Seppi paced and talked with his hands,

"I'm working on a plan to get her father the money but it's going to take a little time. I don't want to give that family the impression that you're the person to hold hostage as collateral. They are not good people, Amelia. You're not equipped to be kidnapped and tortured by the Genovese family, trust me. I've heard stories about what they do to women."

My voice went up an octave,

"What!?"

Seppi moved his hands to mine and I pulled them away. Tears overflowed with a combination of rage and heartbreak, I put my hands on my hips,

"For your information, I didn't mention your name and neither did she. God, get over yourself. She has no idea you and I are...were together."

"Amelia, listen, it's complicated, I need you to trust me. Do you trust me?"

I looked up at him and didn't know how to answer the question. I trusted him with my life. Seppi touched my face in the way he always did and it all came crashing down around me. If he kept his distance, maybe the focus wouldn't end up on me, maybe the hammer would fall on him instead. Maybe I wouldn't be the target of another attack, and maybe I wouldn't be placed in another kill or be killed situation. Seppi scooped the back of my head and kissed me. It was just the two of us in the dark and I could feel the heat from his body.

"I've had your Caddy moved to secure storage. Your aunt's Beetle is a relic with zero safety features besides bumpers and seat belts. You'll let me provide you with something nondescript with airbags, and GPS."

I swallowed hard, I wanted to kiss him, and I also wanted to walk away from him forever. I'm sure he thought I meant the kind with pedals when I said,

"It's fine, I have a bike."

Our eyes met and it knocked the wind out of my soul. The next thing I know, I was opening my eyes to the sparkling ripples and the trees. I sensed the presence of someone on the path in front of me.

"Wake up, wake up for me, I have to go."

I blinked a couple times and Seppi said,

"Just sit here for a bit, Sunny's getting her water bottle out of the car. You're OK, you're safe."

I curled my knees up to my chest and sobbed until I threw up maple creemee in the bush next to the trail. I wasn't a mini mobster and I wasn't good enough for Giuseppi Moretti. Seppi knelt on the path in front of me,

"My heart is yours for as long as you want it."

I looked up at him but he was blurry. Sunny shoved the water into my hands and pushed Seppi toward the car,

"Go, I've got this."

Seppi jogged back and curled something into my palm,

"Nothing has changed. Ti amo."

He held the back of my neck, kissed the top of my head, and then he was gone. The BMW fired up and the taillights faded as they drove away. I opened my hand to see the panic button. I took a sip of water and got up. On our way back to the car, I slid the keyring on my index finger and closed my hand around it. I loved him, and he loved me. Me and Sunny slid into the Mercedes and it was silent until Sunny eventually broke the silence,

"According to Vinny, Giulianna is her father's little minion. He sent her here to fuck with Seppi and see if she can get any information. She does a bump of coke like most of us put on chap stick. She's bat shit crazy."

I scrunched my eyebrows,

"Why would she mess with him, he's a Moretti?"

"She's a crazy, and very powerful bitch, like probably more powerful than Seppi. And she has a large, and very influential mob family. She's trying to prove something to her father, all the while being more vindictive and manipulative than usual. She's blasted out of her fucking gourd most of the time."

I held up the panic button,

"What's with this?"

"Seppi reprogrammed it so it will alert Vinny when you push it. The procedure will be the same as before, only Vinny will call you when you push it, and he'll help you. Right now, Seppi can't be connected to any of it, but he wants you to be safe, and have a lifeline if you need it."

We got back to their apartment and went inside so I could let things settle into my weed addled brain. Right then, I knew Seppi loved me, and maybe he was playing a part, until he could smooth things over.

"Vinny told me they're working on trying to put the money together to pay off Sal's debt, they have an idea but it'll take a little time to put it into play. If they can pull it off, the Genovese family will back off. I'm not sure if that will make Giulianna go away, but at least you won't be dealing with the whole family. The debt will be paid, and maybe we can leave all of this behind us. Then, all we have to worry about is Sal's boss wondering where he is, but it's possible everyone is starting to think he really did just pull up stakes and gallop off into the sunset. Maybe once the debt is paid, everything will be fine."

"How much did Sal owe them?"

She made a face,

"A lot. Like a lot, a lot."

"How are they planning on getting the money?"

She shrugged and went palms up,

"Vinny told me its better if I don't know."

My voice was quieter than I meant it to be,

"OK."

We sat there for a long time. Eventually, Vinny came home and said he would give me a ride back to my apartment. I could still smell Seppi's cologne when I got in the passenger seat. He said,

"I'm sorry about all this. Seppi wants to make sure you're out of harm's way until this is taken care of."

I didn't say anything. He pulled down the alley between Muddy Waters and Giuseppi's Italian Ristorante and watched until I was inside. When I reached the top of the stairs, Kane swung his door open,

"Wanna come in for a drink?"

I pondered the question as I carried the weight of the world on my shoulders, and wondered how long he had been waiting for me to come home,

"Not tonight."

He stepped into the hall.

"I'm sorry for how I've been acting. I don't have an excuse, but the last thing I want to do is ruin a chance we can at least be friends."

Time would tell, but I felt like he was being sincere. I went into my apartment to find Opal and Auggie throwing things into boxes and duffle bags,

"What are you guys doing?"

Opal looked over at me, like it was obvious,

"Duh, packing."

I grabbed some things, snagged Maggie's keys, and tossed the panic button into my bag. My Sig Sauer was in there too but I had no idea if it was loaded. I told Opal I'd see her the next day and made a graceful exit. My eyes drifted to the back of the ristorante and I noticed my car was gone. I felt a pang of something like panic accompanied with burning acid as I started the Beetle. When I pulled onto Maggie's street, I could see the RV in the driveway. Son of a bitch. I didn't even want to go inside. It was late and I just wanted to be alone. I texted her that I didn't need to stay over, and drove back into town. Fifteen minutes later I was unlocking the apartment above the studio.

I curled up and cried in the twin bed with the Care Bear sheets and thrifted quilt. At two in the morning, I woke to someone in the room with me and I didn't know what to do. My panic button and gun were in my purse and my gun probably wasn't loaded anyway. And then I smelled a hint of expensive shower gel, and Tobacco Vanille. The quilt lifted and Giuseppi Moretti wrapped his arms around me and pulled me close. We didn't say anything, we didn't need to. I rolled over so I could see his face. His hand came to my cheek and he rubbed my scrimple. When our lips touched, my body ignited, and I cried as I kissed him. He touched my breast, and stomach, and it sent a jolt of arousal to my privates. I cupped his face in my hand and our tongues touched. One piece at a time, we lost our clothes and made love in the most tender way I've ever experienced. That time, it was about saying I love you, and I trust you, and I need you. We laid in each other's arms and fell asleep.

At five o'clock, Seppi kissed me on the cheek, and with his lips close to my ear,

"Ti amo."

He got dressed, and just like that, Seppi was gone. I should admit that I didn't actually sleep at all that night, I just laid there listening to Seppi breathe, because I didn't know when I would see him again. The VW keys were gone and there was a fob for a Subaru. I glanced at my phone and at some point in the night, Sunny had sent, 'Beetle at Muddy Waters, keys with Opal.' I felt like Seppi was with me, even though he wasn't.

I climbed into a brand-new version of my twenty-seven-year-old piece of Swiss cheese and that made my heart do things. It wasn't held together with duct tape, nothing was hanging off, and I didn't have to smack the dash to get the CD player to work. I felt rich and fancy, and the car didn't scream 'mafia.' I made my way back to the cafe, and parked next to the Beetle. When I emerged from the fancy new station wagon, I eyeballed the Escalade in its spot at the restaurant. Even though it almost killed me, I didn't run to him. I didn't even look over there after that, not that day. We were doing a dance, and I wanted to do my part, without stepping on any toes while I was at it.

CHAPTER 27
ENTER STAGE LEFT

I SHOWERED, did my crazy hair situation, swiped on some mascara, and went down the stairs to the cafe. I pulled the black apron over my head and went through the motions that day. I was grateful for Freida because she was single-handedly running the after-school program for the time being, I didn't have it in me. It was going to be a while before we had our first adult watercolor or pottery class, so I had some leeway. I made lattes and cappuccinos and Americanos. I made paninis and breakfast sandwiches and warmed scones. I wiped the tables and changed the trash. We had done this dance enough that Kane knew I needed space. I was pleasant to the customers but did the bare minimum.

I counted the hours, and drank more espresso than any sane person should. I wanted to be alone and I was trapped in a coffee scented box with a man who had seen me naked. I leaned into Kane's office and when he saw me there, his face did something it shouldn't. I asked,

"Hey, can you follow me to Maggie's later so I can return the VW?"

He shrugged and acted nonchalant about the whole thing,

"Sure."

But I think he was just happy to spend time with me,

"You don't need the beetle anymore?"

Apparently, he hadn't seen the Outback in the driveway.

"It's complicated."

Kane knew enough not to ask too many questions. I returned the Beetle to my aunt, and as I was handing over the keys, we were invited to 'happy hour' on the patio. We were also invited for some of Clem's famous grilled chicken with Brook's marinate. I stood on the steps, gestured to Kane, and hopped out of the Bronco. There was a second there where it felt like we were together. Sometimes I wonder if exes can ever be friends. But I also knew we weren't just exes, I knew there was unfinished business between the two of us. I wanted to have a heart to heart with Kane about what was going on, he would keep my secrets.

I stopped a couple feet from the door and turned to him, swallowed the lump in my throat and broke down. It felt like I was living two lives. It's that whole thing again of knowing that choosing a man meant choosing an entire world. Kane put his hand on my arm,

"Everything's going to be alright."

But I didn't believe it.

He kissed the top of my head, and we went inside. In case you weren't here in the very beginning, my aunt shared retail space with Kane way back and they became close after her second husband passed away. Kane would go on bus trips to Atlantic City and Foxwoods with Maggie, and they built a beautiful friendship. They cared about me and it was nice to be in the presence of people who accepted me for who I am. No mask, no facade, no part to play, I left all that shit behind when I walked through that door. I mean, Kane didn't know about all the things I had in little filing cabinets in the back of my mind, but I never felt like I had to pretend I wasn't broken when I was with him.

Maggie came into the living room in a trail of weed smoke and patchouli. A colorful broomstick skirt flowing around her as she moved. Maggie's cream-colored linen tank stopped just above the waist and I hoped I could pull off outfits like that in another thirty years. Her feet were bare and her toenails were painted, she wore strings of silver bells around her ankles. Maggie's silver-gray curls cascaded over her shoulders with the top half swirled into a bun with a sterling silver hair pin. She gestured us into the kitchen and we carried things outside. When I opened the sliding door to the deck, the smells of chicken marinated in poultry seasoning and vinegar hit my nose, good old Brook's chicken, the same recipe my dad makes.

Clem waved to us and I went over and shook his hand. Clem was a retired firefighter who worked as a carpenter most of his life. He was good looking and fit, his salt and pepper hair was tidy and he had a gray five o clock shadow. His cologne reminded me of leather and cedar, much like a beard oil Kane uses sometimes. It didn't take me long to fall in love with the guy and I hoped my aunt would keep him around for a while. There was never a period of learning that we could all be ourselves, Clem was cool from the very first time I met him and I could see why my aunt liked him so much. Kane shook Clem's hand and they chatted about man stuff, you know, grilling and beer.

I joined my aunt on the deck and she handed me a glass of rosé,

"I was hoping I'd get to share this with you. We stopped at a vineyard out west and I think this is the most delicious rosé I've ever had. For some reason, it made me think of you."

We clinked glasses and took sips. Maggie opened a case and pulled out a joint. We passed it back and forth and Kane looked over as soon as he smelled it. Kane made a beeline for the little weed circle we had going. He stuck his hand out,

"Puff the magic dragon, my turn."

We both looked at him and Maggie handed Kane the joint. I tried to assess whether Clem was a pothead but it didn't take long because he took a sip of his beer and said,

"Don't hold out on me now!"

Kane carried the rest of the joint over to the grill and the two of them finished it. I sat in that deck chair watching Kane smoke a doobie with my aunt's boyfriend and everything seemed normal. I was safe. But I had a pit in my gut about Seppi and how long this charade was going to last. I missed him and worried Giulianna would win, not that it was a competition. I wondered where he was and what he was doing. I looked at my watch and knew Seppi was probably at the restaurant. I excused myself and went to the bathroom even though I didn't have to pee. I pulled out my phone and called Giuseppi's Italian Ristorante, my stomach doing butterflies while it rang,

"Giuseppi's Italian Ristorante, Marcy speaking, how may I help you?"

I stood there holding my breath, she said,

"Hello?"

I scrambled,

"I've got the wrong number."

Immediately,

"Amelia!?"

I ended the call. What a fucking idiot, why am I like this? I stared at myself in the mirror and shook my head before I returned to the deck and slid in across from Maggie. She didn't skip a beat,

"How's your sister?"

I pulled myself back to reality,

"She's doing really well. She and Auggie and little Chloe are going to live in the place above the studio."

"That's great, what prompted that?"

I made a face and bit my bottom lip. I was assessing the situation and how much I should say, I was sick of the filters so I said, fuck it,

"Well, I have a lot to catch you up on."

Maggie put her finger up and ran into the house to check on the oven. Once she was back in her chair,

"I'm all yours, tell me everything."

"I started seeing Seppi a while ago..."

My aunt spit out a mouthful of the delicious rosé,

"Wait, *you* started seeing Seppi?"

She thought about it for a second and her facial expression told me she could see it. I said,

"Yeah, it's a longer story than I can tell right now but the short story is that I had been staying at Seppi's, and Opal was staying at the apartment above the cafe. Recently, I had a change of living situation and needed to move back into my apartment, so I offered the place above the studio to she and Auggie and the baby."

"What happened to your fancy car?"

"My situation changed."

She understood that this was a conversation for another time, a time when we were alone. She patted my hand,

"Let's have lunch later this week and you can tell me all about it."

I teared up at the thought of telling the story, it made me realize how chaotic it was. The ins and outs, the feelings, the details, it all sounded insane. Too much to get into in a casual conversation before macaroni salad and grilled chicken. This time, my aunt put her hand over mine and squeezed,

"You can tell me anything, you know that, right? I blinked away tears and nodded.

Kane and Clem came to the table with trays of chicken and grilled veggies. I hopped up and retrieved the macaroni salad and a pitcher of sun tea. My aunt pulled a pan of buttery homemade rolls out of the oven. We settled in and filled our plates with a summer feast. The four of us talked about the weather and about their trip in the RV. We talked about the cafe and about the studio, I told them about Gilly, and how much her poem meant to me. My aunt asked if I was enjoying the studio and I told her I was. I told her about Freida but I didn't tell her that I had been so preoccupied that I hadn't even used a pottery wheel. I left out the part about doing a test fire using a corpse and that the ashes were helping grow flowers.

Despite it all, I managed to have a nice evening and as I sat there next to Kane, reminiscing, and eating dinner, I felt safe,

"Thank you for coming tonight, I appreciate it."

Kane smiled back at me and it felt like he wanted to say something, it just wasn't the time or the place. I also knew he was close to my aunt and hadn't seen her in a while. We had fruit salad for dessert and then helped clean up before we did our hugs. My aunt sent me away with a baggie full of joints and waved to us as we walked down the path to the car. Once we were inside the Bronco with the doors closed, I felt electricity bouncing between us like it used to. I decided during the ride back home that night, I needed to stay as far away from Kane as possible. Work would be fine, but anything beyond that, any extracurricular activities with him would lead to crossing lines and playing what I like to call, pee-pee tag.

When we got back home, I declined an invitation to go over for a drink. The two of us hugged and I kissed him on the cheek before going into my apartment. The place was a mess. I'm not saying it wasn't cluttered before, but now that everything was torn apart, I didn't even know where to sit. Opal came out of the bedroom with a duffle,

"I think we can stay there tonight, I didn't realize how much stuff we had. All our things used to fit in the van so really this is mostly baby stuff, but wow."

I watched my sister realize she wasn't going to be able to pack up so easily and hit the road now that she had a little human with lots of miscellaneous stuff. I watched as my sister changed my sheets and I was kind of glad I'd be able to curl up in my bed and sleep. Auggie had just gotten home from work and was in the shower. I helped them load the van and Auggie's very old short bed Ford pickup truck. Just as the sun was setting, my sister's little family set off for their new home on the other side of town.

I stood in the driveway waving like a goofball to my little niece, even though she was fast asleep in her baby seat. Seconds after the van and truck pulled out, a set of headlights pulled into the alley. I moved out of the way to let the person through and realized it was Seppi. I waved casually, met his eyes, and then dropped my gaze and went back inside. I didn't know how I was supposed to act. I wanted to crawl into a hole and die. My phone vibrated, it was Sunny, 'Seppi says he hopes you're OK.' I replied, 'I'm fine.' I'm sure she was the go-between. I went into my apartment and suddenly it was quiet. My phone vibrated, 'Call me when you can.' I sat on the sun porch, lit a joint, and called Sunny. She answered,

"What's up, fucker?"

"Hey."

"Are you alone?"

I replied,

"Yeah."

"Giulianna found some pictures of the two of you in Seppi's office at the house."

"Oh."

I was ready to be done with this shit already, I just wanted to sit on the sun porch and get high while I pet my cat. That is not a euphemism for rubbing one out.

"She asked some questions and he tried to smooth it over. He told her you were his Event Planner and nothing more, but Seppi's worried she'll start sniffing around. Until things blow over, you need to pretend you're with Kane. If you're out with him, hold his hand, when you're working at the cafe, wink at him or act like his girlfriend."

It wasn't going to be a stretch to play the role of Kane's girlfriend because I had done it for real in the past and it wasn't that long ago. And here's where the dilemma kicked into high gear. I had no idea how long it would be until things went back to normal, if ever. I'd made the decision just hours ago that I needed to distance myself from Kane Buchanan. I could already feel the pull of my soul to his, I was catching myself thinking about him. I knew that by doing what I was told, to pretend I was with Kane to throw off the scent, it was going to cause problems.

"I don't know if I should be spending that much time with Kane, to be honest."

"Amelia, this is important. Seppi wants to make sure you understood that this is not a game, this is not make believe, it needs to be believable. Do you think Kane will be willing to do it?"

She had no idea how willing he was, and that's why I needed to distance myself from him.

"I just got Opal out the door, she's moving to the apartment over the studio. I need to get my bearings and then I'll go talk to Kane."

"OK, good. Let me know what he says so I can tell Seppi."

"Sunny, I understand the logic and I understand the importance of this, but I need you to know, as my friend, I think this is going to cause another set of problems."

"We'll deal with that when we need to deal with that, right now, this is what you need to do."

I stood in the middle of my living room and I stared at the wall of my empty, and very quiet, apartment. I tossed an edible down the hatch and washed it down with lemonade. I swept and vacuumed and started a load of laundry. Opal had cleaned the bathroom so I dug clean towels out of the closet, I put my things on the vanity. I turned on my wax melter. I opened the windows and threw the folded quilt over the back of the couch. It didn't take long for the place to feel like it used to. Give me a week and I'd have that fresh baby smell replaced with stale weed and incense.

I tapped on Kane's door and he opened it in boxer briefs and a t-shirt. I grit my teeth and tried really hard not to look at his crotch. We sat in the living room and I told him I needed to ask him something. You should have seen the light in his eyes. I'm sure the conversation didn't go as he expected.

"You know how Giulianna is trying to cause problems for Seppi?"

"Yeah."

"Sal owed three quarters of a million dollars to the Genovese family to cover gambling debts they paid, and they think Seppi's hiding him. Obviously, Seppi can't be like, never mind, my father's actually dead, I guess you're not getting your money."

Kane waited patiently for the punchline, but he was holding his breath.

"Giulianna found some pictures of me with Seppi and he said we..."

I motioned between the two of us,

"...need to pretend we're a couple to throw off the scent."

I tried to assess his response through the facial expressions he was making. I kept going,

"Since no one in their right mind would cheat on Giuseppi Moretti, it would be obvious that you and I are actually together if I'm going around town holding hands with you out in the open."

Kane turned to me,

"I want to make sure I understand."

I nodded expectantly,

"You and I have talked about having feelings for each other and that we cannot cross a line while you're with Seppi. And now we are being told, by Seppi, to 'pretend' to be together."

"Yeah."

Kane threw his hands around while he talked and his voice went up an octave,

"Do you have any idea how fucked up that is, Amelia!?"

"I know, but this is important, really important. Something really bad could happen to me if we don't do this."

I tried to stay calm but it was impossible,

"I am not making a mountain out of a molehill this time, this is real, and it's scary. I don't ask you for much, and this is really important."

His dark chocolate voice was more emotional than usual. Maybe there were tears brewing under the surface, maybe there was anger, but bubbling over the top there was something else entirely,

"I love you, Amelia. If I could be with you, I would, that's all I want in the world. So, you're really with Seppi but have to pretend you're with me instead? Do you realize how fucked up that is?"

I needed to diffuse him, I needed to make sure he said yes. I had no idea what would happen if he said no, but least of all, my life would be in danger. I'd be a target for a hostage situation if Giulianna wanted information and she felt Seppi wasn't giving it to her.

I tried again,

"I know this isn't fair and if there was any other way, I wouldn't ask. And it isn't me asking this, it's Seppi. My life will be at risk if we don't do this."

Kane was talking with his hands again and the darkness in his voice was sprinkled with emotion,

"That's not fair, Amelia."

I tried a third time. I stepped forward and took his hand, he didn't pull away. When I looked up at him, I saw so many things in his eyes. Then came the tears, I was overwhelmed and scared and my heart was feeling too many things at once. I was desperate,

"Kane, listen, I know this is not a best-case scenario, I know this complicates things. Honestly, I don't know how long this is going to take. I understand if you aren't comfortable doing it. If you want me to be honest, I think it's going to backfire on him."

Kane dropped his eyes to mine and that's when he knew that I was just as confused as he was. He knew that I had feelings too, and that we were being asked to do the opposite of keeping ourselves apart. Then the wall came down and the feelings flooded in. We held each other and cried. There was a possibility I'd be kidnapped, tortured, ransomed for information or money enough to pay Sal's debt. In a way it was only fair, an eye for an eye. I was a twenty-something with broken pieces, magnificent ringlets, and one and a half dimples. I wasn't someone who'd fair well if I was shoved in a trunk, or tied up in a hatch under somebody's house. Both of us let out a sigh and Kane held my hand in his,

"I'll do it, but…"

He paused,

"I can't be held responsible for wanting to believe that it's real and not just some act. I need you to know that."

I saw love and hunger in his dark chocolate eyes. I said,

"Thank you for doing this, and I'm sorry."

Right then we were still in our own pens, but the next day would be the first day of the charade. I imagined some comedic caricature of a circus, and I was dressed in an elaborate clown costume. Balancing atop a tight wire, people throwing tomatoes at me as I tried to get from one side to the other. That night was the precipice of I went home shortly after and let Sunny know that Kane was on board. I brushed my teeth and curled up in bed with Indie. She purred and made biscuits on my belly. The exhaustion lent itself to a magnificent night of sleep. When I woke, there wasn't a whole lot of dread about pretending to be with Kane, I shifted it into the compartment with the obligatory dysfunction.

In the morning, I showered and worked curl cream through my ringlets. I put on some mascara and lip-gloss. I spun around in a mist of Coco Mademoiselle. I was heading into the belly of the beast, onto the stage, it was time to sell it. I bounced down the stairs to the cafe and kissed Kane on the cheek as he ground beans for the house blend. He gave me a squeeze and I went about my day. The problem was that there had already been two almost kisses and a hand on my lower back that lingered a little too long. We were going to be in trouble if the audience wanted an encore.

CHAPTER 28
IN FRONT OF YOUR FACE

I SAW ISABELLA ROSSI almost every week, in her impressive office in the sky. I was manic at work, way too much energy for the emotional load I was carrying. I smoked more pot, but had all but stopped drinking, and I started taking my cemetery walks again. I kind of forgot about the panic button, and some days it felt like my time with Seppi was lifetimes ago. I know it's my trauma, the way I can so effortlessly compartmentalize difficult feelings into little boxes. It's some broken part I have that doesn't work just right, but sometimes it keeps me from losing my mind, and this was one of those times. It didn't seem real, maybe it had all been a dream. I wasn't going to the ristorante, I wasn't driving the mini mafia sedan, or sitting in my office digging dark chocolate covered blueberries out of the jar with my grubby fingers. And I definitely wasn't sharing whiskey across the desk from Giuseppi Moretti.

I changed out of my work clothes and into linen overalls with a white sports bra. I slid my feet into Birkenstocks and bounced down the stairs to the Outback. I was officially a soccer mom, or needed to buy a kayak, or something. It was a nice day, the sun was shining, birds were chirping, flowers were abloom. But deep inside of me was dread, and a realization that if I didn't play my cards right, I could end up traded for three quarters of a million dollars. I thought of Seppi's bed head and the way he fed Indie pieces of cheese and fried egg. I was sentimental for the times I sat on the lid of the toilet and watched Seppi shave. I wondered if I'd forget the way he smelled or the way his hand felt in mine. I cried in the car before getting out and smoking a joint in the parking lot.

I went through the glass doors into the lobby and took the elevator to the sixth floor. I checked in with Elaine and sat on the couch, but didn't look at the magazines. I stared at the wall. I missed him so much. I held it together in the waiting room but once I was curled up in the overstuffed chair across from Dr. Rossi, I fell apart,

"I don't even know where to start."

She was patient with me, like always,

"Start at the beginning."

I didn't even know where the beginning was. How far back did I need to go?

"Seppi's ex-wife is here, and apparently Sal owed her family three quarters of a million dollars. They think he ran off to escape his debt, and Seppi is worried I'm in danger, that they'll hold me hostage if they realize I'd make good collateral."

Dr. Rossi looked concerned but she was trying to hide it. I could see it in her face, the line of her mouth, the tightness of her eyebrows. I called her out on it,

"I know you're concerned."

She needed to stay neutral, she needed to stay professional, but I could see the look of one woman feeling for another. In that moment we weren't doctor and patient, we were just two broken little girls.

"Seppi said I need to pretend I'm in a relationship with Kane, to throw off the scent, if that makes sense."

She nodded,

"I understand. No one is stupid enough to cheat on a mob boss, so if you're going around with someone else, then it's pretty obvious you're not with Seppi."

"Yeah."

"Are you OK with this plan?"

I went palms up and shrugged but my face was filling with emotion, and I was chewing the inside of my cheek. I felt the first rumblings of panic,

"I wouldn't say I'm excited about it, but it's better than getting tortured, or beaten, or traded to cover a dead man's gambling debt."

I made eye contact with her,

"A man that *I* killed, don't you find that poetic? That it just keeps coming back to bite me in the ass?"

She kept me from derailing,

"Do you have any contact with Seppi?"

"Not right now."

"How are you doing with that?"

I was moving my hands and raising my voice,

"That's the other thing. I was working at the restaurant the night she came in and we sat at the bar for a long time, drinking and talking about life. I didn't mention him, thank God. But when Vincenzo saw her, he dragged me into Seppi's office and gave me the scoop. He told me she's vindictive and manipulative. And then Seppi told me to stay at my apartment that night, so I did. In the morning, I returned the car and the panic button. I went into my office to grab my things and found the stuff I had at his house. It was like she came into town and it was immediately over. Oh, and she's also on a cocktail of coke, benzos, and alcohol."

Dr. Rossi crossed her legs and folded her hands in her lap, waiting patiently. I said,

"Giulianna told Seppi about Sal's debt, and the short story is that the Genovese family wants their money, yesterday. Seppi has an idea, but he said it will take time. He's going to get the money to pay off the Genovese family, and hopefully he'll get rid of Giulianna while he's at it."

I clarified,

"Out of town, not like kill her."

"Do you think she'll stick around after the debt is settled?"

I shrugged again,

"I don't know. I forgot the other part of the story, Giulianna's relative left something for Seppi when he died. I don't know what he got, it could be anything from a pair of cuff links to a private jet, who knows."

The rest of the session consisted of bouts of crying and hyperventilating while Dr. Rossi made sure I felt safe. I made another appointment with Elaine and slid the reminder card into my purse. In the elevator I started to lose it again, but tried to hold it together until I was in the car. If things hadn't been completely fucked, I would have been pushing my panic button. Not that day, folks. That day, I was going to hike up my big girl panties and drive home all by myself. I pulled the Outback down the driveway between Muddy Waters and Giuseppi's Italian Ristorante and parked next to the Bronco. I made it inside without glancing longingly at the Escalade. I went into my apartment and plopped my purse on the chair next to the door, tossed an edible down the hatch, and fed Indie. There was a tap at the door and I opened it to Kane,

"Have you eaten?"

"Nope."

And since I was going to be high as fuck in about forty-five minutes, I was also going to have the munchies. Kane asked,

"Wanna get pizza again? We can go out this time"

That sounded pretty good to me,

"Sure."

He smiled,

"OK, let me know when you're ready to go."

I washed off the day and started from scratch. I worked curl cream through my hair and looked at myself in the mirror. I threw on some eyeliner and some lipstick. I threw on a lightweight blush cardigan and danced around in a spray of my expensive perfume. I slid my feet in my Birkenstocks and sat on the sun porch. I guessed this was supposed to look like 'date night.' I texted that I was ready and heard Kane on the phone with his sister,

"That's what I'm saying."

Pause.

"You know how much I care about her."

Pause.

"This is torture."

And then the rest of the conversation was about Constance's boyfriend and her new puppy. I tip-toed into my kitchen so he wouldn't see me eavesdropping if he went out on his sun porch, which was right next to mine. A couple minutes later, there was a tap at the door. Kane's brown waves were resting on his shoulders but he had a black elastic on his wrist in case he changed his mind. Kane was wearing his favorite Levi's and a button up shirt; I was pretty sure I had unbuttoned them both at one point or another. He smelled like beard oil, six-dollar coconut conditioner, and natural deodorant. He kissed me on the cheek and we set off to get pizza. I wondered if we were going to take the Outback or the Bronco. We didn't need to take either car because Kane had the bright idea to take me on a date to Giuseppi's Italian Ristorante.

I hadn't been in the building since I dropped off the keys and panic button. It had been less than a week but it felt like an eternity. I prayed Seppi had been called off somewhere important, anywhere but there. The hostess made a face like I was a bitch or a whore and I think I made it worse by winking at her. Like I was saying, 'winky-winky, don't tell Seppi.' I wanted to tell her she smelled like an ashtray and a bad knock-off of expensive perfume. Dumb bitch.

I did a casual visual, I didn't see him or hear him or smell him. Oh God, I wanted to smell him. We ordered wine and shared fresh bread with olive oil and roasted garlic. The two of us laughed in the way two people do when they share memories, and that part wasn't pretend. At one point Kane held my hands across the table, and in that moment, I was having a moment. I tried to hold it as long as possible but midway through my shrimp scampi, I needed to pee. If I haven't drawn this out before now, there is a hall off the back of the dining room that leads to both offices and the restrooms. I really couldn't hold it any longer. I excused myself and my heart pounded as I speed-walked to the bathroom. There was darkness under my office door and I could see that Seppi's door was open. I sniffed at the air to see if I could smell Tobacco Vanille. I went a few steps past the bathroom but knew I had no good excuse to be near Seppi's office, especially if I was there on a date with Kane Buchanan. I detoured into the women's room and took the power piss of all power pisses. Sometimes taking a good piss is better than sex.

I managed to make it back to the table without running into Seppi, maybe he wasn't there. I hadn't heard him on his rounds around the dining room so I let my guard down a little. I leaned into it, the wine and the old feelings that were becoming new feelings. Kane and I shared tiramisu. We paid and then had a drink at the bar. At first Joey side-eyed me, he knew I was Seppi's. I winked at him and he understood the assignment. Kane and I chatted with Joey and we debated if dark chocolate versus milk chocolate. I was two glasses of red wine in, on my second shot of tequila, edible on board, feeling good on that stool next to Kane. Joey threw me a kiss. I pretended to catch it, shook it like a Magic 8 Ball, and squinted like I was trying to read the result,

"Sources say the person who threw this is a dipshit."

The three of us were laughing like the joke was much funnier than it was and out of nowhere, Giulianna Genovese hopped her perfect little ass onto a bar stool. I elbowed Kane, bit my bottom lip, and moved my eyes in her direction. He pulled my stool closer and put his arm around me. Kane kissed me on the cheek and blew in my ear. I squeaked and Giulianna swung her head to our end of the bar,

"Amelia?"

I pretended I hadn't seen her five minutes ago and knocked her down a peg or two,

"Oh, hey...Julie, right?"

Giulianna seemed offended, but reigned it in, played the part, self-consciously wiped at her nose,

"Actually, it's Giulianna."

She scanned the ristorante like she owned the place, sat up a little straighter and fingered the stem of her wine glass,

"Actually, it's Giulianna Genovese."

I almost gagged as a tidal wave of acid and heartache lurched into my throat. Kane squeezed my thigh. Fuck her, she didn't matter, she was no one. I wanted to get into my first cat fight with Giulianna Genovese, the cunt. I turned to Kane,

"Babe, this is Julian, I met her the other night at the bar, she's visiting."

She corrected me again,

"Giulianna."

I thumbed in Kane's direction,

"This is my boyfriend Kane, we work together at the cafe next door."

I leaned over, winked and whispered,

"He's my boss."

I giggled and I didn't do it on purpose, I was actually having a little fun. The mask was all the way over my head and I was trying to breathe through the tiny little nose holes in the plastic. Kane wrapped his hands around my waist and buried his nose in my curls. He whispered,

"This better be worth it, because your boyfriend is going to kick my ass if he comes out here."

As a knee-jerk reaction, I pushed Kane away and he diverted her attention by thrusting his hand in her direction,

"Nice to meet you Giulianna Genovese, I'm Kane Buchanan. You should stop by Muddy Waters for a latte and a breakfast sandwich before you leave town."

He gestured at the wall,

"It's right across the alley."

Kane winked at her and I think she was caught off guard that he used her full name, I think a little bit of the real Giulianna came through. Someone was being human with her, personal with her, showing interest. Giulianna seemed nervous, but maybe she was just jonesing to powder her nose,

"Umm, actually, I'm only here for a visit. But I'll try to stop by for a latte and a breakfast sandwich, maybe you'll be there, and we can have a coffee."

She smiled with her perfect teeth and subtly pushed her boobs together. He asked,

"How long are you planning to stay?"

She slid her wineglass to Joey and dug around in the burnt popcorn kernels, shrugging,

"I'm not sure how much longer I'll be in town."

She shifted gears, on a fact-finding mission, looking at Kane in the way of a rich whore who plays with men like a cat batting at a feather on a stick,

"Do you own the cafe?"

Giulianna leaned toward Kane flirtatiously, chin resting on the back of her hand, giggling or something adjacent. I wanted to tell her she missed some of the white powder when she wiped her nose. Kane leaned into the interaction with her, it was obvious he was assessing her. Scale of one to ten? Craziness level? Who knows. Or maybe he just enjoyed flirting with a beautifully unstable coke-head, who used to share a bed with Giuseppi Moretti. He changed course,

"Well, I own the business, Amelia here owns the building, I better behave, or she'll jack up the rent."

We all had a good chuckle but there was a flicker in her eyes when she looked at Kane, and I didn't like it one bit. It was like she let her guard down with him, he wasn't like the men she knew. He was vanilla safe, had a seven-year-old pair of Levis and six-dollar coconut conditioner. He had a second-hand acoustic guitar and not a million dollars to spent at Tiffany & Co or a trip to Sicily. I bet that woman had never felt safe in her own head or her own body. The whole time that was going on, I was worried Seppi would waltz out and see me with Kane. And there I was getting the tiniest bit jealous of how Giulianna Genovese was looking at my fake boyfriend, even if she was probably going to get up in five minutes and do a speed-ball in the bathroom.

I tried to shake it off but it wasn't working. Whatever. I had reached my limit, I grabbed Kane and we said our goodbyes. But, just as Kane and I were leaving, Seppi emerged from the inner sanctum to see if everyone was enjoying their meals. We made eye contact for a split second and I tried to scream 'I'm sorry' the best I could. He came over to us and put his hand out to Kane, they shook hands. I could see by the look on Kane's face that Seppi was squeezing a little too hard. Seppi kissed Kane on both cheeks and I froze. Seppi moved to me next. He was slow and deliberate, kissed my scrimple, leaned in and whispered,

"I miss you, Dimples."

My nipples pressed against my bra. He moved to the other cheek,

"If that long-haired hippie touches you, I'll snap his neck like a twig."

Seppi pulled away and I wanted to wrap my arms around his neck so I could smell whiskey, Cubans, and Tobacco Vanille. I tried with all my might to stuff those feelings way down deep inside, or way in the back of my mind in a filing cabinet I'd never open, crammed in there with one of my demons. I waved at Joey, Giulianna, and Seppi, and then didn't look back. Kane held the door and I burst onto the sidewalk, gulping in air like I had been drowning. My entire body was buzzing and my head was spinning. I glanced in the front window and Seppi was looking out at me, it just about killed me. I broke down, it was too much for me to handle. I stopped in the alley and Kane asked me why I was crying, I didn't know where to start. I felt alone and like the walls were closing in. My heart was being ripped out of my chest and handed to me on a silver platter. Kane tucked a loose curl behind my ear. I needed to drown it all, extinguish all the heartbreak and pain. I stood there rooted in place, staring at the exterior wall of Giuseppi's Italian Ristorante. Eventually, Kane took my hand and dragged me inside. I didn't turn to look at the Escalade or run through the back door into Seppi's arms. I didn't sit in the chair across from his or share a whiskey. I walked away from that world and went up the stairs to the other one.

I brushed my teeth, braided my hair, and scooped Indie under my arm before going over to Kane's. When he came out of his room, Lola bounded out and sniffed at Indie. In fact, the two of them spent like ten minutes sniffing each other's assholes, and then played like old friends. My insides were mushy and confused. I leaned against the counter and Kane came to me, pressed himself against my body with his. I closed my eyes and took in the scent of him, but that night, I was good. I fell asleep in my own bed under my thrifted vintage quilt. I knew we were playing parts, wearing masks, and I needed to remember that we were like actors, we were only together when we were on stage.

So, there I was, in a relationship with one man, pretending to be with another, and I was so incredibly lonely. I didn't want to bother my sister, or Sunny, with any of it, they were dealing with their own shit. So that left Indie, and she was starting to think I was a certifiable lunatic. I was afraid she would call Isabella Rossi and let the cat out of the bag, no pun intended. But really, Indie knew my deepest, darkest secrets and feelings, and she never seemed to judge me. It didn't matter if I was in an expensive pantsuit or Seppi's sweats, Indie loved me. I curled up with her and told her about my day. I told her I missed Seppi's hands and his voice and his Tobacco Vanille. She told me she missed the fried eggs and the cheddar.

CHAPTER 29
MATCHSTICKS AND ALIBIS

THINGS WENT ON like that for a couple more weeks. And given the duration of this little charade, things began to get complicated with Kane. Don't get me wrong, despite his advances, I never did anything with him. But, sometimes I think it's even more damaging if you cross a line with your heart. I'm not saying I fell for Kane or wanted to be with him, I'm just saying it blurred the lines a little. The thing is, our time together made me more certain I wanted to be with Seppi, and it made Kane more certain he wanted to be with me. I'll always have feelings for Kane, I've just changed in ways that wouldn't have meshed with his moral fabric. And at some point, I would have gotten sick of eating vanilla ice cream.

But, I was forced to live a lie while trying desperately to find the truth. That little costume show or soap opera, or whatever, solidified my disdain for playing a part, wearing a mask, and maintaining a facade. I asked Sunny to tell Seppi I loved him. She also told him I missed his pancakes. Seppi said he loved me back and that he missed something else entirely. I noticed the Escalade wasn't in its spot as much, maybe things were happening. I asked Sunny if she knew anything and she said they were cashing in some favors. She reminded me that Seppi has friends in low places.

"Oh, and get this shit. Tomorrow night, me and Vin are going to dinner with Seppi and Mary at the ristorante. Vin told me to post pictures on my socials, said we're celebrating Seppi's Downtown Partnership award. You know, advertise the fact that the Morettis are respected now, instead of feared."

I had a pit in my gut that I couldn't celebrate with Seppi. Although, given the fact that I wasn't born yesterday, I was pretty sure they were establishing an alibi. Wait and see, but I had an idea that something big was going to happen while the four of them were dipping bread in roasted garlic and olive oil. Maybe someone would die while they were clinking glasses of fifty year old Cabernet Sauvignon. Or maybe I was just trying not to give in to an epic case of FOMO. Sunny gushed,

"I need to get my nails done for tomorrow, my God, they look like shit."

Sunny went on and on about doing her hair, and which outfit to wear. I'm thinking, it doesn't fucking matter what you look like, you're going to be taking all the pictures. But, whatever, I let her think she was a part of something, and maybe I was just jealous. It didn't matter, at that point it was a wait and see situation, and the next twenty-four hours were going to drag like molasses. Obviously I spent most of it high. I didn't leave my apartment the night before the big family dinner with selfies on social media. I binge-watched Psych and cleaned my bathroom. I did a face mask, painted my toenails, and took a couple healthy rips from my bong.

I daydreamed about dinner, and wondered if Giulianna was going to be there. And then I realized maybe it would be better if she was, at least everyone could keep an eye on her then. Hopefully Sunny would hold her little white trash bad-ass in check instead of trying to spit in Giulianna's wine. For fuck's sake, I pinched the bridge of my nose and took a deep breath. I knew the truth, he was mine, and she was history. We were all playing parts, and wearing masks, even though I wanted nothing more than to toss my masks in the kiln, and run them through the meat grinder in Mary Moretti's shed. An hour later, I was on the couch under my ratty quilt and Sunny sent me a flurry of texts, but then called me before I had a chance to read them,

"Hey."

"OK, so something is happening."

No, 'what's up fucker,' I knew it was serious. I sat up and hugged my legs to my chest,

"Is Seppi OK?"

"It's nothing like that."

There was a long silence, was she waiting for me to say something? I didn't, I just waited.

"Seppi came home, and Giulianna was blacked out in the pool, just floating around on the big inflatable beaver. He got in the pool, pushed the float to the steps, and waited around for her to wake up. But then he got impatient and ended up dumping a glass of ice water on her sun burnt stomach."

We looked at each other, beaver. Yup, we were twelve-year-old boys.

"Then Vinny said he was over at Seppi's, and Giulianna was looking at photo albums or something."

"OK."

"When Vinny left, he forgot his smokes, so he went back inside."

"Sunny, the suspense is killing me, get to the fucking point, you're giving me diarrhea."

She laughed at me,

"OK, OK. Vinny heard the two of them arguing upstairs. Giulianna went through Seppi's phone."

Oh, fuck. Also, how did she get into it? I had tried at least ten times, and couldn't do it. With my luck, his password was still their anniversary.

"Seppi deleted your contact info, pictures, and texts, but he didn't think about deleting texts from anyone else."

Oh.

"Vin texted Seppi about the panic button, asking if he needed to reset it on your end. On top of that, Mary asked Seppi if something was going on between you to because she hadn't seen you around. She gave him a lecture about treating you right, and Giulianna read that too."

Adrenaline fired off in my belly,

"Then what happened!?"

"He woke up this morning and she was gone. She just packed up her shit and left sometime during the night. The thing is, she knows you're with him, and we don't know where she is, so you might want to lay low."

When the call ended I stared at the wall with my heart beating in my ears. I was awake most of the night and I made countless trips to the front window to make sure she wasn't casing the joint with a sniper rifle. When the sun came up, I had latte while I smoked a joint on the sun porch. The morning was clear and the sun was shining. The birds were chirping, but I had a pit in my gut and the first rumblings of a panic attack. I worked curl cream through my ringlets and let my hair air dry while I put on mascara and lip gloss. I strapped the Sig Sauer inside of my ratty vintage overalls before I slid my feet in my dingy white Chuck

Taylors. I went down the stairs to the cafe and did my thing. Lunch came quickly, and before I knew it, we were closing shop. I wiped the tables on autopilot, dwelling and making assumptions and trying to put two and two together.

I went to the studio after the cafe closed and ran into Gilly, which is exactly what I needed that day. I sat with her as she made butterfly ornaments out of clay. I was preoccupied. She asked,

"Do you have the paints that go on the clay?"

"Glazes? Yes,"

I pointed to the shelf,

"There are a bunch of glazes over there, I'll show you when it's time to do that."

"Can we paint them on Monday?"

I explained the process of pottery. The way you have to let it dry for a long time, until there's no water left in the clay. I showed her the kiln (not the one I used to cremate the dead guy) and explained how long it takes, and how hot it gets.

"Well, my mom says patience is a virtue."

I found myself smiling again,

"Your mom is right."

I wondered if Giulianna would come back in time to grind all over Seppi's lap while they shared spaghetti like Lady and the Tramp. I asked Sunny if Giulianna was there. Sunny took a picture of the table. I saw an expensive bottle of wine and no Giulianna. I got a couple more pictures, one of them was Seppi blowing a kiss and I felt it in my entire body. My phone vibrated as they were waiting for dessert and coffee, 'Something happened.' My mind went to bad places, catastrophic places, I assumed something happened to Seppi. 'Seppi got a phone call and the three of them went to the office. I'll text when I know something.'

Ten minutes later, Sunny came tapping at my door. I swung the door open and she crossed the threshold with her head spinning. She plopped into a kitchen chair and lit a cigarette. I put an ashtray in front of her and she said,

"Umm."

"Did they come out of the office!? What did they say? What happened?"

She stared at the cherry on her cigarette,

"I think they had someone burn down the beach house."

"What!?"

"I think the dinner and all the pictures and Facebook posts were so they could establish an alibi."

I put my finger up and said,

"Oh, I bet they're going to use the insurance money to pay off Sal's debt."

"There's more, come sit down."

I sat across from her,

"He's okay though, right?"

"Seppi is fine."

She took a deep drag and snuffed out the cigarette, she was learning what it was like to be a part of it,

"The fire fighters went through the place to make sure no one was inside."

I leaned forward, she continued,

"There was someone burnt up in there."

My mind raced,

"Someone? Like a person?"

"Amelia, yes, it was Giulianna."

I flew to my feet,

"Where's Seppi!?"

"He and Vinny are on their way to Kimbrook Beach, the mansion is a total loss."

Then it was as if Sunny pulled a mask over her head like a trash bag,

"Everything's going to be fine now."

"What makes you say that?"

"Well, they'll have the money to pay off Sal's debt, and Giulianna won't be a problem anymore."

I ran to the sink and thew up in the garbage disposal. I cracked a can of ginger ale,

"Sunny! Don't be so cold about it, it's a person's life we're talking about!"

She shrugged,

"Sometimes, it's like taking out the trash"

Giulianna was in the house, in the bedroom to be exact. She was coked up, full of vodka, tossing back klonopin like candy. The fire fighters identified her by her jewelry. Her purse was found inside of a little red Ferrari. She essentially raced there to die, so maybe it was a blessing in disguise. Giulianna Carmella Genovese was thirty-six years old at the time of her death. She was a tortured soul who spent her life trying to prove herself to her father. She died alone, either on purpose or by mistake. And even though I didn't know her, it made me sick to my stomach. At some point late in the night, I fell victim to my exhaustion. I was startled to life by Kane pounding on my door, I scuffled over and answered with one eye open, tired and hungover,

"What!?"

"Were you planning to come to work today?"

I stared back at him,

"It's Sunday."

He threw his rag over his shoulder,

"It's Saturday, you were scheduled to come in at seven."

And then he turned around and went down the stairs. Moments later, I was steaming milk for the first in a long line of coffee orders. Time went on and I was working my way through another decent-sized line when Seppi came around the corner. My breath caught in my throat. He pointed at one of the other baristas and she took my place at the counter. Seppi gestured to Kane,

"We're borrowing your office."

Seppi grabbed my arm and locked us in Kane's office. We stared at each other then tears bubbled up. Seppi wrapped me up in his arms, a day's worth of stubble getting caught up in my hair as he cried. He smelled like stress sweat, smoke, and yesterday's Tobacco Vanille. Seppi was disheveled and clearly running on fumes,

"My father left a seven-hundred-and-fifty-thousand-dollar gambling debt when he died, it was less, but there was interest."

I held my breath.

"My father went to Tony Genovese and Tony fronted the money to pay off the debt, my father had loan sharks nibbling at his toes."

Now, he had actual sharks nibbling at his toes.

Seppi continued,

"Long story short, the entire Genovese family thinks my father skipped town to get out of paying his debt and they think I know where he's hiding."

Seppi had his hands on my shoulders, to steady me in the storm,

"I cashed in a favor and had a buddy torch the house in Kimbrook Beach. It's been in the works for a week, lots of moving parts. It's nothing more than a pile of cinder and ash."

"Sunny told me about Giulianna."

I could tell by his response that he hadn't known she was in the house, he cleared his throat,

"I, umm, I'm not really sure what happened."

He paused,

"According to her fiance, Adrian, she'd been blacking out. She was inside of the house when it went up."

"Seppi, I'm so sorry."

And I meant it.

"What about your father's debt? Is there going to be enough insurance money to pay it off?"

"The house was worth ten million dollars."

I choked on my spit,

"What did you say?"

Seppi ignored my question, and waved me away,

"And I'll have plenty left over if I decide to buy another house on the water."

Seppi shifted,

"I just wanted you to know what was going on."

He needed a warm meal, a shower, and a couple hours of sleep.

"I have to go."

Seppi kissed me on both cheeks and the top of the head, and then he was gone. I was standing there staring at the office door when Kane poked his head in,

"Is everything OK?"

I nodded and lied as I stared at the wall,

"Yeah."

"Good, because we're getting slammed."

I made the basic bitches their fancy lattes but really wanted to follow Seppi out the door. The action was a distraction and I made it though the rest of my shift, showered, and got high on the sun porch. I dropped in on Opal and we talked while Auggie played video games. I told her the story as I rocked my precious niece,

"Apparently, when I killed Sal, he owed the Genovese family three-quarters of a million dollars, and they think he skipped town to avoid paying his debt."

She stared back at me flatly, and I could tell she was interested, but not amused.

"Seppi was afraid the Genovese family would take me for ransom, so I've been pretending I'm with Kane.

I shook my head and waved it away,

"That's a whole other thing I'll tell you about later."

"What!?"

I flapped my hand,

"It doesn't matter. Anyway, he had an associate torch the house on Kimbrook Beach."

Her eyes were like saucers,

"Are you fucking kidding me!? I loved that house!"

"Yeah, well, I think the whole shovel-murder kind of put a damper on the vibe."

She shrugged, but I had a point.

"Giulianna found out we were together, threw a temper tantrum and took off."

Opal's mouth hanging open so I reached over and closed it. Chloe changed positions and I lowered my voice like I was telling a bedtime story,

"The fire fighters found her body in the bedroom."

Opal flew up and whispered,

"What the fuck, Amelia!? Jesus Christ! And you believe that bullshit story!?"

I nodded my head,

"Well, yeah."

"You've got to be fucking kidding me, it's obvious, he had her killed, Amelia!"

"What the fuck are you talking about!?"

She leaned in,

"Oh, don't be naive! Jesus, this is the mob we're talking about. That woman was causing problems and if there's one thing Seppi's good at, it's solving problems."

That's how the night ended, I believed him, and she didn't, whatever.

"They're going to use the insurance money to pay Sal's debt."

"Is there going to be enough?"

I leaned in,

"Oh, yeah. The house was worth like ten million dollars."

Eyes wide, choking on the last of her White Claw,

"Excuse me!?"

"The house was worth ten million dollars, and Sal's debt was seven-hundred-and-fifty-thousand-dollars."

"Jesus."

"Yeah, the whole thing is like an episode of The Sopranos, the amount of money we're talking about is insane."

I got into character, some rich asshole,

"Oh? My dad owes you a million-bazillion dollars, and you think he skipped town? No biggie, I'll cash in a gazillion-jillion dollar insurance policy to pay it off."

I paused and went palms up, I mean what the fuck? My sister chuckled,

"We're like boxed mac and cheese people, not burn down your mafia mansion at the ocean to pay off a gambling debt kind of people."

I looked at her,

"We're like paper napkin, jarred spaghetti sauce, and wine with a spigot kind of people."

And with that, we laughed until we snorted and some of the tension lifted. There was a sort of irony that Sal burnt down Seppi's restaurant and then Seppi burnt down Sal's house. Even though Sal was long gone, it felt satisfying to take something from him.

CHAPTER 30
HEAVEN ON EARTH

I WAS STARING AT THE ceiling when I got the call I had been waiting for. The conversation went a little something like this,

"Seppi?"

"Come to me."

The call ended. I jumped into a pair of sweats and slammed my ringlets into a frantic mess on the top of my head. I fed the cat, brushed my teeth, and shoved my feet in my dingy white Chuck Taylors. I flew down the stairs and threw up a little gravel when I backed out of my spot. I arrived at Hidden Hills Estates and the gate swung open as I approached. There were tears teetering at the brim when the house came into view. I parked next to the Escalade and felt like I was home. I ran for the door and Seppi opened it before I got there. He held me to his chest and his stubble got caught up in my curls. I broke the silence,

"I love you."

The wave took him down, and it took me along with him. I put my arms around his waist and held on for dear life. Neither of us said anything, it was as if it was a dream and neither of us wanted to wake up. Seppi held my tear-soaked face in his hands, his left thumb caressing my scrimple. We left a trail of clothes on our way up the stairs. That time was different, being back in his arms was like heaven on earth. We fell asleep in each other's arms and woke up a little after noon. Seppi was gazing at me when I opened my eyes. I stretched,

"Morning."

He smiled but it was replaced with something else entirely,

"I want to show you something."

I pushed up so my back was against the headboard. Seppi handed me an envelope he retrieved from his nightstand. I undid the clasp and pulled the papers out of their hiding place. I read a letter written to Seppi by Giovanni Genovese, the dead uncle of Giulianna. Seppi held his breath as I read,

"Is this real?"

"Yes."

I turned the letter over and examined the back. I read it again and leaned into him and he said,

"Before I was even married to Jules, her uncle Giovanni took me under his wing. Years later, when I was struggling to get my restaurant off the ground, he gave me more than one pep-talk. Gio confided that he wished I could leave the family business. He said I had potential to do great things, no one else had ever said that ton me before. He saw something in me that no one else did, he had faith in me from the start. I'd serve Gio my dishes and he'd give me feedback. We'd share whiskey and cigars, he's the one who got me into Johnny Walker Blue, he was like a father to me."

Seppi got lost in his head for a while before coming back to me,

"There was a situation where the feds raided a front, and they tried to say Giovanni killed a lady and a cop, he was going away for life. I managed to give information that got him off. He was innocent, but the police department was corrupt. They fudged some evidence and bribed a witness. Those cowards couldn't admit that they got the wrong guy, they needed someone to blame. My testimony got him off, and Giovanni promised to repay the favor."

My stomach growled and I realized I hadn't eaten anything. Seppi slid out of bed and I followed. We got dressed on our way back down the stairs. I sat on one of the stools and Seppi ground espresso, it was afternoon but felt like six AM. He sat across from me and we sipped our lattes,

"I wanted out a long time ago, if you're in the mob you've always got a target on your back. I know I've been desensitized to some things. I killed that Arnault character and never thought about it again, I just thought, good riddance."

I cringed, remembering that night,

"So, Giovanni called in a favor and then never told you about it?"

"Yeah. I think he realized it would cause too much fallout, maybe it would put him at odds with his family if it came out that he scratched the back of a Moretti, who knows. The Genovese family is big on loyalty, whatever the reason, Gio never gave me this letter, but he saved it and wanted me to have it after he died."

I swiped at some steamed milk on my lip,

"Isn't that kind of a mind fuck?"

He nodded and emptied his mug like I didn't know the half of it. I slid a joint out of my flip-top tin and Seppi lit it with a fancy Zippo. I hugged one knee and read the letter a third time. The document was written by Giovanni Genovese years ago, it stated that he was eternally grateful to Giuseppi Moretti for helping him avoid a life in prison like Al Capone. Gio plead his case that Giuseppi Moretti had potential as a legitimate businessman and chef, and as a favor to the Moretti family, Gio pulled some strings. And although the favor had been called in a decade ago, at that moment, we were at a crossroads. The whole thing was playing major head games with Seppi,

"It turns out, once the debt is paid to the Genovese family, my father's boss will wash his hands of it. My old man was more trouble than he was worth, I think his own boss would have put a bullet in his head if he had the chance."

"So, once the slate is clean, I don't have to look over my shoulder anymore?"

Seppi reached across the counter and rubbed the back of my hand with his thumb,

"Amelia, it's over. Somehow, my father's horrible reputation and shit decision-making skills, saved you. I'll have the money in a week and it will be over."

I swallowed a year and a half of panic and hyper-vigilance, eighteen-months of something bubbling under the surface. I imagined what Seppi's life would have been like if he wasn't involved in the mob. Driving a regular car or wearing a pair of old blue jeans. Seppi's get out of jail free card died a long time ago but he realized he needed to get out of Bunman for a while. Mary and Vincenzo would take care of things at the ristorante while we were away, it was time for a much needed vacation. I wasn't sure where we would go and I didn't really care, he told me he would take care of the details.,

We packed our bags and left town for a while or maybe longer. It was the first time I saw Seppi in cargo shorts and a T-shirt, his feet in a pair of Vans.

He let his beard grow out a little and it suited him, but it completely changed his appearance. Seppi nosed the mini mafia sedan down the alley between Muddy Waters and Giuseppi's Italian Ristorante and parked in his spot. Mary was buzzing around the ristorante, smiling ear to ear, in her element. She'd oversee things, for now. Seppi and Mary hugged and it brought tears to my eyes, she hugged him like she loved him and he had done bad things. She held me to her chest, I took in the scent of Chanel No.5 and her skinny cigarettes. She handed me a stack of hundreds, and patted my hand,

"Do something nice for yourself, darling."

We shifted our attention when Vinny and Sunny came through the back door,

"What's up, fucker?"

Sunny picked me up off the ground with her hug,

"I know it's just a couple weeks but I'm going to miss you."

I moved from her arms into Vinny's, he kissed me on both cheeks and then hugged me,

"Until next time."

And I hoped it wasn't any time soon, since it usually meant dumping a body, but I smiled and said,

"Until next time."

We were both crying when we got back in the car, even a vacation can be bittersweet. I tried not to worry about the demons, I tried not to take them with me. We made our way to the other side of town because Opal had a loaf of sourdough for me. I wasn't even out of the car when she banged through the door with Chloe strapped to her chest,

"I'm going to miss you so much, and so is little Chloe."

I choked up as Chloe made raspberries in my direction,

"You have to Facetime me so I can see her. And I need to continue with my story, I've been telling her about all the losers I've dated. I left off with a real cliffhanger, I'm surprised she can sleep at night."

I kissed Chloe on the head and put my face close to hers, taking in the scent of her. I hugged Opal and thanked her for the sourdough. Seppi waved to them with a couple fingers and Opal waved back, he said,

"If you guys need anything, don't hesitate to call me, day, or night. I mean it."

She smiled over at him,

"I know."

My dad said he had something for me so we drove to my parent's house. As soon as we were in the driveway, he came onto the porch. He jogged down the steps, wrapped his arms around me, and picked me up off the ground,

"Hi, Boo-Boo Bear, I love you. Have so much fun. Life is too short to be miserable!"

When I was done blubbering on his shirt, he kissed me and then turned to Seppi. They shook hands and Seppi pulled him in for a hug and cheek kisses,

"Take good care of my Boo-Boo Bear."

Seppi smiled,

"You have my word."

My dad handed me a twenty, and winked,

"Get yourself something cool at a thrift store while you're on your vacation, think of it as a souvenir."

"I will dad, thank you."

"See you soon."

It was a monumental occasion that the two of us were leaving town together, even if it was just for a little while. We were off. I hugged my knees as Maple Street went by. The park, the pizza place, the food co-op. Soon, downtown was behind us and we headed north. Seppi had rented a house on Lake Elysian, ten miles south of Burlington. We stopped at a gas station in Brandon and we hugged when we got out of the car. The palms of his hands were planted on my shoulder blades, a real hug by someone who loved me. He exhaled slowly, the weight of the world lifting for a while. He put his palm out,

"Give me the panic button."

I dug around the bottom of the vintage bag that used to belong to the woman with the cute hat who was really the redheaded woman with the pantsuit. I handed over the panic button and he dropped it onto the pavement. We stared down at it for a second and then Seppi smashed it with the heel of his sneaker and threw the pieces into the trash,

"You won't be needing this anymore."

We stood in that gas station parking lot holding each other, just a crazy-haired girl with a scrimple and the patriarch of a mob family. I nuzzled into Seppi's warmth and protection, took in the scent of shower gel and Tobacco Vanille. Sometimes running away from home is the smartest thing you can do. You're running away from one thing, but you're running toward something else for a little while. It was the end of an era for us, the end of the beginning part where I came into town for a fresh start, and that was just the beginning of our story. We held hands the rest of the way to Elysian and I couldn't wait to make love to him in a place where no one would knock on the door with gourmet pastries from Eliana Mazelli'a place. I couldn't remember the last time I took a vacation.

Seppi nosed the car onto a gravel road and after a mile of trees, Seppi pulled into 1313 Enoch Lane. I took in the scent of the woods and the water. The house was just a normal house by the lake. It was a two story farmhouse with chipping paint. It had a screen porch door that squeaked when it opened and slapped when it shut. I stepped onto a dock that had seen better days and there was a rusted flat bottom rowboat anchored to the post, water and leaves collecting in one end. We sat in a pair of weathered Adirondack chairs facing the water, clinked mismatched glasses, and swallowed fire in another town. I lit a joint and he lit a Cuban. I glanced over at him,

"Why did you pick Lake Elysian?"

He put his head back,

"Because Elysian means heavenly, and that sounds nice for a change."

I abandoned my chair and sat on Seppi's lap. I nuzzled into him and he wrapped one of my ringlets around his finger,

"Ti amo."

I kissed his cheek,

"Ti amo."

We were taking a much needed break from the chaos, the bullets, the dead bodies. We had three weeks to forget about life, to forget about the mob. Who am I kidding? You've been around long enough to know things never go as planned.

THE END.

THE
TROUBLED TIES
SOUNDTRACK

BY THE AUTHOR

TWISTED TIES

TIES THAT BIND

TROUBLED TIES

CHECK OUT VANESSA'S PODCAST!

ABOUT THE AUTHOR

VANESSA FELL IN LOVE with writing in the third grade and spent hours typing stories on an old Smith Corona. After pursuing degrees in Sociology, Nursing, and Education, Vanessa returned to writing. She became obsessed with Sue Grafton in the mid-nineties and was inspired to create an equally relatable female main character.

A survivor of childhood trauma, Vanessa is no stranger to battling her own demons. The unapologetically broken main character in this series will feel like an old friend you'd meet for coffee or a glass of well-aged whiskey around the fire. Vanessa's no-filter writing style cultivates an immediate familiarity and connection to the people and places in a world that's shrouded in ruthlessness, mental demons, and self-medication.

This series is planned to have at least ten titles. Vanessa is currently writing a gritty southern novel about a woman on the run, and a young adult fiction about trauma.